LAST SPRING WAS BITTERSWEET

Book II

ARDAIN ISMA

Printed by Village Care Corp.

Village Care
99 King Street #1822
Saint Augustine, FL, 32085

Table of Contents

Praise for Ardain Isma

Praise for Ardain Isma

I love many things about Ardain Isma's novels – the elegant, glittering prose, his beautifully drawn characters and sweeping plotlines – but what *really* fascinates me is his rich and cantilevered view of the Haitian American community. With an unfailing eye for whimsical detail, Dr. Isma draws a resplendent portrait of an ancient culture on the rise in the new world. *Last Spring was Bittersweet* welcomed me as a temporary member of this vibrant community with its innate aristocracy, beautiful Old-World manners, and compelling cultural heritage. What a literary gift and an education!

It's one of the best novels of 2023.

Anne Merino, author and award-winning playwright

It is not necessary to read the first of the two books, Bittersweet Memories of Last Spring (Book One), though the first is excellent and gives a great backdrop to this second edition. Book Two is filled with sadness, joy, loneliness, connection, heartbreak, family, hopelessness, and hope. There is something in this story with which everyone can connect and feel. Yrvin's life journey is filled with all the stumbles, hopes and dreams of humanity. I highly recommend both Book One and Book Two.

Gabriel Constans, scholar, novelist, and award-winning screenwriter

A true masterpiece of the human condition. Yrvin's struggles and triumphs are a perfect representation of the American dream through the eyes of an immigrant. *Last Spring was Bittersweet* is an absolute must read!

Lauren Masterson, literary critic, critically acclaimed writer, poet, and editor

Beautiful story of love, longing, regret, and joy. The novel is a testimony to Dr. Isma's powerful storytelling which is soaked in delicate sensitivity.

Rashmi Bora Das, author and essayist

-One can only fall for Yrvin, impeccable protagonist penned under the craftmanship of an impressive writer. *Last Spring was Bittersweet* is the pure expression of hope, courage, and triumph over all that seems unsurmountable in life.

Jacob Davis, coeditor of CSMS Magazine

Brief Bio

Ardain Isma was born in Haiti, where he lived until he was 18. He migrated to the United States during the mass migration of the 1980s. He is an essayist, novelist, and the Chief Editor of CSMS Magazine (www.csmsmagazine.org). He teaches Introduction to Research Methods at Embry Riddle University. A prolific writer, Ardain has written extensively on three main issues: writers' tools for success, social justice, and multiculturalism. Ardain Isma lives with his wife Maryse in Saint Augustine, Florida.

Also by Ardain Isma

Bittersweet Memories of Last Spring
Alicia Maldonado: A Mother Lost
Midnight at Noon

Acknowledgments

In memory of my parents, Tibince Cédieu and Anne-Rose Isma, who continue to be my main point of comfort in moments of uncertainties.

To my sister, Erna Isma Jules, with whom I spent my earlier years as an immigrant in the United States. We had nothing, but we had each other.

To my other siblings, Guyto, Compa, and Royo, from whom I also draw inspiration to write this story.

To my children, Ardine, Ardain Junior, and Ardy, who had encouraged me to write a story they could easily identify as the spring of their father's life.

Pou Ayiti cheri. Pout tout yon pèp kap goumen pou la vi miyò. Kenbe la. Pa lage.

(For my beloved Haiti. For a people fighting for a better life. Hold firm. Don't give up.)

Book 2

— Paul Laraque

Chapter 1

On a typical Friday evening, I would have sat on the couch with my eyes closed chatting with Mica over the phone. We would have talked about our unsustainable yearning to meet again, about our thirst to breathe once more into each other's arms, our shared responsibility of raising our son-to-be, our lives in marriage, and the low moan of despair escaping our breaking voices as we said goodnight. Those days were gone, lost in the air like dust in the wind.

Tonight, in this eerie silence of the Miami summer, I sat upright, my head resting against the back cushion, deep in thought. Outside, a bird chirped, and I turned toward the window, my eyes musing upon the darkness. I saw nothing but the hollowness of the vast, empty courtyard dotted by royal palms and river birches. The chirping then faded into the hollowness but was soon replaced by a soft rustle from the branches floating in the night breeze. I went back to the couch, a beaten man trapped in an endless continuum of nothingness.

Three weeks after Michaela had left for Strasbourg, I had yet to hear from her. Every day, I would wait by the mailbox, a desperate man who longed for the news of his girlfriend who had gone astray. The mailman would come and hand me a pile of billing statements mixed with advertisement flyers. Then, in giant and apathetic steps, he would go on to the next unit. I would stand there with shivering lips, fading optimism, and a faint hope that perhaps the next day might be *the day*. The day would come and go, and with it, my diminishing hope and endurance to continue to wait. I loathed those days with uncontrolled passion and emotion. It was not the first time Michaela had traveled overseas since we met. Her diary from the Dominican Republic served as unequivocal proof that we both knew proactive communication could spare a vibrant love from the dreaded sinkhole of oblivion. Then, lovesick and miserable, there was not an opportunity to recharge the power of our love that was left unused.

As the days turned into weeks, like pitching waves on high tides, a degree of certainty began to creep into my subconsciousness. Somehow, I thought, Michaela's interests may have been lost in the blurry hope of far-off love. I was well aware of the price one must pay to keep alive a long-distance relationship, for I had experienced it before. My misadventure with Régine had turned out to be a vivid reminder, an ugly recurrence against which I struggled daily.

As realities started to sink in, so did my growing awareness of the inevitability to reclaim my old self, for despite my afflictions, life must go on. To help me heal my unshared pain, I had developed an interest in romance novels and started reading the stories of men and women whose love had been the victims of misfortunes, whose hopes and desires had been dashed by the searing pain of unreachable distance. Since the dramatic morning when Michaela had knocked on the door to say goodbye, my sister Lorna, who greatly admired her, had ceased to talk about her. After a brief moment of grief and deep disappointment,

Nana had been encouraging me to redirect my focus toward finding my dream job.

Nana recognized the devastating effect of living in solitude. She, like me, had realized Michaela had mistreated a love she once alleged to be the love of her life, although she never openly expressed her displeasure for fear of exacerbating my agony. As a matter of mutual understanding, we refrained from referring to her. I no longer hoped for a phone call from Strasbourg. I avoided the mailbox, and the mailman would knock on the door before leaving the pile of mail inside the box and moving on. Though we never exchanged words, albeit a short greeting, a "hi" and a "see you", I sensed he had the feeling that I longed for something he could not deliver. Perhaps, over time he had come to share my unspoken disappointment, and because of that, he had grown wary and wanted to be the bearer of that mysterious missive.

"Vinco, have you seen the brand-new gym on Biscayne?" Nana asked one morning before going to work. The look on her face was the worried stare of a concerned big sister.

"No, I haven't. Where on Biscayne?"

"Near the Morningside Park. You're going to have to get a membership. I'm worried about you. Staying in bed all day long will ruin your health." Her eyes were red. She did not have to say anything further.

After countless sacrifices to earn a college degree, I could not let my new torment with Michaela wash it all away. I realized that I must live on or I would be destroyed. I would lose my dignity, Nana's sanity, my parents' high hopes for me, and the high esteem that all my friends had held dear for me. I could not let them down. So, I rose from my bed and walked out to the living room to talk to her, but she had already stepped outside. The door vibrated as she slammed it behind her in anguish.

Nana was my heroine who had led me to victory in the long and difficult struggle to navigate safely through the painful life of a young immigrant. She was the constant support behind me to earn a decent education, win every pitched battle, to place me on the front door of mainstream America where opportunities were plentiful. I peered through the window, and my eyes caught her diminutive, weather-beaten frame moving in the morning breeze like a phantom of her old self. My once brave sister was now wrestling against invisible odds, fighting vicissitudes against which she had no magic bullets. How selfish I would be to let her down.

That morning, her words and attitude reminded me that we were indeed one and indivisible. Losing Mica would be devastating, but it would not be the end of an ascendant life. Attentive to my needs, my hopes, my fears, Nana was the woman in my life I could *not* live without, the one who, no matter the odds, would not leave me stranded along the banks of the river of hope. In a reverse form of speech, I borrowed this line of hers, most notably when she stood before her church group, bragging about how much I meant to her. We had each other in the most holistic form of brotherly-sisterly love, and that was golden and sacred. That morning, her unuttered words had struck deep in my heart, ushering an awakening that I urgently needed to save myself from the brink of mental despair. Unexpressed words that reminded me of how quick it was for Michaela to capitulate to her parents' desire, agreeing to go thousands of miles away from the man she claimed to have loved unconditionally.

I ran to the shower, got myself refreshed, put on my clothes, ate breakfast, and drove to the new gym. I had to break free from this vicious cycle of sadness and regain the positive mindset that once gave me the pivotal energy I had mastered during my undergraduate years. An exercise regimen would help bring back the strength I now lacked as I embarked upon a new struggle - reentering the job market to find a position in my field of study. I went to the new gym and purchased a membership. So, every morning I was there, pumping iron alongside other motivated faces, including some of old classmates. Before long, I began to regain self-confidence. Although the last, painful minutes with Michaela still haunted me, they no longer played the spooky ghosts of my lonely nights. Nana was pleased by my renewed optimism.

Life, however, has never been a worry-free journey. So, as my devotion to job hunting grew, so too were my anxieties. "Where do I go for that dream job?" I kept saying to myself. Every day after my regular morning exercise and breakfast, I spent two hours digging through the classified pages of the *Miami Herald* and the *Fort Lauderdale Sun Sentinel*, but I could hardly see anything remotely close to software engineering. I spoke to my dear friend Pedro about my frustrations, and he suggested that I go to a job agency. He gave me a list of employment agencies specializing in technology firms. On the list was an agency named IT Services with offices all over town. One of the offices was in midtown Miami, the option that was closest to where I lived. I wasted no time. A day after I spoke to Pedro, I showed up at IT Services well-dressed with my credentials in hand. It was a two-story building with wide windows; filled with men and women that had unsmiling faces. They were all in business suits, talking business in tones difficult for me to decipher. I walked up to the receptionist, a red-haired woman in a tight dress with a mean attitude.

"How can I help you?" She asked.

"I'm looking for a job in either computer programming or software engineering," I replied.

"Do you have a degree in these fields?"

"Yes, I do."

"What school did you graduate from?"

"Barry University."

Her stiffness loosened, and she flashed a vague smile. "Do you have your transcript with you?"

"Yes." I handed her an unofficial copy.

She glanced at it. "You just graduated," she said.

I did not answer, and she did not press for clarification either.

"You'll have to meet Anabel. She handles entry-level positions. She's not here yet. In the meantime, here. Fill out this application."

I took the application, walked to the corner of the room, and began my assault on the mountain of forms. I was midway through when a petite woman in a dark suit walked in. She had wavy, peach-colored hair, a nose ring, and was moving fast toward the elevator, suitcase in hand. The receptionist called to her, and she stopped.

"Annabel," she said. "This young man is here for employment services."

"Good morning, sir." The petite woman said, walking back to meet me.

"Good morning," I replied as we shook hands.

"Follow me," she instructed. "What kind of job are you looking for?" She asked while we were in the elevator.

"I'm a software engineer, but anything along those lines would be fine."

At her office, she requested my transcript, and I handed it to her. She spent about five minutes analyzing the transcript while I sat near her desk, finishing the application process. She picked up the phone, making several phone calls as she jotted down some information.

Then, she hung up the phone and called me. "Yrvin Lacroix. Did I pronounce your name right?"

"Yes," I replied.

"I'm Anabel Villaviciencio, but my colleagues call me Ana," she said, taking the forms from me and examining each one with the eye of a hawk. "Young man, you seem very smart," she said, surprised. "But it's not easy to secure an entry-level position right now in your field of study."

"I'm also a computer programmer," I said, trying to conceal my nerves.

"I see that, Mr. Lacroix. However, it's the entire tech sector that doesn't seem to be hiring young college graduates. At least, not at the moment."

"Really?" A rising tension boiled inside of me, and I could feel the muscles on my face tighten.

"But that doesn't mean it's mission impossible. In fact, I just got off the phone with a gentleman named Jake Ortega. He's a recruiter at Lawton Enterprises. They have an opening. He's willing to give you an interview, Thursday at ten a.m."

She gave me Ortega's business card and address. She then went on to explain the role of IT Services. If hired, five percent of my paycheck would go to service fees for a period of six months. She asked me to sign, and I did. We shook hands and I left.

I was pleased with Anabel, as I liked professionals who promised little, but could deliver what was promised. Scheduling the interview for Thursday so quickly had reinforced my impression of her. That day, soon after I left Anabel's office, my optimism grew. When I came home and checked the mailbox, I found my green card. I had been waiting for mine, praying to God every day. Nana and most friends I knew had already received theirs. Now, I could travel overseas, go see my mother in Haiti, my father in the Bahamas, and Michaela in France if necessary. I felt liberated from the shackles of humiliation and the threat of being deported someday. Besides, that green card put me on the right path to citizenship.

Thursday morning, I was there, arriving half an hour before time. Lawton Enterprises was located in one of the high rises near downtown. I met Jake Ortega, nut-skinned and red-haired, near the front desk. Tall and slim, he wore no business jacket, and the top of his button-down, collared shirt was left undone. His sleeves were rolled up to his elbow and the necktie was loosely knotted, appearing both professional yet relaxed. He stood alone in a vast reception area. We greeted each other with a handshake. He then instructed me to follow him to a grand office decorated with fancy artwork where he invited me to take a seat facing him at a small table near a polished wooden cabinet.

He held copies of my résumé and transcript, and seemed to admire my credentials and my multilingual skills. He said they would be an asset to the company which was now in full expansion, seeking new business overseas. As if flipping a switch, in the flick of a light fixture, he changed the conversation.

"Where are you from, Mr. Lacroix?" he asked, smiling a bit.

"Haiti."

"That's what I thought. I'm impressed for a young Haitian man."

"How so, sir?"

"No offense, I meant your transcript looks quite impressive." He realized the gaffe he had just committed. "My parents spent years sponsoring an orphanage in Haiti," he added as if his parents' acts of charity would make up for his misspoken words.

But I took no offense at his bias. Belittling Haitians for having been from one of the poorest countries on Earth was common for well-established business folks in South Florida. Adding to their nonchalance was the reality of Haitian refugees whose main methods of survival in Miami were working as hotel housekeepers, factory workers, restaurant workers, and construction laborers; all without fair representation. I wanted to tell him how I felt about his callous words, but I needed a job.

"So, is there a possibility that I can be hired?" I asked, looking him straight in the eye.

"*Sure.* If I didn't think you were qualified, I would not have said yes to Anabel when she called on Monday to talk about your credentials."

He went on to explain the nature of the job, taking me on a tour of the building, in particular to a floor with well-designed offices where groups of young professionals congregated, discussing job assignments.

"You would be working with them," he said with such an awesome pride that I was almost convinced the position was already mine—if he did not use the conditional "would".

Then he led me back to the front door. "If you don't hear from me in two weeks, call me," he said as I stepped down and made my way toward the parking lot.

In the car, I realized that it may take more than just my college degree to reach the height of my golden dreams. Still, I went home with cautious optimism that if it were God's will, I would get a call from Jake. I told Nana about the interview, about my worries, but she reminded me of where we had come from, where nothing was given, where everything had to be earned with persistence. Of course, I was not going to wait for Jake to call me. Besides the recommendations I received from the employment agency, I continued to do my own research. I built a network with my former classmates who had found themselves in the same predicament.

One Sunday afternoon while going through the *Miami Herald* classified section, I discovered an ad from a Coral Gables company named Zenith Software Group. It was an entry-level position, and that raised my hopes. I called first thing on Monday morning. A lady answered the phone and asked me to come in. Within an hour, I was there. Zenith Software Group occupied a small one-storied complex on a busy street at the edge of Coral Gables. I could hear Cuban salsa music coming from the western side of Red Road, one of the main boulevards of Little Havana. Unable to find a visitors' parking spot, I had to park across the street in a Wendy's parking lot. As soon as I arrived, I met a short, oversized woman with a round face. Customary to job hunting, politeness played a key role in the shrewd maneuvering of job market savvies, hooking the interviewer with a knockout smile while hoping for a happy ending. So, I threw a warm smile, enthusiastic and cordial as we shook hands. She introduced herself as Darling Dardesky, the hiring manager.

"Over the phone, you said your name was Lacroix?" she asked. Wrinkles popped on her forehead, as if wanting to make sure it was indeed me, the gentleman with whom she had spoken to an hour earlier.

"Yes, I'm Yrvin Lacroix."

As instructed, I followed her to a tiny office right next to the reception desk. It reminded me of the small office I had shared with Pito Fuentes during my summer job in Las Calinas a few years earlier. Darling wore low-heeled shoes and a tight knee-length skirt, and when she sat behind her desk to speak to me, extra rolls spilled over and splayed on her waist and belly.

"I thought you were French-Canadian," she said, inviting me to take my seat in an armchair, facing her.

"No, I'm not," I replied.

"Obviously," she said in an unfriendly tone that left me perplexed.

That tone was quite different from the same jolly and inviting voice I had heard over the phone earlier. I handed her my résumé. She skimmed through it with disengaged glances while grabbing an open bag of thin pretzels out of the desk drawer and stuffed her mouth with a handful. Tiny salt bits dropped all over her unorganized desk as she bit and chewed. She seemed unconcerned. Perhaps she wanted to show me how my presence annoyed her. I was *not* who she had expected. Then, she put the résumé aside.

"Haitians are nice people. I have a young man about your age who does the landscaping for my house. He's very good at what he does."

I did not reply, but my face was transformed into a tight frown which revealed my displeasure. I felt my chest tighten.

"We're currently in the process of interviewing for an entry-level computer programming position. I have a half-dozen candidates to interview today. One way or the other, you'll hear from me."

She then rose swiftly from her desk. I also got up and we both walked out. When she reached the door, she pushed it open, and with her index finger, showed me the way out as if I were blind. Despite feeling hurt and humiliated, I was resolute in the pursuit of my dream job. Certainly, I was not going to let an insecure, ill-mannered lady break my will to succeed. Her reference to her Haitian gardener was an implicit way of telling me that I only belonged in her backyard. She did not even bother interviewing me. Maybe she had reserved her challenging questions for the other candidates she would be interviewing throughout the day.

Chapter 2

After that disastrous experience, I began to realize that if I were to find the job that matched my college degree, I would have to start thinking of widening the scope of my search. It was something I heard from a job fair for new graduates at the university. The market in Miami had become saturated, and entry-level positions were practically nonexistent. I now took aim at Broward and Palm Beach counties, thinking if I found a job in the greater metropolitan area, I could still commute. Instead of going home, I drove to the employment agency to speak to Anabel. She was on her way to a meeting when I arrived, but she stopped to talk to me when she saw the look on my face.

"What's wrong, Yrvin?" she asked, a bit worried.

"I've been going from one interview to the next, but nothing seems to be going my way."

"It's the nature of the job market. Patience is the key here, and you must get used to rejections. I know it's hard, after making countless sacrifices to get this far. But the people who interview candidates are usually plain and cold-hearted individuals mainly interested in their company's well-being."

"If it's for their company's well-being, I'm absolutely positive I can make the effort to contribute to that well-being, and more importantly, to the company's business growth."

"I have no doubt, Yrvin, that you're one of the best candidates out there among the young college graduates. You have a competitive edge."

"What 'competitive edge,' Ana?"

"You've graduated from a prestigious university. BU is a private religious institution and that says a lot."

"That may be true, Ana. But I get the sense the people I met saw *me* first, a young black male, before they looked at my degree and the university I've attended."

"What do you mean, Yrvin? Have you experienced racism in the places you've been to?"

"I'm not sure if I can call it racism, blatant or camouflaged, but the negative attitudes directed at me were unmistakable. I was always unwelcome."

Her lips froze in embarrassment, and I went on to tell her about what I had just been through with Darling Dardesky and Jake Ortega. I also told her I wanted to widen the search, and my eyes now focused on Broward and Palm Beach. She was hesitant, saying Palm Beach was too far. I insisted, however, that she look for tech companies in those counties as well.

"Yrvin, I know it's tough for job hunters these days, but you must not be deterred by unprofessional individuals. Believe me, a year from now, when you look back, you won't even remember those dark moments. Be strong, be yourself. I believe in you. If I didn't think you were qualified for a software engineering position, I wouldn't have signed you up." She asked me to wait while she ran to her office and came right back with a form. "Sign this form so that we can extend the search."

I signed it, and we both walked outside to our separate cars. Before I got into my car, she called to me. "Have faith, Yrvin."

I came home and found my sister in bed, reeling from stomach pain. "I had to come home, Vinco."

"I know, women's problem," I teased her.

"I wish it was, but my period came two weeks ago."

She was in such terrible pain that I got freaked out. "You want me to take you to the ER?"

"No, not yet. I'm making some tea. Did you call the Coral Gables company?"

"I just came from there. They said I would hear from them. So, now we wait."

I did not dare share my awful experience. I stayed in the room with her until the pain diminished and she fell asleep. Later in the afternoon, I decided to go for a walk down the neighborhood as an attempt to beat back the waves of uncertainties that never ceased to come my way. It had not been long since my life had a sense of purpose, a reason to get up in the morning, to be active and productive. Now, as a young man, I could not understand why I had to feel so besieged by the complexities of life. I had a college degree with which I should be able to succeed. Already, I missed school when things were manageable. I missed the friends I cherished, the professors who believed in me, and, most of all, Michaela, the girl who had brought meaning to my life. All seemed lost in a tangled mess of survival and greed. The journey through life is one roadblock after another.

Two blocks away, I saw Chantale with her little brother moving toward the ice cream truck stationed on the corner. I drifted off to the next street, avoiding her, where groups of men played cards in a large backyard, chatting and laughing. Chantale would have been happy to see me, for we had rarely talked since graduation day. But I needed to be alone, until I had something newsworthy of sharing. So, I strolled on.

When I reached Fosia's house, it was quite a surprising scene. I saw her talking to Susana. I waved, and they both waved back as they talked inside their respective fenced-in yards. Sworn enemies had now turned into good neighbors, and I wondered at whatever had happened to Esmeralda. A block away, I met Travon, Mr. Jackson's son, who told me a month before rumors spread that Esmeralda had gone missing, later to find out she had moved to Boone, North Carolina, where she wedded an excommunicated Trappist monk. I was stunned. Susana now lived alone with her little hound dog whose barking had become a vile annoyance.

My neighborhood had not changed. Under the weight of their mountains of problems, they lived on, with their cries and laughter, their ups and downs, of course, but with the same determination to keep on going. As the afternoon sun slanted to the east before giving way to the hot summer night, I sauntered up, retreating to my apartment, feeling trapped in a web of thoughts and worries and fears, not knowing how far my dream would carry me.

I went in, checking on Nana. She was still asleep. Quietly, I tiptoed to my bedroom, a young man in a war against odds that seemed insurmountable. Among them was the battle against an invading solitude. I must win this one, and my tour around the neighborhood had given fuel to my conviction. Loneliness will pin a man down, expose his fecklessness to every living being whom he encounters. His devotion to heal, to beat the odds, however, will ultimately usher him to new heights where he would gain crucial confidence in his every step toward his dream. Papa used to tell me that during hard times in the old country.

The next morning, Nana went to work, feeling much better. By eleven am, she came home, saying she and a group of other workers were let go. She worked as a housekeeper in one of the hotels in Miami Beach. Her supervisor said business was slow. What surprised her most was that all the people who had been let go were Haitians. I was on the couch, making phone calls to some tech companies that were hiring when she broke the news.

I dropped everything in horror. Eyebrows lowered, lips pouting, she joined me on the couch, seeking a renewed hope that I could not deliver, a comfort I could not provide. We both were now jobless, and if we remained jobless for another month, we might become homeless. We had been living from paycheck to paycheck. Minimum wage had long forced us to a tight budget, resorting to live within our means. The pressure to find a job had grown to an unbelievable depth. But the chance at finding that dream job was becoming more and more remote.

Morose and silent, Nana lay speechless, trying to digest this latest humiliation. I glanced across the table, and my eyes caught a pile of utility bills that we could not ignore. There was food in the fridge, and the rent money would cover us for one month. My car was running low on gas, and I needed it more than ever for my job hunting. I had been calling place after place, trying to win an interview. "We're not hiring" was a common answer, and when I said I found the job ad in a newspaper, the response took a negative tone. "We know nothing about that." And the interlocutor hung up. Two weeks had gone by, and the dream job had yet to come. I now began to think beyond finding a job in my field of study. Finding any kind of work had become a matter of survival.

Nana did not remain idle either. She too was desperately looking. From hotels, to restaurants, to supermarkets, she searched in vain. Every night, we spent two hours praying for a miracle to happen. We would wake up the next morning feeling empowered by a divine spirit. By late afternoon, however, hope had once again diminished. The search had produced no result, and we would go back into the tiny bedroom again for another round of night prayer. Every time I called the employment office, Anabel would say "Don't worry, Yrvin. I'm on it," I was too ashamed to tell her how desperate I was.

A month later, the search remained fruitless. All our savings had been used. Now penniless and facing a pile of bills, the monthly rent, groceries, and more, we had to find something to avert an imminent crash. Nana, a dignified, introverted young woman who never talked about her financial hardships in public, now felt compelled to ask her friends from church for help. Every day, she would be on the phone networking, for not all the time she had the bus fare to go job hunting. One Tuesday morning, Anabel called me saying she had secured an interview at Novatech International, an architecture firm in Fort Lauderdale. She sounded upbeat, which also raised my expectations. A gentleman named Steve Colombo, the hiring manager, expected me there the next day at eleven a.m.

Wednesday morning, bright and early, I took Interstate 95 North to Fort Lauderdale. Back then, that city just north of Miami was unfamiliar terrain; I drove there occasionally to visit some distant relatives. Heavy traffic north of Hollywood near the Fort Lauderdale International Airport pinned me down. An unwanted nervousness crept into my tormented mind. The traffic jam lasted close to an hour. Luckily, I had left home two hours ahead and Novatech International was headquartered in a ten-storied building just off the interstate on Cypress Creek Road. I arrived twenty minutes before the scheduled time. I wore a jacket and tie, and carried my folder in hand. I was cautiously hopeful. I walked into an empty lobby with a sparkling marbled floor, where I met a tall, fit gentleman in a blue business suit, standing by the elevator.

"Are you Mr. Lacroix?" he asked.

"Yes, I am."

"Come on up."

We got into the elevator and went up to the sixth floor. He led me to his well-organized and spotless office furnished with shiny, cherry-finished office furniture. Behind his desk was a conference table. He invited me there, where we sat side by side. I handed him my résumé. He glanced at it.

"Anabel has already faxed me a copy." He looked me straight in the eye. "You have quite an impressive transcript," he said as if praising me. I was not moved by his compliment, for I had been through this before.

"Have you worked in a technology environment before?" He asked.

"No, I haven't. I've just graduated from Barry University," I replied.

"So, you're more interested in an entry-level position. Right?"

"Whatever position that fits me. I'm a quick learner. If hired, I'll do my best to learn the business culture as fast as I can."

"We have two positions available. One is entry level. If Novatech hires you, you would work as a software engineer on the second floor. It's a busy place, and you'll have to be able to work under pressure."

"I love working under pressure because it keeps my mind busy and more focused on the task."

He went on to give me some details about Novatech's history, which was founded by a group of venture capitalists from Calgary, Canada; they held offices there as well. They had been doing business with a lot of developers in both Florida and Latin America.

"Do you speak Spanish, Mr. Lacroix?"

"I can get by in Spanish, but I'm not fluent enough to use it in a professional setting."

"Anabel told me you're multilingual. Is that right?"

"Yes. I'm well-versed in both Creole and French."

"I see. Where are you originally from?"

"Haiti."

He then took me down to the sixth floor full of busy people. Some were on the phone. Others were typing in front of giant computer screens. We went on to a large cafeteria swamped with young professionals, ordering, chatting, eating. He ordered chicken sandwiches for both of us.

"Mr. Colombo, this is quite an interesting place to work," I said as we walked to a table near the entrance door.

"Call me Steve. Colombo sounds like the movie actor." He laughed.

"You call me Yrvin, then. That suits me better."

"Yrvin, this place is an ideal location for a firm like this one. However, you would be traveling overseas a lot on conferences and other business-related issues."

A tinge of optimism began to creep in, but I concealed it within. In a flash, I saw the unpaid billing statements on the table, and Nana's struggle to pay the rent. I felt I was a step away from conquering that elusive dream and putting my life on track. Steve Colombo looked charming and spoke with meticulous diction. He was fair-skinned with straight dark hair and walked in imposing strides. I noticed he liked to stroke his hair while talking. I thought maybe it was a way to show self-confidence.

After a good half hour of talking about the business, he switched to Haiti. "Your country seems to be going through some difficult moments in history," he said.

"Yes, like many other countries around the world."

"When I lived in New York, I had Haitian neighbors. They were nice people and very industrious. I knew this family who owned a clothing business on Utica Avenue in Brooklyn."

"Yes, we're a dignified and hardworking people. Of course, no one can attain his full potential if not given the opportunity. In Haiti, opportunities are scarce, and because of that reality, great minds are being wasted. Like many citizens in the world,

Haitians live inside a vicious cycle of poverty, which provokes mass migration as people seek to better their lives."

"I know that story too well, Yrvin. My parents are immigrants from South America—from Peru to be precise. Living through hardships is something I'm used to." His eyes narrowed, shrinking his now pale face as he remembered those difficult moments in time. After we ate, he walked me down the lobby and promised to call me very soon. I left a bit disappointed, but still optimistic about the prospect of getting hired.

Three weeks went by, and I had yet to hear from him. One morning, there was a knock on the door. When I opened it, I saw Mrs. Jane, a gray-haired woman. She was the building manager, coming to collect the rent, something she had never done before. We had always paid ahead of time. She was a friendly woman who always greeted us with the biggest of smiles. That morning, however, the smile had disappeared, giving way to a stone face like that of an iron woman.

"Where's your sister?" She asked.

"She's in the shower. Is there anything you want me to tell her, Mrs. Jane?"

"Tell her I'm worried. The rent is two weeks late, and she's never done this before."

"I'm aware of it, too, Mrs. Jane. My sister lost her job, and she and I have been looking."

"I can't wait for too long, not knowing when she'll start a new job. I'm just the manager, not the owner."

"Mrs. Jane, can you give us another month? We'll pay two months the next payment cycle with interest if necessary. Let us know if this is possible. If not, we'll have to move out. The last thing we want is to put your own job in jeopardy." I was frank and firm. I spoke loud enough for Nana to hear so that she did not have to come out to face the embarrassing moment. But she came out anyway, hoping to spare me the shame.

"Mrs. Jane, we will pay if you're willing to give us a couple of more weeks," Nana pleaded.

"Don't worry, the young man has already told me. You're one of my best tenants. I certainly don't want to lose you." She left.

The minute after I shut the door, I called Steve Colombo. "Hey Yrvin, I know you've been worried. I wanted to call you last week, but I had to leave for a conference in Chicago. Unfortunately-"

He did not have to say anything further. I was back in the same hopelessness. "Thank you for letting me know." For the first time, I could feel cold sweat under my skin. I went to my room, nosediving into bed.

Nana followed me, but she did not have to ask. "Don't worry, Vinco. God will provide."

"We've been saying this for the longest time now. If this is a test of faith as you always like to say, this test seems to be the longest one—EVER." I wanted to crawl out of my skin and cry to the highest pitch.

The phone rang, and Nana picked it up. "*Mica*," she said. Her voice shuddered with emotion. She set the phone on the table and came to get me. "Vinco, Michaela, *Michaela.*"

"Tell her I'm busy." My heart pounded.

"You can't do that."

"I can't talk right now." I was not prepared to deal with Michaela as more pressing problems besieged my tormented mind, and I knew whatever her excuses, nothing could get rid of the pain she had inflicted in my heart. Now I was on the verge of moving beyond, reclaiming my old self, and Michaela's call meant almost nothing.

"You tell her that yourself." She brought me the phone.

"Mi amor, sorry. I'm *so* sorry."

I did not reply to her implausible apology. I was angry, and her voice made me angrier. I kept the phone in my ear, and I was wordless.

"Vinco, I don't know if I can ever heal the pain I've caused. I've been sick since I arrived here. My uncle lives in a very small apartment. Six of us live here. No air-conditioning unit. It's been hot like hell. The baby is making me sick. I've been suffering from dizziness, vomiting. I think of you day and night. I feel ashamed. I should not have let my parents send me here. I don't know the culture. I don't speak the language. I'm sick. I'm penniless, but I refuse to call home for help. I told them if anything happened to me here in this strange place, they're the ones who will bear the responsibility." She paused for a quick second, hoping I would say something. I was unmoved.

"My uncle can barely make ends meet let alone take care of me as he promised my parents," she continued. "My dream is for the two of us to be reunited as soon as possible. We would rent a place. We'll live however we can. Our love must not die because of the malicious decisions of others. I have yet to see a gynecologist. I can feel the baby kicking inside my tummy, and my heart vibrates each time. It gives me hope, thinking a part of you begins to take shape inside of me. Our baby must live. Vinco, my love, my prince, I'm sorry." Her voice was breaking between the words. Still, I said nothing. I was unconvinced. I listened to her tale with contemptuous dismissal. "Vinco, are you there?"

"Yes, I am."

"But you're not talking to me, Vinco."

"What do you want me to say? That I believe you? That you're a victim of your parents' shortsightedness? That it was true because of me, shame would befall you?"

"Mi amor, it wasn't because of you. It was because of my pregnancy."

"If I were a prince from Westminster, their decision would have been quite different. But, I'm not, and never will be. You know, Michaela, it wasn't their decision that hurt me the most; it was the quickness with which you decided to go along with it. As if I had no say in what would become of you, our future, our baby. They treated me as an insignificant, good-for-nothing lad. You yourself admitted their decision to send you to France was made shortly after the party. Yet, it took you more than twenty four hours to inform me of your decision. You ignored my calls, my worry, my love and affection, and waited until the minute before you left to drop your bombshell. By then, you were convinced there was nothing I could do to stop you. The images of you in the back of that minivan shedding crocodile tears as I begged you to reconsider still haunt me. And for three months, I waited in vain to hear from you as promised."

"Vinco, mi amor. Forgive me. I want you more than ever before. I'm alone and scared."

I wanted to tell it all to her, but I still loved her. Besides, she was the bearer of my child. My sister listened in horror; her face hardened to those gut-wrenching words. I refrained from saying anything further. I restrained myself from expressing how raw and emotional I felt on that nightmarish morning. I avoided telling her how I despised the naiveté that dwelled in her mind, body, and soul, and that I no longer believed in that love she had been claiming to be unconditional. I held it all back because Manman used to say that you don't bury your enemy deep in a hole when he's pinned down, let alone someone you love.

"Can I have an address?" I asked.

"Yes, Vinco." She gave me the address. "You can keep this number, too. You can call me in the morning hours, your time. I have to go now. I'll call you when I have another opportunity." Annoyed, I wrote them down.

As soon as Michaela hung up the phone, Nana rose from the floor. "How could you talk to her like this?"

"I'm still hurt, Nana. You know that. Don't you?"

"Still..."

"Still what? Even if everything she just said was true, do you think I can take this huge responsibility? Nana, don't you see, we're all alone, not knowing where we might be next week if we can't get a job? Michaela will always be sheltered by her relatives in France."

Nana said nothing more. Once again, our blighted reality had set in her mind. I understood she wanted me to behave like a gentleman, expressing empathetic words to comfort Mica. What Nana did not understand was that when under the spell of misfortunes, no one behaves according to the expected norm. I jumped out of my bed and walked out to the living room, evermore resolute to be successful in my job hunting.

Chapter 3

One week before the rent was due again, Nana and I had yet to find a job. Desperation grew beyond our control. Friday morning, I was ready to hit the road for yet another round of job hunting when the phone rang. The voice of a man who introduced himself as Jean-Luc Parizeau boomed from the other end of the line.

"Can I speak to Mr. Yrvin Lacroix?" He asked in a French accent.

"This is he," I replied.

"Your résumé has come to me from Anabel Villaviciencio from IT Services. I'm the hiring manager at A. J. Partners. We are an engineering firm in Miami Shores. I'd like to schedule an interview."

"Sure."

"Let's say Monday at nine a.m."

Monday morning, I was there. Upon arrival, I met a middle-aged gentleman who stood right outside of the main entrance, smoking a cigarette. "You are Yrvin Lacroix, I presume," he said, taking the last drag of his cigarette before throwing the butt over a tree-line.

"Yes, I am," I replied with a tight smile.

"Let's go inside then." He led me to a small office located at the end of a narrow hallway. After settling behind his well-polished desk, he invited me to sit in an armchair, facing him. He took off his jacket and rolled up his sleeves while reviewing my résumé. "Both your transcript and résumé impress me," he said, pulling the transcript out of his folder, peering through the lenses of his owl-rimmed spectacles in search of the strongest point of my transcript. "Mister Lacroix, that's very interesting," he squeaked like a mockingbird in distress, stressing the "r" in its purest phonetic sound the way educated francophone individuals speak English.

He went on to explain the nature of the job, the culture at A.J. Partners, and what my tasks would be if hired. Nothing he said was different from my previous interviews except for a mutually inclusive acknowledgment of our French heritage. I went home, trying not to even think about it.

Nana was out job hunting as well. At one p.m., the phone rang. Another man called, saying his name was Bryce Rhodes, hiring manager at Harrison Asset Management. He said his secretary had referred my résumé to him, and he was wondering if I could come in immediately for an interview. He gave me the address as well as detailed instructions on how to get there. Within seconds, I was back in my car, driving west to Miami Springs. That was when I remembered an ad I had seen in the *Miami Herald* about a system information engineering position at an investment firm near the airport. When I arrived, I met a young woman, golden-haired and purplish-blue-eyed, in a velvet dress with a red-striped shawl around her neck, sitting at the reception desk. I introduced myself as Yrvin Lacroix and stated that I came to see Mr. Bryce Rhodes for a job interview.

"Ha, I remember having spoken to you over the phone. Yeah, Dr. Rhodes is waiting for you. He's in his office, the second door on your right."

"Dr. Bryce Rhodes?" I asked when I walked into his office, trying to confirm he was indeed referred to as a "Dr." instead of a "Mr.".

"Yes, I am, Mr. Lacroix. It's a pleasure to meet you. Thank you for coming. I'm glad I was able to find you on the phone." He spoke with a measured voice. He was Nordic white with a giant's height. A red pimple perched on the tip of his nose. He pulled back a bit from the desk, and from his movement, his belly sprawled and extra fat sank to just off his knees.

"The pleasure is also mine." I grinned.

"I see you've graduated from Barry University."

I nodded.

"That's extraordinary. BU is a prestigious institution." His smile catapulted into restrained laughter, and I did not know what to make of such a muted, unemotional laugh. I showed no reaction, remaining serene to those little lies that had long become familiar to my ear. Already, I was well-prepared for what would be coming next.

"Regrettably, we don't have a position available right now in your field of study," he said, pulling out of his chair to get closer to me. His knees skewed left and then right as he moved under the weight of his heavy upper body.

"Your secretary did not see what was in my résumé?" I asked. I looked at him straight with reddening and unblinking eyes.

"She should have," he acknowledged, attempting to soften the disappointment on my face, a frustration I tried and failed to contain inside of me.

That rejection was the quickest and the most hurtful. The man glanced at my credentials, and less than a couple of minutes, he had concluded that I was not qualified; but he understood my reference to his secretary was transitory because through her, I saw an unprofessional individual who admitted he should have indeed read the résumé before calling me in. With face tightened, I rose from the chair, readying to exit.

"Mr. Lacroix, we have a data-entry position, which is not entirely in your field, but I'm sure this is something you can undoubtedly do. I've already interviewed several candidates, but you're welcome to apply. Is this something you would be interested in?"

Frankly, I wanted to leave, but I could hear Nana's voice saying, "Apply! Apply!"

"Yes, I would love to, Dr. Rhodes." I felt defeated, not finding the job of my dream after so many sacrifices, so many tries.

"Do you type?"

"Yes, I do."

"Your knowledge in computer programming and WordStar amazes me." He handed me an application packet and returned to his desk, pulling a small plastic bowl full of rice pudding from his desk drawer.

I moved to what looked like a student's desk in the back of the room to fill out the forms. He took a couple of spoonsful.

"This is my afternoon snack," he said, almost choking himself while chewing. His cheeks swelled on the second spoonful. "A nice snack!" He repeated as if trying to tell me he was not obese, and that his heavy body was the result of an undesired inheritance rather than the consequence of an eating disorder.

But I paid no attention to him, busying myself with the task of completing the forms. Ten minutes later, I was done. He was halfway through the pudding when I handed him the application packet.

"You're done already?" He put the food away.

"Yes, sir."

"My wife has put me on a rice pudding diet," he said, retrieving the packet from my hand. I did not react to his unrealistic revelation for fear of embarrassing him. "This position, Mr. Lacroix, doesn't require much but a good discipline and the ability to work cooperatively. Harrison Asset Management has branches in many parts of the country. We're an investment company, and sometimes, you might have to work overtime."

"I'm used to working under pressure. But my performance on the job will give you a better idea of my professionalism."

He grabbed the bowl of rice pudding and took two giant bites. "I'm glad you mention the word professionalism," he said, swallowing the last spoonful, grabbing a water bottle, and taking a gulp to cleanse his mouth from the rice residue stuck between his yellow teeth and gums. I stood there, looking at the miserable fellow who seemed to have fallen victim to food addiction. "Mr. Lacroix, you would be the sole male specialist if hired. Are you uncomfortable working with women?" He spoke like a humble individual who perhaps understood the exhaustion and humiliation usually associated with job hunting.

"No, not at all."

"Here, the code of ethics is strictly enforced, and as part of the company's policy, discrimination in any form is not tolerable. We value our employees, and we evaluate them based on performance, not on gender, race, or religion." He coughed and sneezed after taking the last gulp of his water bottle, snatching a tissue off the desk to clean out his nostrils.

"Yes, sir. But what is the base salary for this position?"

"Six dollars an hour with the possibility to work overtime as I just mentioned. Will that work for you?"

"It will."

"And I see that you're multicultural."

"Very much so." My anxieties lessened a bit.

"*Parlez-vous français?*" He asked in an interrogative fashion, like most educated Americans in their ambiguous honesties, using words, phrases, and even expressions from the language of Voltaire to project intellectual dominance. When pressed further, however, you would find out their *parler français* is usually shallow at best.

"*C'est très bien, monsieur,*" I replied in French.

"What was that?" He startled.

"It's nice to know that, sir," I meant.

"My French is very limited," he admitted, chuckling. He then switched the conversation. "Haiti is such a small island with an impeccable history," he said, showing off his knowledge about Haiti and its role in the nineteenth century's independence movements in the Americas.

He knew I was Haitian, and to make me feel comfortable, he edged closer to tell me about his own foreign origin, taking pride in revealing that he was the son of an Icelandic sailor and a seamstress from Reykjavik where he was born but raised in the New England town of Pittsfield. He grew up speaking both Icelandic and English, aware of the sharp differences between the two Germanic languages. He said he had a younger sister who married a black South African businessman, gleefully describing the exotic features of their mixed-race children.

"Oh, they're so *cute*, so *beautiful!*" He let out to unconsciously glamorize lighter-skinned blacks, an unspoken reality in society at large.

Soon, the conversation took a friendlier tone, like the chat of two friends. In the end, he walked me to the door, giving me his business card before we said goodbye. He did not hire me, but he promised that I should hear from the company. I thanked him for the time and the opportunity to apply for the data-entry position. Then, I walked to my car with a tinge of optimism, but still feeling trapped in a web of blighted hope from which I had yet to find an escape.

It had just been raining, and heavy gray clouds lingered on the horizon. The road was slick, and that worried me. My car needed a tune-up, and a rumbling noise coming out of the muffler added to my worry. On the dash, the oil light flashed a warning. I drove to my cousin Hilaire, who owned a small garage on the edge of Liberty City. He was closing shop when I pulled into his driveway. Short and stocky, his hands had a firm grip on the latch and were readying to pull the garage door down when he noticed me. He stopped, let go of the latch, and approached the car.

"Vinco, what's going on? Haven't seen you in a while," he said, hands inside a filthy blue overall, laughing.

"Man, I've been busy, trying to get a job."

"Marie-Louise told me you graduated last month. You should be a big shot now." With a dirt-stained handkerchief, he wiped the lingering grease and sweat off his forehead.

"That's what you think. Life is not that easy. Listen, man. My oil light is flashing and I'm hearing some funny noise coming out of the muffler." I climbed out of the car, shaking his dirty hand, and waited for him to diagnose the problem. He pulled up the hood, checking the engine oil and spark plugs.

"Vinco, you'll have to leave the car here overnight and you can pick it up tomorrow afternoon."

"Coz, isn't there anything you can do now? I just came from a job interview, and there's a great chance they might call me back."

"I wished I could do it now, but Marie-Louise is waiting for me. We have to go to Winn-Dixie for groceries. As you can see, my guys are gone."

"Coz, I really need your help. I'm penniless. I have no money for parts let alone for labor. Can I talk to Marie-Louise?"

"Go ahead. Good luck."

The small garage was connected to the house where he lived with Marie-Louise, his domineering wife, and their three children. I left him with the car and went inside. I met her near the dining room table. She was wearing a short-sleeved, loose garment and a red-striped headcloth.

"Vinco, so glad to *see* you," she giggled, gesticulating in frenzied joy, putting aside a tiny blusher puff box with which she was using to blur the pores and enhance the glow from her square face.

"Glad to see you, too, Louloune," I said, giving her a little hug.

"Vinco, at the church last Sunday, everybody was talking about your progress at school, and Nana was *so* proud." Hands on hips, she stood tall and robust, laughing with an authoritative stare, like an African queen at the height of her glory.

"Yeah, she told me."

"Sit down, *mon beau petit garçon.*" *My cute little boy.* She pulled me down onto a chair, giving me a little peck on the cheek, and snatched a velvet lipstick and gave a gentle brush to her plump lips. She liked to drop French phrases into her broken English to intimidate Hilaire, who was younger and had been living in Miami since he was three. "Didn't you see Hilaire outside?" She turned around. "*Hilaire*," she crowed, without giving me the chance to reply.

"He's replacing a couple of spark plugs in my car."

From the garage outside, Hilaire, forever compliant, cried, "Louloune, I'm right here finishing up Vinco's car."

"You're too hard on him, Louloune," I teased her.

"With these men, you can't be too soft, Vinco." She laughed, putting the final touches on her plump lips with a lip gloss.

"Are you going to church?" I teased her again. Hilaire had already told me where they were going.

"No, Winn-Dixie." She burst into uproarious laughter. From one of the bedrooms, the children became rowdy, and with a tiny bounce, she went to discipline them. She was braless, and her unrestrained breasts swung as she moved back to me.

"But you're going to have to wait for him to cleanse his body from the grease."

"*Hell*, no. He should have known better. This man is lazy. I'm fed up with him. He's going to follow me, or I'll have him wait in the car. Miami now has so many folks from Hinche, and they walk around spreading gossip. I have to look the best I can, Vinco. So, their mouth would be shut when they see me in town. You know, Hinche is the worst town in central Haiti to be from. All they do is spread lies, play dominoes, and eat fried chicken. Vinco, you remember Dorcelia?"

"No, you know I'm from Saint Louis, not in the Central Plateau where Hinche is."

"Vinco, don't do this to me. Everyone in Little Haiti knows fat-butt Dorcelia who was one of the best quickies at Chez Popo on Forty-sixth Street. She fucked with two dozen men there a night. That's why she was nicknamed the best quickie in town. They said she used a magic wand inside her panties, a kind of magnet that trapped the men and forced them to keep coming. And I was so upset when a good friend from church told me Hilaire was one of her customers."

"Louloune, I don't believe this. Hilaire is always under your watch."

"That's what you think. Last year, I caught him masturbating in the bathroom. Then I punished him, putting him on a sex diet for five months, giving him a two-minute blow once a month to empty his urge." She laughed, folding back the traces of hair that had escaped the headcloth.

"So, where's Dorcelia?"

"A friend called me last week from Hinche. She told me two months ago that the whole town was in jubilation after Dorcelia arrived from Miami with a suitcase they said was filled with money. She held the biggest party in Hinche history after marrying walleyed Dorville, the elder son of a rural chief. I was stunned. Soon after my friend told me the story, I went to that little convenience store on Second Avenue, not far from Chez Popo. Dorcelia's story was on everybody's tongue. You know, the womenfolk love to spice stories to make them more laughable. But they said Dorcelia became a prostitute to raise money for that wedding."

"But Louloune, rumors spread like wildfire. That Dorville must have found some people in Hinche to warn him against who he was about to marry."

"My baby boy, you still need to grow. In Haiti, people never question the source of your money. I'm sure this man knew."

At last, Hilaire walked in. "Vinco, I got you squared away."

"Thank you, coz." I rose from the chair.

"I put new spark plugs, changed the oil. But you'll need to bring it back in two weeks. When I test-drove it, I noticed the shocks need to be replaced," he said while handing me the keys.

"Coz, how much do I owe?"

"Don't worry. It's on me."

"Hurry up, Hilaire. We're running late. Hurry and take a shower. You smell like a wild goat." Before the iron lady launched another barrage of insults, Hilaire ran to the bathroom and shut the door. I walked to my car and sped away, feeling sorry for Hilaire, a man now enslaved by the mother of his children, the very woman who was supposed to honor him.

As soon as I got home, the phone rang, and it was a woman from Human Resources at Harrison Asset Management. "Is Mr. Lacroix available?" The woman asked.

"This is he," I replied.

"Can you come in tomorrow morning to fill out your hiring package?"

"Who is this, please?"

"I'm Mrs. Olivia Shriver, HR supervisor at Harrison Asset Management. I believe you have spoken to Dr. Rhodes this afternoon, and I am pleased to let you know that you have been hired."

I did not know what to say. An urge of *joie de vivre* took control of my heart and soul. "Thank you. What time do you want me to be there tomorrow?"

"Is eight a.m. okay for you?"

"Sure."

"When you arrive, have Alice, the young woman at the front desk, direct you to my office. Happy to have you on board. See you then."

After I hung up the phone, I felt I had just been rescued from a cliff's edge. At last, Nana's prayers had been answered. God had spoken; but deep, in my heart, mixed emotions lingered. A data-entry position was far from being what I went to college for, but it would spare Nana and me the humiliation of being evicted from our apartment. The fog of despair, in which we had been dwelling, vanished in an instant. That woman's voice over the telephone, poignantly filtered, had heralded a new dawn in my professional life. It had helped me understand how hardships and desperations can turn lofty aspirations into faint moments of hope. In that critical junction of my life, however, this job was golden.

Nana came home around six p.m. just when I was making spaghetti for the two of us. She looked beaten. Stress and anxiety had taken a toll on her body. "How was your day?" I asked.

"No change in the story. I walked more than ten miles today looking for a job," she said, dropping her purse on the table and going to lie down on the couch, her eyes half-closed.

"Well, there's a change in the story, Nana," I said with a teasing grin. "I got a call this afternoon from a management company. A woman from Human Resources there called me and congratulated me for becoming their newest employee."

"Really?" She sat right up—sleepy eyes turned feverish. "When do you start?"

"I'll know tomorrow."

"Glory to God, the Almighty!" I joined her on the couch, holding hands while shedding tears of joy. Then, we both went to the kitchen, and she took command in finishing the spaghetti. "Where's the bell pepper, the onion, and the tomatoes?"

"They're still in the fridge. I was boiling the spaghetti first."

"What? How long do I have to teach you?"

"As long as I live, dear sister."

"Go take your shower, naughty boy." She was alive again.

Later, we sat at the table, eating. "Nana, I'm worried about you. You need to take time to get yourself rejuvenated. By the grace of God, we can now breathe a sigh of relief."

"I can't relax. I also need a job. Tomorrow, I have an appointment at the food stamp office."

"I'll be paid six dollars an hour with the possibility to work overtime, Nana. For now, that will be enough to meet our obligations."

With a quick shrug, Nana dismissed my offer. She knew a second paycheck would ultimately erase any possibility of eviction. Besides, she feared her big sister's role would suffer a setback if she let her younger brother take control of household expenses. I did not insist either. This was something, I thought, that would happen in due time. That night, we felt as if the river of hope had rushed its way into our little apartment.

Chapter 4

I walked into the building, feeling confident in a slim-fit suit. Instantly, I ran across Alice, the front desk secretary, in a tailored belted dress. She was about to go into her office when our eyes met, and we both smiled at once. "I'm here to see—"

"Mrs. Shriver," she said, preempting me with tittering laughter. She stepped back and came to join me.

"Yes," I replied.

"Let's go." We walked down a long hallway leading to a double backdoor behind which was a small office building. "This is HR. Have a nice first day," she said, hurrying back to her front desk. Her wish further reinforced my positive attitude.

I went in, and there near a glass door cabinet stood Mrs. Shriver, a pale-skinned woman in a top-notch knee-length dress. "Good morning," I said. I felt my face twist as unease gripped me.

"Good morning, Mr. Lacroix," she uttered as we shook hands. "Dr. Rhodes is so proud to have you on board. Let's walk to this back office where you'll fill out your paperwork."

We walked past a large room where several employees, men and women, sat at their computer desks, getting ready for the day at work. Soon we reached a well-furnished office room. Fancy artworks hung on the wall. The room was spotless, and the impressive décor revealed her taste for neatness. "Is Dr. Rhodes here?" I asked.

"He's at his office. You won't see him this morning. From here, you'll be going to orientation, and that will last the whole day. There, you'll meet a young man named Frank, who teaches Harrison's culture to new employees."

She invited me to sit at a table across from her desk, which was accessorized in a meticulous fashion. A computer was at the center, next to which was a coffee mug. I saw no push pins, but some notes in colorful holders and well-polished bookends displayed on her fancy desk. Instead of going to her desk, she came and sat next to me as she gave me detailed instructions on how to fill out the forms. Good-humored, Mrs. Shriver spoke with a midwestern tone, making sure everything was done seamlessly. Then she requested my identification papers to make copies for record keeping.

I handed her everything, including my green card. A sense of pride seized my mind. Before receiving my green card, I used to feel like a diminished character each time I had to hand over my old Cuban-Haitian immigration paper designed for Cuban and Haitian refugees who arrived in Florida during the great migration of the nineteen-eighties. Then, those refugees lived in legal limbo as politicians in Washington debated their final status. I was never comfortable displaying that card, particularly in corporate venues such as this one.

"Mr. Lacroix is Little Haiti helpful in keeping the nostalgia at bay? I'm sure it affects most Haitians in this town." Mrs. Shriver asked in a blend of sympathetic smile and politeness. I sensed this was designed to appease the wrinkles of uneasiness popping up on my face.

"I'm sure it is. As for myself, I can speak with absolute certainty that the Haitian community has placed me a lot closer to home in many ways, including language, culture, and ethnicity," I replied.

"Haitians are indeed a proud people; they're smart. I have two young men who go to Miami Dade Community College North Campus. They have Haitian friends."

"Really?"

"Yes. One of them, the younger one, dated a very pretty girl from New York whose parents were Haitians."

"So, whatever happened to that romance?" I asked, facing her now as we talked like two friends.

"You know, kids are kids. Never committed to anything, certainly not to anything serious. So, the romance went up in smoke. My goal is to make sure he graduates this year. Then, I'll have him transferred to Barry, *your* school."

She stressed the "your" to show me how impressed she was with my academic progress for having been a refugee, and despite the odds, was still able to graduate from a prestigious Christian institution such as Barry University. We talked for a few more minutes, which she used to tell me about her parents' Creole origin from Paramin, Trinidad where they speak the same French-based Creole they speak in Haiti. Although she was born in Orlando, she said when she was a minor, her parents used to take her to Paramin for the annual Creole festival there where people from all over the Caribbean would congregate to celebrate the Dimanche Gras, eating tasty Creole food and dancing to the beat of the Crèche.

While talking, tardy employees slowed their hurried footsteps to peer through the glass window and appeared stunned to see a cordial Mrs. Shriver, relaxed and smiling while talking to a stranger. Later, as we became friends and coworkers, some of them told me how surprised they were to see Mrs. Shriver looking so cordial and welcoming in that morning meeting. They said they had never seen her laughing with anyone before. In fact, they nicknamed her the Iron Lady. I guessed I was lucky to start off in such a friendly atmosphere.

She took me on a tour of her organized building to see the employees on task, becoming more focused as we strolled by. In the end, she walked me to a conference room in the main building. "Frank, this is Mr. Yrvin Lacroix, our new hire." She presented me to a gentleman in sharp attire, wished me good luck, and then left.

Frank was tall, sun-tanned, with hair in tousled curls. "How's it going, Mr. Lacroix?" He said in a deep voice. I thought maybe it was a way to compensate for his slim posture, which made him look younger than he would have liked.

"I'm fine," I replied with an air of optimism. "Am I the only student?" I asked with a repressed laugh.

"Yes, you are the only sacrificial lamb today," he joked back.

The room was vast and furnished with cherry-finished wooden tables arranged in rows of four. Each table housed two IBM computers, and he asked me to come and sit in the front row to be closer to a large whiteboard. As in most corporate businesses, video presentations play an important part of professional development training, thereby reducing the trainer's role to little more than a facilitator. After giving me a detailed reintroduction of Harrison Investments, he narrowed the orientation down to data entry. He rolled in the videotape, which lasted forty-five minutes, covering a wide range of skills a data-entry clerk must master, including entering account information into a database for clients, compiling and sorting information, reviewing data for deficiencies, and establishing priorities.

Meanwhile, he was on the phone, speaking to what seemed to be a woman. His baritone voice of earlier had changed into a dovish, filtered one, like a foxy bachelor, pleading for forgiveness. The video soon paused, and that seemed to irritate him.

"Don't worry, I can switch it," I said.

"Okay," he replied and then refocused on the phone conversation. "Lolo," he pleaded, "I promise this is the last time, the last time, babe, the last time." He became coy and lost in his guilty plea.

In the end, the video presentation was over, and I called his attention again. "Is there another one?" I asked.

"Yes, there're four more in this same topic, *great* for reinforcement. By the way"—he looked at his watch, grimacing— "I'll give you an early lunch. It's now ten-thirty. Be back here at twelve."

"Can I leave my folder here?"

"Sure, sure. Listen, Yrvin. The cafeteria is on the second floor. There are a variety of things there to eat. But if you like Chinese food, there's a restaurant around the corner on 47th Street." Before I had the chance to say thank you, he was back on the phone, begging. "Lolo, please, Lolo."

Shortly after noon, I returned, and he looked relaxed this time, breathing a sigh of relief. "Man, with your credentials, I don't think there's a whole lot for me to present. It looks like Mrs. Shriver is on your side, and that's awesome. I'm in my third year here, and I can't remember the last time I saw her laughing or even smiling. As you already know, she supervises HR, but she makes it seem like she is the general manager of this whole building."

So, we spent another hour going over policies and procedures. Then he led me to my office, a square cubicle in the next room, containing a small desk, a computer, and a two-drawer file cabinet. He told me that I could stay there, try to organize my office, and that I could leave at four.

On the way home, I stopped by Denise Boutique, a small beauty shop at the entrance of Little Haiti. I wanted to see Joe Le Coiffeur, a popular barber among the youth. He rented a tiny room in the back of the store where he set up his barber shop. He alone ran the business. "No credit card, no personal checks are accepted—only cash," was written on a small sign hooked onto the glass window. He was a dark-skinned fellow, salt-and-pepper-haired, tall, extroverted, and always laughing at his own jokes. When he was off work, he wore nothing but the latest fashion designs of Pierre Cardin. Women easily fell prey to his seductive charm.

I knew him since my first days in Little Haiti when my sister took me for a haircut one Saturday morning. I liked him not just for his jokes, but for his skillfulness, trimming my hair in the newest popular trend among the young folks, short, tapered sideburns well-crafted to enhance a puffy tail-end haircut.

"Hey, Vinco! *Sak pase?*" He cried upon seeing me stepping into the shop. *What's going on?*

"Man, *n'ap boule!*" *I'm doing okay.*

"Look at you! Nice jacket and necktie like a businessman. What's going on?" Denise asked, she was the beautician and store owner with whom Joe shared the place.

She also was a hairdresser, and stood by a high-arc-faucet utility sink on the other side of the room where she ran a nail and hair salon. A thin, red-haired lady in a floppy dress stood before her, neck craning forward like a starving pelican as water droplets from her hair sprinkled around. Denise was a happy-faced woman and wore a knee-length t-shirt cinched tightly on the side by a single knot. She was of average height and moved with a youthful weave.

Her hair extension swung, flapped, and trailed down toward her buttocks as she hurried up to serve new customers who came to purchase cosmetic products. The store was well equipped with all kinds of beauty supplies, from cosmetic bleaching creams to hair extensions, wigs in all sizes, etc. Like all beauty salons in this town, gossip played a central role in keeping the clientele. Both Denise and Joe were masters in sharing gossip, using unrevealing stories and spicing them in the purest form of Creole tales that made one laugh until his eyes turned moist and the muscles of his jaw began to ache.

"Vinco," she said with a theatrical gesture. "I saw Bernise last week. Oh, she's charming, the prettiest Haitian girl in this town."

"Where?" Bernise was a girl I used to like back in the days when I was a senior in high school. She was then a junior at Curly High, a Catholic high school run by the Saint Mary Sisters.

"Right here when she came to purchase some hair extensions."

"Denise, you're right," Joe intervened. "That girl has the face of an angel. Vinco, did you ever fix things up with her?"

"No, it's been four years since the last time I saw her."

"Really? It's unfortunate." He paused for a moment as if scrutinizing me in my well-dressed professional outfit. "You look so sharp, Vinco. I'm sure Bernise would be pleased to see you today," Joe said.

"Stop joking, man," I said with a laugh.

"Vinco, do you want your same regular haircut?"

"You *know* it."

"Just checking." He was finishing a client's hair, a fellow with weathered and wrinkled skin akin to Langichatte Debordus's, a legendary standup comedian that middle-aged folk tried to emulate. So, I took a seat in a highchair in the corner, waiting for my turn.

"Vinco, tell me," Denise said from across the room, raising her voice a little. "You mean you never even got a kiss from Bernise?"

"No."

"How could that be, Vinco? I remember she showed me an acrostic poem you wrote to her. She was so happy reading the poem to us. Remember, Joe?"

"Of course. She was in a blue dress. She came in to purchase some extensions."

"I don't remember ever writing an acrostic poem. Maybe she was referring to another bachelor."

"Vinco, Marie-Louise told me she saw you two in Haulover Beach naked and interlaced in the water."

"Everyone knows Marie-Louise is a pathological liar. She makes things up. And did she tell you whom she herself was at the beach with on that fictional day?"

"Certainly not with poor Hilaire," Joe said. "Poor petit Hilaire. With so much cheating, he will someday have no hair left on his tiny head."

We all laughed. I then got up, stretched a bit, and sank back into the chair.

"Vinco, you look tired. I just introduced a massage service in a room in the rear. Come this weekend. I'll give you a free one. You have to promise to bring me clients."

"Thank you in advance." The front door squeaked and a woman in a blousy dress walked in.

"*Wow*, Clautide! You look like Irene Cara. Your face looks suave. *Tu es belle!*" Denise meowed in a kittenish fashion. *You're very pretty.*

"I wish I could sing like her," Clautide said, touching her face with her well-manicured fingernails as if to show off her light complexion, a shade which its fakeness appeared obvious, for sure not the one she was born with because its luster was too shiny, her elbow too dark as if her folds of skin had stubbornly succeeded in staving off the effect of the bleaching cream. In a rush, Denise folded the young lady's hair into a white towel and ordered her to go sit on a butterfly stool.

She ran to Clautide. "*Pitit*, did you see the loser Jean-Noel?" she asked Clautide, lowering her voice.

"No, *pitit*. His brother told me he moved to Fort Lauderdale with Célimène, that fat-butt slut."

"Jesus, Marie, *Joseph*! You *lost* him for good."

"I never had him, but don't worry, *pitit*. I can survive. Now, I got my green card. I'm going to learn a trade and apply for government assistance for now so that I can pay for my daughter's daycare."

"No, Clau. You can't let him go so easily. He got you pregnant. Now, he's gotta take care of his child."

"You don't know me, Denise. I'm a woman with a strong character." Clautide shrugged, dismissing Denise's advice.

"Sister, with that kind of thought, you'll be the loser, not him." Denise's words pounded my heart. I remembered Michaela's words during our last phone conversation. Now that I have a job, I felt the time had come to face my own reality with Michaela.

Joe was eavesdropping. "*Clau*," he crowed from the back like a sleazy rooster. "Can you call me tonight?"

"What for?" Clautide adjusted her dress a little and moved to the center. "You think you can fool me?"

"Leave Clautide alone," Denise warned him with an inoffensive grin, twinkling her eyes, facing Joe.

"What a fine young man you have here, Joe!" Clautide said. Her big black eyes now aimed at me.

"And he's from your hometown, too," Denise giggled.

"No way. Saint Louis men don't look so *handsome*," Clautide purred with an infantile curiosity.

"Now, you know," I said.

Joe was now done with the middle-aged man who, in a prompt gesture, rose from the barber chair and headed for the door without giving the tiniest of attention to Denise and Clautide. Their gossip seemed to annoy him.

"Big man. *Come* on over," Joe teased me.

"I hope you'll be the next president of Haiti," Clautide said, stepping closer. Denise returned to her station to finish arranging the young woman's hair.

"What part of town are you from?" Clautide asked, quite inquisitive. "You know Saint Louis is now a booming town."

"I'm from Vertus, the northern suburb."

"I'm from lower Saint Louis, near the riverside. Are you related to Laurette?"

"Yeah. We're also good friends and collegemates."

"Your name is Vinco. Right?"

"How do you know?"

"Laurette told me. I live down on the same street. She used to tell me—"

"Don't believe what she says. She likes to make fun of people." I preempted her. Laurette's name sounded like a hammer hitting my heart. "Did you guys hear the story about General Regala?" I changed the subject.

"Which one?" Denise raised her voice a little.

"What do you mean 'Which one?' How many stories they have on this man?" Joe inquired.

"There're a lot of shady stories." The young woman in the butterfly stool injected with a burst of laughter.

"How do you know?" Denise asked.

"I heard my parents talk about politics in Haiti every day," the young woman chortled. "If they're not fighting over the TV remote, they're out in the backyard tending their garden while talking about Haitian politics. Last week, I heard them say the general fathered more than two dozen children with a dozen concubines."

"General Regala is not the only womanizer among the pack," Joe intervened. "All of them are crooked and cold-blooded murderers. Duvalier may be gone, but Duvalierism is very much intact."

"Someday, Haiti will be free from the scorpion's claws," Clautide affirmed in a firm tone of patriotic fervor.

"You're so right, sister," the young woman on the stool replied.

"They said they saw the general downtown last weekend. Six stooges were with him. Some were carrying suitcases, others were trailing him like house dogs in upscale Port-au-Prince," Clautide said in disgust. "And some of them were folks who live right here in this town," she added.

"Shame on them," the young woman said with obvious repugnance.

I had succeeded in shifting the conversation. They got so involved in stories of powerful men who father children out of wedlock and whose greed had cost the lives of thousands of innocent men and women in one of the poorest countries on the planet. They did not realize Joe was done cutting my hair until he dropped the electric shaver on a small table behind him and folded into his shirt pocket the five-dollar bill I always paid him for the job. Then, like the weathered-skin man, I snuck out, leaving them lost deep in their shared passion for Haiti and its struggle to defeat poverty.

Chapter 5

The mailman had gotten what I had been waiting for, but he seemed disappointed for not being the eyewitness, the harbinger of an ascendant joy. As every day, before I stepped into the house, I emptied the mailbox. That afternoon, my eyes caught a note glued on the box. "Today, I hope I was the messenger of the best of news—your loyal mailman." Unsure of what he meant, I yanked my hand into the mailbox and retrieved the piles of advertisements within which a brown envelope stood out. It was from Michaela.

I hurried inside dropping everything onto the table but the envelope. To better digest what was in the letter, I went to my room and lay face up in bed, ripping it open. There she was in a large white nightgown that revealed the glow of a swollen face, her tender breasts, and her sprawling belly on which both of her hands rested. Her long golden hair had been shortened, and she beamed a smile that seemed frozen in the fear of the unknown. She also sent a note.

Mi amor, I'm sending you this snapshot to show you how my body has been transformed. As you can see, I no longer look like the girl who folded into your arms and melted like ice cream in the heat of sunrise. I cut my hair because the long tresses had become unbearable. In this strange place, I feel so lonely but not scared because I know inside of me our baby, the product of our love, nestles, develops, and will soon see the light of day; and, every time he moves, he gives me a sensation I can never describe, as if he's asking for you. Every time he moves, it feels like a sorrowful refrain of a sad song which brings tears to my eyes, tears of self-reproach, of self-inflected guilt. Being so far from you, nothing is the same, and Strasbourg seems surreal.

Late summer nights echo the autumnal mornings, gray and windy. Thinking of you feels as if a part of me has been extracted. The memories never cease to haunt me, sweet and omnipresent. Mi amor, the weather is changing. It's now getting cold. Last evening, outside my window, I watched the first, brief snow flurries swirling through, and Josefina said the Alsatian winter will soon turn Strasbourg cold, white, and milky. Oh Vinco, these cold nights have silenced my words, ushering a frisson of nostalgia and lovesickness that only you can heal. Now, I only have the sweet memories, the secrets that we shared, the love that we made to cherish and treasure until we meet again.

I'm now seeing a gynecologist. He's prescribed me prenatal pills. I continue to have morning sickness. He told me the baby is due in three months. Mi amor, I long for your love. I long for your touch. Amorecito, I'm cold, and I'm all to blame for this misfortune that has befallen us. It's pointless to tell you how much I miss you, but I'm confident our love will endure as it has before. Remember? If all goes well, we'll be reunited next year. Like I told you last time over the phone, I never felt so uncomfortable in a household. Although my uncle tries his best to accommodate me, he can ill afford to support me the way he promised my parents.

Josefina is teaching me some French, but I want to take French classes so that we can talk and make love in French when we meet again. I know you have plans to look for a job, but remember to register for graduate school as we have discussed. As soon as I return to Miami, I will register for the rest of my courses. There's so much I'd love to share with you, but my hand now swells, and I feel tired too easily. I hope to hear from you soon. I have faith. Next year we'll be together, we'll live together, and our baby, our primrose in the herald of spring, will also be happy to be raised by his beloved parents.

Bye, my love.

Mica

I wanted to cry. A sudden urge to reach out and rescue my girlfriend took hold of my tormented mind. I wanted to call her, but I knew it was past midnight in Strasbourg. So, I slept with the note laid on my chest. I woke up in the middle of the night and I could not go back to sleep. I became restless. In my stomach, there was an unsettledness, a frenzied lust steaming in a web of passion. Irresistibly, I grabbed the phone around four am and dialed the number. She picked it up on the first ring. "Alo," she replied in French thinking it was a local call.

"Baby, it's me," I replied with a quivering voice.

"Mi amor! My love!" She was ecstatic.

"I received your letter late yesterday, and I can't sleep. I wanted to call you right away, but I knew it was too late on your end. Mica, I miss you, too. Like you, I can't wait for the day when you and I can meet again."

"Vinco, why didn't you call me?"

"I have been going through a lot in my personal life."

"Baby, what's wrong?"

"Nothing for you to worry about. I'm okay, now. My problem is your absence. I've always wanted to be the breadwinner for my child and wife. God seemed to have decided otherwise."

"Mi amor, the suffering is mutual. Reuniting with you, being able to be with you, to hug you knowing that our lives will forever be blessed with our baby-to-be. How's Nana doing?"

"She's doing fine. She asks for you all the time. She's worried."

"Tell her not to worry. I'll be home next year."

"Baby, I found a job at an investment firm in Miami Springs. Yesterday was my first day."

"Wow! I'm happy for you!"

"Happy for you, too, and Junior."

"Don't worry about me for now, and the baby, too."

"What do you mean, Mica? Are you saying that I should let your relatives in France take responsibility for something they were never interested in? Something they were never proud of?"

"But my parents will send money for me. I think it would be best for you to save so that you can better prepare for when the baby and I return."

"Here, you go again, baby. You make your own decision without consulting me. How can you deny your baby's father the right and the privilege to take care of his child? I may be three thousand miles away, but I'm committed to doing anything in my God-given power to make sure that you, the woman I love and mother of my child, have all that's necessary to live in dignity until we meet again."

"Vinco, you misunderstand. My parents will send for me."

"So that they can continue to prove their points. Right?"

"What point?"

"That the man who got you pregnant can ill afford to take care of his own child. Don't get me wrong, Mica. I respect your parents' love and emotion, but I reject their impulsive decision as well as your inability to stand up for me. And if we're gonna create a family like they did, you'll have to restore my dignity before their eyes. I love you more than anything else in the world."

"Baby, sorry. I wish I could be with you right at this moment."

"Mica, if I had money, I would travel to France right now."

"Do you have your green card?"

"Yes."

She rejoiced over the phone. "Can you come, now? I wanna make you feel your baby kicking inside my tummy. Baby, please."

"I want it, too. But I will have to save for that. Like I said, I just found this job. It's not what I had hoped for, but it's something that I can live with, for now. I know you're safe in Strasbourg. My job here is to prepare for our eventual reunion."

"And you need money to do so. But what do you mean when you say this job is not what you had expected?"

"Baby, there's a big difference between dreams and reality. After graduation, I began to learn about the real world of corporate America. For weeks I searched in vain to find a software engineering position. I went to interviews. I was given false hope. Nothing came of it. I was desperate to get my foot in the door, and last week I was lucky to come across the hiring manager at that investment firm who decided to hire me as a data-entry clerk."

"Oh, baby."

"Don't worry. I'm convinced God has a better plan. We'll be all right."

"Vinco, I hope to find a job when I return so that we can better plan, even if it means going back to that shoe store where we first met."

"Mica, focus on the baby. Let's pray for a safe delivery. Baby?"

"Yes, darling," she replied. Her voice softened.

"I wanna touch you, Mica."

"Don't make me cry, Vinco. Your voice, just your voice makes me wanna make love."

"And that's what put us in this predicament." She laughed.

"Vinco, it's best to call around this time. It's ten am here, and everyone is at work. Josefina is at school. So that we can talk about our problem without any fear of anyone listening."

"Baby, I have to go. I'll call you before the weekend."

"Friday, same time?"

"Yes, *amorecita*. Take care of Junior."

"You make it seem as if you already know the baby is a boy," she chuckled.

"I have this gut feeling. One million kisses your way, Mica."

"Two million to you, my prince."

#

When I walked past the front desk, Alice had not yet arrived. I was on time and eager to begin work. The room was modest and partitioned in rows of cubicles, and mine was in corner of the room. I liked its isolation, which gave me greater privacy. Knowing how dusty my space was the day before, I had brought a feather duster, a clean rag, and a dust spray cleaner with which I used to keep the place tidy. I had just begun cleaning when a young lady walked in. She was a strawberry-haired brunette, petite, and wore fashionable tennis shoes.

"You're our new coworker?" She asked, strolling up to me with a welcoming smile. She offered her hand, and I shook it in a respectful manner. "I'm Angela Robinson, but you can call me Angie," she said with a burst of laughter.

"And I'm Yrvin Lacroix," I said with a grin, and she seemed to sense my unease.

"Any nickname?" She giggled, stepping a bit.

"Yes, of course. You can call me Vinco."

While we were talking, two other ladies walked in. One of them was a tall, blond woman with well-coiffed short hair. She was tanned, and it seemed this was due to too much exposure to the Florida sun. That was later confirmed by her stories of the long hours she and her husband spent in the sandy shores of South Point. The other was a young woman about my age, wearing stylish hoop earrings, high-heeled shoes, and blue jeans. She was a stunning milk-chocolate shade, and moved about with a smiling face. Upon seeing Angie and me talking, they both came up to us. We shook hands. The blond woman introduced herself as Betsy and the other, much younger, said her name was Adriana. Later, she told me she was Haitian-Mexican American, born in Southern California.

"Are there any other coworkers in this room?" I asked.

"No. Just the four of us," Adriana said with tittering laughter.

"I'm glad we now have a man to protect and defend us against unwanted attacks from the big boss," Betsy said, edging closer to me as if seeking shelter from an invisible enemy.

"You're funny," I said. We all laughed. Betsy, the oldest, seemed to have understood that her birthright gave her the advantage to lead the room. The other two girls appeared to have been fine with that. That morning, it was apparent.

"Yrvin, you don't know how to clean. Do you?" She teased me and grabbed the dust cleaner out of my hand and began to clean for me. I let her do so as the other girls looked on, twinkling their eyes to send an unspoken message to me.

"Vinco, it's nice to have you on our team," Angie said.

"Ah, he's Vinco already?" Betsy snickered with a half-suppressed smile.

"Yes," Angie said, sniggering. Both she and Adriana retreated to their respective cubicles.

Betsy and I were now alone. She continued cleaning. "I can do it, Betsy," I said.

"Don't worry. I do it all the time, even for the girls." She laughed, and I began to be convinced of her assuming role. By continuing to clean, I understood she wanted to tell me she was a control freak, and tidiness was her prime way to display her domineering position. Unexpectedly, Dr. Rhodes in a starched khaki jacket walked in.

"I knew it," he let out, laughing. "Yrvin, don't worry. You're in good hands. The ladies will take care of you. Bet, you hear me?"

Betsy stopped, one hand on her hip, her eyes fixated on Dr. Rhodes. "Of course. Don't you see? Lunch is on me, too, today."

"No. I brought lunch," I replied, showing off my little lunch box Nana had prepared for me the night before.

"Hey, ladies," Dr. Rhodes raised his voice so that everyone could hear. "I delivered on my promise. Didn't I?"

"Yes, you did!" The ladies said, laughing out loud.

"Listen, I know you guys are working on this project, and the document must be ready by Monday. I'm sure Yrvin will help to meet this deadline. So, today, take some time to show him the task." He then left.

Betsy was done cleaning. I sat at my desk, and she stood facing me. "I don't know how to thank you," I said.

"This is how we work here in this room. I love the workmanship. We cover for each other because it doesn't matter who finishes the job as long as it's done in a timely manner."

"Do you always have lunch break at the same time?" I asked.

"We always do. Usually, we go to the cafeteria to grab a sandwich. But when we want to eat something better, we go out and have lunch at one of the restaurants nearby."

"Yeah. I'm told there's a Chinese restaurant down the street from here."

"We can go next week if you like. They have great food." She dropped her hands off her hips. "By the way, Vinco, how fast can you type?"

"As fast as the job necessitates. But I'm not a professional typist."

"We're working on a large project that is due next week, and today you'll work with me."

"That's fine." That reminded me of my days at Las Calinas when I had to work with Pito Fuentes for a few days at the beginning.

With a couple of great strides, she returned to her cubicle but came right back. "I'll work with you instead. I think that'll make you comfortable in your own quarter."

"Okay."

She got her chair closer to mine at the desk as we both now faced the computer monitor. "Before we get started, I have to download this program onto your computer. You know how to use WordStar?"

"Yes, I do."

"Where did you learn it, Vinco?"

"At school."

"Which one? Lindsey Hopkins?"

"No. Barry University."

She looked surprised, even astonished. "You're Haitian, aren't you?"

"Yes, *ma'am.*"

"You're a smart young man."

"I'm not sure what you mean by being 'smart,' Betsy. School is school, a place where every human being, whether young, old, Haitian, or otherwise, can go and be empowered with education if given the opportunity. Did you go there, Betsy?"

"No. After high school, I went to a trade school. Then, I got married, and I've been working as a clerk ever since."

"You've always worked here?"

"No. I was the head clerk at Herald Holdings, an investment firm in South Miami. Five years ago, the company filed for bankruptcy and laid off all lower-level employees."

"Then, you found this position and have been working here ever since?"

"You got it, Vinco."

By now, she was done downloading the program to my computer and uploading the file we were supposed to work on. It was a large file containing a multitude of financial assets of the company's clients. It was divided into several components. Each of us had to sort a component. The job was easy, for it required no strategic thinking. All it required was brute force and the speed to get everything done before the deadlines.

Chapter 6

After an hour of going over the routine, she left me alone and returned to her space. She would come back periodically to check on me, making sure I was on track. By eleven am, I heard the timid sound of an alarm bell, and all the ladies rose at once from their seats and walked out of their cubicles. I remained seated because I did not know what to make of it. Then, Adriana rushed toward me.

"Vinco, we usually eat lunch together, and we use that little bell to alert us. Can you come with us?" She asked in a sympathetic way. The narrow squint of her tired eyes disarmed my resistance.

"I would love to, but I brought my lunch," I replied with a grin.

"Vinco, we always eat lunch together. This is our culture. We wouldn't want you to feel left alone on your first day."

"How about you go buy your lunch and come back? I won't eat until you guys return." She agreed. It looked like the others were listening.

"If this is the case, I'll go and bring the food for everyone," Angie said, standing by the exit.

They all agreed. While Angie was gone, I asked Adriana where I could find a microwave to heat the food.

"There's one in a little room next door. Let me go do it for you," she said, eagerly wanting to make me feel comfortable. Already, I felt I was being pampered.

"I'll go with you, Adriana."

Betsy drifted away, returning to her cubicle while waiting for us. While in the little room and my food was being warmed, the aroma wafted in the air, and Adriana was tempted. "Your food smells good. You made it?"

"No, my sister did."

"Your sister is a *hell* of a cook," she giggled.

"You bet. We can share it."

"What is it?"

"It's yellow squash soup."

When we were back, Angie had not returned. So, we went to Betsy's place. From some empty cubicles, we grabbed some chairs. Soon, Angie strolled in, bringing bags of sandwiches and drinks, including a can of mango drink for me. "For you, Vinco. I know folks from Miami love mangoes," she chuckled, handing Betsy and Adriana their respective sandwiches.

"Are we having a welcoming party here?" Betsy asked, always in her domineering fashion.

She unwrapped her sandwich and the other girls followed suit. I realized that the girls seemed comfortable in deferring to Betsy the supervisor and her big-sister role—something I noticed she enjoyed immensely. But I was not interested in being scooped up by anyone. I was not also sure if she would want me to be a conformist junior clerk. On my first day at work, playing along seemed the right thing to do. Besides, these women's attitude toward me was a warm, accommodating one. I took out my own food and began to eat.

"Wow!" Betsy shrieked. "Your food smells good."

Angie lowered her sandwich and craned her neck, eyeing my soup. "Hmm, that must be delicious," she said with a smile, voracious and tempting. Her hair was in a bouffant like a ravishing female from the sixties, swept forward and nearly covered her entire face.

"*Tell* me about it," Adriana said, taking a bite of her sandwich and roughly choked herself as she chewed. "He told me his sister made it."

"That's what I was gonna *say*," affirmed Betsy. "A young man like you can never make such impressive food."

"Since you all seem impressed, we all can share it," I proposed.

"Don't worry, Vinco," they replied with one voice.

"So, you live with your sister?" Adriana interrogated, apparently scrutinizing my personal life.

"Yes."

"What about your folks?" Betsy inquired.

"They don't live here. And you, Angie?" I tried to turn the conversation on her.

"And what?"

"Do you live with your parents?"

"Yeah."

"Me, too," Adriana said forcefully. "But it won't be for long."

"Why?" I asked, peering into her fierce gray eyes.

"This is the moment in life when one has to assert herself. It's time for me to break free."

"Really?" Angie inquired.

"How do you free yourself?" Betsy intervened.

"Find Mr. Right and get married," Angie teased her. "My best friend is from the Dominican Republic, and she was literally expelled from her home for being pregnant by her Puerto Rican boyfriend," Angie added in disgust.

My heart sank at her revelation. Michaela popped into my mind, and my appetite had all of a sudden vanished, to be replaced by the unspoken persistence of sadness, lovesickness, and the bitter taste of melancholy that seemed to forever enslave the minds of those who live in solitude. A mix of lassitude and gloom flickered within me, and before my change of mood betrayed me, I wrapped my food and rose from my chair.

"I just remembered that I have to sign a form for HR. See you guys later." I lied and left.

At my cubicle, I struggled to finish my assignment for the day; I did it with stoic determination. The first day ended on a successful note, and each passing day, my confidence grew. The environment became friendlier. Although going to work every day no longer bore the loathed sensation of anxiety, the work itself was too shallow. Entering data in a computer file reminded me of the transitionary nature of the job and the condescending feeling that came with it, in particular in moments of pressure to meet deadlines. So, I continued to look for an alternative, for a software engineering position. I kept in contact with Anabel from IT Services, reminding her of my continued effort to find my dream job. Friday had arrived. Four in the morning, I called Michaela.

She was ready on the other end. "*Amorecito*, I've been waiting."

"Me, too, Mica. So, how's your week?"

"It's fine, the anticipation of your call now makes my days a little easier to go through."

"How's Junior?" We both laughed.

"He's been fine, kicking and asking for Dad. I can feel him now. I guess he knows Dad is on the phone."

"Oh, baby. I wish I were by your side, in bed resting my head over that sprawling tummy."

"Don't make me cry, Vinco. So, how was your first week on the job?"

"Okay. But I'm determined to find the job I went to school for."

"And I pray to God every day for that job to come by."

"Mica, I'm going to register for graduate school. It's expensive, far more than I anticipated. I'll have to take student loans to pay for at least part of the cost. I've realized if someone wants to succeed in the corporate world, he has to have the means to maximize his chance, and a higher education and a good discipline can provide that."

"Vinco, I agree. I can't wait to be with you next year so that we can plan together."

"Me, too, Mica. When is your next doctor's appointment?"

"In two weeks. And the doctor says he'll be able to give me a more-or-less date of delivery. But you know, this experience of going to the doctor in a foreign country has opened my eyes in many ways. I now know what it means to be an immigrant. I can barely understand what the doctor says."

"Who goes with you?"

"Josefina. Last time, we took the commuter train. But on the way back, somehow, we failed to transfer to the train that goes to the eastern side of town where we live."

"And then what?"

"You won't believe it, *mi amor*. We ended up in Germany, in the town of Kehl, a small city across the Rhine River."

"So, what did you do?"

"We had to get off and take the train returning from Offenburg, another German city farther away, going to Strasbourg."

"I'm gonna fire Josefina. She's supposed to be your eyes and ears."

"She usually does a good job, but that day, she was busy reading a magazine. We didn't realize we missed the exit until we heard the common French phrase '*Prochain arrêt, Kehl*!' which means, 'The next stop is Kehl.' Then, Josefina raised her rosy cheeks. Her eyes were inflamed."

"I wish I could be in Strasbourg with you."

"*Mi amor, no puedo vivir sin ti.*" *I can't live without you.*

And we began to cry, shedding tears of pain, sorrow, and grief, longing for the day when the uncertainty of time would be lost in the merriment of infinite love; but despite our suffering, our solitariness no longer defined our loneliness. I could hear her lacerating cry, and because of this, the stillness of my bedroom had become a welcoming interlude in my difficult journey through life. The echo of her voice pounded my heart but heightened my hope, powerful enough to repel all gloom and darkness. Through her vibrating voice, the bell of love jingled in the faint distance, heralding a new dawn, a new life with Mica, the shared existence we had always wanted. There in my bedroom, I held onto the phone not willing to let go, even as the time to get ready for work had arrived.

"Baby."

"Yes, *mi amor.*"

"I have to go."

"Not yet, baby. I crave your lips."

"I want yours more."

In my ear, she breathed softly but intensely, and the soft hum of her voice echoed the lusty passion boiling inside of her. When we ultimately let go, and her voice vanished, her body unreachable, I knew once more how lonely I was. Drifting to the bathroom, my eyes soaked in tears, I felt powerless against overwhelming odds. My anxiety now deepened. I wanted her voice in my ear until we could touch each other again, or at the very least keep our little, romantic chat every morning. I knew it was impossible. Neither of us could afford a daily long-distance phone conversation. It was too expensive.

Later as I was leaving, Nana walked me to the car, something she had never done. When we reached the passenger door, she held my hand. "Vinco, be yourself. Keep your eyes on the road. I hear your pain. Mica will return. Have faith."

I did not reply. We hugged and kissed goodbye. On the road, her words resonated. She had been listening to my conversation and, as always, was afraid my painful chagrin would swallow every part of my body, absorbing it until a human shell emerged, too numb to feel the pain.

I arrived at work, breezing through the day, almost stress-free. The positive attitude toward me at work had helped boost my morale. The ladies reminded me every day of my own sister, protective and eager to make me feel appreciated. We brought lunch to each other on a regular basis. I told my sister about my special treatment at work and about how the ladies loved her cooking. I never knew why they were so kind to me; to please them, I made sure all assignments were done ahead of time. I helped them when they were running late on their assignment deadline.

I registered for graduate school, pursuing a Master's degree in software engineering. Nana and I had gained control of the bills. However, she never stopped looking for another job. One afternoon, she came home elated. "Vinco, I got a job!" She cried, both hands in the air in celebration.

"*Where?*" I was equally happy.

"At a doctor's office on Biscayne Boulevard, just north of the television station."

"You mean Channel 10?"

"Yes."

"How did you get the job?"

"A sister at the church recommended me. They were looking for a Creole speaker to deal with a growing number of Haitian patients. I called yesterday, and they called me back this morning right after you left, asking me to come in for an interview. When I arrived, I met a tall woman named Dorie. She was very nice, explaining the nature of the job. I'll be working as an office assistant, servicing the Haitian patients."

"Wow! How much will they pay you?"

"Four bucks an hour. It's full-time, too. I praised the Lord. I was always afraid that you would lose your job, and we would be right back in the same humiliating situation as before."

"Don't worry. God would never let us go down that low again."

"I have more news for you, Vinco."

"Tell me, sister." My eyes widened.

"I got rid of Lucien."

"Now, this news is even *sweeter.*"

"I knew you were gonna say that."

"I got my sister *back*!"

"I knew I had to get rid of him, but I wasn't ready."

Since that day, Nana was rejuvenated. With a new job and a recalcitrant boyfriend off her back, her youthful glow had resurfaced. She had enrolled in a nursing assistant program, saying it would increase her profile at work and put her on track for a promotion. I could not agree more. I continued to have my weekly chat with Mica. On the final days of her pregnancy, she sent me another picture. Naked from the waist up, both hands rested on her belly, stretching like a balloon. "Look what you've done to me, *amorecito*," she wrote in a quick note. My heart pounded at her words. So, I redoubled my effort to save more money for when she and my baby came home.

Chapter 7

It was just past midnight when the phone rang. The sound was long-pitched and distant. I sensed Mica was on the other end. "Mica!" I cried, bolting out of the bed.

"No, it's not Mica," Josefina voiced cheerfully. "Your baby boy is here! He looks strong, just like his dad, with the same forehead as yours." She was gleeful, cooing like a roadrunner, heralding the dawn of a brand-new day.

"When did he come? Where's Mica?"

"Junior came late this afternoon, and Mica is recovering with the baby at the maternity hospital on Rue Philippe Thys. My brother and I are with her. She's in pain, but she wanted me to come down to call you to let you know."

"Can I talk to her, even for a minute?"

"Wait. Let me go see if she can." I held onto the phone. She came right back. "The nurse is now with her. I'll call you in five minutes."

I ran to Nana's room. "You got a nephew. Yrvin Junior is here!"

"Mica just *called?*"

"No. Josefina just did. She's in the hospital with her. She said she'll call me again in a few to let me talk to her."

"Thank you, *Jesus!*" Nana rose from her bed and joined me in celebration. "You're a dad, a penniless dad!" She pecked my cheek.

"You got that right, sister."

"I'm joking, Vinco. Even if it was true, this is not the moment to think about the uncertainty or even fear with the coming of a child. In any event, it wouldn't be fair to Junior. Remember Manman's old saying?"

"Which one?'

"Babies never ask to be born. You make them, you need to take care of them." Nana burst out laughing. I laughed with her; and, in this explosion of laughter, the phone rang again.

"*Mi amor,*" she uttered feebly. She was in pain.

"I'm here, *amorevita.* I know you're in pain. Where's Junior?"

"They took him to the nursery. He looks just like his father. Too much like him."

"Really? You're kidding."

"The same forehead, eyes, and when he's grimacing, he looks even more like Dad, especially when Dad makes funny jokes to soften Mom and make her laugh."

"Do you know when you'll go home?"

"Not yet. They'll have to run some tests on him. That might take a day or two."

"Mica, how can I help?"

"Baby, I'm okay for now, and I think it's all that matters for the three of us."

The expression "the three of us" had all of a sudden become our new reality. I felt frightened. "Baby, I know. I'm gonna let you rest for I can hear you're breathing heavily."

"I already told the nurse Junior's name."

"And what is the name?"

"Yrvin Junior." I could hear her trying to laugh, but she was in pain. "Call me later, Vinco."

"Of course, I will, *amorecita.*"

She then asked Josefina to give me instructions on how to reach her by phone, and she did. After I hung up the phone and Nana returned to her room, I became quite pensive. A stew of thoughts boiled down in my mind. I felt like a feckless loser in a sentimental narrative, a man who had been prevented from holding his newborn child, a man who had been forced to recognize his true limit in a world plagued by unexpressed prejudices. The coming of Junior, however, in a blur had allayed all feelings of resentment, until now, that my heart had harbored since Mica left.

Her parents' shortsightedness had also trapped them, leaving them, I supposed, to wrestle with their own self-inflicted guilt. Previously, I had not doubted their love for their daughter, but that love had been called into question the minute they decided to ship Michaela to Europe to avoid "humiliation." In my mind, their action had exposed how much they feared my precarious living conditions, how terrified they were when Michaela admitted she was indeed pregnant. In a world where money and status are so overvalued, consumption always takes precedence over one's inherent dignity. They knew I was a refugee and lived on the fringe; but they also knew I was an ambitious university student determined to beat the odds, to break through that glass ceiling to reach my full potential. Every parent wants what is best for their child, and financial stability generally tops the priority list. Nevertheless, in their lack of forethought, they had blundered in their rush to keep Mica away from me.

On that critical day, being forced to live in France, away from those she held dearest in her broken heart, Mica's eyes had grown even wider, and her loneliness deepened. She no longer saw in her mother and father her reliable parents. Her uncle, who had promised to shelter her just as his brother would, was not there by her side that day. Later when I called, they had yet to show up at the hospital to check up on her as Mica told me. Josefina and her brother had gone home, and she was left to rely on her own survival instincts to understand the nurses' instructions. An old English woman who was a doctor on the floor would sometimes interpret for her, but she was frequently busy with other patients. My phone call was a savior.

"Vinco, I haven't seen Junior since this morning. Can you talk to the nurse for me?"

"Let me speak to her."

She passed the phone to her. "Alo!" The nurse responded.

"Oui. Je suis le père du bébé. Maman veut lui voir. Depuis ce matin elle ne l'a pas vu." I'm the father. Mom wants to see her baby. She hasn't seen him since this morning.

"Ah, bon. Je vais lui chercher." Okay. *I'll go look for him.*

"Merci beaucoup," I thanked the nurse.

"Je vous en pris, monsieur." You're welcome, sir. And before she passed the phone back to Mica, she asked me to tell her she would be going home Sunday afternoon, providing the doctor signed the discharge papers. When I told Mica what the nurse had said, she reacted with mixed emotions, knowing she was not going to hear from me until she got better.

"Do your folks know?" I asked her.

"I guess so. But I haven't talked to them."

"I'm sure your uncle has already called them."

"You may be right. Earlier, the phone rang, but I told Josefina not to pass me any overseas call unless it's you."

"Baby, you can't ignore them."

"I've never ignored them. They've abandoned me, placing me on the train to the unknown."

"Don't say this. You and your parents were inseparable until the very moment they knew you were carrying my baby. You may say their action, however cruel it may seem, was an impulsive miscalculation rather than a dishonorable rejection. They never expected that from their lovely daughter, principally when they knew I was the father."

"I'm not going to dispute your thought. No one ditches what he loves. He shelters and cherishes it. I know someday they'll realize that my choice of you was the perfect one for me."

"I'm sure they will. But if they call, don't reject their call. You don't wanna make things harder for the two of us."

The nurse came back with the baby, and I could hear Junior's repetitive cry, low-pitched and rhythmic.

"Junior's crying for you," she said, laughing while baby-talking him.

"I can't wait any longer, Mica. I wanna hold both of you in my arms."

"I have faith. It won't be long for that to happen."

"Take care of Junior. I'll call you tomorrow morning."

But tomorrow when I called, she was gone. I tried the house. The phone rang but no one picked it up. Five days later, I received a package from Strasbourg. In it, were two pictures of her, holding Junior in her arms, face grimacing as if lip-smacking. There was also a note with a new phone number. She told me not to worry about money. Her parents had sent for her. She suggested that I save for when she and Junior came home. She said she had no intention of going back to her parents' home and would marry me as I had asked her before. We would do it at the downtown courthouse. She said her Catholic faith would not allow her to live with me out of wedlock.

My worries vanished instantly. I had become more optimistic about a speedy reunion with Mica, and Nana's new job had helped me a lot in that frame of thought. I could save more than what I originally anticipated, and to save faster, Mica and I agreed to chat once a week, every Friday evening, my time, when the international call was cheaper. During every chat, she would place the phone next to Junior's bassinet so that I could hear his movements.

A month later, she told me she had registered for a French class at the University of Strasbourg. I reluctantly agreed to the idea because that would certainly delay our reunion. However, she was determined to learn French to make sure it was part of one of the languages we would speak in the household besides English, Spanish, and Creole. She said it was a tuition-free class offered for foreign students at the University of Strasbourg. She said the class would last one semester, and then she would head home. At every chat, we tried to have a limited conversation in basic French, and we would switch into English when she encountered words she had not yet learned.

#

One day, Nana came in with a gentleman named Paul Emile. He was tall and well-built. He bore an Afro hairstyle and seemed proud of it. He wore khaki trousers and a black jacket without a necktie. Nana presented me to her new boyfriend, who wanted to marry her. He appeared to be a nice individual, and a deeply religious one. He would quote a passage from the Bible every time he stressed the emphasis on something he deemed important to him. He stayed for about two hours, speaking in meticulous grandiloquence, hoping his pomposity mixed with his well-educated manner would leave a lasting impression in Nana's beloved brother's mind. A few days later, he took us to the Walt Disney World resort in Orlando. We had a lot of fun, and as he walked hand in hand with my sister, now genuinely in love, I was busy looking for Michaela's beauty and demeanor in every Hispanic girl who came across our path in that theme park. Later that day, when he dropped us off at home and left, I asked Nana if she honestly thought he was the one.

"I think so," she replied with a dubious undertone. "What do you think, Vinco?"

"It's very difficult to jump to a conclusion because I barely know him. But I can see the difference between him and Lucien. They're like day and night."

She smiled to confirm my assertion. "He asked me to marry him, but I told him I wanna marry him after you finish the graduate program."

"No, Nana. Don't ruin your chance. Besides, Mica returns in a few months, and she won't go back to her parents'."

"She told you that?" Her voice rose and then quivered.

"She's adamant, although I tried to convince her not to. She's bitter for what they did to her."

Nana said nothing more, and went to her room. A month later, as I was getting ready to go to work on a Tuesday morning, Nana came to my room. "Vinco, Paul and I have agreed to get married. But I'm still hesitant. I don't want to leave you alone. Would you come to live with us?"

"Nana, don't worry. I already told you. Mica will be here soon." I hunched over and gave her a little hug to reassure her.

"Vinco, I've been giving some serious thoughts about this. I'm not convinced Mica will return so quickly. I'm sure she'd love to. But will she have the courage to defy her relatives in France to get on a plane back to America?"

"Nana, we talk every day. She sounds excited each time."

"Anyway, young man, you need to get a plan B if the plan of return runs into a problem."

Still skeptical, she walked me to the car that morning. I sensed she had more to say. "Have you guys already settled on a date?" I asked, sounding cheerful, to tell her once more it would be okay.

"Not yet, Vinco. We could have but my worries continue to pin me down."

"Nana, I want you to focus on your wedding, knowing your brother will be okay. You're marrying your soulmate; you're not abandoning me. I know I will forever count on your support, and that's enough for me."

Three months thereafter, Nana and Paul tied the knot inside her little Baptist church in the presence of an elated group of relatives and well-wishers. Uncle Philippe, Uncle Tony, and our dad, who flew from the Bahamas, were all dressed in white suits fit for the occasion. As per the tradition, my father walked Nana down the aisle, and when they reached the altar where the groom stood, he handed Nana over as his eyes swelled with tears. Nana was molded inside a white gown and her face was covered with a wedding veil. She then took position near Paul Emile, her husband-to-be, attired in a black tuxedo, smiling at the attendees.

When the ceremony was over, the wedding reception was held in a small room outside the church building. The crisis group members decorated it in the purest Haitian tradition with tropical flowers and red roses. The food was plentiful—*Gryo* (deep fried pork), *pikliz* (hot pickles), and dark rice were served with a variety of Haitian party drinks.

In the midst of this memorable moment, one of the maids of honor, a young lady with hollowed cheeks dressed in a pink gown, rose from her seat and walked to a small podium where a spiky-haired master of the ceremony waited behind his microphone for the maid of honor to come to deliver some remarks. When the young woman passed by the table, where my father and I sat, on her way to the microphone, my father smiled.

His eyes fixed on her. "She could be yours if you make a move tonight," he said with a burst of laughter.

"You think so, Papa?"

"Sure. She's very beautiful. Can't you see, Vinco?"

"I'm happy for Nana tonight, Papa." I changed the conversation, although I was tempted to tell him about my story with Michaela. Until now, a few of my relatives knew about it. I thought my father would not have approved of me getting my girlfriend pregnant. I had preferred to wait for the right moment to do so—when Mica returned.

A day after the wedding, Papa flew back to the Bahamas, and I was left to face a new reality, living without Nana. My first night without my sister in the apartment was a sleepless one. I had never lived alone in my life. The place was empty, apart from my little bed and few belongings. But her fragrance, the aroma of her delicious cuisine seemed omnipresent, even the echo of her filtered voice still lingered in my subconsciousness. I kept on surveying the naked walls with saddened eyes. Her pictures, her favorite paintings, her clothes, her shoes in the closet, all were gone and appeared lost in the harsh transition of life.

At the time Nana told me she was getting married; I did not feel the impact right away. I was too deep in my preparation in anticipation of Michaela's return. I even thought of myself to be lucky that my sister had found her soulmate. After all, it was the fear of leaving Nana without the means to cover all the bills that paralyzed me the minute I proposed to Michaela at Morningside Park following the pregnancy test result.

The newlyweds rented a modest cottage home in southwest Miami. I remained in the apartment while intensifying my effort to get ready for Mica and Junior. I bought new furniture, a new bedroom set, and kitchen utensils. In every chat, I shared with Mica news of some items I purchased, and she would give me her opinion on certain furnishings based on her preferences. I was alone, but I no longer felt lonely. Between work, school, and getting ready for Mica and Junior, my hands were full.

One Friday evening, two months after Mica started learning French, I called her as usual for our regular chat, but she did not pick up. Normally, she would pick up on the first ring because on her end it would be late at night. I did not insist on calling her again. I was hoping for a collect call. It never came. I went to bed without hearing from her. The next morning, I called her again. Someone picked up the phone saying she was not available. The person sounded like the voice of a young man. He was very polite. So, I identified myself as the baby's father and left a message for Mica to call me. Mica never did. I spent the whole week feeling disturbed. I feared another episode of what happened months ago when she went to France without sharing her decision with me. Friday night had arrived. I was on the verge of drifting off to sleep when the phone rang.

"Baby, it's me," she said, sounding quite unconcerned. "How are you, Vinco?"

"I'm fine," I replied. "So, what has happened?"

"I could not call you on Friday. Junior cries at night, and because of that, I had to move to another room without a phone."

"But I called you and left a message the next day."

"I know. I just could not call. I'm so tied up with Junior. When I can call you, you're at work."

"So, how's Junior doing?"

"He's being the bad boy, crying to be breastfed." She laughed and forgot that everyone was asleep.

"Are you breastfeeding him?" I teased her.

"Hell, no," she replied sarcastically.

So, we talked about our problem as always. Soon, Junior started to cry, and I could hear his voice in the distance, chirping like an angry bird.

"Baby, I gotta go. I'll call you."

I didn't hear from her until two weeks later, basically to tell me she had found a job at a cosmetic boutique in downtown Strasbourg. "Mica, you already know enough French to find a job?" I asked, choked with emotion.

"They hired me because I speak English. They have a lot of English customers, British and Americans. I didn't know there were so many Americans and other English-speaking folks in the city..."

I let her talk and talk and talk until she ran out of words and realized she had long been plunged into an arid, inexcusable monologue. I did not have the courage to reply. So, she stopped, and I remained silent.

"Vinco, are you there?" She asked in a weak voice.

"Of course, I am. I just don't know how to reply. Are you trying to tell me something you know will not please me?" My voice was hoarse.

"What thing, Vinco?" She became defensive.

"You know I've been preparing for the three of us. And I give you an account of everything I do each time we talk. I just don't understand this move, Michaela. If you're changing your mind, let me know *now*."

"Baby, what do you mean by 'changing my mind?' I've figured some extra cash is always better."

"Even at the price of making me wait until *you* decide, without me again, when *you* think it's the right time to come home." I was angry.

"Vinco, that's not true."

"If it isn't, show me how to interpret your sudden decision to find a job in Strasbourg. Maybe you have yet to realize how your absence has left an emptiness that only your presence can fill." My voice began to break.

"Vinco, I miss you more than you could ever imagine. I didn't tell you about my decision because I knew it wasn't gonna please you."

"And you did it anyway, Mica? Goodbye, Mica."

"No, Vinco." She tried to stall me, but I was gone.

I could not believe that once again I was deep in the trance of an unreachable love. The harder I fought and the closer I got to winning over this great barrier, the more I found myself losing against the odds. This elusive romance drifted further away into the bewildering perplexity of time.

95

Chapter 8

Michaela and I continued to hold our Friday night chat, but the talk revolved mainly around Junior, and it lasted no more than ten minutes. She no longer talked about going home, and I ceased to raise the issue. Her loss of interest and intimacy over time had become obvious. Like a climber going down from a mountaintop, our Friday night chat had become a gradual and scary descent into uncharted territory. Gone was the anticipated and exciting rendezvous. To Mica, I could tell, it was more like one last task in an already stressful day. Then, I offered to hold off the chat and to talk whenever it was comfortable for both of us. She rejected the offer and insisted that we maintain the same format. I guessed she did not want me to uncover her change of attitude.

Love, however, carries uncontrolled emotions with boundless desires. Pure love, that is. The one Mica had always expressed in words and actions. But when interest dwindles, so too were the sacrifices required to cherish a long-distance relationship. She tried as hard as she could to hide her diminishing appetite to chat. As the father of her son and the sole man she had ever loved, I would be the last person on this earth whose feelings she would want to hurt and whose hopes she would want to dash.

Yet, it appeared she was fighting against something greater than herself. First, our Friday night chat had turned into a monthly one, and solely when time permitted. Then came a shambling procession of little white lies. "Junior is asleep, and he had such a bad day." Or, "Vinco, I'm very tired, worn out by this new job." Or, "Learning French is so hard. I need time to study." In the end, after an agonizing eternity of small talks and empty promises, the chat went cold, frozen in the icy fog of faraway romance. I expected that. Coming home with a baby to me, whom her parents disapproved, would not set her free from her nightmarish state of mind. She still had to face her parents and seek peace and approval. So, I began to question the very existence or feasibility of true love unless it is linked through blood. It had been three months since our last chat, and these thoughts felt like an endless angst for which I had no cure.

Work now became a holy sanctuary, the place that offered me a sense of appeasement. I started showing up earlier than everyone, and I was one of the last employees to leave the premises after work. Among us was a slim girl, chocolate-skinned, who walked with sharp strides, particularly when I crossed her path on her way to and from the cafeteria. She would throw a superficial smile when our eyes met and weave on. She worked in Account Services. I thought maybe she was an introvert, a gentle and reserved girl.

One afternoon, I met her in the front building waiting for a ride home. The minute she saw me coming, she turned her face away. Maybe she sensed I was going to engage her in some form of conversation. I walked by without acknowledging her presence. As I reached the parking lot, a blue Toyota pulled in.

"*Kote-w te ye?*" She asked a young man in dark attire sitting behind the wheel. He looked nervous. *Where have you been?*

The gentleman mumbled some words in Creole I could not hear. In this whole building, there were five black employees: Mrs. Shriver, my coworkers Angie and Adriana, that young lady, and me; working in the middle of a slew of white folks. One day, I was running late, and I heard an explosion of laughter. I made an abrupt stop, and my eyes squinted.

"*Blondine*, girl, you're so funny!" One of her coworkers shrieked.

The black girl, whose name until then I did not know, took center stage in a joke-telling ambiance, flirting with everyone. In an instant, I understood her meanness was reserved for me alone. Indeed, she was a friendly girl who did not want my friendship.

Adriana was carless. So, I drove her to her place after work almost daily. She had moved out of her parents' home and lived in an apartment in northeast Miami. One afternoon, as we were leaving our workstation, Blondine walked right by us, moving in swift, gigantic steps.

"You know this girl?" Adriana asked. Her voice lowered.

"No."

"She's a Louisiana Creole."

"Really? Let's hurry, Adriana. I have to study for a final exam." I changed the conversation.

I knew Blondine, an insecure girl, ashamed of her roots, her identity, had lied to everyone. A Creole from Louisiana would suit her perfectly, better than the ones led by Dessalines. Those Creoles had successfully battled Napoleonic soldiers in Saint Domingue, freeing the slaves when Louisiana was still a French territory from which its slaves wanted to flee at all costs to reach the shores of Haiti. But ignorance is more than a hindrance on the road to progress. It can be fatalistically dangerous.

Of course, I was not about to share this with Adriana, whose Haitianism seemed limited to what she had learned from her father. She would not have understood the identity problem so rampant among the Haitian youth, mimicking African Americans in the way they spoke English as they tried desperately to bleach the stain of shame, they thought, that forever stamped the dignity of Haitians living in America.

That afternoon, the disturbance on my face could not be hidden. "Why are you so quiet this afternoon, Vinco?" Adriana asked.

"I'm not feeling well," I said. Both hands took a firm grip on the steering wheel.

"I can see that. No jokes, no music." She tried to stir me up.

"It looks like I'm catching a cold."

"Oh, no."

When we reached her apartment building, she invited me inside for the first time. It was a modest place furnished with basic furniture, but her imposing picture in the golden frame hooked onto the wall shed the charm and neatness that, in an instant, captured my attention. "I know you have to go study for a test but give me a minute. I'll make you some lemon tea."

She invited me to sit on the couch while she went to make tea. So, I sat there watching her decisive moves, shifting from the stove to her small kitchen cabinets, pulling out teabags, mugs, sugar, and spoons. Her sharp curves moved about in relaxed motions.

"I know you're happy to be in your own place," I said, rising from the sofa and joining her.

"I'm not sure, Vinco."

"What do you mean?"

"Vinco, living alone brings mixed feelings, let alone for a young woman like me."

"I thought that was what you've wanted."

"Yes, I have. But as you know, Vinco, reality can be far removed from a dream. I'm not gonna lie to you. I feel vulnerable in my apartment at night, and I have to call my mom before going to sleep. I miss home, Vinco."

"Why don't you go back?"

"I would never go back. I know my folks would be very happy, but I'm not sure how I would feel." She was done with the tea, and we went back onto the sofa, chatting. Her hollow cheeks became deeper when she smiled, exhibiting her pride to be a free and independent young woman. She smiled like Mica. She spoke Spanglish like Mica.

"Adriana, I hear you. I now live alone."

"*Se vre? Kote sèw?*" She asked in Creole. "*Really? Where's your sister?*" It was the first time we spoke in Creole. Until then, I did not know how impressive her Creole was.

"My sister got married a few weeks ago. Adriana, I guess you and I share the same worries, minus the vulnerability. I miss my sister. I've never lived alone in my life."

"Welcome to the club, Vinco. But you have your girlfriend to talk to, even if she's now in Europe."

"We do, but it's expensive to keep a long-distance relationship."

"Tell me about it." She laughed, but a laugh charged with an upsurge of disgust.

We both said nothing more, but I could tell she had more to say. For now, I refrained from pushing her to reveal her unexpressed words. So, we sat there, sipping the hot tea as if diving into the swollen silence of the room.

I broke the silence. "You seem disenchanted with long-distance relationships. Don't you?"

"I'm not sure if it's a sort of disenchantment with the idea. It's the pain associated with it. It's painful in the sense that love is like a flower that needs to be watered and sometimes daily if not every hour."

She was done with her tea, and adjusted herself on the sofa, taking off her hoop earrings and resting her head on the cushion. "I was involved in an abusive relationship when I lived in San Diego."

I sat right up, taking the last gulp of my tea. "How abusive was that?"

"He was tearing up my heart with lies, cheating on me."

"How could anyone cheat on an exuberant girl like you?" I gave her a big brother's stare.

She smiled, welcoming a compliment she could not ignore. "Vinco, why are men so difficult to trust?"

"I never knew untrustworthiness was an exclusive reserve for men. Your father is a man, and I'm sure you'll put your life on the line for him."

"You know what I mean."

"Yes, I do, but that assertion can also be attributed to women. My relationship with Michaela is now going through some major turbulence. Though I'm still hoping for a soft landing, I'm not betting on it."

"What kind of turbulence?"

"It's not the time to talk about it. I'm going home, and I need to concentrate. Remember?"

"Yeah, you have to go. But I wish you could stay a bit more."

"Next time." She walked me to the car, and we hugged.

Later, just before bedtime, I called her. "As if I knew you were gonna call me," she giggled.

"I've been thinking of you, Adriana, since I left. I think you and I now share the same burden in life. You haven't called your mom yet?"

"Not yet. Let me do so, now. I'll call you right back."

Five minutes later, she called me back. "So, tell me what happened with *you* and Michaela."

"Adriana."

"Call me, Adi."

"I have to get used to it." We both laughed. "I can't get into this conversation, Adi."

"Why not?"

"Because this will awaken issues I would otherwise prefer not to talk about. After all, we're going to say goodnight, and my night will be long and sleepless. Forgive me, Adi. I hope we can talk about it someday. But I can tell you this."

"What, Vinco?"

"Like Michaela, you're a very charming young woman, but you and Michaela have two different personalities."

"How different, Vinco?"

"I'll tell you in due time."

We changed the conversation to our busy work schedule, the things we like in life. We hung up the phone with an eagerness to meet again the next morning. Since then, we had been holding nightly chats. At work, she made lunch for the two of us. On weekends, we went to private parties and danced all night long. One Saturday night, I dropped her off, and before I drove home, she stopped me.

"Vinco, I want you tonight." She was blunt.

The minute we entered the apartment, we threaded to the room. We both undressed at once and then we made love. We were lovers ever since. At work, we fought as hard as we could to avoid suspicions.

But one morning, Angie came to my cubicle and asked, "Vinco, are you and Adriana lovers?"

"What kind of question is this, Angie?" I was aloof.

"Anyway, I think she is madly in love with you. And Betsy made the same observation."

"Is it because she rides with me?"

"Not at all. The way she looks at you…"

"Don't start it, Angie. This is pure imagination," I lied, but they never believed me, rejecting my standoffishness.

I got caught one Friday night, when Adi and I showed up at a little bar on Calle Ocho. Angie was right there with her boyfriend, a well-built fellow with a funny laugh. Angie stared at us, and we soon burst out laughing.

On Monday at work, Angie came up to me again. "I knew you were lying."

"We're just friends, Angie."

"Friends don't French kiss and slow-drag on dancefloors. I feel sorry for your girl in France."

"Angie, my story is complicated. We'll talk." She left.

Michaela continued to flash across my mind, for sure, and I still wished to get a ring from Strasbourg, but my feeling of hopelessness no longer bewitched my mind. Nana called me almost daily to make sure I took care of myself the way she would. When I told her that Michaela would not return to America, she asked me to join her. Once again, I refused, reminding her I wanted her to focus on her marriage, on the new family she had just created. She would make me deep-seasoned fried fish, fried plantains, and Haitian pickles, dishes she knew I loved. I would come to eat and would leave with the rest that I would share with Adriana at work.

The year went by, and I graduated. Now, with a Master's degree in software engineering, the urge to find another job had never been greater. Adriana and I had gotten closer. She wanted me to move in with her, but I resisted that. Some nights, however, mostly on weekends, I slept with her. On a Friday afternoon as I drove her home, she said she had to go to San Diego for a wedding. A cousin of hers was getting married. She left and never returned. It hurt me a lot, but Michaela's experience had helped me a great deal in overcoming yet another unexpected turn of events in a skin-deep relationship. My focus was to find a job in the software engineering field.

Chapter 9

One Wednesday afternoon, I was leaving my cramped office when Dr. Rhodes approached. He started complimenting me for how my coworkers admired my workmanship. He asked me about my school, and I told him I had just graduated, and I was back on the job market. He understood and promised to use his contacts to help in that effort. He went back to his office but came right back.

"Yrvin, are you free this weekend?" He asked.

"I just have to go to my sister's this Saturday."

"Listen, a friend of mine is having a party near Las Olas on the intracoastal, east of Fort Lauderdale. Many of those folks you would need to know in your search will be there. I will present you to some of them I know as personal friends. Remember, in the corporate world, it's mostly about who you know."

"Yes, I would love to," I replied without hesitation. He jotted down the address on a sticky notepad and handed it to me.

#

Like two crafted sculptures in the evening twilight, two doormen dressed in red tuxedos and bowties stood upright on opposite sides of gigantic double doors with gold handles. As soon as I showed up, they stepped back and bowed. Hands on the handles, they pulled the doors wide open and made way for me to step into a vast entrance hallway of shiny beige marble. Crystal chandeliers, hooked on the ceiling foyer, sparkled overhead. No guests were in sight. I felt intimidated and quite uncertain, not knowing which way to go until I heard a squeak from the door behind me.

"To your right upstairs, sir," said one of the doormen with a bewildered stare and shut the door.

I turned right and ran into a palatial Mediterranean-style staircase that meandered up to a reception room where groups of men in casual jackets and slim women in tight dresses chatted, sipped wine, and laughed in perfect harmony. I looked like the youngest person in the room amid well-mannered business folks. With caution, I strolled on.

"*Yrvin*," I heard the high-pitched voice of Dr. Rhodes calling to me.

He sat not far from the entrance at a well-garnished table. By his side was a smallish, Asian woman in a décolleté, leaning on him, but in a brisk move, she straightened herself when she saw me coming. When I reached the table, Dr. Rhodes presented her to me. She threw me a gleeful smile and let her soft hand fall into mine as I greeted her with a handshake. A diamond necklace adorned her tiny frame, sparkling in the dim light.

"Glad to meet you, Yrvin," she said while inviting me to sit next to her.

"Look at you!" Dr. Rhodes said with a burst of laughter. "Was it difficult to get here, Yrvin?"

"No, not at all," I replied, adjusting myself in the chair.

"This is my wife, Katina, and we were wondering if you got lost," Dr. Rhodes said with a beaming smile.

"I was cautious, making sure I drove to the right address." I laughed.

"I see," Katina said, leaning on Dr. Rhodes as if seeking comfort from her husband's oversized body. "Yrvin," she continued, "Rhodes always speaks highly of you at home, taking pride in your punctuality and frankness." Her lips parted in a smile that underscored finesse, pride, and self-confidence commonly found among those who dwell in the opulent, uptown world.

I glanced across the room, and my eyes caught a myriad of golden-faced men in timeless attire, expensive wine in their glasses with their elegant women dressed in the latest haute couture clothing, chatting in low tones; the accepted norm in high society. Our table was in a great location, providing Dr. Rhodes an opportunity to see who came and went, and who left their seats to go to the restroom. A man who looked as robust as a heavyweight boxer walked by. His eyes, gray like a wolf, seemed buried beneath thick, bushy eyebrows. Dr. Rhodes introduced me to him. He stretched out his muscled arm to shake my hand and nearly missed it when his straight, blond hair followed the pattern of his head, blurring his vision. In haste, he pushed his hair backward and laughed.

"How are you?" His voice boomed in the quiet atmosphere.

"I'm fine," I said. He then moved on.

"He's George Posky, a hedge fund manager in one of the investment firms downtown," Dr. Rhodes said as the man left.

"What's a hedge fund manager?" I asked.

"Someone who hires many portfolio managers in an investment firm," he replied. He looked at me up-close as if peering into my eyes. "Don't worry. I'll tell you some other time," he said to temper my anxieties and chase away my confusion.

Shortly thereafter, a couple walked in, both tall and slim, sauntering down toward our table. Dressed in a V-neck, velvet vintage dress, the woman clutched her husband's arm like tightening the leash of a dog to prevent it from breaking free.

"Laurine," Katina tittered, sitting upright. "Rhodes and I thought you and Paul had opted out of the party."

"Yeah, we were wondering," Dr. Rhodes added.

"You know Laurine. She takes forever to get ready," the husband said with a commanding stare that soon dissolved into a funny smile.

"Don't listen to him," the woman said with a little tap on her husband's stomach. "He was too busy talking to his foreign investors."

"Yrvin, this is Paul and Laurine Nadal," Dr. Rhodes said, pushing me forward in a friendly gesture.

"Hi, Yrvin," they both said at once in an abrupt and dry tone. They then left.

We now turned our attention to the food on our table, which was filled to the brim with all kinds of delicacies I had never seen before. Uncertain of what to choose, I resorted to having some fresh salad and fruits, and watching Dr. Rhodes and his wife bicker over what was best for him to choose. It was by now late in the evening, but people never stopped coming.

Just before I started eating my salad, an announcement came from a gray-haired gentleman who stood behind a makeshift podium on the opposite side of the room.

"Ladies and gentlemen, it is with great honor I welcome our friends Paul and his lovely wife, Laurine, this evening. The stock market has not been friendly these days, but Paul has the magic wand to turn things around," he said from the base of his throat.

The man stepped out of the podium to make way for Paul and Laurine to get on. The chatting ceased. Tableware no longer rattled, and all eyes were now glued on Paul, his wife by his side, taking up position behind a microphone to speak to the audience. His turquoise eyes now grayish blue, he seemed to tower over the elite group of guests as he began his address, speaking in an extemporaneous fashion, a business language of which I knew very little.

"General Motors took a nosedive last week, but this is no cause for concern," he began, in full control of himself. Like a solicitous coquette, Laurine stood by her husband, throwing smiles and affectionate glances with muted lips.

"In fact," Paul continued, "this is a buying opportunity, a golden one, I must say. Earnings report on Thursday, though missed Wall Street consensus estimates by a trickle of two cents per share, confirmed or reaffirmed once more GM's strategic position as the ultimate leader of the auto industry. Despite the miss, the company still retains its competitive edge. At the P&P firm, we maintain our sixty-dollar price target for the company stock. At its current fifty-two-dollar level, as of Friday's market close, the stock still stands above its ten-day moving average, and I do not expect it to fall below it. In fact, there was a sense of leveling up in after-hours trading. I know there will be a short-term overhead resistance around fifty-six dollars as the stock struggles to break through some major headwinds. But I'm sure, the stock will find support around fifty dollars.

"In any event, that close-range trading won't last for long because the underlying fundamental trend of GM remains strong. Yes, sales were disappointing in the last quarter. This was due in part to investors' negative sentiment, the threat of raising interest rates by the Fed, and the growing competition in the global market. But do not forget, these are temporary headwinds, which will soon fade. The stock will undoubtedly retake its upward trend, and all the beautiful faces here in attendance tonight will once again sit back, relax, and enjoy the ride. Remember folks, buy the dip, increase your position to average the cost down." He then let his hands follow the curve of his splendid wife, and like a politician in full-campaign mode, he led her down the steps and walked toward their table under showers of applause.

In my ignorance of the Wall Street language, when spoken by a savvy guru in particular, I was stupefied. "Dr. Rhodes," I said with a whispering voice. "I knew nothing about what this man was talking about."

"Don't worry. You'll know soon," he replied with absolute confidence.

Katina smiled. "Yrvin, I'm just like you. It's too much to digest."

Now, the party officially began under a renewed rattling of silverware and low-tone chatting like chirping birds in the foliage at dusk. An occasional burst of laughter would break the quiet talks. At our table, we returned our attention to the food. I sprinkled a little light dressing over my garden salad, grabbing a couple of wheat rolls, and taking a bite. Katina and Dr. Rhodes had resumed their bickering over the food and its ingredients.

"Yrvin," Dr. Rhodes said, facing me. "Remember what we talked about on Friday?"

"Yes, sir."

"There's someone I'm going to introduce you to." He raised his head and craned his neck. He was looking for that "someone." He rose from his chair to survey the room and then fell back into it. "Did you see John?" he asked Katina.

"No. It looks like he's not coming anymore," Katina replied, taking some bean sprouts out of the salad bowl and dropping them onto her plate.

"What makes you think so?"

"You know John." She raised her head a little. "Wait. There he is," Katina said, wide-eyed, looking at the entryway.

Dr. Rhodes and I raised our heads at once. My eyes caught a couple making their way to their reserved table. The man wore a tight jacket over oversized trousers. He was a blond man with wavy hair and a well-trimmed beard that lifted his square face. A chubby woman in a short pink velour dress moved along with him. In careful strides, the couple walked hand in hand, waving here and there to friends who seemed eager to get their attention. When they reached our table, they stopped and greeted us with warm handshakes and happy smiles.

"Katina and I thought you weren't coming anymore," Dr. Rhodes said.

"I came home late. I have so much to do these days in my office, even on a Saturday," the man said.

"I know, you're a workaholic!" Dr. Rhodes laughed.

"It's not just that, Rhodes. You know I lost one of my engineers last week. I'm in urgent need of a replacement," the man said, touching his jacket, making sure it was properly suited.

"You have one right here, John," Dr. Rhodes said, pushing me forward. "This is Yrvin Lacroix, smart, disciplined, and a Barry graduate."

John turned to me. "How are you?"

"I'm okay," I said.

His wife, gray eyes turned feverish like that of a wolf, moved to get a closer look at me, a young black man with a serene demeanor obviously out of place in this high-end gathering.

"The young man you told me about last week, Rhodes?"

"That's him, John."

"Yrvin *Lacroix*, did I pronounce it right?" He looked at me and smiled.

"Yes, you did," I replied.

John then retrieved a business card from the pocket of his jacket. "Here, meet me at my office Monday at ten a.m."

"Thank you." I took the card and inserted it in my wallet.

John then switched the conversation. "Has Paul spoken already?" He asked Dr. Rhodes.

"Yes, he has. He delivered an important speech, by the way, on technical analyses of the current market conditions and GM stock price prediction."

"Really? What was his prediction?"

"A possible rebound next week."

John edged closer, letting go of his wife, who moved to the side to talk to Katina. "Listen, Rhodes. I'm bullish on the stock," he chortled.

"Not more than I am, John. I added to my position yesterday in after-hours trading."

"I'm taking a cautious attitude. Rhodes, you gotta move with prudence because talks about a market correction continue."

"You may be right, but I'm a great believer in the buying-the-dip strategy. I'll be watching the stock closely during premarket trading on Monday." Dr. Rhodes took a huge gulp of his margarita.

Katina edged to his side and gave a little tap on the head. "You're such a stubborn boy," she said with clenched teeth. We all laughed.

"Meanwhile, John," Dr, Rhodes said. "I'm building a watch list of some growth stocks."

"Is Home Depot in that list?"

"HD is my number one. There are rumors of a stock split."

"I haven't heard. If that's the case, there'll be a rush to the finish. But remember, Rhodes, we're long-term investors. So, daily market fluctuations shouldn't be a concern."

"I agree."

John glanced across the room. Chatty folks wined and dined over golden plates and crystal champagne glasses. "Honey, let's go," he then took his wife's hand and they left.

Dr. Rhodes now turned to me. "Yrvin, congratulations!"

"What for, Doctor?"

"John Nasser, his full name, will give you the vacant position." He was elated.

I was about to say 'How do you know that?' but I stopped. The look on my face, however, must have revealed the expression of an unconvinced young man, even after his gleeful boss announced the coming of a brand-new day.

"Don't worry, Yrvin. I've spoken to him. We've already had an agreement on it. On Monday, go straight to his office. It's in the heart of downtown. So, leave early to beat the traffic."

"Yes, sir." In my mind stirred a stew of confusion and bewilderment. I had yet to digest the moment.

"Here, eat, my young boy," Katina tittered while her eyes were glued on Dr. Rhodes, controlling everything he grabbed from his plate.

"I think I have to be spoon-fed," he let out.

"Who's gonna do it?"

"The iron lady who watches my every move when it comes to food."

Both Katina and I laughed. "Maybe that's what I'll have to do," Katina teased him, dropping on her plate a couple of wheat rolls and some broccoli cheddar. "Yrvin, I gotta watch him closely. His doctor has put him on a low-salt diet. He has to shed some pounds quick. Otherwise, he might have to undergo some serious procedures to tighten his stomach."

"Dr. Rhodes, you need to listen to your wife," I said with a repressed laugh.

"Yrvin," Katina said, pulling me closer to her. "Do you have children?"

"Yes, I have a son." That was the most painful response for me. Michaela flashed across my mind, washing away my appetite. Yes, I had a child, but certainly I was not a father.

A few minutes later, a freckle-faced man stopped by our table on his way to the restroom. "Rhodes, I didn't see you last week in Ponte Vedra."

"Katina and I had a prior engagement."

"Rhodes, you missed a lot," the man said, mumbling the words like that of a drunk man.

"I can imagine. You know how I love golf tournaments. I'll catch the next one."

"For sure." The man left and disappeared amid happy campers enjoying their extravagant lifestyles, eating rare delicacies, and drinking French Bordeaux wine while making business deals.

"Yrvin, this man was a former swing trader turned hedge fund manager, a Wall Street billionaire from the World Golf Village in north Florida."

I was about to ask him to define swing trading, but I chose not to. I began to memorize the business terminologies so that I could do my own research later. I became curious about this world, a clannish world where money dominated, where shortsightedness ruled. I wanted to know if beneath the surface of glamor, wealth, and boundless privilege one could still find some sense of humanity. Each table was sumptuously garnished with the rarest and fanciest food items. Except for the champagne and scarlet red pomegranate juice, few people paid attention to those mouthwatering ingredients.

Yet, I did not feel rejected. On the contrary, I felt an odd sense of being welcome. Bigshot men and their flashy women streamed toward our table like the rushing current of a crystal brook. In each wave, I was the first to receive the warm and strong handshakes, while the women threw affectionate smiles. I did not know what to make of it. I resorted to thinking that maybe I was being used as a tool of redemption, a golden opportunity to redeem old sins of prejudices, a natural inheritance from the exclusive world in which they belonged.

Shortly after midnight, a stylish young woman in a velvet dress walked to our table for a greeting. She was about my age. Her hair, hued like a brushfire, washed over her shoulder when she bent forward to shake my hand. She had soft strawberry lips, glossy skin, and mesmerizing blue eyes. "I'm Lany Schnell," she said. She was quite polite.

"I'm Yrvin Lacroix," I replied with a grin, letting go of her hand.

"Lacroix," she said with a smile. "I know another Lacroix. He's friends with Paul."

"Who's Paul?" I inquired.

"Paul Nadal. The gentleman who gave the speech earlier."

"I've always thought all Lacroix are Haitians."

"So are Paul and his wife, Laurine."

"Really?"

"Yeah. I work in the same company with Paul. We're in the same building, too. He's a senior manager at Dean Witter."

While Lany and I were talking, Dr. Rhodes and Katina strolled to the dancefloor. A bolero was being played. "Where do you work?" Lany asked, taking a seat next to me.

"At Harrison Asset Management."

"Ah. That's why you're with Dr. Rhodes. He's funny. Isn't he?"

"You know it. He's one like no other." We both laughed, taking our attention to happy couples on the dancefloor, dancing cheek to cheek.

"How do you know Dr. Rhodes?" I asked.

"He's my fiancé's uncle."

"I see. Where's your fiancé?"

"He's at a conference in Zurich, Switzerland."

The music stopped and Dr. Rhodes and Katina returned. "Are you a manager at Dean Witter, too?"

"Yes. I've been working there since graduating from college."

"Which one did you attend?"

"BU."

"I'm a Barry University graduate, too."

Her golden face beamed in the dim light. "When?" She edged closer. We found common ground, both BU alumni. "I majored in business."

"Software engineering."

"I see. You look like a boy who shared one of my statistics classes."

"Not really. I remember most female classmates, mainly the extroverted ones." I laughed. Lany stayed at our table until it was time to leave around one a.m..

"Lany is a smart girl, engaged to marry my nephew," Dr. Rhodes said with measureless pride after she left.

"Yes, she told me," I replied.

"She works in the same building you're going to on Monday. Her firm is three floors on top of you. Yrvin, I know you're a smart and dignified young man. Those two traits will carry you a long way. When you get there, keep your eyes open. Learn the culture. Walk with your head high. Look your colleagues straight in the eye, always. Never let anyone think or act as if he's more important than you are. Ask questions when you don't understand things. Stand out in every assignment. In corporate America, it's all about making profit in lofty investments. Befriend Lany. You'll be seeing her a lot. Learn how to make strategic investments, the kind of things Paul was talking about earlier." He took a glass of champagne and drank a little.

"I wish I had a notepad, Dr. Rhodes. So much to digest." I was worried.

"Son, I said many things, but they all could be summarized into two words: Be *wise!*"

"By the way, Dr. Rhodes. Lany told me Paul and his wife are Haitians." I said, changing the conversation.

"Yes. I forgot to tell you," he said, taking another gulp of his champagne. "Meeting you and Paul," he continued, "has given me a whole different perspective about Haiti and other countries in general. Both of you are well-mannered and smart."

"What does he do at Dean Witter?"

"He manages rich folks' portfolios, including some from Haiti."

I was stunned. Later at home, alone in my little apartment, I thought of this couple, Paul and Laurine, whose shrewdness was an asset for many of these rich folks. So, I concluded that the Haitian elite was not a bunch of backward and out-of-the-norm individuals as I had previously thought. They have the *savoir faire* in their exclusive high society, its lucrative investments, and the means of their global financial success. They knew how to live the good life, and Haiti's misfortune guaranteed that good life. It was a conscious decision they made to forgo their historical mission as bourgeois of a deprived country. A weaker Haiti well served their selfish purpose.

Chapter 10

Monday morning, I arrived at the Bedell Tech firm. A young woman in a crosshatch blazer, who was at the front office, greeted me. "How can I help you?" She asked.

"I'm here to see Mr. John Nasser," I replied.

She raised her pencil-thin eyebrows slightly. "Are you Mr. Lacroix?"

"Yes."

"He's in his office. Two doors down on your right."

"Thank you."

When I stepped into John's office, he sat behind a well-polished desk in a room decorated with fancy antique artworks, two glossy brown reception sofas, and several ornamental items, the names of which I did not know. Not knowing what to expect, the countless rejections I had to face a few years ago flicked across my mind. I kept cool, however, showing no signs of anxiety.

"How are *you*, Yrvin?" He seemed ecstatic.

"I'm fine, Mr. Nasser," I replied with a smile that concealed my worry.

"Call me John. Here, we keep a brotherly atmosphere."

He laughed, pulling out of his chair, and meeting me halfway through the room. This time, he wore no oversized pants, looking fit in a dark suit without a tie. We shook hands, but he held mine firm and strong, like grabbing a very important catch after a long wait.

"Listen, Yrvin. The software engineering position is yours. Starting salary is a hundred thousand dollars." He let go of my hand and he laughed, looking at me with indescribable respect and elation. "You must sign an agreement to not compete with the firm for at least five years. Is that all right?"

I hesitated a bit. "That's fine," I answered in a firm voice. He looked relieved.

"Yrvin, you'll be working with some sharp, tech-savvy people. Your first five months here will be dedicated to learning the culture. As Rhodes told me, punctuality could be a suitable middle name for you."

I smiled without replying. He then wrapped his long, hairy white arm around my shoulders and walked me out of the office like two longtime friends who had not seen each other for a while. Necks craned and faces baffled, employees in nearby offices wanted to get a glimpse of this young man whom John was walking with in jubilant steps.

He led me to Human Resources. On the way, we stopped by the front desk. There, he gave formal introduction for me to the same young woman I had just met.

"Yrvin, this is Kayla, your new secretary." He pushed me forward.

"Nice to meet you, sir," she said with a broad smile.

"Nice to meet you, too," I replied with a grin.

John then walked me down a long hallway in the middle of which was HR. John opened the door to let me in while he stood there, waving at the busy employees who also stopped working, seeming surprised and throwing curious glances.

"Go see Marisol, the lady in the red suit." He then left and came right back. "Yrvin, when you're done, return to the front office. Kayla will walk you to your office."

He then disappeared. I spent about a half hour at HR filling out the forms and making sure the base salary was exactly what John had told me. Marisol was cordial, attentive to my words, smiling to make me feel at home, and offering a sugarless drink.

When I returned to the front office, I found Kayla waiting. "Mr. Lacroix, come with me." A dazzling smile lit up her face. I followed her.

I did not know what to make of this attention. My journey through life had reached an elevation unthinkable an hour earlier. I could not process what was happening to me. We arrived at an imposing mahogany door. My name and title had already been printed on a golden plate with "Engineer Yrvin Lacroix." She handed me a magnetic card with which I used to open the door. We entered a room almost half the size of my apartment.

"This is your office. It is now empty. I purposely emptied it last week."

"Why?" I asked.

"Last Friday, John told me about a new engineer to start today. Since I did not know your taste, the kind of furniture you like, or the artwork you prefer to have in your surroundings, I thought it would be best that you told me. But don't worry, Mr. Lacroix. We have a budget for this," she said, waiting for me to approve her explanation.

"You mean there's is a budget to furnish offices in here?"

"Yes, sir. And I've put aside thirty thousand dollars for you."

"That's very kind of you, Kayla."

She smiled and flashed white shining teeth. "I have to go back to my office. Tomorrow, we'll sit together to decorate the room to your liking."

"Thank you for your generosity."

"No. That's part of my job. Oh, I almost forgot."

"What is it, Kayla?"

"Whenever you need something, push the button behind your desk or dial zero from your phone." She left.

#

Later in the afternoon, I came home feeling dazed, oddly so. I called Pedro. "Man, I think I got it!" I cried aloud.

"You mean, you found Mica?" He now worked as an engineer for the city of Miami. He and Chen got married and had a two-year-old son named Charlito. I was the best man at the wedding.

"No, man. I was hired today at the *Bedell*."

"The giant investment firm downtown?"

"*Yes.*"

"God is great, *man*! God is great!" He kept on saying. He knew I had been suffering. And I went on to fill him in on the process that led me to the new job. We celebrated over the phone. He was thrilled.

"But the joy is halfhearted for me. I wish Mica and my boy were here. But I'm now convinced I've lost them for real."

"Vinco, I have a different take on the situation."

"How so?"

"I never thought you honestly believed Michaela would have come back to Miami to be with you a few months after she flew to France under pressure from her parents. Many girls I know would have resisted. But she chose not to. I have no doubt Mica loves you; maybe you're the only man she'll ever love. But that love seems trapped in her inability to *stand up* for what she believes in." He knew I lived alone and was dwelling in the painful web of loneliness.

"I hear you, Ped."

"When Chen took me to meet her parents, Vinco, she presented me as the man of her life. The man she intended to spend the rest of her life with."

"And what was their reaction?"

"Did it matter? Of course, parents always have reservations or even objections over their children's choices, like my dad who, I remember correctly, asked me more than ten times if Chen was really the girl. And every time, I gave him the same firm response:

'Yes, Dad.' So, I'm convinced that Mica doesn't have the guts to fight for the man she claims to love so much. If she did, she wouldn't have left to go *this* far."

"I guess she shared her parents' fear. I wasn't ready."

"It could be, I'm afraid, Vinco. It could be. Of course, she'll never agree to that assertion. However, she had her chance to prove how strong her love was. At the park after the pregnancy test, as you told me, she had agreed to marry you, agreeing to a plan the two of you worked out; and she reneged on it the minute her parents objected."

The phone went silent. Then I could hear him clearing his throat. "Vinco," he continued, "every time I think of this sad story, I see Judy, the girl who spoke her mind. If Michaela were Judy, this story could have been *very* different. Despite everything, she would have stood her ground and fought."

"Ped, remember she went off to Oxford, across the Atlantic, like Mica."

"It was after *you* told her it was over. Now, I'm not trying to say she was a better person. But Judy would not have abandoned you if she knew she was carrying your baby."

"You think so, Ped?"

"I'm almost certain. And if Michaela is the woman with whom you want to live, you'll have to go find her. In fact, this is becoming more and more a possibility now that she's raising your child."

He could hear me crying. "Man, tonight is your night. Don't let Michaela steal the joy from you. I'm almost certain Michaela's parents would not have opposed a wedding if you were then what you *are* tonight: a software engineer from one of the most prestigious investment firms in town."

I did not reply. "Think of it, Vinco. Your victory tonight is a victory against prejudices in all its forms, and that's what makes it so sweet. This is your moment, brother. Celebrate it, even if you have to do it alone. We'll talk over the weekend."

Long after we hung up the phone, I kept thinking of Pedro's words. It was the first time he talked to me so bluntly about what he thought of the affair with Michaela. "Mica's love seems trapped in her inability to stand up…" Then Judy came to my mind. I met Chen the very night Judy deceived me at the school party. Chen was drunk and bleary-eyed, leaning on Pedro as if begging to be petted. I took the moment as nothing out of the ordinary—certainly I thought she would not have been the girl who could steal Pedro's heart. But she did—in a big way. Maybe Judy was sincere, and perhaps she needed my support, psychological and moral, and needed the romantic courage to break free from parental greed and sentimental ruthlessness. That night in my little room, she was in my mind, at least for a couple of hours.

Then, I was back to reality, my new reality. A one-hundred-thousand-dollar job, a secretary, a credit card for business traveling, thirty thousand dollars for furnishing my office; I could not believe it was "little me" at the receiving end of all these. I was not sure if I had just woken from a strange and surreal dream. Twice, I was tempted to call Nana to celebrate, but my hand compulsively shook. Although she had known me for always telling the truth, I was not certain she would have believed me. I tried to find the proper words, simple words to use, but I could not, for I was still struggling to digest this rapid transformation of my life. Our world was too far removed from the lavish world of corporate America.

So, I decided not to call. I wanted to call my mom and dad, my siblings. Although they would have been overjoyed that I had a new and better job, they still would not have had any clue of the powerful glass ceiling through which I had just broken. So, alone I celebrated with a glass of wine and a pint of shrimp fried rice I bought at a little Chinese restaurant on the way home. Then, exhausted, I went to sleep shortly thereafter just to be awakened a few hours later to the jingling of my phone.

"Vinco, I waited for you. You didn't come by," Nana's voice growled in anxiety.

Big sister had long ordered her brother to stop by every day after work where she cooked dinner for me. I never felt comfortable with that. She was married, and I wanted her husband to see me for who I was, not as an intruder to his marriage and an unavoidable annoyance.

"I had to go for a job interview that took me longer than expected," I replied with a laugh to lessen her anxiety.

"But you told me last week your current job was stress-free."

"Nana, you know I didn't go to school to be a data-entry clerk."

"I'm afraid you might drop a pretty good job in exchange for something you might not be able to hold."

"Sister, I can't believe you already forgot the sacrifices you've made in my education."

"What do you mean?" She sounded more worrisome.

"I mean those sacrifices would be in vain if I had to remain a clerk in some corporate building. I don't think that's what you want for me."

"So, did you get the job?"

"Yes. And that was why I could not stop by on the way home. It's been a long day."

"Did you call your old job?"

"My boss knew. He was the one who helped me find this new job."

"Better salary?"

"Oh, yes. I'll be working as a software engineer, now, with my own office and a secretary."

"Wow! My prayers have been answered."

"The struggle is not yet over. My task is now greater and more challenging. But that was what I went to school for. So, continue to pray. Some difficult days still lie ahead."

"I know, Vinco. I sleep with my Bible. God is great. He and *He* alone will protect us."

"God always watches out for us."

"To add to the good news. I have some of my own." She burst out laughing.

"Let me guess. Papa's coming."

"No. You're gonna be an uncle soon. A niece or nephew is on the way!"

"Really? When did you know?"

"This morning when I went to see my gynecologist."

On that news, we joked, laughed, and prayed. Then we said goodnight with a promise to see each other the next day after work.

Chapter 11

The next morning when I arrived at work, I found Kayla waiting by the front desk. I came ahead of time and that seemed to please her. "I like the punctuality," she said with a grin.

"I know you have the list ready," I said as we greeted each other.

"Let's go to your office," she suggested.

She brought in the list of items we needed to purchase. I had no clue what I needed because the things I honestly needed were my desk, a computer, and some file cabinets. They were all there. I knew she was not referring to those basic items. To conceal my ignorance, I let her choose.

"Let's see, Mr. Lacroix."

"Call me Yrvin. This suits me better."

"Yes, Yrvin." She smiled and I smiled back. "So, Yrvin, these are the items I have checked after you left yesterday."

She opened an office furniture catalog. I took a deep look at the items she bookmarked, crystal pens, writing utensils to jot down all important notes, agenda with tiny golden binders, bookends, fancy sharpener to make sure my pencils were in tip-top shape, leather desk pads, two reception sofas with luxurious cushioning and solid hardwood legs, and more.

"Kayla," I said. "Do you have a team that helps you decorate?"

"You mean an occasion like this?"

"Yes, no." She laughed.

"What's that for?" I also laughed but at my own stupefaction.

"Aren't we a team, Yrvin?"

"Absolutely, yes, and I'm counting on you, Kayla, to help me learn the culture of this new work environment."

"You got it, sir."

"You go ahead and purchase the items, and we'll set a date to begin putting things together."

"This sounds like a great plan," she said smiling.

"So, Kayla, how was your daily routine with the engineer before me?"

"We would have a quick meeting, going over the tasks of the day, making sure deadlines were met. My job was to organize new projects before he would start working. We had a great rapport. I hope that will continue."

"The hope is also mine, Kayla."

"I have to get back to the office. Call me if you need anything."

"I certainly will." She left.

Fifteen minutes later, John walked into my office. He was upbeat, elated to have me in the firm. "Morning, Yrvin. I hope you don't feel overwhelmed with a heavy introduction."

"Not at all, John. I'm learning the culture, though." We both laughed at once.

"Listen. I want you to finish this project Robert started last month. Follow me."

I followed him to a conference room where he presented me with a blueprint of the assignment. I had to develop software for a company based in the Cayman Islands. I had to create and install software solutions to make it user-friendly. It was a tricky project because it required SDLC (software development life cycle), an important component for effective testing and deployment. I knew at the Bedell, faultlessness was the norm.

Understandably, John took time to meticulously review every detail. I bombarded him with pointed questions that impressed him. To make sure I had a good grasp of the work at hand, I took the materials home with me. The stakes were high, for each contract ran in the millions, and I wanted to secure my new job. One aspect that worked for me was the blueprint the former engineer had left for his successor. I did not have to start from scratch.

Building a high-quality and innovative design fully complied with coding standards was not a problem. Meeting the deadline was. I worked on the project day and night and brought work home, which reminded me of my undergrad days pulling all-nighters to get the job done. Each day, the task became easier as I got closer to finishing. Kayla helped a lot in taking the job of decorating my office upon herself. Once, I offered to stay with her to decorate. She refused, saying I had to go get some rest because my eyes were weary. In the end, I finished the job two weeks in advance.

Since the first project, the job became literally mine. The other engineers seemed proud of me and even seemed surprised by my strong work ethic. Kayla and I had developed a cordial, professional relationship. Most of the time, we ate lunch in her office, which had a cozy room just for secretaries who were not interested in going downstairs to the cafeteria.

Kayla did a fantastic job, decorating my antique-white office. She made sure my working area was as pleasant as it could be. I had a desk made of mahogany-stained wood with a brown granite top. I hated clutter. So, a desktop IBM computer and a couple of folders containing pressing projects were found on my desk. Kayla, who knew how I detested untidy masses of papers, did her best to make sure she did not spoil my day. The room itself was a conventional size compared with other offices in the building, which were engraved with swirls and elegant designs. Across from my desk was a brown leather sofa to receive clients and other visitors. There was also one file cabinet in the corner and a few other accessories.

No more than half of the thirty-thousand dollars for refurnishing was used. Per Kayla's advice, I kept the rest in an expense account for future expenditures. Although my office lacked materialistic luxury, its strategic location had brought a natural taste that no money could buy. From my desk, I just had to glance down and the stunning turquoise water of Biscayne Bay, jet skis, and fancy boats cruising around were in full view.

Then, the moment had come for me to move out of that Little Haiti apartment. Six months later, I moved into a much larger one at the Grenoble, a gated, middle-class community. My first night in the new apartment gave me mixed feelings. Mica and Junior invaded my mind. "How happy we could have been together!" I sighed.

The next day at lunch, Kayla brought rice pudding. I teased her. "Is that part of your culture that people eat rice pudding for lunch?"

"No, Yrvin. I knew you were going to bring fried chicken. Mine is just a dessert."

"I forgot." I became pensive.

She noticed my sudden change in attitude. "What's wrong?" She asked.

"I was moving last night, and I was exhausted."

"Didn't you have movers?"

"Yes," I lied. I did not have much to call a moving company. I rented a small truck to move my few belongings. The rest, like my bed and a little dining set, I gave up to the Salvation Army. But I did not want Kayla to know that.

"You should be happy," she said, still trying to pinpoint the reason for my change of attitude.

"I dated my college sweetheart, and that relationship had produced a child. When she told her parents she was pregnant, they sent her off to France to stay with an uncle."

"Is she still in Europe?"

"Yes. Do you have children, Kayla?"

"Yes, I have a boy."

"My child is also a boy. Where's your son's father?"

"Not sure."

"What do you mean?"

"Obviously, I mean we no longer have a relationship. It was an ugly story." She rose from her seat and strolled toward the telephone. "Can we order Italian food?" She asked, grabbing the phone while turning to face me.

"Yes, and it's on *me*."

"Of course," she tittered. She ordered the food and then joined me again at the table. "So, the mother of your child is still in Europe?"

"Yes. My son was born there. Last night, I really missed them. She is Hispanic like you."

"But you two communicate. Right?"

"We used to. It's been two years since the last time we talked. Anyway, did you see Anny this morning?" I purposely changed the conversation.

"Anny Schnell?"

"Yes."

"She came looking for you earlier when you were in the meeting. She said she was going to call you."

"I didn't hear from her."

"Is she your stockbroker?"

"She will be."

"I heard she's a great portfolio manager."

"She's so friendly, too. We're both BU alumni."

While chatting, the food arrived. She had ordered pasta and garlic bread. She knew I loved that. But as soon as I grabbed the food to take my very first bite, the phone rang again, and it was Anny this time looking for me.

"Talk to you later, Kayla." I rose from the desk and headed for my office.

I hurried and picked up the phone and called Anny. "Sorry I missed your call. Going from meetings to other work-related urgencies, I've been busy. I'm sure you know the drill."

"I know, Yrvin. No need to explain. Listen, I have some papers I want you to sign. Would you come up before going home?"

"I won't be able to wait for long because I have to beat the traffic and make a couple stops on the way home. By the way, did you prepare the balanced portfolio we've talked about?"

"Yes, I did. And that's precisely why I want you to stop by so we can talk it over. But we can talk over the phone."

"What do you mean by a balanced portfolio?"

"A diversified one, meaning you'll need to invest in companies from different sectors of the economy, and their stocks' performances must match their fundamentals. Diversifying also means that you do not want to invest just in stocks. You want some mutual funds, etcetera."

"I agree, but what are the companies you are referring to?"

"Home Depot, Disney, IBM, and General Electric are some of the few. And a couple mutual funds."

"And how much money do I need to jumpstart?"

"Whatever you can."

"Ten grand?"

"That's more than enough. I'm not going to spend it all because it's always good to have cash reserves in the portfolio."

"Why?"

"Because the market fluctuates daily. If a stock drops for whatever reason, you need some cash to buy more. In doing so, you'll average your cost down and increase your position. Remember, you're building a portfolio."

"I'm with you, Anny. I'll follow your good advice."

"You're a wise young man." We both laughed.

Chapter 12

My new life did not bring new happiness, for every night I kept on thinking of the day I would be able to meet Mica and hug my son. Days, weeks, months, and two years went by; my sense of gloom remained immutable. In fact, it had exacerbated. Despite my ceaseless torment, I felt I had never been doing so well in my young life. For the first time in my immigrant journey, I could safely say I had conquered the stubborn and treacherous heights to financial stability.

I had purchased a brand-new car, a convertible BMW, a symbol of affluence. My new place was not fancy, but it was well furnished in the style of any clean and professional bachelor. I made sure of that. Modest, one may say, the living room was blended with a neatly built café area adorned by a four-by-eight mahogany table above which was a five-arm golden candelabra hook from the center of the ceiling. Without a tablecloth, the candelabra took most of the space, but it was impossible to ignore the glow besetting the well-crafted table, in the middle of which was a large stainless-steel bowl filled with fresh oranges, green apples, and ripe, reddish mangoes. From the dining area, I had a fringeless runner of Persian design woven in gold and red that led to a mid-size kitchen of cherry cabinets and granite countertops.

I had a passion for fresh vegetables. So, they were always plentiful inside my fridge. I worked out daily, something I had learned from one of my cousins and a hobby I was addicted to since my teenage years. A strong believer in eating *right*, I thought this was necessary to preserve a firm and imposing posture—thin waist, flat belly, and robust upper body.

For a Haitian man who was raised in a machismo culture, I had an unusual fondness for cooking. Those days, though, I rarely stood in front of my kitchen stove to make dinner. After a long day at work, I would come home, spend most of my time in my living room and lay face up on my two-piece right arm double chaise sofa. I would lie there using two cushions stuffed under my head, reading my favorite novel or old letters from Michaela. Adjacent to my sofa was a bookcase full of my favorite historical novels and a collection of memoirs and scientific documents. Next to the bookcase was an impressive photo of me displayed in a poster frame on the wall, a smiling Vinco surrounded by his college buddies, a vivid remembrance of the good old days.

I loved music, and to satisfy this craving, I had purchased a brand-new Bose audio system from which I would play my preferred Caribbean jazz or Frederic Chopin's collection of classical music. When the pain felt insurmountable, I would go to my bedroom, leaving the French doors ajar that separated my bedroom from the rest of the apartment, and lay face down on my silken mattress, pressing my cheeks on my soft pillow until I succumbed to sleep.

One Friday evening after work, while thinking about these painful realities, I rose from the couch and walked to the kitchen. From one of the cabinets, I grabbed a three-star bottle of Barbancourt, the famous Haitian rum. Without a second thought, I gulped down two full cups of that strong alcoholic drink. It was so strong, vaporous gas trickled out of my nose. I then retired to my room, lying face down in bed with my clothes on, and fell asleep. I didn't wake up until seven a.m., feeling beaten, lost in a race to Bliss Land.

The next morning, I tried to get up, but fear of loss crippled me, weighing down my anguished mind. I wished I had never taken my girlfriend to that hotel room where we made love unprotected. Losing my son as well as Michaela scared me to the core, although I knew the best way to fight off solitude and suppress invading feelings of sadness was to clear my mind of all self-defeating thoughts. While struggling to get out of bed, there was a knock on the door, which was followed by giggling and laughter outside on the porch. I rushed to the door and pushed it right open, and Nana walked in with Nanouche, her two-year-old daughter, who ran up to me, arms outstretched, begging to be picked up.

"Nana, what brings you here at this time?" I asked, stifling an unwanted morning yawn.

"We're going to Aventura Mall."

"This early?" I grabbed elated Nanouche by the shoulders and lifted her up. "Are there some seventy-five-percent-off sales going on today?" I teased Nana.

"You know you're in trouble." We all now moved to the couch where I laid Nanouche. Sitting in the middle, her cute face buried into my shirt, she wrapped her little creamy arms around my neck.

"Why would I be in trouble, Nana?"

"You have to carry the bags."

"No way, Nana. That was then."

"And now?"

"Well, I've lost all energy."

"From work?"

"Part of it is overstressing with mounting piles of work."

"And the other?"

"I can't explain."

"No need to, Vinco. Mica is eating away your sleep, even mine, too, sometimes."

"I'm worried about my son, too. Is he well-fed? Alive?"

"Oh, Vinco. How could you be so pessimistic?"

"This is nerve-wracking, Nana. I feel betrayed. Big time."

"Be careful, Vinco. Michaela is not the girl who would turn her back on the man she once loved unconditionally. You know her. Give her the benefit of the doubt."

"I tried, sister. But three years is a long time. When a man runs out of options in the pursuit of the girl of his life, nothing can stop him from thinking the worst."

"And what do you think that *worst* might be? She's found another man?"

"It could be."

"I honestly don't think so. Have you tried to contact her parents?"

"I've been resisting."

"Because they sent Mica to France?"

"It was humiliating."

"If you still love Mica, her parents' attitude should not deter you."

"Before I go to her parents, I need to make sure Michaela did not personally decide to sever all contacts with me."

"And how will you find out?"

"I don't know."

"You need to know. Otherwise, you'll be doing nothing but crying like a worthless romancero."

Nana rose from the couch and made her way to the kitchen. I had never seen her so snappish. Despite the fact I thought myself a freed bird that could fly on its own, Lorna still saw in her younger brother's eyes a novice child who had yet to learn the ups and downs of this complicated world, and deceptions and betrayals are key components of the learning process. No man knows for sure the content of his character until he runs into hardships. Consequently, Lorna felt she still had the responsibility to play her big sister's role.

Leaving Nanouche on the couch, I followed her to the kitchen, knowing that despite my loneliness, in the reality, I was never alone. There, she was pulling ingredients out of the cabinets to make a vegetable omelet. She then turned on the stove, grabbing an aluminum pan and laying it on a burner, humming old country songs with the same gaiety as when we lived together in the old Little Haiti apartment. I could see in her eyes and demeanor the sheltering love that bore fear and anxiety as she sought the assurance that her younger brother could fend for himself.

She turned around and saw me standing right behind her. At once, we both burst out laughing. She moved a step away from the stove as the sunrays trickling through the kitchen window caught her nut-brown visage, piercing her eyes with pain. I was about to thank her for the surprise, enchanted morning visit, but she preempted me.

"I guess I need to come here more often," she uttered with a repressed laugh.

"Why, Nana?"

"To get your food prepared."

"Don't worry. You know I can do this."

"Are you *sure?*"

"Uh-huh."

"This kitchen seems like a place that hasn't been used in a long time."

Leaving the couch, Nanouche joined us, begging for sweets. From the fridge, I yanked out a carton of vanilla ice cream, scooped a large cup, and handed it to her. She was overjoyed. A few minutes later, all three of us sat at the table. Nanouche sat on Mommy's lap while Nana and I savored a delightful breakfast of French toast, vegetable omelet, and delicious, sugar-free, fresh tropical fruits pureed with milk. Lorna had the magic touch when it came to Haitian gastronomy, meticulously fashioned with an unquestionable love and adroitness.

After that generous meal, Nana did not have to ask me again to follow her around the shopping mall. The load was as heavy as always, but I was in no way burdened by the weight, for I welcomed her motherly instincts, something I needed now more than ever as I struggled to repel the feelings of intense sadness that kept me awake at night. That Saturday was my best in weeks, and when Nana and Nanouche left late in the afternoon, a sense of abandonment crept into my mind, thinking about the lonely night that awaited me.

#

Running late for work was never a sensation I wished to experience, but Monday morning I found myself amid a traffic jam on Biscayne Boulevard, a direct path to work. A procession of cars snaked down for miles, creeping along. Tires screeched in a commotion of horn blowing, yelling, and bitching as some impatient drivers surrendered to their mounting road rage. Others turned up their favorite music, trying to kill the time. They looked consumed by their hermetically odd indifference.

I must be at work at eight a.m., and it was now past seven-thirty. An alternate route came to mind, and it led to Interstate 95. To get there, I had to drive by Jade Garden, the Chinese restaurant Michaela, Josefina, and I ate lunch at several days before her departure for France. I had always avoided that restaurant going home, for it brought unwanted, painful memories. That Monday morning, however, it did not matter. Zigzagging, I pulled my way out of the traffic on Biscayne and headed west toward I-95, passing wealthy suburban homes with wide front yards, well-designed gardens, and spotless walkways along which moved slow, oversized older women and fat-bellied men walking their dogs.

By then, it was twenty minutes to eight. Face contracted, brows hardened, I stepped up the speed as the pressure to get to work mounted. I ran two stop signs without halting my speed until I reached the back entrance of the North Miami Beach Shopping Mall, where Jeff Goldstein, an old Jewish rabbi always dressed in black with his kippah perched on what was left of his bald head, sold cuckoo clocks to the first potential buyers hungry for bargains. From a distance, his headgear looked like the black zucchetto that Father Jean-Juste used to wear back in the day while leading mass demonstrations and fighting for refugee rights.

Next to the rabbi was Coutilien, a retired voodoo priest whose fortune he had lost long ago to sleazy prostitutes who paraded down the sidewalk a few blocks away. He had resorted to selling the remaining tools from his altar as souvenirs he claimed were old artifacts from Haiti's pre-independence era. They both knew me, for this stretch of twisty street had become my preferred backroad on the way home every afternoon, circumventing the grand boulevard that led to the main entrance of the Grenoble.

I pulled up my tinted window and veered to the left, heading west to the interstate highway that ran straight to the heart of downtown Miami where the highway ended, and Brickell Avenue was a few steps down. Just two minutes before eight, I made it inside the vast building lobby swamped with folks in business suits crisscrossing each other, rushing to beat the final seconds before they were late for work.

Their fast pacing over an impressive, crema nuova marble floor created an annoying commotion, making every step echo. Imposing chandeliers hung from golden canopies brightened multiple priceless paintings hung on the wall, underpinning the grandeur of corporate America. As in most executive buildings, a reception desk was stationed a few feet from the elevator, behind which stood a short, slim young lady dressed in a blue blazer, throwing repressed smiles like a baby doll in a toy shop.

Before she threw her smile, I was already in the elevator, jacket in hand, briefcase in the other, squeezing my way among the other employees, hurrying to get to their respective destinations. At last, I walked onto the eighteenth floor, passing Kayla without greeting her on the way to my office.

Breathing a sigh of relief, I dropped my suitcase on the desk, laid my jacket over the cushion of my chair, pulled down my tie while rolling up my sleeves, and surveyed the room to get a grasp of the work at hand for the day. Soon, Kayla walked in, always in her trademark blue jeans tucked inside stylish boots, holding two new folders in her arms. Before she had a chance to utter a word, I interrupted her.

"More work on top of this pile?" I asked, pointing to the file cabinet in the corner where the projects had been stored.

"I'm afraid, you're right, Yrvin," she said, giggling like a young woman caught in childish glee.

"What's so funny? The mountain of work?"

"No, Yrvin. You know I would never make fun of your never-ending projects. Besides, your heavy load is in some ways mine, too."

"I know. By the way, isn't there supposed to be a staff meeting this morning?"

"Yeah, but it was canceled at the last minute."

"Really? Do you know why?"

"John had an unexpected emergency that forced him to leave. He's now at the airport, catching a flight to Manhattan."

"Is it a family problem?"

"I don't think so. I believe he has to meet Dusayev, the Belarusian billionaire. And that's why Mike asked if you could review these two projects before a business meeting this afternoon."

She handed me the folders and readied to go back to her desk. "Hey, Kaykay!" I called to her.

"What?" she asked, turning around and adjusting the bun that held her golden hair.

"You haven't told me what was so funny that got you to laugh earlier."

"Because of that smile."

"How so?"

"Because it was the most natural smile I've seen in weeks, and that's reassuring for a secretary. I could see it extended to your eyes."

"Sincerely?"

She stepped back a bit, edging the desk. "You can't imagine how much I and the rest of the staff miss that smile; the way things were until a year ago."

"I'm sorry, Kaykay. I'm not my old self anymore. Sorry if my personal ordeals have spilled over, disturbing your honest professionalism. I too miss your laughter."

"Really?"

"Of course. Can we have lunch together today? I have something I want to share with you."

"*Sure.*"

I then rose from my desk and strolled to her, giving her a hug, and together we walked to the front desk where I chatted for a few minutes with the rest of the staff. I was amazed to see how happy they were, making me feel like Santa Claus in a rescue mission.

I went back to my office and reviewed John's work. Like every day, at work or home, the quiet moments were the most painful to endure. What I usually did to suppress loneliness and anxiety was to get my heart and soul consumed in the task at hand, and in doing so, assignments were accomplished with almost faultless results. But that highest form of professionalism had produced a reverse effect. My workload was always large, and I suspected mine was the largest one, although I could never prove it because we all complained about our mounting piles of work.

I was still working on the document when Kaykay buzzed me from the front desk. "Are you ready?" She asked.

Her voice lowered. I guessed she did not want her coworkers to hear, avoiding unnecessary suspicion, for we rarely went out to lunch together. In fact, it had been a while since I had been having my lunch in my office.

"Be right there," I replied in a feeble tone.

I hurried and put my work away, grabbing my jacket and walking to the front desk where Kaykay stood purse in hand, waiting. With squinting eyes, she smiled like that of a young woman going out on a blind date. She walked up and met me halfway. We then walked toward the elevator. Some of her colleagues gazed at us as we reached the elevator and pushed the down button.

"Bring me a veggie sandwich," cried Amy, her good friend and workmate.

We could not reply, for we were already on the way down. Seconds later, we walked out of the elevator, busy as usual. The cafeteria was at the tail end of the huge lobby. Hungry professionals filled up the line that led to it. Kaykay and I trailed down, but just before we reached the line, long and noisy, I held her hand.

"Kaykay, we can't eat lunch here."

"Why not?" She asked.

"I want a place where we can talk quietly."

"And what makes me so special today?"

"Kaykay, you've always been special to me," I teased her. "But let's go to La Romanita."

She laughed but said nothing. So, we headed toward the parking lot, got in my car, and drove off. La Romanita was located at the end of Brickell Avenue where the road curved into Coral Way, a busy boulevard that ran down to the heart of Little Havana. We could have literally walked there, but the bustling of cars, pedestrians, and the late morning haze sweeping through the downtown high rises made it quite uncomfortable to do so. After two traffic lights, we had arrived.

It was a small cottage in the middle of an unpaved parking lot. An iron fence enclosed it. I chose not to park inside for fear of not being able to get back to work on time. There were so many cars parked almost on top of each other. So, we parked by the roadside in one of the parking meters that were plentiful all over downtown Miami. The minute we got out of the car, the aroma of Cuban cuisine permeated the air. We proceeded to the front porch, but there was no one at the reception desk. So, we sauntered in, surveying the room. Our eyes caught a cozy spot in the far end corner.

"Let's go," I said.

Side by side, we strolled in its direction amid low, soft chatting over delicious Cuban cuisine. "I'm hungry, very hungry," she let out in a dulcet voice like that of a swallow.

"Be quiet," I teased her.

We sat facing each other, waiting to be served with mounting impatience. "Yrvin, what did I do to deserve such special treatment today?" She reiterated again, adjusting her stylish outfit bathed in a redolent fragrance of meadow-fresh mint from Victoria's Secret.

"Because I know you can help me."

"*Me?* With what?" Her eyes went wide and grew intense.

"Kaykay, have you been deceived in love before?"

"Yes, Yrvin. Twice." She paused for a moment, thinking.

"In both instances, what was your reaction?" I asked.

"Crushed. And why ask?"

"Because now I'm learning how to deal with my own painful stab in the heart."

"From the girl who flew to Strasbourg?"

"Yes."

"But it's been almost five years."

"I haven't heard from her in three years, and she's the mother of my child."

A waitress soon showed up, and I left it to Kaykay to place the order for the two of us. She understood. She ordered one big *pescado frito* (deep-fried fish) and *arroz con frigoles rojos* (rice with mixed red beans). She knew I loved that.

"Yrvin, in my twenty-four years on this earth, I went through a lot, from romantic backstabbing to full-scale betrayal, and now left to raise a child…"

"I know your story as you told me before. That's why I trust you with my suffering. I want you to help me get through this." My eyes turned moist. I turned my face sideways, no longer wanting to make eye contact.

"Yrvin."

"Call me Vinco. I think we're more than just coworkers."

"Despite those unwanted setbacks, Vinco, we're still at the spring of our lives. I think it would be a grave mistake to think it's all finished. I know you're stronger than that."

"Yeah, it's easy to say."

"Vinco, I'm not gonna lie to you. I was wrecked on both occasions, cooped up in my bedroom for days and weeks. But I fought back as hard as I could because I had to reclaim my life, not let it be destroyed by selfish men."

"Kaykay. I'm impressed, but how did you find your way back after being down so deep?"

The food came, and I took two tiny pieces of that delicious fish and a couple of spoonsful of rice.

"Vinco, don't do this to me."

"What?"

"Eat," she insisted in a coy smile, taking a juicy piece of fish and squeezed it between my lips. I laughed, chewing the fish which almost choked me. "If you're so devastated the way you say you are, you need to go find her," she added.

"How?"

"I don't know. Maybe by trying to contact her relatives. They still live here. Don't they?"

"I presume so."

"Presume? Are you sure you want to find out about your son and your girl?"

I didn't reply. I switched the conversation, talking about the morning assignment at work, something totally irrelevant to the purpose of our lunch. The last thing I wanted was for her to realize how vulnerable I was as a man raised in the Caribbean machismo. Kaykay knew how firm I had always been when performing my professional obligations. She did not question why such an abrupt change of the subject. I guessed she was not interested in being drawn into something she herself had previously endured. We spent the rest of the time joking about each other's cultural traits, awkward beliefs, etc. On the way back, surprisingly she returned to our earlier topic of conversation.

"Vinco, I know what you're going through, but I want you to know that life can sometimes be very unfair," she said with a charge of emotion, becoming a transformed young woman. We soon reached the parking lot but remained in the car. "You see, I knew something was not right because for a long time I have been watching you coming and going with very little to say to us in the office. I have missed the smile that lit up my day. I've never had to work with someone whose attitude could be so…." I stopped her.

"Negative, you mean?" I asked.

"No, Vinco, Rigid, I mean, until now."

"But, remember when I first started here, Kakay? We made fun of each other. We ate and joked…"

"If you want me to, I can be with you in the search—although I'm not sure if I can be helpful. But I'll do whatever I can."

"Thank you, Kaykay. Just knowing that you understand my suffering makes me feel less lonely."

"I have a friend who is Dominican. She goes to my church."

"Kakay, there're so many Dominicans in town."

"I speak Spanish, remember? In any event, I'm in the fight with you. Do me a favor, Vinco."

"What, Kakay?"

"Be hopeful."

Then, we went up to our separate offices.

Chapter 13

Since the Duvaliers left the country in 1986, life had not profoundly changed as the people of Haiti had hoped. On the contrary, the sociopolitical crisis had deepened. The popular democracy for which the masses fought so hard had yet to materialize. The day after Baby Doc's departure, a military junta took over with the promise to respect popular demands for participatory democracy. It was a ploy, a scheme to pacify an angry population that was still fighting for social justice. The junta introduced cosmetic changes, allowing Haitians to express their political grievances freely, but refusing to address the pressing, basic needs like putting food on the table, introducing social and economic reforms to rebuild the shattered economy, and speeding up the process for rewriting a constitution as this was one of the key elements in the struggle against the Duvalier dictatorship.

Understandably, it did not take long for the Haitian people to go back to the streets, opposing what they perceived to be a furtherance of Duvalierism without Duvalier. The country soon descended into chaos. What followed was a series of coups and counter-coups as competing forces within the ruling elite fought for control of the state bureaucracy. In the end, in 1990, general elections were held and Jean-Bertrand Aristide, a popular priest turned politician won by a landslide. It was the first time in Haiti's history, free and fair elections were held, but Aristide's victory was a major blow to US foreign diplomacy in Haiti. His closest opponent was Marc Bazin, a true believer in laissez-faire economics. He read verbatim the economic model enshrined in *El Ladrillo*, the Chicago Boys' Bible. Bazin was heavily favored by the ruling elite and its foreign backers. He lost decisively.

A renewed sense of hope took hold in the minds and hearts of Haitians everywhere. Nine months later, however, Aristide was shockingly deposed in a bloody coup that brought general Raoul Cédras to power. Haitians, at home and abroad, were outraged. So were many people in the Haitian community in Miami. Once again, I found myself in the middle of the same struggle for freedom and democracy I thought we had won.

It had also provided me an unexpected opportunity to keep my mind preoccupied, away from thinking too much about Michaela and Yrvin Junior. I became a political activist, being an active member of CAPAM (Committee for Patriotic Haitian Action in Miami), a grassroots organization dedicated to the return of Aristide who lived in exile in the United States. The popular sentiment across the Haitian diaspora as well as Haitians in Haiti was that the coup plotters must allow the Haitian president to return to Haiti to finish his presidential mandate. Every afternoon after work, as well as on weekends, I had to stop by the Haitian Refugee Center on Fifty-Fourth Street to get the latest news from Haiti.

One afternoon, I was returning home from a political event when my eyes caught Soledad walking out of the little grocery store still owned by the Arab merchants. She was ready to get in her car when I called to her.

"*Sole!*" I shouted while making a left turn to meet her.

She raised her head and saw me coming. She was thrilled, arms spread for a warm hug when we met. "I'm excited to see you, Vinco," she giggled, pulling away from me. We still held hands.

"Me, too. Still the same rosy cheeks…." I poked her chin a little.

"I hear you're a bigshot downtown, Vinco."

"Is that right? So, how's the family doing? Henriette?" I changed the conversation.

"Everyone is fine, except for Henriette."

"What's wrong?"

"She's still depressed."

"Over her boyfriend in Haiti?"

"Yep."

"That's so sad. Whatever happened to your dancing career?" I teased her.

"That was a childhood *dream*." She burst out laughing.

"And now?"

"After graduating from Miami Dade Community College, I moved to Savannah with Sony, my longtime boyfriend. Remember? Things didn't work out. So, I left him and moved back home. Now, I'm trying to rebuild…"

"Soledad, you did the right thing."

"Vinco, I heard from Chantale, your Dominican girl left you and moved to France."

"That's true." There was a sudden pause in the conversation. She understood.

"I can imagine what you went through."

"Yeah, this is life, Soledad."

"You remember that girl who was with her when I waited for you by the bookstore that Friday afternoon?"

"Yes. That was Juanita, her cousin. What about her?"

"I saw her last week."

"*Where?*"

"At Barnett Bank, the one on 79th Street. She's one of the supervisors there."

"Are you sure it was *her*?"

"I think so. I was with my mom, opening a new account. She was the one who served us."

"*Thank* you, Sole."

So, we chatted for a few more minutes. We then exchanged phone numbers and hugged each other goodbye. That piece of information felt like a much-needed injection to boost my energy in the search for Mica. In an instant, I thought of Kaykay, who had promised to help in the effort. I had not visited my former neighborhood for more than two years. I was curious to see if my old community had changed. I decided to take a tour.

Surprisingly, I discovered that everything remained almost the same. With unmitigated chagrin, I sluggishly rolled by my old apartment, which seemed to have new tenants. Fresh paint coated the walls. From inside, I heard voices of children laughing while mumbling words in Spanish I could not understand. Then came the authoritative voice of a woman screaming from the kitchen.

"Caya te, Bianca," she commanded. *Be quiet.*

A feeling of nostalgia wrapped my soul, thinking of the happy time my sister and I shared in that apartment despite the precariousness of our lives as refugees. She gave me a sense of home that I would not have traded for anything. The home I now missed, lost in the shadow of my younger years, my college years, a home in which Michaela and I made love with uncontrolled passion. Taking frantic aim at this cozy place, old memories of a not-too-distant past rushed back with a vengeance.

I remembered the enchanted mornings right here in this small backyard, shirtless and sweaty after a long jog, listening to the sounds of crickets chirping in the nearby trees and the indigo bunting birds whistling their sharp, high-pitched notes piercing the morning silence. I glanced at the small window of my old bedroom in which I spent countless, sleepless summer nights, long and torturous, thinking of Michaela, the girl who had stolen my soul, while agonizing over my sense of betrayal vis-à-vis Régine, the childhood sweetheart I left behind in Haiti.

Deep in thought, all of a sudden, I heard the front door slam. Curious, I parked my car by the roadside and then sauntered around the main entrance. I saw a porcelain-skinned young woman in a yellow dress, standing on the porch. Droplets of sweat glistened on her oval face. When our eyes met, she threw a gentle smile. I smiled back with an urge to exchange a few words, but I refrained from taking that step. So, I decided to walk across the street to say hello to Mr. Jackson and his wife. I knew they still lived there because I noticed his Cadillac, now a bit depreciated, there under the carport as in the old days. Unfortunately, no one was home. As I was going back to my car, a boy who lived two blocks down told me the Jacksons had traveled to Louisiana for a funeral. He also told me Trayvon went off to college somewhere in Indiana.

Mr. Yakimono, the sumo wrestler, still lived in the same duplex behind the chain-link fence, but I met a neighbor at the front gates who told me he retired a year ago from the Santa Claus role. He had not been in good health since his domineering wife Kanna left him and flew to Honolulu with a black dude no one knew. Rumors spread in the neighborhood that Kanna told some friends from the church choir, where she was an active member, that she was tired of going to bed every night with a lust that could never be satisfied. She told them Yakimono's impotence had become impossible to tolerate.

The neighbor then left, and I went ahead, unlatching the gates, walking to the front porch, and knocking on the door. I wanted to see him. No one replied when I knocked. I then went to the side of the house and peeked through the window. There he was, slumping in a wheelchair, his chihuahua by his side on the floor, dozing off. His face was drawn. His lips were chapped and bleeding.

My heart sank. He was completely disfigured. I was desperate to get his attention, so I knocked again. At last, he turned his head and widened his eyes. I knew he heard the knocking, but he remained glued to his chair. I then left, returning to my car, and driving to Fosia's home. On the way, I noticed that most of the people still lived on that narrow street, which curved around a line of mango trees, including Onès, the sacristan from the Catholic church. A year before, my sister told me he and Claudette were married and they had a two-year-old boy.

As I drove by Susana's place, I saw the yard was overgrown. Some of the front windows were broken, and the paint on the door was peeled off. The house looked depressing and abandoned. A lone, malnourished hound dog roamed the backyard, wagging its tail while barking. I pulled over by the side of the road, got out of the car, and walked to Fosia's home next door. One of the mango trees in the front yard was in full bloom, and against it leaned a robust young man wearing a hard hat like those of construction workers waiting to be picked up on their way to their work sites. I greeted him with a grin, and he responded in kind. I did not see the domino players in the backyard, bragging while fiercely competing under the avocado tree. I pursued and rang the doorbell.

On the first ring, the door swung right open, and Fosia in a pink garment stood in front of me with both hands resting inside a calico apron. Her face brightened into a wide smile as she looked me over. "Hey, Vinco. Look at my handsome boy!" She crowed. Now approaching middle age, spots of gray hair were visible, and her body had thickened a bit.

I stepped in and hugged her. "Every time you see me, you always say that, Aunt Fosia."

She grabbed my hand and led me to the kitchen where she was making stir-fried chicken and mixed rice and red beans. "Hmm, this makes me hungry," I confessed, sniffing the air filled with the aroma of that delicious Haitian dish.

"You'll get some, my son. Don't worry," she replied with an awesome pride, retrieving an aluminum bowl from one of the cabinets. She poured in some rice and red beans and laid the fried chicken on the top.

"What about the *pikliz* (hot pickles)?" I asked, pouring a spoonful of that rice into my mouth.

"It's coming," she bragged.

"By the way, Aunt Fosia, where's Laurette?"

"She's at work, but she should be here any moment."

"I'd love to see her. I haven't seen her since graduation night."

"Really?"

"But we always chat on the phone."

While talking, Carona, Fosia's youngest daughter, walked in. She was in tight blue jeans, a red shirt, and tennis shoes. She dropped her purse on the couch in the living room, and with sudden elation, ran up to me and almost choked me with a hug while I chewed on a delicious piece of fried chicken.

"*Vinco!*" She shrieked.

"Did you miss me?" I teased her.

"Of *course*! But you never came to visit. I ask Laurette for you all the time."

"I've been busy...."

"Carona, did you stop by someplace on the way home?" Fosia questioned her daughter since she was late coming home from school.

Carona leaned on me and squeezed my hands as if looking for a defense lawyer to come to the rescue. "I went to Cayard's Market to buy some coconut *dous* (sweets) and on the way out, I met Choubouloute."

"*Choubouloute?*" I injected. She was an impetuous girl who had an eye on me back in Haiti, but her impetuousness scared me.

"Don't tell her that you saw me, Carona."

"You got it, Vinco."

So, we chatted for more than an hour. I was hoping to see Laurette. Unfortunately, she never came. It was getting late, and I left.

#

Unless one has dwelled in the icy cave of solitude, he could never understand the anguish that seems to forever enslave the minds of those who live there. That was how I felt one Friday morning at work while sitting at my desk. Kayla had not yet arrived, and I had a couple of tasks for her. I wished she were there to cheer me up as she always did when I felt down.

Ever since Kaykay made the promise to help me in the search to reestablish contact with Michaela, we had been very close, and growing closer each passing day. She was so kind-hearted that sometimes when we were together, I felt I was on the verge of creeping over the forbidden line, the narrow alley of temptation that friends must never be allowed to cross. I noticed how in my presence she held my gaze with shining eyes that never squinted. This was manifested more when I praised her after she had accomplished an important task.

Kaykay was the closest I could get to Mica. She was smart, affectionate, and well spoken, with a stunning grasp of the complexity of life. On top of all this, she bore an unbound passion for social justice. Along with being a secretary in this high-tech firm, Kakay was a senior at the University of Miami School of Law. She would graduate in a few months, and her days as a secretary would be over. This would mean the end of our journey as coworkers sharing the same daily stressors of corporate America. That prospect scared me, for beyond this point, our professional relationship would be jeopardized.

Born in Coral Gables, a wealthy suburb in South Miami, Kayla was a *morena*, the product of a mixed-race woman from Barranquilla, Colombia, and a *trigueño* businessman from Quito, Ecuador. She was slightly taller than Michaela. And like Michaela, beneath her pale wheat-colored skin tone, the impermeable reflection of her African blood showed. There were times at work, mostly during lunchtime, that she used to tell me stories of her upbringing living in the Gables, of her high school years at Coral Gables High where she met classmates, children of wealthy Haitians who lived in lavish homes not far from her parents'.

She would describe how perplexed and baffled she was when she questioned them about the extreme poverty in the Caribbean nation as then stories of Haitian refugees caught on high seas and in police custody occupied a part of the local evening news. The wealthy children, she told me, would shrug it off, saying it was none of their business. She said she never understood their nonchalant attitude until she met me, although she had already recognized the reality of class divisions in every society.

Kayla and I seemed to have shared the unspoken, mutually inclusive worry and grasped the urgent need to move our friendship to a new level, pushing it beyond the rim of the workplace. My suspicion was confirmed that Friday when she pushed the door open, handed me a card, and left without giving me a chance to utter a word. I hurried and read the card; it was an invitation to a party at her home Saturday night as her family was celebrating her father's fifty-fifth birthday. Surprised, I rose from my desk and walked to her office where I met her standing near a wooden cabinet, going through some folders.

"I knew you were gonna come," she said with a timid smile, placing the folders back into the cabinets and turning to face me with a worried grin.

"I'm honored," I let her know. We both burst out laughing.

"I'm equally honored," she laughed, edging closer.

"What's the dress code?" I asked.

"Dress as you always do, minus the jacket."

"Why, Kakay?"

"Because the jacket is meaningless when people talk about dressing formally for in-house parties."

"Listen, Kakay. I'm leaving in a few." I changed the conversation.

"Why so early?"

"I have to pick up my dad from the airport. He's arriving on a flight from Nassau, Bahamas. See you tomorrow evening." I walked back to my office, grabbed my briefcase, and headed for the elevator.

#

Miami International Airport, one of South Florida's busiest airports, was a fifteen-minute drive when the traffic was light. Luckily, it was mid-afternoon, and the congestion down Highway 112 that led to the airport had worn off. I made it there rather quickly. I never liked to go to that airport, finding a parking spot was like playing the lotto. My father knew that, and every time I had to go pick him up, I would find him waiting at the edge of the main entrance where passengers from all international flights exited.

That day, however, his shrinking frame was lost amid fast-moving travelers and three tall taxi drivers gossiping around the taxi stand. I had not seen my father in four years. I almost didn't recognize him. His hair had gotten grayer and his bald head shinier. The traces of hair that once arched his forehead had all but disappeared. He looked thinner than when we last were together at my sister's wedding. A large blue shirt tucked inside khaki pants did not make it easier for me to spot him at first glance. I was able to see him when one of the cab drivers stepped out of the taxi stand, and he came into full view, hand raised above his forehead, looking quite anxious.

I made a daring halt, pulling to the side of the traffic circle, and walked out of the car. We were elated to be in each other's arms. From the airport, he asked me to take him to my sister's home. While riding, I tried to convince him to go home with me.

He refused. "Don't worry, Vinco. Next week, I'll be with you."

My sister lived in the Overtown Neighborhood of Miami, not far from the airport either. We made it to my sister's home in less than twenty minutes despite the traffic that started to pick up again as the afternoon rush hour drew closer.

"Papa," I said, still trying to persuade him. "Why don't you want to go home with me?"

"You can go, Vinco. You can come pick me up tomorrow afternoon," he reiterated, patting me on the head like he used to do when I was a boy.

"No, Papa. I've been invited to a party, and I wouldn't want to leave you alone."

"How about next weekend?"

"Perfect, Papa. It'll be you and I. Father and *son!*"

He then grabbed me with both hands and gave me a tight, fatherly hug.

My sister was home, and the minute she heard my father's voice, she rushed right outside. "Pa*pa*," she cried cheerfully. "Look at you!"

Papa was equally excited to be once again with his two lovely children. We all went in. I carried the luggage to an empty guest room where we all went to talk about the good old times but more importantly about the rest of the family that would soon join him in Miami. Papa was not going back to the Bahamas where he had spent twenty-five years of his life running a tailor's shop. Though he was happy to be with us, he was anxious. He had never lived in the United States before. My sister and I, however, assured him that we were going to do everything necessary to ensure the transition to a new life in America was as painless as possible.

Nana was the oldest child in the family and appeared to be the most beloved. She was Papa's spoiled girl, and she knew how to manipulate him. He believed everything she said and never questioned her funny tricks, including her weird desire to take him on an excursion to Billy Swamp Safari in the Florida Everglades. The latest ploy was to make him taste the Miccosukee Indians' fried bread, which was almost a replica of the Haitian's *pate*, a fried bread stuffed with smoked fish.

That afternoon, she pledged to go down to the Indian reservation with him the following week, along with little Nanouche, who was taking a nap in the next room. In what sounded like icing on the cake, she said that on their way back she would take him for a stroll, the two alone, along the bank of a sleepy lake enclosed by marshlands where alligators bred, and crawfish and mullet swam.

"And where do we leave Nanouche?" He asked. He was curious.

"Don't worry, Papa," she whined. "Nanouche will be fine in the car, playing her video game."

As many times before, Papa was ready to follow her on that wild adventure. He reluctantly declined, however, when he overheard one of my sister's neighbors, a retired, middle-school geography teacher, talking to a group of children about how vicious and sneaky alligators were, and how drivers who ran astray and fell down the alligator-infested canals along I-75, commonly known as Alligator Alley, never got out alive. Papa got freaked out. This was the first time he refused to follow her blindly.

Tired and exhausted after a long voyage, Papa started dozing off and soon began to snore his way into a deep slumber. Nana and I walked to the kitchen where she was making dinner.

"Why do you like to tell Papa those little lies?" I asked, teasing her.

She did not reply. She simply smiled. I then grabbed my car keys and headed for the door. "Don't you wanna wait for your favorite crab and callaloo?"

I was tempted to stay, but when I remembered the traffic on Interstate 95, I turned around and uttered with a grin. "Save it for me."

Chapter 14

Coral Gables was one of the more interesting places to live in Miami, an oasis enclosed by urban sprawls. Its strategic location gave its residents a dual feeling of city and suburban life. It was affluent not just because of its wealthy home dwellers, but because of its picturesque landscape, distinct tropical flowers, sweet fragrant jasmines, and its giant oaks whose extended branches camouflaged the million-dollar homes plentiful in this exclusive corner of South Florida.

At night, the Gables shed an aura of a sleeping paradise, enhanced by twinkling lights, amid tropical fruit trees and well-kept lawns customary to Miami's prosperous neighborhoods. Streetlamps were dimmed, and unless one lived there, it could be difficult to navigate. Unlike the rest of the city, Coral Gables had no street poles, and the streets were not numbered. They rather bore the names of famous people and rare animals engraved on square boulders coated in white on each street corner.

Kayla lived on Blue Road, right off Bird Road, one of the main boulevards that cut through the Gables, not far from the University of Miami. It was nine p.m. when I rolled onto Bird Road. The city noises died here, and I was forced to slow down, following a procession of flashy cars, and then turning left onto

Blue Road where the convoy stopped, and Kaykay's home was two houses down.

It was an imposing white house built in the middle of a courtyard framed by faultlessly trimmed ficus edges. Two royal palms guarded the main entrance, before which lines of colorful impatiens stretched from one end to the next. One by one, fancy guests walked out of their cars and threaded up to the main entrance. Nothing disturbed the silent night except for the whistling of a nightingale perched on one of the palm branches.

I stepped out of my car and followed behind a couple dressed in dark attire, speaking in low tones like fancy people do. The minute I walked onto the porch, out rushed Kayla, molded inside a long-sleeve velvet dress. I placed kisses on both cheeks, and she responded in kind.

"Sorry, Kaykay, for being late," I said with an utmost politeness.

"No, Vinco. You're not late at all. Look around you. Guests are just pulling in," she chortled while inviting me inside.

She then led me to a table in the corner of a vast room softened by a dim light fit for the moment. The guests sat in groups, large and small, around square mahogany tables that were well garnished with a variety of Spanish rums and French wines. There, we sat side by side, facing the room. Busy servers, dressed in black and white, took orders, throwing repressed smiles. Soon a girl in a blue dress strolled in from a back door accompanied by a well-built lad.

"Violeta," she called to her. "*¿A donde esta mama?*" she said in Spanish. *Where is mom?*

"*No se.* I think she is in the back talking to some guests."

Then a Colombian cumbia was introduced, and the two young kids moved to the center of the room to join other attendees dancing to the beat of the popular South American music.

"Who's this girl?" I asked.

"She's my younger sister."

"And the young man?"

"He's Carlito, her boyfriend."

"I heard she said your mom is in the back."

"Yeah. I'd like for you to meet both of my parents."

"No worries, Kaykay. I just walked in, and you know they're busy."

"Wait, Vinco. I'll be right back."

In pure ladylike fashion, she rose from her seat, strode across the room, and soon faded. I was perplexed. A minute later, she was back with a smile on her face, carrying a bottle of *kremas*, a delicious Haitian party drink.

"For you, Vinco," she said. The pride on her face warmed my heart. She knew I loved *kremas*.

"Who made it for you, Kaykay?" I asked, taking a sip.

"I did it myself. Well, not entirely myself. My friend and neighbor, Lucette, helped me."

"Didn't she ask you why you wanted to make *kremas*?

"Yes, and I told her it was for my boss, who loves it."

She took a cup from our table and poured in some *kremas*. I then grabbed the bottle from her hand and filled one for her, too. While chatting, a couple walked by, and Kaykay waved to them. They were a six-foot-tall gentleman with a red cinnamon face and an impressive young woman fashioned in a Versace baroque-print dress. The couple stopped and approached our table. Kayla introduced them to me. She was Lucette and her husband Jean-Marie, two wealthy lawyers who lived next door, Kaykay later told me.

We exchanged a few words in classic South Florida Creoglish, a mixture of Creole and English, a popular form of speech among Haitian Americans. Kayla seemed lost in the brief conversation. Then, the couple left and made their way to their table. All of a sudden, the music stopped, and the dancers vacated the dancefloor as everyone returned to their seats.

A middle-aged man and his wife, hand in hand, stepped onto a raised terrace where an improvised stage awaited them. All eyes were on the couple. Wearing a black jacket, the man approached the mic and snatched it from the stand with one hand while the other was wrapped around the thin waist of his smiling wife's feline body. He stood upright and began to speak. From the depth of his voice sprung the gentle expressions of an educated man on top of his game, greeting the guests in total dominance while thanking them for coming to celebrate yet another milestone of his amazing life.

"He's my dad, Antonio, and my mom, Lupita," Kaykay whispered.

"It's obvious, Kaykay," I replied with a grin.

As soon as the official greeting was over, the music and the dancing resumed. Antonio and Lupita led the way, and the crazy dancers trailed them back to the dancefloor. This time, it was a salsa by Willy Colón. Antonio and his wife were in sheer delight. One could see how the happy couple had mastered the art of salsa dancing. Later, Kaykay told me dancing was to them so much a passion that, alone, they would put their favorite music and dance naked from the waist up until they got exhausted and retired to their bedroom.

"To do the hanky-panky?" I teased her.

"You *stop* it," she laughed.

I asked for a dance. She declined rather politely but invited me instead to go for a stroll, just the two of us. At once, we abandoned our chairs and headed for an alley that opened to a backyard. We held hands. Just before we reached the door, she flicked off the switch that controlled the garden lights. I became quite reticent, not because of the perplexity of the moment, but because of where we were. I felt like a wary soldier moving to unchartered waters. But I trusted her.

It was past midnight, dark and silent. Now, the music was behind us, but we could still hear the waning voices from inside the mansion, like crickets chirping in the distance. We strolled along an invisible pathway, passing two young lovers kissing behind a bushy mango tree. They made no attempt to walk away as they saw us coming. A pair of Akita dogs soon barked in the shadows, moving toward us. In a quick whisper in Spanish, she quieted them down. We then reached the edge of a rosebush behind which was a tiny concrete bench where we sat side by side, still holding hands. My heart was racing.

"This is quite peaceful here," I said, trying to suppress my mounting fear.

"Yes, it *is*, Vinco," she replied, leaning on me. Her voice softened.

"You didn't show me your cutie Miguelito, Kaykay." Miguelito was her son's name. I tried to direct the conversation away from unwanted topics.

"Miguelito was there, the tallest boy among the children in the playroom, the one with the curly hair."

"Yes, I saw him. He's really handsome, and beneath his pale brown skin lies the indescribable beauty of his mother."

"*Stop* it, Vinco," she shrieked.

"You sound like a songbird in the night."

"And I will fly like one if you insist on these little white lies."

We now turned to face each other and burst out laughing.

"Vinco, tell me, do you truly wanna dance with me?"

"Who wouldn't wanna dance with a splendid young lady like you?"

"Don't start it again," she warned with a playful coyness. "I wanna dance, but dancing with someone like you could…"

"Could what, Kaykay?"

"Never mind, Vinco. There's something I feel I must share with you."

Suddenly, we heard her sister's voice and rapid footsteps moving from the back, calling out to her. So, we left the bench and met her halfway. "Violeta, what's wrong?" Kaykay asked her. She was anxious.

"Juanita's here with her husband, and they're asking for you," she said, aiming a cold stare at both of us as if she disapproved of her sister being in the dark with someone she didn't know.

"Tell them I'm coming."

Violeta left, stomping her feet in displeasure.

"Kaykay, I think she's not happy seeing us together."

"In the dark here, of course."

"I may have to leave, then, to avoid unwanted—"

"Don't even go there, Vinco. Let's get back inside. I'll be at your place tomorrow afternoon after church," she whispered in my ear.

The minute we stepped inside, we came face to face with Juanita, Michaela's cousin. She was the young woman my friend Soleda told me about, who worked at Barnett Bank near Little Haiti. We both were stunned. We jumped into each other's arms, shedding happy tears to the astonishing eyes of Kaykay and Juanita's husband, a gray-eyed fellow with an imposing posture and wearing a business suit without a necktie. Juanita presented him as her husband, Jayden Charlemagne. She later told me he was from the Caribbean Island of Saint Lucia where they speak a French-based Creole, the same as mine, as well as English. All four of us now moved to the table where Kaykay and I sat earlier. We began to review our college years, the good old times, telling stories that until now remained untold tales of romance.

Kaykay seemed interested in the conversation and even seemed quite happy, for she was the one who unknowingly had made this unexpected meeting possible, although she never knew if there was a family connection between Juanita and Michaela, the woman whose absence had tormented her boss and good friend. I was not so sure after all if she was genuinely interested. Juanita told me she had not heard from Michaela in two years, but Emilio, Michaela's father and her mother's older brother, with whom she regularly communicated, said Mica was fine. At the end of the party, before I left, we exchanged phone numbers, and she promised to put me in contact with Gabriela, Michaela's older sister. Leaving Juanita and her husband at the table, Kaykay walked me to the door, and we said goodbye.

#

As a young man, I knew I was stubborn and ambitious. Nothing I owned was a gift. I understood that the world I came from was quite different from the one many of my peers had known or were born into. That shaped my character, and I drew my strength from the hardships of the past. I never surrendered my right to fight for what I believed in. Despite such a stoic attitude toward fortitude and temperance, however, nothing tempted me more than the presence and enigma of a beautiful woman.

The next day, I was preparing a late lunch for the two of us when the knock that I had been anticipating came upon the door shortly after one p.m. I looked through the window, and there she was. Kayla stood on the porch, looking relaxed, wearing a flower-patterned dress enhanced by a red scarf wrapped around her neck. I hurried and opened the door. We kissed each other, and the soft cushion of her lips coated in rouge left a lovely red stamp on my cheeks. With a cheery smile, I led her to the sofa, but she did not want to sit. Instead, she followed me to the kitchen where I was making garlic bread and spaghetti.

"For me, Vinco," she tittered.

"For both of us," I replied with a funny laugh.

"So, let me help you, then."

"Kaykay, I'm your host. Just a little reminder," I teased her.

"Let's prepare it together, *Monsieur Yrvin*."

"*Oui*, Mademoiselle Kayla."

Her face lit up, and her eyes went feverish. She took command of the spaghetti while I tended to the garlic bread. I avoided the conversation from the night before, which would have been a celebration between the two of us knowing she was the one who made it possible for me to meet Juanita. Although it seemed a stroke of luck, it had raised my hope for an eventual reunion with Michaela.

Instead, we spent the rest of the meal preparation joking about old gossip from work. I tried to walk a thin blue line, not knowing how to address the sudden change in our friendship. The mere fact she did not raise the subject had left me puzzled. Still, I was confident the moment had arrived for lovemaking. After all, the decision to come here was hers.

I was wrong. Besides her flawless charm and exuberance, Kayla bore in her heart and mind a dignity difficult to overlook. After we ate lunch, we moved to the sofa, sitting side by side, hand and hand. Her head tilted toward my chest, almost touching it. After nearly an hour on the sofa, the needle had not moved an inch, and I began to realize if there was going to be a romantic moment fueled by sexual pleasures, I had to be the one to initiate it. I made several moves, trying to creep my fingers under the flower dress, but she shifted position each time, skewing to the opposite side. "You're such a player, Vinco!" she kept on saying. Still, I had hope, for despite her resistance, the passion in her eyes had betrayed her, turning them into orbs of a raging fire. I knew she wanted to make love. So, I rose from the sofa while pulling her along, still holding hands, standing so close that our lips almost touched. Unexpectedly, she freed her hands from mine.

"Vinco," she said in a firm tone of voice. "We're on the verge of crossing a red line that might prove to be dangerous for both of us. So, let's avoid it while we still can."

"What do you mean, Kaykay?"

"Don't play with me, Vinco. Don't you realize our friendship is fast becoming an unnecessary adventure?"

"Kaykay, don't say that. My feelings for you grow daily."

"So do mine. But I've learned to suppress this emotion sneaking into my heart. I think you and I should avoid taking this train of love that will lead us to a forbidden land. Vinco, the reason why I asked for that little walk last night in the garden was because I wanted to discuss this with you. I can't ignore the main factor that has gotten us so close, and I will never renege on my promise to help you reunite with Michaela, the girl you honestly love."

"Kaykay, I don't want you to think I wanna use this moment as a preamble for an open-ended, temporary love."

"I would never agree to that."

"So, you see—" She stopped me right there.

"Vinco, don't get me wrong. I *love* you, but I know I would violate my own principles, trashing my self-esteem if I were to go to bed with you. I've learned from past mistakes, as I've already told you." She let her hand fall back into mine. Her hazel eyes now turned moist and blue, an ocean of hopeless grief. She glanced across the room, and her eyes caught the bed through the door that was ajar. She turned to me again. "Vinco," she uttered in a faint-hearted voice. "What could a short moment of pleasure do for us?"

"Don't say this, Kaykay."

"I have to, and I think you have to ask yourself the same question. I believe we both *must* fight off these sexual stirrings and face reality. You don't want to turn me into your sex toy. Is that what you want from me? *Is* it?"

"Oh, Kaykay."

"Vinco, that's precisely what I would be, for I know I will never earn your heart, although I may earn just another child out of wedlock."

"Kaykay, I see what you're saying. But I want to be a part of your life. I have to be realistic."

"What do you mean by realistic? Do you want me as your stick-around girl? Your sweet plan B? Vinco, let's get back to the way we were. A friendship will suit us well."

She paused for a moment, studying one of my pictures hanging on the wall. She turned to me again, wrapping both her arms around my neck. "I see why a woman would hastily fall in love with you."

"Why?"

"You have the magic touch that can easily urge a woman to climax."

We were now back on the sofa, her head resting on my chest, sobbing. So, we settled for a few kisses, spending the rest of the afternoon interlaced, wiping away each other's tears until it was time for her to leave, and I walked her down to her car.

#

I went up to my apartment a beaten man. I could not find the words to describe Kaykay's dignified demeanor. With one single stroke, I was disarmed from all arguments. Admitting our shared feelings, she proved to me that, despite her sincerest and profound emotions, she was still able to rise to the moment and say NO. I had no doubt she went home evermore convinced that she indeed had learned from her past mistakes and that her pride went above and beyond everything. Once again, she reminded me of Michaela, a firm young woman with amazing self-assurance.

By nightfall, I had an unexpected visit. It was from Laurette, whom I had not seen in more than two years. When I went to see her a few days before, she was not home, but Carona, her younger sister, had promised to have her call me. I was expecting a call, but not a surprise show-up. She was stylish, the way she had always been during our college years. Now, however, she had the demeanor of a more mature young woman in full ascendance of what shaped up to be a promising life. She stepped into the room dressed in a knee-length skirt over which billowed sprinkles of water from a quick drizzle that came through as she walked out of her car to get to the building. With two soft *bisous* (little kisses), one on each cheek, she greeted me. I was thrilled.

"What a gift!" I cried, ecstatic.

"Ever since my mom told me you came to see us, I couldn't stop thinking of you and our college years."

"Lolo, believe it or not, it's been roughly four and a half years." Lolo was how we all lovingly called her.

"Vinco, it feels an eternity."

Without asking me, she walked to the kitchen, grabbed a plate, and filled it with spaghetti and garlic bread, just like she used to do when I lived down in Little Haiti. On the first bite, she was delighted.

"You've always been a great cook," she laughed with the same big-sister, commanding stare as back in college days.

"You forgot. It was Nana who did the cooking. But I'm glad you like it, Lolo."

We moved to the dining table. There, we spent the moment talking about good old times, her experiences being a nurse, and her failed romance with the preacher's son. I knew she never liked him. She loved Ronel, who was not really interested in her. But I saw no need to raise the issue, certainly not when she came to see me after years of not seeing each other. I did not have to tell her about my professional job at the firm downtown, and I was not about to share my current ordeal with Michaela. She knew. Chantale told her. Toward the end of the visit, she brought up Régine's story.

"Vinco, have you heard from Régine?"

"No."

"I saw her last month. She still goes to Miami Dade Community College, and she has two children."

"Really?" I was evasive. "I'm happy for her."

"So, how's your Dominican girl?"

"That girl has a name."

"I know, and I'm still bitter about this whole story."

"I think you need to get over it. Régine herself has moved on, is happily married, and has two kids as you just told me."

"You haven't told me about Michaela."

"Now, you remember her name. Yeah, she's fine. We don't have a wedding date yet, but when the time comes, you'll know."

She did not react to my answer. I guessed she knew I was lying, and by asking questions about Mica, she was trying to prove a point that she had been right all along and that Régine would have never treated me the way Michaela did. Deep in my subconsciousness, I realized there were some elements of truth in her unspoken words.

That evening, I dared to challenge her. We grew up in the same dusty town of Saint Louis in Haiti, and we had always been the best of friends. She was a year older, and because of that, she would tell me, she had the birthright and obligations to protect me against unforeseen pitfalls in life. In Miami, we were reconnected, and unlike the other old-country friends I met in South Florida who had become estranged, Laurette never alienated herself from me. Instead, she had shown me that good friends could still be found in this cruel world. She was beautiful, intelligent, and witty. Most of the time, I welcomed her domineering, overprotective attitude. This had helped chase my homesickness, giving me a sense of belonging in the community, and making me feel loved—the sisterly love that anyone going through hardships honestly needs.

I disagreed with her objections over Michaela because I had always thought they were ill-founded. I had my own ways of quelling her biased opinions. "Sister, you need to walk your talk," I would say. "You sound like those folks who love to talk about social justice but will do everything in their power to keep enslaved servants in their homes. You can't be Miss Right when you're cheating on your boyfriend." She would stop immediately. However, she was the girl whose friendship I was not prepared to sacrifice. I made several attempts that evening to share my ordeal, telling it all to her, but I fought back the urge. After two hours of chatting, she left but we promised each other to "retighten the rank" as they used to say back home in Haiti.

Chapter 15

I had not been at her parents' home since the night of her birthday party, and every time that dreaded morning of her flight to France invaded my mind, it felt like a self-inflicted wound that refused to heal. For the first time in many years, I reclaimed the road that led to their home. Committed to learning the truth about what had happened to Michaela and my son, I drove on. If they denied me entry into their home, I kept on thinking, I would simply leave. That Saturday morning, the traffic was light. The night before, I had a long conversation with my sister, and she gave me an ultimatum to go find Michaela's parents. I told her to sit tight, and I would call her as soon as I left the Monsalves' home.

When I rolled into Hialeah and drove by the Dominican beauty shops and onward to the street where she once lived, I burst into tears. To regain my composure, I pulled over by the side of the street and took a deep breath. Already, I could see the cottage home a few houses down. I was nervous, fearful of rejection as well as of any bad news they might have told me about Mica and my boy. With maximum prudence, I advanced until I reached the front gate where I used to drop my girlfriend off every day after school. I walked out of the car, stepped up to the front door, and knocked. A short, slim gentleman opened the door.

"How can I help you?" He asked.

"I'm here to see Mr. and Mrs. Monsalve," I replied in a polite, but firm voice.

"No," he said, widening his eyes. "They no longer live here. They sold this house two years ago."

"Do you know where they now live?"

"No. I heard they live in Hialeah Garden."

"Thank you."

He closed the door, and I retreated down to my car, disappointed. I was about to drive off, when a neighbor called to me, a tall woman named Paula who lived adjacent to the home.

"Vinco, how are *you*?" She asked, standing by the side of the street.

"I'm doing okay," I replied. "So *glad* to see you."

I remained in the car, and she strolled toward me. "I heard what happened, and it made me very sad," she said, her voice lowered.

"Life can be unpredictable. Can't it?" I said. "Listen, Paula, I went to visit the Monsalves, and a gentleman told me they no longer live there. He said they've moved to Hialeah Garden. Do you know their physical address?"

"No, but I can certainly ask for you. I'm warning you, though. You shouldn't go."

"Why is that?"

"Because after Michaela left, Lucrecia went into a major depression, and she blamed it all on you for getting her daughter pregnant, which made her send her off to Europe."

"But she didn't have to. She could've reacted differently."

"I know, and several of the neighbors shared the same thought. Do you keep in contact with her?"

"At the beginning, yes; but it's been three years since the last time we talked. Paula, can you help me?"

"How?"

"Can you manage to get Mica's contact info for me? I've lost it." I did not want to get into the details.

"I'm gonna try."

We exchanged phone numbers and said goodbye. While driving, a sense of optimism grew in my mind. I knew Paula, a middle-aged Puerto Rican woman from New York who had lived in the neighborhood years before the Monsalves. She was very funny. As I dropped off Michaela from school, she used to tease us. "What *a beautiful* couple you two would make, uh, uh, uh!" She would say, squinting her eyes. We always laughed.

Although it did not put me any closer to finding Michaela, Paula's promise had raised my hope a bit. One thing this quick talk had given me was a cautious realization that Michaela and Junior still lived in France, and it could have been her own decision to sever all contacts with me. Why? I did not know. Even if she had found a man, I began to think, could she master the strength to prevent me from reaching my son? I rejected such a possibility, for Mica was a dignified young woman who would not have bought in to this dangerous, cold-hearted game. I drove straight home. Although I had not eaten breakfast in anticipation of meeting Mica's parents, I felt no urge to put food in my mouth. The possibility of spending the rest of my life without my son and Michaela terrified me.

I took off my shoes and threw them in the closet. With my clothes on, I sat on the floor, struggling to fight off tears before they started streaming down my cheeks. Then Pedro came to mind. Pedro was a visionary. He once predicted a major setback in the relationship that could result in a long-lasting itch that would require clearsighted devotion to get rid of.

"Why do you make such a horrible prediction?" I asked.

"Because your romance with Michaela seems surreal," he replied. "We're living in an imperfect world so much at odds with this fairytale," he joked.

Then, I had paid little attention to what I called expressions born out of protectiveness. I became retrospective, remembering how Carmelita, my other classmate and dear friend had warned me that morning after class, just before Michaela and I made love in the Fontainebleau Hotel in Miami Beach where she got pregnant. I also remembered so vividly one afternoon when my friend and coworker Pablo stormed out of the financial office where we worked, in complete meltdown, warning me about love betrayal after his girlfriend was caught red-handed making love with another young man. I started thinking that even my Haitian female friends had a point when they bitterly cautioned me about the relationship, although I knew they were doing it out of jealousy and selfishness.

However, I refused to accept what seemed obvious, because despite everything I was still convinced romantic betrayal would be the last pain Mica would inflict on my heart. Some grave incident must have happened, preventing her from reaching out to me. Even if her actions bore the trademark of a changed heart, could she have mastered the deceptive courage to deny me the right to be with my son? These thoughts and unanswered questions stirred in my mind like a river in fury, rushing to an ocean of despair.

I grabbed my phone and called Pedro. Luckily, he picked on the first ring. "Vinco, you wouldn't believe it. You were just on my mind. I was going to call you because we haven't talked in a while," he said, and I could hear him chewing something that nearly choked him.

"I was expecting this first line, and, you think I believe you?" I mocked him.

"No, *man*. You can ask Chen."

"Listen, man. I need to talk to you. It's urgent. Call me when you're done eating." I could hear the cutlery clinking of spoons, knives, forks and little Charlito, a year old, crying "Papi, Papi" and the voice of Chen trying to quiet him down. I heard her telling Pedro to tell me to come over and have dinner with them.

"I'm done, man."

"Tell Chen, I'll let you know when that'll be possible. My dad is in town, and you know what that means, man."

"I will. So, what's up?"

"I need your help. I'm on the verge of losing my sanity. I can't stop thinking of what she did to me. I have to find her."

"Let me step outside on the balcony. Charlito is making some noise as you can hear in the background."

"And this reminds me of that father-and-son love I may never get the chance to enjoy."

"Have faith. Michaela *might* come back to you. Just last night, Chen and I were talking about it. You know Chen knew her. They had a philosophy class together."

"Pedro, you think faith will someday turn into a miracle, and Michaela and Junior will emerge out of the blue?"

"You know I never believe in miracles, but I know if you try hard enough, your courage and determination will eventually take you to *el camino real*."

"Translation?"

"To the real path that leads to her and your son."

"This is too subjective. You know I like to speak in concrete terms. I need to take actions, and my mind is now blank. Help me, *man*."

"Last time we talked, you said you were going to speak to her parents."

"I just came from there, but a man told me they'd moved to Hialeah Garden."

"Really?"

"Yeah. But a neighbor told me she could get her sister's phone number for me."

"That's encouraging, but I think we need to do more than that. Calling her sister, you'll probably get a fake, hypocritical response. But we could use her boyfriend to find out the truth."

"How? Is he your friend?"

"No, but I know someone who is and can help. We need to find the answers to some critical questions. Is Mica still in France? If she is, where and what had happened to cause such a dramatic turn of events? If she's still in France, we'll have to look for an address or a phone number. Things have changed, Vinco. You're no longer the penniless immigrant boy struggling to get by in a Little Haiti neighborhood. You now have the logistics—everything at your disposal for the search. Money is no longer a problem. I hope Michaela, wherever she may now be, is thinking about you, too. We also need to concentrate on the possibility that she might be back home, although I seriously doubt it."

"Ped, do you think such possibility could exist?"

"You never know. People can change, sometimes in the most dramatic fashion. If she's back in Miami and makes no attempt to get in touch with you, you'll know it's over. At that point on, you'll be facing a new fight, the fight to be a part of your son's life. And you'll have to be prepared for the worst and hope for the best-case scenario."

"Thank you, man, for your good support. You're a brother, more than just a friend."

"Hey, Vinco. I want you to know I'm much more concerned about your well-being, more than anything else. Give me until next weekend. We'll talk."

#

After I hung up the phone, I fell asleep. I did not wake up until late in the afternoon when the phone rang, but it went silent before I had the chance to reach it. Then I remembered my sister and her *stern* order to call her as soon as I left the Monsalves' home. I hurried and dialed her number, and she picked up the phone on the first ring.

"What ever happened to you, *naughty* boy?" She asked with her usual commanding tone.

"Nana, I forgot, but there was no serious news. Well, there was some news, but not what you and I had hoped."

"What do you mean?"

"Mica's parents don't live there anymore."

"*What?*" She was stunned, but before she had the chance to ask another question, I preempted her.

"I'll be over soon. Then I'll tell you all about it."

"You'd better get your tail here fast. Papa's been waiting…"

It did not take me long to get there after a quick shower. My father was excited when I arrived at my sister's home. Hands on hips, he stood like a commander-in-chief at the pedestal of his glory.

"You made me *wait* all day," he reminded me with love and authority.

I knew I was supposed to bring him over as we had agreed on Friday, but the current circumstances had paralyzed me. A good time with Dad had always been the best of times. He loved to tell stories of past romances, of his machismo, of his struggles to be a man, and of his vicissitudes of fortune in the unforgiving landscapes of the Bahamas.

"Sorry, Papa. I had some unfinished work at the job." I lied, and he didn't seem to buy it.

"I didn't know you also work on Saturdays," he growled from the base of his throat.

I hunched over and gave him a tight hug to soften the attitude. "No, I don't. But remember I had to leave work before time on Friday to go pick you up from the airport? Am I in trouble?"

"Not yet." He laughed, pulling me against his chest like he used to when I was a young boy back in Saint Louis.

We walked in, joking. He then left me and strolled straight toward the back door, pushing it open and shutting it behind him. From inside, I could hear him leap off the back porch and walk down a graveled pathway that ran up to a mango tree in full bloom.

My sister was in the kitchen, humming "*Ayiti Cheri*" ("Haiti, my Darling"), her favorite folksong. Nanouche sat in a low chair a few feet from her. She jumped off the chair and ran up to me when she saw me coming, showing me her new baby doll, a gift from Grandpa. I lifted her up while she wrapped her little creamy arm around my neck.

Nana made a sudden stop. She was no longer humming. "*Vinco*, I'm nervous to know what happened this morning with Mica's parents," she uttered, facing me with mounting fear.

"Give me a minute because if I start talking now, my sense of taste will vanish. I'm a hungry wolf right now, Nana." I joined her. Wooden spoon in hand, she filled my plate with deep-fried grouper and mixed rice and red beans. "*Hmm*, can't wait," I cried, putting Nanouche down, snatching the plate from her hand, ready to wolf down the food.

"I'd better get out of here before that wolf jumps on me," she teased. "So, let's go sit at the table next door," she added.

We both moved to the table, and Nanouche followed behind. After a few giant bites, I was done.

"I need to know what happened," Nana insisted.

"When I arrived, a gentleman, maybe in his late thirties, told me Mica's parents have moved."

"Jesus, Mary, and Joseph. Now, we're back to square one."

"Not necessarily."

"How so?"

"Because Pedro and I now have a plan."

"And?"

"He's going to try to get Mica's number through a mutual friend. Someone who knows Gabriela, Mica's older sister."

"Let's hope and pray."

"You bet."

Chapter 16

My father soon walked in from the backyard. "Vinco, let's go," he said with a great sense of urgency.

I rose from my seat, keys in hand. Papa was already at the door. Kissing both Nana and Nanouche goodbye, we drove off, heading straight to northeast Little Haiti, less than a fifteen-minute drive. That part of Little Haiti was the center of Haitian culture and traditions. This was where homesick immigrants, starving for a piece of *lakay* (home), would find it. Voodoo jazz and konpa, a well-known popular music beloved by Haitians—the younger generation in particular—could fairly compete. Our first stop was Chez Titine, a woman from Saint Louis who ran a *fritay* business from home, which was customary to Haitian refugees struggling to survive. She lived just off 67th Street in a back-street cottage near Notre Dame d' Haiti Catholic Church, not far from where I once lived.

"Papa, why do you wanna go to Chez Titine? We just ate fried food. Remember, your doctor says low sugar, low salt, and no greasy food."

"Vinco, I know *fritay* is fried food, but you know I don't like *fritay* too much."

"Papa, do you know Titine?" I slowed the speed to almost zero.

"Of course. Back in the days, we lived in the same courtyard made for Haitian immigrants on the island of Abaco. She was one of the chicks."

"*Really?*" I was stunned.

He turned his face sideways and threw an uproarious laugh. I said nothing more.

It was six p.m. when we reached Chez Titine, which was in front of a duplex apartment painted in white without a driveway. As if in a rush, the sun sank down and darkness started creeping in. We got out of the car and strolled in silence down a tiny walkway that led to the backyard where Titine lived. Doors swung and porches screeched in the neighborhood stillness. We then reached the edge of a decaying palisade behind which we could hear soft-night murmurs of hungry customers waiting for their food. Through a small gate, we walked in and ran into a line of men and women standing in a single file like parishioners in a church procession.

"Where's Titine?" I asked in a low tone.

"She's under that tent," said a gray-haired fellow in a trench coat pointing out to the tent, which seemed like a wall-less hut built off the wreckage of a destroyed awning. "But you can't skip the line," the man added.

"Don't worry, sir. We're not ordering food," said my father without looking back.

We moved toward the tent where we met Titine sitting in a low chair in front of two big frying pots filled with deep-fried pork and sliced plantains. A crunchy, crackling sound echoed when she dropped pieces of meat into the pots. Rushing footsteps caught her attention. She turned around and jumped off the chair when she saw my father coming.

"*Tibince!*" She screamed, putting away the wooden spoon, coated in grease.

"*Titine!*" My father reciprocated. "*A pa nou!*" He added. *Here, we are!*

Oblivious to my presence, the two old friends fell into each other's arms, rejoicing. Titine looked chubby in a white calico dress stained by grease and dust. She wore a red headband tightened around her forehead to keep sweat from pouring down her oily face.

"Tibince, I thought I was never gonna see you," she said with an awed pride. "Who's this handsome boy?" She asked, moving away from the tent and grabbing our hands to move along.

"He's my son, Yrvin," replied my father.

"I'm sure lots of girls are after him," she joked. I plainly smiled.

"Where're the children, Titine?" Asked my father.

"There're no children anymore. Paul's now married and lives in Sanford near Orlando. Arthur lives in South Beach with a Puerto Rican woman. Jésula is inside. She has a month-old baby boy." Titine now freed our hands, and my father stepped back a bit.

"Is Jésula married?"

"No, and this is a long story. Another time, we can sit down to talk about it."

"How come?"

They both lowered their voices so customers could not hear them. Already, there was a growing impatience in the yard. People wanted their food, and Titine seemed to have forgotten that she was both the cook and server.

"Jésula got pregnant, and nobody knows who the father is. She's out of school because she's bad with all her teachers. Tibince, you go inside with your handsome young man, and I'll be there in a second. Let me deal with these hungry hawks."

"Titine, I have to *go*!" Yelled a stocky man from the back of the line.

"Me, *too*!" Growled a fat-bellied dude who was ready to leave and asked the other folks to do the same. So, we left Titine to go manage her starving folks.

The small house was a two-bedroom rental unpainted on the outside with steep front steps tied to the tent by a graveled pathway. So, we walked up the steps and opened the door, which was unlocked. The minute we stepped inside, we heard the voice of a young lady in distress and the voice of a woman scolding her.

"Stay put, Jésula, stay put, *goddamn* it!" She yelled at Jésula. "The only way to retighten your *chocolate* is to let that vapor sink into it."

"I'm trying, Aunt Fauvette!" Wailed the girl in severe pain.

My father and I were shocked. I let him stand by the door, and with muted lips I tiptoed, passing a room where a baby cried alone in his crib. Next door was where Fauvette held Jésula by the shoulders, pinning her down while she sat on an aluminum bucket. Like a gas chamber, vapor trickled out of the pail and filled the room with unbearable heat. The poor girl moaned like a woman in labor. Her dress got soaked in sweat and her legs widened as she sat over the bucket to let the heat penetrate her. When the procedure was over, Fauvette handed her a rag, hot and steamy, with which she cleaned her genitalia area.

Titine came in just as Fauvette walked out of the room. "How did she do?" Titine asked Fauvette.

"The same as yesterday. But you know we have to do this to ensure her *chocolate* is tight again. Otherwise, no man will ever take her seriously."

"I know. Anyway, what kind of a man would want a girl like her?" Titine said in disgust.

"Don't say that, Titine," said my father.

"The girl is lazy. Her report card from school is a heartbreaker. All she wants to do is to go after the boys."

Fauvette left. "Bye, everybody," she said in hurried steps.

My dad swept off his hat and bowed as Fauvette pushed the door open and disappeared into the darkness. Her face seemed familiar, and she reminded me of Susana, the mother of Esmeralda. I left my dad for a moment and went after Fauvette. In the still of the night, I nearly missed her, if it were not for the barking of two mad, stray dogs that leaped off a fence and ran after me, foaming at the mouth. Fauvette turned around and saw me coming. She stopped and ordered the dogs to vacate the deserted street. The vicious dogs vanished as fast as they were coming at me.

"Where're you going, young man?" She asked, startled.

"To you, Mrs. Fauvette," I replied, almost out of breath.

She was a tall woman with a plump body. Proud of herself, she stood near her front door, resting her hands at the curve of her hips. With her strange, gray eyes shining in the dark, she watched me coming. "How can I help you?"

"You may not remember me. I lived in this neighborhood three years ago."

She took an up-close look at me. "This is *Vinco*!" She cried, pulling me to her and holding me against her chest. "I was never going to recognize you. You're a big boy now!"

"I need your help. I remember you were a good friend of Esmeralda's mother, Susana."

"Yeah. We're still friends, despite all that happened between her and Fosia."

"She had a friend named Ramona, who was the sister of a man named Emilio."

"You mean Emilio Monsalve?"

"Yes."

"Whose daughter you got pregnant?"

"Yes." I softened my tone out of embarrassment.

"Ramona still has that stand in the flea market in Hialeah, next to mine. We see each other every Saturday. And Emilio comes by every now and then to buy fresh vegetables."

"Can you put me in contact with Ramona?"

She paused for a moment as if pondering. "Sorry, Vinco. I can't."

"How come, Mrs. Fauvette?"

"It's not prudent to wake the sleeping cat,' as our old Haitian proverb goes. Vinco, you don't wanna play with fire."

"Mrs. Fauvette—"

She stopped me. "I know the story. Emilio and his wife never got over their daughter's pregnancy, and they blamed it all on you. As Ramona told me, both Lucrecia and Emilio have no problem having their child marry a Haitian boy. They never thought, however, you were daring enough to get their daughter pregnant."

"Mrs. Fauvette, I haven't heard from Michaela in three years. I called and wrote letters, but she never replied."

"I'm not sure if she'll ever reply. She was under heavy pressure to stop communicating with you. Maybe that's why you no longer hear from her. Vinco, I wish Yolette was here to see you." She changed the conversation. Yolette was her sole daughter, who was a popular girl in the neighborhood when I lived there.

"Me, too, Mrs. Fauvette."

"So, what do you do now?"

"I work as an engineer, downtown."

"Wow! Can't wait to tell Ramona when I see her Saturday. You make me feel proud."

"I have to go, Mrs. Fauvette. My dad is waiting. He must be worried."

"Tibince?"

"You know my dad?" I was astonished.

"I used to live in Abaco, too. He was a sweet talker, and women were all over him, but he always told them that he was a married man. Don't worry, Titine will keep him for the night if he wants to." We both laughed, and I handed her my business card.

"We'll be in touch, Vinco."

My conversation with Fauvette had added more pain to my endless suffering. I wished I had not run after her, for every one of her words of frankness felt like a sharp knife, piercing my broken heart. From then on, I lost all interest in meeting Michaela's parents. In making it possible for neighbors like Paula and strangers like Fauvette to know about their legitimate anger, I believed they had mistreated their daughter. Both Paula and Fauvette warned me not to go. I had to heed their warning.

Then came the vexing question: How could Michaela master the strength to deprive me of my son? I refused to believe in such a possibility. One thing remained certain, however, Michaela still lived in France, and she had purposely decided to renege on her promise to return. I started to believe she had been assimilated into French society, and as a result, she no longer viewed her future as one with someone who lived across the Atlantic Ocean. These awful thoughts, racing through my torn mind, terrified me.

The odds had become overwhelming. I felt like a defeated superman weakened with kryptonite, trapped in his failed plan of action. Three years of indifference seemed an eternity in a struggle for romantic freedom and everlasting happiness. I should have trusted my gut instincts, which, many times during sleepless nights, urged me to give up living in such solitude and to work harder to mitigate my pain as the unique way forward. That option eluded me.

Leaving Fauvette, my legs quivered at each step to go join my father. If desperation took hold of my mind, I asked myself, would it give me the chance to fight and win against the bittersweet memories, the priceless moments, the loss of my son, which would inflict upon my heart the worst of grief?

Losing my son was not an option because this would leave me with an uncontrolled, frenzied bitterness for which I would never forgive Michaela, but also for which I felt obligated to search the world in the pursuit of my son and romantic salvation. I still loved her, although after three years of neglected romance it was hard to keep alive a dying love. In the game of passion, anger and resentment do not ebb; they multiply. Consequently, I now found myself morphed into a prisoner of his own feelings, unable to turn back the clock and start anew even in the face of growing evidence of rejection and even as everything my friends had predicted came true. Or did they? Michaela alone had the answer. Thus, making the path that leads to her even more urgent for me.

Chapter 17

When my father and I arrived at my apartment later that night, I could hardly find the strength to even undress. I needed to relax my restless mind, but finding some sleep, like many other nights before, proved to be an unreachable treasure. Papa, however, seemed delighted after his meeting with Titine. As soon as he took off his clothes and put on his pajamas, he grabbed the phone and called Titine. I stood in the middle of the bedroom, listening to him chatting with that woman whom I barely knew, telling each other stories of their younger years in Nassau, Bahamas. I wished he could lend me some of his contentment.

A dull, unwanted pessimism had crept beneath the veins of my broken heart that was now in rapid pulsation. It was not the attitude of Mica's parents that bothered me the most, but the manner in which she had turned her back on me. I felt as if I had been pushed off a cliff and left to plunge to my oblivion. Trapped down in darkness, the way forward looked bleak. I could not reconcile the unfettered love for which she once would rather die than lose and the repulsive way in which she abandoned me. I tried as hard as I could to keep a positive frame of mind, but the circumstantial reality offered me no such comfort. No matter what her parents might have said or felt, I said to myself, the decision to turn on the father of her child would rest with her and her alone.

Afraid of being consumed by rage and hopeless grief, I joined my dad on the couch in the living room just as he hung up the phone. "Titine must've been a *very* good friend, back in the day, Dad?" I teased him.

"Oh, yes, my son," he replied while looking at a picture of Michaela on the wall. "What a beautiful young woman!" He said with childlike glee.

"She was a friend from school. But Papa, aren't there many good women in the Bahamas?" I wanted to change the conversation.

"There're plenty good women there, whether they were Bahamians or Haitians. But like everywhere else, there're some good people and bad people, too."

"Why did you never bring Manman to go live with you there? Was it because of women like Titine?"

"Titine was always a good friend. That was all. I never felt it was necessary to bring your mom to a place where Haitians were so mistreated. You know your mother is a dignified woman. She would have never liked life in the Bahamas. Besides, all of you would have been left to be raised by relatives. Your mom and I never wanted such tragedy to happen to our children."

"Really?"

"Yes, my son." He rose from the couch and walked to the kitchen as if looking for something to eat.

"Papa, I have some rice pudding in the fridge. Do you want some?"

"No. I'm not hungry. I just need something to drink." He then grabbed a cup from one of the cabinets and poured in some water. He was back on the couch, his eyes once again fixated on the picture on the wall. "She's very pretty. This is the girl I want you to marry or some girl who is as pretty as she is."

His interest in the photo became like a sudden itch. "Papa, this girl you're looking at is the mother of my son."

"You have a *son?*"

"Sorry, Dad. I thought Nana told you."

"She told me a vague story of a Dominican girl…"

"That's her."

"I sensed it, son. I'm proud of you. When will you bring the girl to meet your father?"

"I don't know, Papa."

"How so?"

I fed him with the whole story. He was speechless. "How do you plan on seeing your son?"

"I'm trying to find some contact information that could lead me to where she now lives."

"You mean you will go to France if necessary?"

"Yes, Papa. I did some preliminary searching by speaking to people who know her parents. They all think Michaela still lives in Europe, and perhaps still in Strasbourg."

"Vinco, don't fool yourself. That girl is no longer interested in you. If she is still alive and well, and she hasn't called you in three years, why in the world do you still think she's yours?"

"And that's what all my friends and colleagues are telling me, Papa."

"It's not easy to rekindle a frozen love. Perhaps if you two were to meet again, this love might have a chance to survive. And when you meet her again, what would she say to convince you she still loves you? I think you need to focus on rebuilding your broken heart. Open your eyes, son. You know if that girl wanted to continue the relationship, she would do it. She knows how to reach you. Now, trying to find your son is a just cause, but this will also depend on her goodwill."

"What if she is being prevented from contacting me, Papa?"

"Who could prevent her from calling you? She is twenty-five. Isn't she?"

"Yes, Papa."

"Who can stop a grown woman from reaching out to the man she loves? I think you need to stop fantasizing about this past romance. I'm confident you'll be able to meet your son someday."

He rose from the couch and strolled to the bedroom, a disappointed father seeing his son destroyed by a deceptive love. I trailed him there. He sensed my embarrassment and turned to me.

"Vinco, you're not the first young man who has been the victim of insincerity. I'm speaking from experience. I've lived it, not just once. I can tell you the story of a girl named Philomena

I met at a festival in Chansole, a small town just south of Saint Louis."

"I know Chansole. I used to go there with Mom to that big flea market." I felt hope kindle in me.

"She was very pretty. But it wasn't just her beauty that seduced me. It was her good manner. She was polite, attentive to my joy, well-spoken."

"And what happened, *Papa*?"

"One day, I was standing on my parents' front porch when a boy came to me and handed me a note and left." He paused for a moment. His face hardened.

"And, Papa?"

"I read the note, and it was a message from her telling me we could no longer continue to maintain the relationship. Her mother found a man for her, and he wanted to marry her."

"Just like that?"

"Yeah. Just like that."

"Didn't you try to get in touch with her?"

"I did, but not because I wanted her back in my life. It was because I felt it was necessary to meet her, to be able to look her in the eyes to see if she was not going to blink. She never gave me that chance, and as time went on and my emotion disappeared, I realized I did the right thing."

"And you never met her again, Papa?"

"Yes. Years later inside a shoe store in Nassau."

"Did you have a talk?"

"When I saw her coming up to me, I turned my face away and walked out of the store. But I realized my heart was not ready to forgive her. Son, I can't say the mother of your son will never give you the chance to meet your son, but I'm almost certain her love for you is dead. I wish I could tell you something different because your sadness is my worry. Your career is one of the most important things to me, and I'm sure you'll find a beautiful girl like her to tie the knot, if you decide to do so one day. Now, let's get some sleep."

Within minutes, he was snoring. The next morning after breakfast, we got dressed and off to church we went. A fervent Catholic, Papa never missed his Sunday morning mass. So, we headed for Notre Dame d'Haiti where all services were in Creole. I had not been in my Little Haiti church since the old days. Taking my father to church was golden. As we neared 62nd Street, where the church was, we saw large waves of parishioners pouring out of the church and into the parking lot amid a thunder of foot-stomping, engine rumbling, church bell jingling, and joyous laughter.

"It looks like we're late," Papa said. His face hardened, revealing scary wrinkles on both cheeks.

"It seems like it," I replied with embarrassment, bracing for another round of complaining.

Despite his good-hearted manner, mishandling disappointment was one of Papa's major flaws. I drove with muted lips and greatest care, moving through the intersection on 62nd Street, and Notre Dame d'Haiti was on the right. With utmost care, I rolled into the parking lot and luckily found a spot near the main entrance. Papa had passion, uncontrolled elation each time he met fellow immigrants from his hometown of Saint Louis.

The minute we stepped out, something stunning occurred. Groups of parishioners surrounded the car, wanting to have a chat with Papa. Standing tall and proud, he greeted the crowd with pontifical authority, like a priest from his confessional giving penance and absolution to devoted, faithful worshipers after making sacramental confessions. This led me to believe my father was more interested in meeting old friends rather than making the act of contrition with which he prayed to God, asking Him to whiten his soul. Surprisingly, I knew some of the people, too. I had befriended many of their children during my high school days.

Papa's pleasure was equally mine, for amid the crowded lot, forgotten tales of my high school years resurfaced in a blur. Old classmates rushed my way as soon as they spotted me standing next to my father. One of them was Paul-Edouard, a jolly, handsome, kind-hearted boy, now a married man with two children, he told me. We chatted for a few minutes, exchanging phone numbers with a promise to keep in touch. Then a group of female classmates came toward me, all sisters who played a pivotal role in my English acquisition period.

Béatrice, a midnight beauty with starry eyes, whose dignified bearing I admired a lot. She was a shy girl, a good friend who always wanted to make sure we ate lunch together on one of the remote benches outside of the cafeteria. She told me she was now married to a young man of Dominican origin she met in college. My heart sank. The memory of Michaela's promises suddenly hit my heart, like a sledgehammer beating down on it in relentless fury. I fought hard to keep a calm demeanor.

Next to her stood Louloune, with a smooth ebony complexion. She was the prettiest of them all. Louloune was always late for a chemistry class that we shared, and she would sneak through a backdoor where I sat. I would always leave an empty seat near me just for her. She was an extroverted girl with a flaming visage that seemed ever ablaze. She had thick dark hair arranged in two pigtails secured at the end by multiple barrettes. She had become a refined young lady, but still single and, with eager heart, waiting for Monsieur Right.

Behind Louloune was Goldie, an Amazon, she was striking with an oval face and wondering eyes. She had golden hair floating in the late morning breeze. A young boy wrapped his little arms around her legs. Needless to say, she was his mother. And there were more whose names I could not remember. These girls were all born in the United States. Their Haitianism, however, could not be ignored. They loved dancing the konpa, cooking tasty Creole food, and speaking in perfect Creole as unblemished as mine. Papa and I chatted for a while and left elated as forgotten memories had found their way into our consciousness.

We then decided to take a more comprehensive tour of this Haitian corner of Miami, a cozy place inhabited almost entirely by fellow countrymen who had chosen to live there, not because they were barred from moving elsewhere, but because it was the closest they could get to their homeland, both in language and in traditions. For five years I had lived in this community for the same reasons many Haitian immigrants had opted to make this place their new home. For the three years since I left, Little Haiti had changed in many ways.

The first generation of Haitian children had reached adulthood, and they saw themselves primarily more as Americans than as Haitians. To them, Haiti was an ancestral land to which they felt they owed almost nothing, like a blurry, distant dream that had become an annoying itch. So, moving out of town was in no way a matter of choice but an educated decision in their persistent chase of the American dream. Their parents followed suit, and so did other refugees like me who had migrated north to where the grass looked greener, and the opportunities were plentiful. Sustaining a successful life in this immigrant community with all the complexities and intricacies of modern living required a higher degree of balance.

Consequently, local businesses had dwindled and the poverty level had risen. Many of those who remained did so out of necessity rather than an intense nostalgia for Haiti. Under the harsh rays of the rising sun that morning, this Miami neighborhood looked woefully humdrum. My dad and I rode in silence. We turned into 54th Street, Little Haiti's main boulevard. At the peak of its ascendance, no out-of-towners could skip this famous street of Miami. It was *Creoliciously* famous for its restaurants, delicious pastries, sidewalk cafés, doctors' offices, boutiques, nail salons, and record stores. The Haitian Refugee Center was also located there.

The glory days, however, were gone. A few bakeries survived as well as one lone record store and the refugee center that continued to operate. Even the afternoon crowd protesting for the restoration of democracy in Haiti had considerably diminished as I observed during my many stops on the way home from work. Survival instincts had forced the change of attitude. Many refugees had concluded that integrating into society at large had become far more important than the fight for socioeconomic justice in Haiti, particularly those, like me, who immigrated here at a young age and who now saw in Haiti a dim relic of childhood.

The rosy life in paradise they were promised back in Haiti had yet to materialize. There were too many barriers to overcome, barriers of class, language, and ethnicity; all this had led them to interpret their life in the new country as an unexplained, dark fatalism that perhaps only God in due time could save them from this continuance of marginalization and hopelessness. Miami was supposed to be the place where everyone dwelled in paradise as they were taught. Instead, what they faced here was a world that asked little of them, and their meager contribution to society was greeted with indifference. They felt trapped with their backs against an untold number of hindrances. Incapable of finding the way forward, they naturally sank into a self-defeating shiftlessness.

As these thoughts stirred in my mind, I remembered a Haitian family that lived a block away from the refugee center. They rented a one-bedroom apartment in a large housing complex, paint peeled off, in apparent neglect. I used to visit them a lot in part because I lived not far from them, on the other side of the Catholic church, and also because their story made the local news in September of 1980 when the United States Coast Guard rescued them at sea in the middle of the Windward Passage on their way to Florida just as their rickety boat was about to capsize. I took Michaela there several times before she went to France. Mica and I used to buy sweets and burgers for the children.

"Papa, I know you wanna go home, but can we make a quick stop to check on a family I haven't seen since I moved to North Miami Beach?"

"Sure, why not. This place looks a dying town, son."

"That's what catches my attention. They were from the island of La Tortue."

Subdued, Papa tried to conceal his emotions. He expected these scenes somewhere in the Bahamas, where Haitians were inhumanly treated. Papa and I were equally eager to see if the family still lived there. Back then, they were a family of five. Louison, a fifteen-year-old boy, energetic and ambitious with a quick and authoritative restless tongue. He was the oldest of the children, and Mica and I had an immeasurable admiration for his constant scolding, berating the other siblings for laziness, and urging them to do better. We saw in him a father-in-training.

Next came twelve-year-old Zanine, petite and vivacious, who loved to dance and dreamed of becoming a Hollywood star. Then was eight-year-old Claireline, homely but very motivated about her school obligations and always bragged about her academic progress. She was a jolly, well-mannered girl who looked after her little three-year-old brother Christophe, who was red-haired, bow-legged, and chubby. He cried for ice cream each time Mica and I showed up.

Manasé, their mother, was a dignified woman with a milky coffee complexion. She loved to smile and sighed as a way to suppress what appeared to be a hopeless life in solitude. Her face showed signs of invading wrinkles. Prolonged hardships had taken their toll. She spoke little English, and she worked washing dishes in a South Beach hotel. One could see the pain on her beaten, oval face as she tried to care for four fatherless children. Their father had drowned during the rescue operation.

Reaching the housing complex, we pulled into guest parking near a dumpster filled to overflowing. We stepped out of the car, hiked up the stairs, and went on to apartment twenty-three where they lived. I was not sure, however, if they were still living there. Manasé walked to the door as soon as she heard the knock.

"Who is it?" She asked.

"It's me, Vinco," I replied.

Papa stood behind me. The woman did not seem to know who was outside but opened the door anyway. We fell into each other's arms in jubilation as soon as she realized it was me. She widened the door to let us in and invited us to sit at a small dining table near the kitchen. I noticed she was home alone.

"Where are the kids?" I asked, puzzled.

"Two years ago, after high school, Louison moved to Florida City with a Puerto Rican girl. He calls every now and then. Sometimes, he stops by when he wants some Haitian food. Zanine quit school a year ago. She went away with a Jamaican boy. I didn't even know where they lived until three months ago when she came home with a nameless child. She works as a cashier in a supermarket in North Miami. Claireline is now in her first year of high school, doing well as always. All her teachers adore her. She's also at work now."

"Where does she work, Mana?" That was what I used to lovingly call her.

"At a Burger King on Biscayne Boulevard."

"Where's little Christophe?"

"He's no baby anymore." She laughed, and soon Christophe walked out of the bedroom. He looked tall, and now straight. The bowlegs had gone. He was in fifth grade and spoke English like an American boy.

"Vinco, where's Mademoiselle Mica?" He inquired, curious.

"She's home," I answered. "But how's school, Christophe?" I avoided the conversation.

"School's all right." He paused for a moment. "I missed her," he said, thirsty for an answer.

"I know what you miss. Your favorite vanilla ice cream, huh?"

"You know that. Do you guys have children?"

"Yeah, one boy."

"Wow!" Both Christophe and Manasé cried with one voice.

I fought hard to put forth my best face. My father understood my embarrassment. "That boy is driving me *nuts.*"

"I hear you, sir," Manasé injected.

"I commend you for raising four kids on your own," my father stated.

"It's not been easy. Life in this country is hard for poor folks like me."

"I know, madame. But do you work?" My father asked her, trying to get an idea about how difficult it was going to be for him as he embarked upon a new life in Miami.

"Yes, I do. I work at a meat packing plant in southwest Miami. It's tough work, but I have no other job. I think of home a lot. I think of my husband… of how he slipped out of my hand and drowned. I was hopeless, powerless when he went under. I keep thinking how different life might have been if he was here." Her eyes swelled and turned teary, and Papa intervened.

"Lady, you've already demonstrated how strong you are as a woman. I'm sure your husband is in heaven looking down and proud of you."

I wrapped my arms around her neck and held her tight. "Mana, we have to go, but I promise never to take this long to visit again. I'll do whatever I can to help."

She nodded in agreement and walked us to the door. Christophe followed behind. Just before I stepped out, I pulled out my wallet, yanked out a twenty-dollar bill, and gave it to him. "Here you go. Get some ice cream." We hugged as I patted him on the back.

"Bring Mademoiselle Mica when you come again!"

"Sure, I will."

We stepped down, walked to the car, and left. Behind us lay a heap of unsolvable problems, unmet challenges, unreachable opportunities. How should a man measure progress where weather-beaten faces like Manasé live? How many heartfelt griefs, echoes of pain should be required to raise awareness of the plight of those who live at the raw edge of poverty? Life is never a foregone fantasy, certainly not for those who dwell in poverty-stricken communities, and certainly not for people like me who seemed to have entered the ridgeline of success but were still pinned down by vicissitudes of fortune, of love and betrayal, of sorrows and deceptions. How hard it was to speak the truth to young Christophe? It was even harder when he insisted on seeing Michaela. In mutually inclusive silence, Papa and I drove home.

Chapter 18

Since my conversation with Fauvette on Saturday night, I had been trying to keep my mind preoccupied, away from any thought about Michaela. However, no matter how hard I tried, I could not get rid of the priceless, intimate moments, the expectations to share a married life, and the dreaded prospect of losing all hope. More and more I realized I must find the road that would lead me to wherever my girl and my son were. Three years of hoping and waiting had worn me down. Work had become the place of salvation, although my pile of projects grew daily.

It was Monday. My head bent down, I sat at my desk, but I was not thinking of the long week that lay ahead, nor did I feel overwhelmed with so much to do. In fact, I welcomed the challenge. The irony was that my reclusive pain had pushed me ever closer to Kakay. Since the day at my apartment, we had maintained a loose form of relationship. I was tempted many times to invite her for dinner. I knew it would have been difficult for both of us not to yield to the boiling lust, the heat of which grew hotter each day. Whenever she entered my office either for a document review or for some other office-related work, we made sure we left the door open, not because we did not want to create suspicions, but because we knew an open door could restrain us from crossing that feared line.

That Monday morning, my door was closed when she pulled it open, got in, and shut the door right behind her. The squeak caught me by surprise, and I startled a bit.

"Vinco," she said, softening her voice. "You won't believe it."

"What, Kakay?"

"Jason is leaving."

"Where is he going?"

"Amy told me during a meeting this morning, he submitted his resignation, saying he has an offer from a firm in Washington, and he's accepted it."

"Good for him. I'll miss him, though. I remember he told me last month that he and his wife would love to move to Alexandria to be closer to their daughter, who attends Georgetown University."

"Guess *what?*" She raised her muted voice and edged closer.

"What, Kaykay?"

"Mr. Goldberg has proposed to the board that Monsieur Yrvin Lacroix take over his position. The board has agreed."

"Really?" I was stupefied.

"What do you mean? Vinco, do you think I could fabricate a story like this?" She handed me a copy of the drafted letter that

Amy wrote per Jason's order. Amy had worked with Jason Fieldman and has been his secretary for over five years.

I walked out of my desk and grabbed both of her hands. "I'll agree under one condition," I uttered, peering into her bluish eyes, seeing a faint reflection of those of Michaela's.

"What is the condition, Mr. Lacroix?" She tittered. Her hands still rested in mine, and she made no effort to remove them.

"That you come with me."

"*Vinco*. You really wanna stir up gossip in here. So, what will become of Amy?"

"I'll make sure she's promoted to a supervisor position up on the nineteenth floor."

"She's talked to me about it, Vinco. But this makes no sense. You know I graduate soon, and I won't be here afterwards."

"We'll talk it over at lunch, Kaykay."

"No. I'm leaving before lunch time. There's something I have to do for my dad. Call me tonight."

"Okay, *mi amor*."

"*Stop* it. Bye."

I released her hands.

Later, when I went out for lunch in the cafeteria and walked by her office, she had already gone. On the way down in the elevator, I decided to stop on the third floor to meet my investment advisor Anny Schnell. The minute I walked out of the elevator, I had a pleasant surprise. A young couple with their daughter, maybe two years old, stood right before me. Dressed in a black suit, the gentleman held his daughter's hand, wearing a pair of fashionable Louis Vuitton glasses. His wife stood by his side, wearing a long-sleeve turn-down collar dress, flashy in all its form. In a quick reflex, I recognized it was Judy McCarter.

"Vinco!" She screamed to the bewilderment of both husband and daughter.

"Judy!" I cried.

"I can't believe my eyes. Mark, this is Yrvin, an old friend from Barry University," she said turning to her husband. She tried to control her emotions. "Vinco, how have you been doing?" She asked.

"Okay, I guess."

"Not just okay, Vinco. You look like a successful businessman."

We exchanged a few more words as well as business cards. We then went our separate ways. I went on to a reception area where Anny, dressed in an Ann Taylor Peplum jacket, was waiting.

"I didn't know you knew this couple. It looks like you can run for office," she giggled.

"Why?"

"You know everyone. Every time you walk into this office, you always meet someone you know."

"She was a good friend from long ago. Is this couple one of your millions of investors?" I teased her.

"Yes. They're loyal and smart investors." She walked me down to a hallway with multiple offices, and hers was the fourth one on the left. There, she invited me to sit on a couch adjacent to her desk where she sat.

"Listen, Anny. I'm worried about the current market conditions."

"The Dow has been in a downward spiral, for sure. But your stocks are holding up well. In fact, when the market is down, it's always a buying opportunity."

"You mean pumping money in stocks that are trending down?"

"Vinco, it wouldn't be a bad idea because now is the time to reinforce your positions and wait for the nice rebound."

"Are you *sure?*"

"I'm positive. Remember back in 1987 when the market crashed?"

"Yes."

"But it was recovered. Patience is the key here."

"Anny, don't you think it would be wiser to exit before any bad news like an unexpected downgrade, a bad earnings report, and wait for that rebound as you say?"

"Of course, yes. The truth is that no one knows when lightning will strike, except for those who have insider information, and they won't share it with you."

"Why?"

"Because it's illegal."

"Anny, I might have to travel to France."

"In the search for your Mica and your son?"

"Yes, but not immediately. More and more I realize I may never meet my son unless I take this necessary step."

"I agree with you. Your son can't be unreachable. And of course, you'll need closure in the estranged relationship. If Michaela found someone and settled with him…"

"I know. I would be devasted, but I would get back on my feet. With regard to my son, I can't foresee a scenario where she would deny me access to the very symbol of what was once a promising romance."

"So, I'm sure you need money for the trip."

"That's exactly right."

"Be specific."

"I can't, because I've never been to Europe."

"I'll make some adjustments in the portfolio because you have a couple bullish stocks, extremely volatile. When do you travel? In one month, two months?"

"Most likely in late November or the beginning of December."

"Okay, we have some months ahead of us. Let's wait, and I'll take all precautionary measures to make sure when the time comes, the fund will be there."

"Great, Anny. I must go. I'm starving."

"I wish I could go with you."

"No worries."

#

On the way home that afternoon, I met Jeff Goldstein, the old Jewish rabbi on the edge of the parking lot north of the back entrance of the shopping mall. He was without his headgear and not in his usual spot. Coutilien, the voodoo priest, was not there either. That Monday afternoon, I nearly missed him as he trundled up and down the entrance with long muffled strides, wearing a trench coat patched on all sides. His deep voice, trying to sell his last cuckoo clock of the day, caught my attention.

"Where's Coutilien?" I asked.

"You just missed him. He left about an hour ago. One of his daughters is getting married. He was busy all day, buying gifts for the bride."

"I see. Happy for him. Do you know the name of the girl getting married?"

"No, I don't. I think she's the third child, the one who was with him last week. Remember?"

"I know now. I gotta go. Tomorrow, Jeff."

"Wait, Vinco! Don't you wanna get the last cuckoo? I'll give it to you for half the price."

I pulled out of my wallet, handing him a ten-dollar bill, and the clock was mine. Balding and tall, Jeff was an unkempt old man who always wore steel-rimmed glasses perched on the tip of his pointy nose; but he also was a clearsighted, dignified fellow who combined the divine scriptures with human values to preach good manners to a society ravaged by polluted sinners. I sought his guidance whenever I felt down or out of strength to fight off my inner demons. Sometimes, after a grueling day at work, I would stop by, looking for his jokes while preaching his seventeenth-century, allegorical fables to feel a sigh of relief. I was about to leave when he called to me. He sensed that I was not my old self.

"Vinco, don't tell me you're still thinking about that girl. Are you?" He asked, looking worried.

"I'm not gonna lie to you. I can't sleep at night."

"Hold on a minute. Pull into the parking lot," he ordered in his usual mixture of fun and authority.

"*Yes*, sir." I wheeled over and pulled into an empty spot.

"Vinco, I want you to take a good look at yourself," he said, hands on the hips.

I glanced at my body and laughed.

"This is no laughing matter. You're a good-looking, successful young man. I want you to stop agonizing over something you have no control. Obviously, if that girl wanted to reach out to you, she could've. I know you worry about your son. But what can you do?"

"It's my son. My inability to reach out to him is killing me."

"Don't tell me this, Vinco. It's her, her love that you're so afraid of losing. But you must ask yourself if you can lose something you no longer have. Whatever the reason that keeps that girl from calling you, you should now move on with your life. Or, you may have to go the extra mile."

"What do you mean by extra mile, Jeff?"

"Travel to France, and if you can find her there, that might bring you closure. But I'm not optimistic about that girl still seeing her future in communion with you. Now, go. Be yourself."

I stepped out of my car, stretched out my arms, and asked for a hug. "Go, Vinco." We hugged each other in a tight embrace. Then, I left.

I came home thinking about Jeff's comforting words of wisdom. A man must be strong in the face of adversity. But there is no strength that can spare a man from the heavy weight of a vanquished love, as my father used to remind me. Dropping my keys, briefcase, and jacket all at once onto the dining table, I lumbered past the couch, kicking it with an uncontrolled rage while I almost stumbled on the way to my bedroom. Jeff's every word pounded my heart like a hammer smashing a bar of iron.

There, in my bedroom, I felt I had seen the end, the death of a dying love, the extinguishing light of hope, of painful memories, of afternoon strolls, of wild caresses, of lovemaking, and of all the promises for a rosy future in wedlock. All seemed to have washed away in the rushing gutter of a cruel life. From now on, I must start thinking of the way forward, but every time I came to the thought of moving past Michaela, Kayla was the person who showed up in my torn mind. So, I started to believe somehow deep in my subconsciousness, that her love resonated.

Since that day, I began to take a closer look at my relationship with Kayla. She had all the characteristics that any man would look for in a woman. She was impeccably stylish, articulate, smart, and assertive. She bore the same attributes that Michaela possessed, but she was not the mother of my son as I was not the father of her cute, innocent boy. Therefore, I hesitated to make the move of no return, of throwing myself onto her pristine love to find myself raising another man's unwanted child. My mind was on fire. Through my bedroom window, I took aim at the darkening sky, staring at the crimson glow above the yard that streamed toward darkness. Nightfall came too quickly, I thought.

Another fearsome night in solitude awaited me. From the window, I staggered to my feet, lurching toward my bed. "I have to fight back," I muttered to myself. In bitterness, I got out of the bed as my eyes roamed around, searching for any trace of a past that tied me with Michaela. Inside of me, an unmitigated rage grew, ushering an urge to keep out of sight the dearest, treasured memories I was desperately trying to hold onto, symbols of a dazzling past that now became reminders of a failed adventure.

Her smiling photo in the living room was the first to be taken off the wall. Then came her well-crafted letters penned with meticulous expressions, her favorite fancy perfume, and all other remaining vestiges of our long-ago romance. I assembled them and put them all in a large silver box. My eyes turned red and moist, watching in horror the final traces of memorabilia chronicling an unforgettable past romance. With watery eyes, I retired them into a corner of my bedroom closet.

Exhausted, I wanted to call my sister, but I decided not to. I knew how she would feel, sharing my pain. Instead, I opted for the gym, which was just a block away. When I arrived, the gym was packed with people, some weaving, some chatting in a cacophony of sounds of music mixed with the echo of foot falling from the aerobics class next door, the clanking of exercising equipment, weights being pulled and put down, all designed to share an atmosphere of camaraderie, a family ambiance where everyone worked toward one goal: great physical fitness. Here, loneliness, at least for the moment, vanished.

229

Chapter 19

After an enjoyable exercise session, I went home, feeling reenergized. For the first time in a week, I felt hungry rather than eating out of necessity. On my way to the kitchen to fix a sandwich, I noticed the voice recorder from my phone was flashing, indicating a new message. Thinking it was Kaykay, whom I was supposed to call, I hurried and listened. It was not Kaykay, instead it was Judy McCarter.

"Vinco, it's me, Judy. You couldn't believe how I felt when we met earlier today. It was a stroke of luck. I had been praying for a miracle, and it happened today. I wanna meet you so bad. Mark went off to Orlando, and he won't be back until tomorrow. Call me when you get this message."

I was astonished. I never believed Judy could somehow return to my life. I pondered a bit, thinking if I should even reply to her message. I went back to the kitchen and fixed my sandwich. Before I took the first bite, the phone rang, and I picked it up.

"Vinco, it's Chouchou. Did you get my message?" Chouchou was our secret name back in college, a name that means sweetheart in Creole.

"Yes, Chouchou. I just listened to it, and I was about to call you."

"Can we meet now?"

I hesitated. "Yes. Where are you now?"

"At the Sheraton on Biscayne, just north of Aventura Mall."

"Really? I'm ten minutes away. Give me fifteen minutes."

"Okay. I'll be in the lobby."

I put on my clothes and grabbed my keys off the table. In less than fifteen minutes, I was there. As soon as I pulled in the front, there she was, standing tall behind the huge glass door, eyeing the vast parking lot. I got out of the car and headed up to the main entrance. The minute she saw me, she waltzed out. In awe, I watched her impressive figure, fitted inside a plunging neckline dress with padded shoulders and leopard print. The flashy dress was topped by a stylish front buckle leather belt. She was moving in long swinging strides to meet me halfway. We fell into each other's arms in a mixture of cries and tears of joy. "Chouchou, Chouchou…"

Soon, I realized this was not the place for such a theatrical scene. "Chouchou, we need to get out of here before our craziness starts to attract attention."

"You're right, Vinco. Let's go somewhere."

"Where do we go, Chouchou?"

"How about my place, Vinco? You live alone?"

"It's been three years, now."

"Take me there."

We got into the car and took off. "Judy, where's your daughter?" I asked while we rode.

"She went with her dad. That girl is crazy about her father," she tittered, adjusting herself. "I can't believe I'm riding in a car with the *sole* man I've ever loved," she added and laughed. Her fancy perfume filled the car.

We reached an intersection, and the light turned red. "Chouchou, don't start it," I replied with a grin.

"It's true, Vinco."

"Me, too, Chouchou. Never in my wildest dream did I think you and I could someday meet again."

The light turned green, but an unexpected downpour started. So, I drove with caution. By the time we arrived at the apartment complex, the rain was heavier, pouring down in wet gray sheets.

"Let's wait here, Chouchou," I said.

"No. I wanna go in."

"In that rain? Chouchou, I don't want you to get wet and sick."

"It doesn't bother me. I'd be sick in your arms."

I knew then she was just the same. Her love had never withered. Fortunately, I always had my jacket hooked on the back of the driver's seat. I snatched it and wrapped her up. I unlocked the passenger door, and she flew like a tropical bird toward a roof-covered alleyway that led to the elevator. I was right behind her. Still, the run didn't stop us from being drenched. Heavy raindrops plastered her hair. At last, we went in. I rushed to the bathroom and retrieved a towel. She followed me there.

"Chouchou, I think you'll have to take off your dress so that it can dry."

"And what do I put on?"

"One of my pajamas."

She laughed, taking the towel from my hand with which she fluffed her hair while gazing at the man with whom she was once madly in love. Her body shivered inside the wet dress. I helped her take both dress and shoes off while she wrapped herself with the towel. I ran to the bedroom, taking off my wet clothes and putting on a blue robe. From the closet, I picked up another robe, walked out, and shielded her feline body with it.

"You remain the same gentleman who once upon a time set my heart and mind on fire," she let out as I enveloped her flawless tan shoulders in a hug.

I said nothing, trying to avoid the conversation while taking aim at her imposing, exuberant, and coquettish figure. But with Judy, nothing followed the natural order, and I could not believe such a dramatic turn of events, living in an unexpected wild moment with someone I had thought had dropped off my radar. She herself seemed dazed by this spectacular development. I then laid the dress on the cushion to dry and put her shoes down on the floor by the sofa. We sat on opposite sides of the table, facing each other while she still covered her body with the towel. I purposely dodged the sofa for fear of melting into her charming body, which was soaked in a fancy perfume.

"Chouchou, I have a tuna sandwich in the fridge."

"I haven't eaten a thing since our brief meeting earlier. Yes, I wanna eat some."

So, we rose from the table and headed for the kitchen. "Chouchou, you want a footlong or just a half?"

"You know I've never been a big eater. Remember back in the days at that little Jamaican diner on Second Avenue?"

"Of course, I do. The one right outside the school. We used to go there, having Jamaican patties and guanabana milkshakes. I cut the long sandwich in two halves.

"Oh, Vinco, times just fly, like rushing rivers in rainy seasons." Her sensual lips instantly froze on a giant bite. I dropped my half on the kitchen counter and edged closer, holding her by the shoulders. She dropped hers, too. Her eyes were swelled with tears.

"Chouchou, you were always on my mind, and the memories of those moments still ache. I was petrified when we had to say goodbye for the last time. It took me an eternity to accept the fact that I was never going to see you again. How could I forget our first meeting, our first embrace, our wild caresses, our pain, and my impossibility to adjust to a love that was too fancy for me to handle? I never thought I'd loved you this much until our last shared moment at your place when you nearly choked me with the shocking news of your decision to leave for Europe to go finishing school at the University of Oxford."

"Me too, Vinco. The decision was one of the toughest in my life. It took me a long time to learn to live with my hidden solitude." She wrapped her arms around my waist, sobbing.

"That afternoon, I trembled in fear and embarrassment, realizing how I had broken your heart, leaving you to wade across a river of tears, letting your voice soak into your choking words. Sorry, Chouchou, for not being able to compromise, to meet you halfway. Sorry for treating you in such an inconsiderate way. But I want you to know that your passion, your sincerity, your love will always have a special place in my heart."

We strolled toward the bedroom where we sat side by side on the edge of the bed. Her soft fragrant scent filled the room, ushering a taste of *joie de vivre*. But sadness seized our souls. Michaela came to mind, and I began to think perhaps I was wrong for not heeding Judy's cry for a long-lasting relationship. As Pedro reminded me few years earlier, Judy was a girl with a tenacious attitude who followed her heart to wherever it might lead her, and that path had led to me, a man who was unable to share the depth of her romantic conviction.

"Chouchou, how did you come to marry Mark when you told me it was a relationship of convenience?" I asked, peering into her eyes.

"What *choice* did I have?"

Her reply struck deep in my guilty heart. "I know you, girl. You could've done otherwise."

"With whom? With some freak at Oxford? There were many of them who had their eyes on me, but I paid no attention to their sneaky lies. If I couldn't settle with you, I'd rather be with someone I knew who has been very attentive to my wants and my pain." She now collapsed into my arms, melting.

"Vinco, tell me. What have you done the last five years?" She asked, pulling me down with her like playful children diving into a backyard swimming pool. We now lay in bed, facing each other. Our lips almost met.

"Chouchou, life hasn't been treating me too bad. Remember, when you left, I was in my third year. I graduated a year later. I went to graduate school and became a software engineer. I now work at a firm in the same building where we met this morning."

"After I left, my sister told me she always saw you around campus with a Spanish girl named Michaela. So, Vinco, whatever happened to that relationship?"

"Things didn't work out—unfortunately." I avoided the conversation. "And you, Chouchou?"

"After graduating from Oxford, I went back home."

"And?"

"Then, I worked for a while at my father's real estate firm as a regional director at a branch in Treasure Key on Abaco Island. Then, Mark asked me to marry him, and I agreed."

"How long have you been married?"

"Two and a half years, now."

"Do you still live on the island?"

"Yes, but we plan on purchasing a vacation home on Key Biscayne."

"Really?"

"Yes. Actually, Mark and I were on our way to signing the contract when I bumped into you. We'd just walked out of the Dean Witter office seeing a young woman named Anny. She's our financial advisor."

"Wonderful!"

"Vinco, don't do this to me. You know I'm never going to be happy without you. Mark and I were under pressure to get married because of our parents' selfish interests, but I'm not sure if he genuinely loves me."

"I remember you once told me this. But why did you guys decide to bow to your parents' selfishness?"

"For me, it wasn't a question of accommodating my parents in their ambitions. I married Mark because I couldn't get you. You've prevented me from showing you the depth of my devotion." She pulled away from me and rose from the bed, but we still held hands. "You've never changed, boyish as the first summer night when we made love," she chuckled, falling back into my arms this time, searching for my lips.

My heart leapt at the sudden move, but I fought back, refusing to fall prey to her charm, her curvaceous, revealing outline. But, could I really resist a beautiful woman whose love for me was unquestionable?

"Chouchou, it feels like we never left each other."

"I feel the same way, Vinco. But if it was difficult then for us to be together, now it's almost impossible, unless we're prepared to make terrible sacrifices, which I hope not to," she admitted, appearing fully aware of the precarious and embarrassing moment. Her face was now drawn as sadness crept in. I took an evasive posture, avoiding a reply. She understood. She then edged closer and laid her head on my chest. I pressed her feline frame hard against me, my fingers running through her dark wavy hair and onto her firm, naked breast, causing her to arch and moan softly. She reached out for my lips, and I met her halfway. Our bodies now interlocked as we kissed. My fingers tenderly skimmed her flawless skin, and I sensed we both yielded to the pressure of our shared emotions that forced us to a frisson in total pleasure and ecstasy. Then, in a brisk gesture, she bounced away.

"Chouchou," I uttered in a faint voice.

"Vinco, I can't do this. Please, help me. I feel I'm at the paroxysm of my desire. I haven't felt this way since the last time we made love. I'm at your mercy. My body is yours and yours for as long as I live. If you want to take me now, I will reciprocate in kind because I'm helpless in your presence. I love you more than I can ever describe. But it's *wrong* what we're about to do, and only *you* can stop it," she said with a breaking voice. Tears sprang from her eyes.

"*Chouchou—*"

She stopped me. Her face wrinkled, wracked with pain. "Vinco, I'm old enough to know that I can never duplicate my love for you with another man, no matter how handsome or well-off that man might be in the eyes of others. I can travel the world in the pursuit of happiness, but I know I'll never find it, because as far as I'm concerned, the road to my happiness leads to one man: Yrvin Lacroix. It feels as if my life begins and ends with you. Vinco, you've never loved me the way I loved you because from the start of our on-and-off love affair, you showed no interest in making the sacrifices necessary to give our love a chance. I respected that. But I've always trusted you because I knew you would never do anything to shatter my pride, my dignity as a woman."

"Chouchou, let me explain."

"There's nothing to explain, *mon amour*. You can have me now, and I will enjoy it as much as you will. My love is endless, and I'm sure of it. But if I do this now, I will *never* make love to

Mark again. I would have to file for divorce. Sleeping with two men is not part of my character. Are you prepared to assume responsibility for this?"

"Chouchou, I know how you feel, but the fact that we can meet again is indicative that it was meant for you and me to be—
"

"Be *what?* Well, if something was meant to be, then it *will*—in due time."

She folded herself inside the robe as she walked out of the room in despair, straight to the sofa in the living room where she collapsed face down. I followed her, holding her in my arms. We sobbed together. The guilt was too raw, for I knew she was right. Years ago, one evening when I met her inside the university gym, I underestimated her character. So did my Haitian female friends who called her a "sluttish," spoiled girl for her open display of love and affection when she was with me around campus. That was before I met Michaela. I honestly loved Judy then, but I despised her upper-class demeanor, her nonchalant attitude toward average folks, primarily when I raised the issues of refugee rights and the fight for social justice. Although I acknowledged her sincerest feelings, I was afraid the Bahamian bourgeoisie in which she was born and raised would have never accepted me, knowing how Haitian immigrants were treated in her country.

Now, as she lay on my bare chest, weeping, I realized how my shortsightedness had blurred my vision, making it impossible to love Judy for who she was, not for what she had been. How wrong I was to blame her for her indifference vis-à-vis the plight of others. Growing up, she was molded inside the lavish world of "between themselves" where status and abundant wealth took precedence. Tonight, her ability to resist a sexual adventure, despite the powerful urge boiling inside her and my lusty advances, proved the kind of strong and noble young woman she had always been. She turned around, facing me, smiling. Her sexy lips gently brushed mine, but our lips parted, and she straightened herself on the sofa.

"Vinco, you know?"

"What is it, Chouchou?"

"When you touch me, it gives me a strange feeling, a sensation I can never describe. It's overwhelming. This is how I feel now, as if the flame of love is carrying me to a dangerous fire. I feel I love you like a puppy does—loyal, lively, and naïve. Because of this feeling, because of you, Vinco, I am now able to acknowledge my own fragility."

"I'm sorry, Judy, for all the pain I've caused."

We remained interlaced and fell asleep. We did not wake up until two o'clock in the morning. Realizing it was late, we both rushed to get dressed. Then I drove her back to the hotel. Before she got out of the car, she asked me something that I thought was very dear to me.

"Promise me, Vinco, that you'll always be there when I call you. I leave tomorrow, but Mark and I will be back next month for the closing."

"I will, Chouchou."

Chapter 20

The conference room was packed with smiling colleagues and other coworkers chatting in low tones, waiting for the meeting to begin. I sat on the front end of a long mahogany table fit for the room where the top leadership of the firm was seated, including application architect Jason Fieldman, who was leaving for a new post in another firm in Washington DC, and Jeff Goldberg, a lanky fellow, who was the chairman of the board. Kayla stood against the wall next to Amy on the other side, facing me. Her eyes brimmed with pride.

Goldberg rose from his seat and trod up to a small podium where a microphone stood.

"Can I have everyone's attention?" He smoothed his wrinkled red tie while straightening the blue jacket that had long become his trademark. The room soon went silent.

"Today is one of those days that you wish would never end," he paused for a moment, glancing at the packed room as all eyes gazed upon him. "It is with mixed feelings that I am announcing the departure of one of our best and brightest here at the Bedell's Tech Firm, architect Jason Fieldman. He leaves us after receiving a job offer from Gasby's International in DC. In the four years since he's been with us, the board has had nothing but praise for Jason. His positive attitude, notably during some of our difficult moments, will certainly be missed. However, we understand a man's desire to stretch his wings, flying to new horizons like adventurers at the prime of their lives and the zenith of their professional careers do," Goldberg concluded. There was a mixed reaction after everyone listened to Goldberg's brief remarks. Some employees were saddened, others were happy for Jason. A small group of them that stood in the back room had a passive attitude.

Jason trudged up to the podium to join Goldberg. Golberg then stepped back to let Jason address the staff. With wolfish eyes, as usual, his unkempt blond hair gave the telltale impressions of a tech-savvy computer whiz, lost in the upscale world of corporate America.

"I must say it is with a bittersweet feeling that I stand before you this morning to thank you for all the support and encouragement that I have enjoyed over the years. Software engineering can be challenging sometimes, but in the presence of such an impeccable team, as we are, nothing is impossible. We've demonstrated it time and time again. But there are moments when family obligations must take priority. The decision to move to Washington DC has agonized me for months, but I felt I must bow to my wife's desire to be with our son attending Georgetown University in DC…"

He paused to catch his breath. His eyes squinted, zeroing in on me as everyone looked on. "I know my departure may disappoint many of you if not all of you, but I must say some good news has also come out of my leaving for DC. This morning, the board unanimously decided to promote Monsieur Yrvin Lacroix to my current position. As of now, our Vinco is your new project manager. We all admire Mr. Lacroix's data-driven, client-focused professionalism on top of his unmatched competence as a software engineer. I'm leaving Mr. Lacroix with our skilled application architects, Mike Colombo and Tony Baez."

Just before he concluded his remarks, Jason drifted his gaze about the room, and when his eyes caught mine, he called to me. "Vinco, *come* up here," he commanded. "Come say a few words."

I asked John to come with me, for after all, he was the one who hired me. He refused, saying, "Vinco, I'm proud of you. Go!"

Jason stepped back to where Jeff stood, making way for me to address the staff. Kaykay and I made eye contact as I crossed the room in a couple of long strides to join the gentlemen at the podium. She appeared very excited, not just because of the promotion, but also because of my appearance that morning. Dressed in a blue suit over a button-down striped shirt, I seemed fit for the gracious moment. I wore a gold wristband Seiko watch, a gift from her, to sweeten her heart, making sure she saw it as I reached out to grab the microphone. Unconcealed emotion, however, forced tears to stream down her face, but everyone knew it was because she was my secretary and, perhaps, they thought my promotion would have interrupted our professional relationship.

"I don't know what to say. This announcement leaves me speechless. Words can't explain my gratitude for the trust the board has placed in me to lead the project management team. Jason Fieldman can never be replaced, as you all know. But I will do my best to continue his work, so detailed, so impressive, because of which Bedell's Tech Firm has earned the respect of our clients. It's going to be a tough challenge, I can tell you this; but I always welcome challenges, especially when I know that I'll be working with great minds and daring, tech-savvy leaders like Mike and Tony. Once again, thank you for recognizing me."

Words stuck in my throat, but the staff understood the moment. Showers of applause swept the room. Shortly thereafter, a sumptuous breakfast was served in my honor as incoming PM, as well as in honor of Jason, for acknowledging his contributions to the success of the company.

When breakfast was over, everyone returned to their respective offices to formally begin their day at work. I walked back to my workplace, still trying to control my emotions, and wondering if I was one of the luckiest among young immigrants of my generation, some of whom held college degrees like me but were struggling to get a foothold in the competitive world of corporate America.

Back at my desk, I surveyed my office space one last time, which for three years had been my little cozy place away from home. From my office window, I took a last look at the bay area, empty and silent. Over the crystal blue water sparkling in the morning sunshine, a few boats moored on the edge of the embankment. Slowly, I began to pack up my files, my university diploma, my mother's photo, boxing them up and readying to move to my new office. While emptying my desk drawer, I found a *thank you* card signed by Kayla, which read:

Monsieur Lacroix, it's been a pleasure to be your secretary, and I've enjoyed every moment of it. Words can't explain how much I'll miss working with you. But I know you'll just be a few doors away, and I can still count on you for your thought-provoking advice. Equally, I promise to be at your disposal for anything you might need as you transition to your new post. I'm proud of you. Thank you for allowing me to get to know your immeasurable kindness and professionalism. Really, I'll miss your jokes, our jokes. The past three years have brought nothing but a joyful experience. They'll forever be memorable.

Besitos, Kaykay.

Shocked, I stopped packing and ran to her office. She turned her face away when she saw me rushing toward her. "Kaykay, I read your card. Can we talk?"

"I'll be there," she replied. A suspicious smile stretched across her lips.

A couple of minutes later, she walked in and found me leaning against the edge of the desk, holding the card. She looked reticent as she shut the door behind her. "Vinco, I know what you're gonna tell me," she said, avoiding eye contact.

"You can't do this to me, Kaykay."

"I think this could be best for both of us."

"How?"

"I think so."

"An opinion is in no way factual. This is your judgment."

"Vinco, the last thing you want is for us to be prejudged out of suspicion."

"Kaykay—"

She stopped me. "If you really love me, Vinco, you certainly wouldn't want me to be your secretary. It would shatter my dignity, demean your status in here, and perhaps destroy your bright career. So, whatever might come out of our friendship will have to come outside of this building."

"I understand, but you know I'm at my best when we work together. It's work blended with personal experiences."

"That was then, Vinco. You can't imagine how happy I am to see you—a young black man now leading an important department in our company. It makes the African blood running in my veins so special."

Her statement warmed my heart. I stepped over and hunched for a kiss. "Vinco, let me go. *Mi amor, por favor.* I'm cold. I'm hot. Please." She offered no resistance, but her submissive demeanor disarmed and watered down the fire raging in my heart.

"Go, Kaykay. We'll talk later."

"You made me wait last night, and I waited. The call you promised me never came."

"Sorry. An old friend came to see me. Listen, if I have to work with Amy, I wanna make sure that you work with someone who—"

"Whoever I work with, I'll be fine. You know me, and it won't be for long anyway. Bye."

"Bye, Kaykay."

#

Later at my apartment after a quick supper, I lay on the sofa, thinking of Kaykay. It was around seven pm. So, I picked up the phone and called her. On the first ring, her sensual voice was there. "I anticipated your call. *Espera me un poquito.*" *Wait for me, a little bit.* A brief pause followed, then I heard the swinging of a shutting door. "Sorry, Vinco. I was on the back porch with my folks. I'm in my room, now."

"Where's Miguelito?"

"He's with his grandma, spoiling him." She laughed.

"Don't blame it on grandma. There're other spoilers, too," I teased her.

"Vinco, I've been giving serious thought to our relationship. And I'm sure by now you understand my reticence."

"I do, Kaykay. You have every right to feel this way. Besides, as you've reminded me time and time again, we've got to where we are, now, because of your offer to help me find Michaela, an offer that has taken a major turn and run into an icy, slippery road. I think about the same thing you're thinking. I'm sure you can sense my uneasiness each time I'm with you. But there's something inside of me that's deeper and more powerful, beyond reason. I know I've lost Michaela but losing you is my biggest dread."

"How do you know you've lost her?"

"It's obvious. She's unreachable, and the silence of my relationship with her is still hard to digest, but I take comfort that I wasn't the one who caused it. Kaykay, would you please try to understand my predicament? Waiting for unresponsive love feels like driving slowly down an endless road. Kaykay, you may not love me enough to hold my hand and help me cross this foggy trail of solitude unharmed, but I'm convinced you understand the painful sinkhole in which I now dwell. I must find a way out. I wanna fight back, like you did in the wake of your last betrayal. I can't promise you paradise, for I myself don't know how to get there, but I can say with certitude that I will always be there for you, attentive to your desire, sharing your pain, your worries, and your joy. Please, Kaykay. I *love* you." I let my voice drop on the word "love" to stress my desperation.

There was a pause on the other end of the line. "Kaykay, are you there?" I asked.

"Of course, I'm here, attentively listening, pondering."

"If you're tired of my rambling, we can talk at work tomorrow."

"Vinco, my love. I'm scared. I've made some bad choices in the past. Please, forgive me if you find me unresponsive to your words of assurances. Vinco, I can't describe how much I love you, but I don't wanna play the risky game anymore. You set my heart on fire the very first day you walked into the corporate building, and I did my best to conceal this odd feeling I could not describe, and it was for good reason. When you spoke about Michaela with such pride, it gave me goosebumps. I wished I were her. I wished I had a man like you, a man whose love is indisputable. Now, here we are deep in the trench of love, sinking deeper each passing day."

"Kaykay, there isn't much I can say that will convince you that I'm not on a rescue mission. But there're things I can do to prove I'm not just another player sneaking his way into your honest heart. I know even sentimental expressions at their purest forms have never been enough to solidify true love. Trust me, and time will tell."

"Vinco, the prospect of people at work finding out about our secret love affair terrifies me."

"And how will they know?"

"Our demeanor will ultimately betray us, no matter how hard we'll try to hide it. Love is like the fluorescent light in a room that *cannot* be contained unless it is extinguished."

I knew then I had won the fight. Or did I? We went on to talk about this milestone we had just crossed and our plan to celebrate soon. In the end, we said goodnight with a thousand kisses thrown from each end.

After we hung up, I was deep in thought, thinking about Kayla, a dignified young woman who seemed to have sincerely learned from her past mistakes and was now determined never to repeat them. Our conversation earlier in the day was the best clue of how she started thinking of our developing relationship. Although her impressive bearing was a constant reminder of Michaela, Kayla was not Mica in many ways. Her strong character had me convinced of the sharp differences, a girl who would not easily bow to any dictate from her parents, most noticeably one that would require sacrificing the love of her life. My persistence had dissolved her resistance. She had concluded that staving off stirring feelings could do one thing: prolonging the inevitable. Her feelings had become irresistible. Furthermore, she may have thought her chance at succeeding in securing a long-lasting relationship was for all practical purposes quite realistic, knowing the impractical nature of a man in search of a lost romance.

Love can best be sustained through affection, not hope, and certainly not through a hopeless dream. These thoughts may have been raging in her tormented mind. So, surrendering to my plea bore the strongest of pain for her. I could tell. That had terrified me because I knew I would never be at peace with myself without knowing what had happened to Michaela and Yrvin Junior. I had to intensify the quest for the truth.

I lay in bed with two pillows stuffed under my head, thinking about my current dilemma. Then, the phone rang, and I could see Pedro's number flashing. "Man, I've been waiting for your call," I said, pulling the long extension cord toward my bed.

"You gave me homework to do, remember?"

"Any news?"

"Yes, sir! I was able to locate a phone number for you as well as an address."

I bounced off the bed, throwing off the pillow along the way. "You're kidding."

"Why would I? Remember Angelica?"

"No."

"The girl who worked at the library. We used to tease her because she couldn't speak Spanish."

"Yeah, now I remember. She was from Belize."

"You got it. Chen and I met her at a Toyota dealership in Kendal, South Miami. She was sitting in the waiting room, and the moment she saw us, she jumped out of her seat and ran to us. She said she was waiting for her fiancé. That was when she told us she was marrying Hector. I wasn't sure if she was referring to Gabriela's Hector until he turned around and called to her."

"*What?*"

"Hector and Gabby are history. While we were talking, Hector walked out, looking neat and sharp as always in a business suit. I pulled him over, leaving Chen and Angelica together."

"Then?"

"I asked him directly for Mica's whereabouts. He said he did not know. But he knew she was still in Strasbourg. I told him you haven't heard from Mica in more than a year, and you're deeply hurt."

"What did he say?"

"That was when he said he wasn't surprised because Gabriela was the mastermind behind sending Michaela to France."

"Really?"

"That's not all. Hector said Gabby went on to fabricate an ugly story, using your photo supposedly with other women. She was jealous of your relationship with her sister. He wrote this number and this address. He said he would like to talk to you. Can I give him your number?"

"Yes, yes…"

"But how did he and Gabby go their separate ways? Didn't you ask?"

"Of course. He said he found out she had cheated on him with a fat-bellied guy who owned a shoe store in the Dadeland Mall. At first, she denied it, but when he brought pictures of the two going in and out of hotel rooms, she had to admit it."

"Michaela once told me that girl changes boyfriends every six months."

"Vinco, listen. Chen is calling me for something. We're inviting you this Sunday for dinner."

"You bet. I'll be there."

Chapter 21

Pedro's revelation struck a chord, like a pinched nerve tingling my increasingly restless body. I sauntered to the kitchen, snatched a bottle of *kremas* from the fridge, and poured it into one of my crystal wine glasses. I swallowed it down with a couple of gulps while pacing up and down like a prisoner in his jail cell. The difference was that I was a prisoner of my own feelings, contemplating the way ahead. I had hoped the news could have been different—weirdly so. This was one of those moments I feared the most. I would rather tolerate the uncertainty and give my heart a little space to beat at a normal pulsation, at least for the time being, as my ascendant romance with Kayla began to take shape. I retreated to the sofa, pondering my next steps.

"What an irony!" I cried in disgust, lying face up, arms and legs splayed.

After months of living in unrelenting bleakness, in fading desire for other times and in unadulterated dreams, the harvest suddenly provided an abundance. But how could I reconcile the promises I had just made to Kayla with my moral and sentimental attachment to Michaela and my son? My eyes turned misty in self-absorbed nostalgia and indelible sentimentalism stemmed from an unreachable, irretrievable romance. That was not me, although the fear of becoming the victim of a dubious cause or falling prey to irrational thoughts horrified me.

There on the sofa, I dove into my deepest reflection to try to make perfect sense of what Hector had said about Gabriela. Even if what Pedro told me was true, and that Gabriela, awash with vindictive passions, succeeded in convincing her parents to send her sister off to Strasbourg and then went on to spearhead a coup against me, fabricating my photos with other women to hoodwink Michaela, it should not have removed Mica from her intellectual and romantic duties to vet her sister's stories. I was almost convinced she also bore part of, if not all, the blame for not having reached out or confronted me with these baseless allegations. Michaela was a submissive girl, for sure, but not a gullible young lady. These stirrings mused me. Still, Pedro's news had put me ever closer to uncovering the mystery surrounding Michaela's actions. If Mica and I met again someday, could I ever forgive her?

Conquering Kayla's heart felt like the perfect gift when loneliness seemed inescapable. I no longer felt like a man besieged by waves crashing upon his inner self. But Kaykay was not by my side. So, my state of gloom persisted. I knew, however, that I, not someone else, held the key to my salvation. The more I pondered my ordeal, the more I needed to be somewhere with ordinary people, where life seemed normal, where jolly faces camouflaged the evils eating away the thirst for happiness that all men and women, hungry for a life in perfect contentment, craved.

My mind soon took aim at *Café Des Trois Colombes*, a small café and bar restaurant near upscale Aventura on Biscayne Boulevard. Without a second thought, I grabbed my car keys and headed there. While driving, I realized how ridiculous I had become. On Monday night, it sounded strange for any rational individual to choose a bar as the place of redemption, a sanctuary against invading stressors. But when one lives alone and is paralyzed by languishing loneliness, days and nights no longer carry their strategic significance as they morph into a monotonous, timeless journey. These thoughts raced in my head as I drove.

Located in the northernmost corner of Miami-Dade County, Aventura was an extraordinary community where some of the richest people in the land lived. Movie actors, football players, Wall Street stockbrokers, and shady billionaires had all made Aventura their enchanted oasis, their perfect place in paradise. Though a very small city, Aventura possessed the country's third largest shopping mall, Aventura Mall, full of exclusive shops where glamor and wealth intertwined to create a dazzling replica of life in wonderland.

Café Des Trois Colombes was nestled on the southern edge of the mall, just below the main entrance. It was a one-storied building bedecked by a remarkable landscape garden designed not just to impress but also to showcase its fancy cuisine of multiple dinner courses made from delicacies unknown to average folks. The mall's sprawling parking lot stretched out to a verdant ficus edge that enclosed the restaurant's inviting location and made it easily accessible and certainly worry-free for the rich and famous who lived in the opulent world of the *one-percent*, offering them a unique venue to maintain their lavish lifestyle. A few feet from the front porch stood two gumbo limbo trees trimmed in artistic designs, providing the ideal cover for loners in search of wild romance. At any given time, three turtledoves could be seen perching on one of the top branches. Thus, came the French name *Café Des Trois Colombes*, which translated in English is *The Three Doves Café*. French Canadians, who were not well-versed in English, had built and named the place.

It was just after nine p.m. when I pulled into the parking lot, where a few cars were parked in the front near the gumbo limbo's extended branches. I stepped out of my car, passing a middle-aged couple sitting at one of the outdoor tables, chatting tête-à-tête like newlyweds enjoying the balmy night. An attentive young man dressed in a black-and-white uniform and guarding the main entrance greeted me with a faint smile, widening the double doors to let me in.

I moved toward the welcome stand, and without delay, a young hostess asked for my name, wrote it down on a clipboard, and then instructed me to follow her. She led me to a cozy table in the corner facing the bar filled with hideously expensive beverages where a steel band played a rendition of Harry Belafonte's "Yellow Bird." Before long, my eyes caught a serene atmosphere in which gentlemen and women clothed in casual elegant outfits engaged in intellectual and captivating conversations over vintage wine.

I took my seat, and she asked me to wait for one of the waitresses to come and serve. I was not interested in food, but the lovely ambiance and the high-toned English spoken there entranced me. Meanwhile the band continued to play "Yellow Bird," and I noticed two ladies in cocktail dresses and high heels sipping wine at the next table, menu in hands, selecting their entrées, singing the same song but in Creole, and humming over the words they did not remember. Diamond rings and necklaces sparkled in the dim lighting as they hummed. Their flawless Creole mixed with the uptown Port-au-Prince domestic French led me to believe they were womenfolk from back home, as my fellow Haitians liked to say. I've known that song since I was six years old. Manman used to sing it in the home, usually when she was preparing the afternoon meal in her outdoor kitchen while the neighborhood children and I listened and sang along.

Ti zwazo nan bwa ki tape koute	Little bird in the wood listening
Ti zwazo nan bwa ki tape koute	Little bird in the wood listening
Le mwen tande sa mwen genyin lapen	
Le mwen tande sa mwen genyin lapen	When I heard all this, grief overcomes me
Kan depi jou sa depie mwen nan shen	When I heard all this, grief overcomes me
	Since that day, I have been in shackles.

"It's amazing to see how they can take a Haitian's masterpiece and use it for their own purposes without giving credit to the Haitians who created it," I said to myself.

The women at the next table overheard me. "*Alors, vous êtes haitien?*" they both asked in a pure Port-au-Prince French accent. *You're Haitian, then?*

"Yes, I am," I replied in English, and there was a purpose for that.

In Haiti, French is often used to create an invisible caste. Not being able to communicate in French demeans an individual's social status. Obviously, when I arrived, they were chatting in faultless Creole. They switched to French for a reason.

"No speak English," said one of them with an embarrassed smile.

She was tall, light-skinned, and dark-haired. The other, a slender dark-skinned woman with a lustrous visage and who smiled with a peculiar capriciousness. She looked younger.

"Young man, you're right," she affirmed "The title of this song is 'Choucoune,' a poem written in 1883 by Oswald Durand, one of our nineteenth century's best poets. In 1909, a Haitian composer immortalized the poem through this melody," she added as the other woman was humming through the music still being performed at the bar.

I then changed seats so that I could be closer to their table and introduce myself. "My name is Yrvin."

"I'm Laurene," she said. "And this is my sister Josette." She pointed to the light-skinned woman.

"Are you ladies residents of Aventura?" I asked with a blend of sarcasm and childish glee.

"I am," again replied Laurene, who seemed quite extroverted.

"And you, Josette?" My direct question forced her to react.

"I'm visiting from Port-au-Prince," she replied between tight lips, trying to suppress her displeasure. My interrogative statement did not sit well with her.

"And you?" she asked, fixing her wide black eyes on me.

"No," I replied. "Not far from here. I live in the Grenoble."

"You do?" Laurene injected. "A good friend of mine lives there. Do you know Dr. Michel Léandre?"

"No."

The waitress arrived, and I ordered a piña colada without alcohol. Both laughed at once. "What was so funny, ladies?"

"We've never seen a fine young man like you ordering a virgin colada."

"Really?"

"I wish my daughter were like you," Josette joked.

"My sister is the family's satirist," Laurene said.

"Don't listen to her, Yrvin," Josette let out but still in her introverted manner. "Why don't you come and sit with us?" she demanded in a very polite manner, and I obliged without replying.

The front doors were pushed open, and a young woman stepped in wearing a collared shirt atop well-fitted jeans. Her eyes surveyed the room in an investigative fashion as she moved forward. "*Mom*!" She cried when her eyes caught those of Josette's, and she hurried to join our table. That was when I realized it was Élodie, a collegemate from back in the day. We jumped into each other's arms to the bewildered gaze of the women.

"You two know each other?" Josette said, baffled as Laurene watched in astonishment.

"Mom, he's Vinco. My best friend from Barry University."

"And you never told me about him."

"He was too busy in life, as I was. Understandably, we drifted apart."

The piña colada came, and the waitress asked if I was still undecided on the main course. "I'll let you know when I make my choice," I replied. She left, and the table became very animated.

"Mom," Élodie tweeted, "you won't believe how much fun we had back in college."

"I can see that," Laurene intervened while adjusting herself to display her gracious demeanor.

"Tell me, Vinco. What have you done the last five years?"

"After Barry, I went to graduate school for two years, and I've been working as a software engineer at a firm downtown ever since."

"So proud of you, Vinco. Just last week Arianne and I were talking about you."

"Intelligent young man!" Josette uttered.

"Indeed," Laurene agreed.

"And you, Élodie?"

"After graduation, I went back home. Worked for a while. I got married, but it didn't last. Now, I plan on going back for my Master's. I live here with my Aunt Laurene."

"How's Arianne doing? Did she marry the redneck boy?"

"No." She laughed. "Things didn't work out. How about your beautiful Dominican girl?"

"It didn't work out for me, either." I turned and faced Josette. "So, how is Port-au-Prince?" I asked her. I wanted to change the conversation, for it was a golden opportunity to know how the privileged few in Haiti felt about the *coup d'état* against Aristide.

"Well, the country is fine, doing better than what Aristide was trying to do," she said, and in a clumsy move to suppress the embarrassing lie, she turned her face sideways. Her eyes were now glued onto the musicians while trying to adjust the tight outfit that drew the lines of her swelling belly.

"Oh, Mom. How could you say things are better? There's an embargo on food supplies, on money transfers, and on many other things. Even in our family, some folks are struggling. A lot of people, who depend on their relatives abroad to send them money, are now dying from hunger. People in Port-au-Prince looked like skeletons, like walking zombies," Élodie said, contradicting her mother's statement.

"And I heard people are disappearing day and night. Those who openly opposed General Cédras are in hiding, including popular folksinger Manno Charlemagne. Doctor Henriques called me yesterday, and we were talking about it," Laurene said in a firm and patriotic tone, seconding Élodie's rebuttal.

"I didn't know that." I lied. I knew all about the systematic repression that followed shortly after Aristide was overthrown. In popular neighborhoods across urban Haiti, resistance leaders were being hunted down and killed or disappeared as was confirmed by several human rights organizations.

"Vinco, you remember Lucson, the short boy with a scarred face?"

"Yeah."

"He said Manno's younger brother, Fat, told him Manno fled in the middle of the night to an embassy."

"Is he still there?"

"He said yes, but he wouldn't tell me which one."

"Mom, things are dire in our country, and you know it."

I let them talk because their conflicting accounts reflected the self-inflicted guilt eating away the hearts of a tiny portion of the Haitian elite and the self-indulging cruelty of the Haitian bourgeoisie, unpatriotic, wealthy people. Shortsighted, these folks remained frozen and immune to any change that could place their country on the path to industrial development. Each passing day, Haiti sank deeper into oblivion while most nations in the Americas fought tirelessly to emerge from a painful past encrusted in historical injustices stemming from foreign domination and neocolonialism.

"I know you two, ladies. You blame the military for everything," Josette growled in a melodramatic fashion, throwing a suppressed smile blighted by bitterness and veiled nonchalance.

"I know one thing," I said with a profound patriotic conviction. "Haiti will not perish. One day, democracy and the rule of law will come to the land of Dessalines."

"I guess you're right, young man," Laurene conceded.

The music resumed, and the two women rose from their seats and moved to the dancefloor, leaving Élodie and me at the table. We felt thrilled for being left alone, a golden opportunity to relive our dazzling college years. I sensed she was dying to know what had happened to Michaela and me, but I went on the offensive to preempt her. "Whatever happened to you and Evens?" I asked.

"Vinco, it's a long story." She changed her seat and moved closer to me.

"Tell me," I urged her.

"Evens was a player if you remember. I found out he was cheating on me with Ana Sosa, that Brazilian girl. I confronted him with evidence that he couldn't deny. So, I left him."

"So, what happened to him after that?"

"He went to live with Ana in an apartment in Kendal."

"What? Did they ever graduate?"

"Not sure. I was wrecked and nearly failed the semester. The next year, I transferred to the University of Puerto Rico, where I graduated. The news of our breakup made a splash around campus, and I'm surprised you didn't know. I guess you were too busy flirting with your Dominican girl. So, tell me. Did you two tie the knot?"

"Unfortunately, not. We had some major disagreements."

"I can't believe it. If you and Michaela could drift apart, I'm now convinced love is indeed a deceptive endeavor. I remember the last time I saw you two was at that party at the YWCA, dancing your night away, dragging on the dancefloor, cheek to cheek." She threw a disgusted glare at the roving lights as if reviewing her own romantic failure through the lenses of my revelations, realizing when you are young and free, pleasant surprises proved hard to come by.

"You said you were married. So that, too, had failed?"

"Yes. I met this young man in San Juan. We both were seniors. We started dating and I got pregnant. He then proposed to me, and I agreed. He lived in San Juan then. But he was a lazy punk who couldn't keep a job. So, I left him and moved back home."

"I'm sorry to hear this." The music subsided and the women were back at the table.

"I thought you two were going to have a dance to celebrate. Look how happy you guys look," Laurene teased us. But we stood up at the teasing to get up and walked to the dancefloor as the band played a hot calypso.

"Vinco, where is Michaela?"

"She lives in Strasbourg, France."

"Strasbourg? What the *hell* is she doing there?"

"She has relatives there."

"My cousin lives in Strasbourg, and I was there a year ago. She works at the European Parliament."

I soon realized she could help, and now felt compelled to tell her about my ordeal. She was stunned. "I had that gut feeling something bad was going to happen."

"How so?" We talked as we danced.

"Every Haitian I know who has dated a girl from the Dominican Republic had some pretty bad experiences."

"Élodie, she didn't cheat on me. She simply was too weak to fight for her man. My main struggle is to be able to meet my son and be a part of his life."

"Then, you'll have to fly to France."

"I plan on doing so before the end of the year."

"Do that, and if you need my cousin's help, let me know, and I'll put you in contact with her."

"I'll let you know."

The night went on as an unexpected, enjoyable surprise. All four of us seemed to have succeeded in suppressing concealed longings, at least for the time being, to live a pleasurable moment, the closest we could get to being in a tropical paradise. In the end, we exchanged phone numbers with a commitment to staying in touch.

Chapter 22

"Gentlemen, being a project manager could have been a serious challenge. However, I know I have nothing to fear because I'm working with impeccable professionals like you," I said as Mike Colombo and Tony Baez listened with utmost attention All three of us sat at a conference table in a room that was two doors down from my new office.

"Yrvin, you didn't have to say this. You know we work like brothers do," Mike said, showing a wide smile.

"Of course, we're a team," Tony burst out, seconding Mike. "But we'll follow your lead. I respect the corporate hierarchy."

"Tony, while this is my first meeting, speaking in this capacity, it is by no means the first time we meet as colleagues. I don't intend to deviate from the same workmanship that has made us so successful. Yes, we're a team, indivisible…" We all laughed in acknowledgment of our new reality.

"By the way, did Jason leave the blueprints for the work in Palm Beach?" Tony asked.

"Yes, he did," I said, grabbing my folder and showing him a disk that contained a copy of the computer file. "But the Palm Beach work is not the most pressing, right now," I added.

"I think the deadline is November fifteenth," Mike inferred.

"Yes, but we're going to try to get it done before that day. I'm taking December off for a vacation," I said looking at the clock, trying to wrap up the meeting.

"A well-deserved one," Tony responded with a laugh.

"I couldn't agree more," Mike reinforced. "This is the first time I hear you talk about going on vacation. Where will you be going?"

"I'll be in Europe, in France in particular. I know November is still some months away, but we have a much more pressing assignment before the conference at the Intercontinental Hotel. It's an information system that needs to be updated for this company based in Alberta, Canada. The conference is next week, and their CEO will attend."

"So, we need to get right into it, then," Tony and Mike said.

"Also, he and his delegation are invited for lunch here. I'm going to ask Amy to make preparations. I won't be here for that lunch, though. I'll be in a meeting with John and two clients from central Asia. So, you guys can handle it, right?"

"Of course," both gentlemen boasted.

"Now, I have to get back to my office. Amy is waiting."

At once, we all rose from our seats and made our way to our separate offices. Seconds later, I stepped into my new office, a grand room decorated in the fashion of a presidential suite.

Reception and café areas lay dormant against the backdrop of a half-dozen windows draped in red velour fabric. A few inches away from my desk was a built-in bookcase filled with books related to the job. Two mahogany armchairs framed my desk, designed to make an impressive statement as soon as a person walked into the room.

This new décor, however, had a lesser impression on me. I guessed after five years of working in this upscale environment, grandiosity no longer fascinated me. I met Amy sitting in the reception area, but she rose from her seat as soon as she saw me coming to meet me halfway.

"Sorry to keep you waiting," I said.

"No. Like you, I just walked in." She grinned. "Yrvin, I know the drill. Meetings here and there, it feels like living in a surreal world where everyone is always on the go. It was very difficult for me to get a hold of Jason," she added, smiling.

"But I will never make it difficult for you to get a hold of me. We're more than just coworkers. We're teammates. You'll hold my schedule, and you'll have the power to pull the strings and retrieve me when you think it's necessary, Amy." I teased her.

"You have such a great sense of humor," she said, smiling.

Amy was a fashionable young black woman, the one black female in this corporate building. She bore a dignified posture that was difficult to ignore. She was articulate, with admirable punctuality. She had a cordial and professional relationship with Kayla through whom she learned about my story with Michaela. We walked over to the café area where we sat at a table, going over the work of the day. Then, we joked a little.

"Vinco, you make me feel so proud," she said.

I smiled. "Did you see Kakay?" I asked her just before she exited the room to go to her own office located a few doors down, not far from Kakay's.

"She's down in her office," Amy said chortling, turning around to face me. "I know you miss her already."

"Not really. We'll continue to maintain the same camaraderie. Certainly, my responsibilities have changed, but it's the same *me*. In fact, we'll have lunch later at her office. Can you tell her?"

After Amy left, I called Kaykay. "Already, you look presidential," she said, joking.

"How do you know that, Kaykay?"

"I saw you earlier rushing to the conference room. Are you coming down for lunch?"

"Absolutely! The three of us like before. I already told Amy to tell you. Do you want me to order food?"

"No, I will. Now, go, Mr. Big Shot. You have work to do."

"Is this an order?" I mocked her.

We both laughed at once before saying goodbye with the same mellow stress on the word *goodbye* like lovers do, and we hung up. I then returned to my desk, thinking of what Kaykay told me the night before. "Love is like a florescent light."

I was late for lunch when I walked into Kaykay's office. I found the two ladies waiting. The food was still hot and served in Chinese bowls. Kaykay looked incredibly striking wearing a dark jacket over black jeans.

"We were about to start," Kaykay said, giggling.

"You ladies should have. I was on an overseas call, and it looks like my job has really changed."

"I know, and I already told Kaykay there will be times we might have to eat without you," Amy said, supporting my statement.

"I'm hungry like a wolf," I said, grabbing my bowl.

"I miss the chat already," Amy admitted, laughing.

"Me, too," I said, chewing on the food.

"Worst of all, you'll have to get through me now to get to Monsieur Lacroix," Amy tittered. Kaykay said nothing, but she seemed amused.

Throughout lunch, I fought hard to keep a professional demeanor. I could see Kaykay struggling to do the same. Later at my office, I called her. "You have a minute?"

"Let me call you instead," she replied.

Ten minutes later, she called. "I'm leaving. My son's school just called me."

"Is Miguelito okay?"

"I'm not sure. A lady at the school told me he was complaining about a headache. I'll be at your place later. Bye." After we hung up, Yrvin Junior right away came to mind. I could see how caring she was as a parent. My son was unreachable, and it hurt.

After work, I drove straight home, avoiding the Haitian Refugee Center where I had wanted to stop. They were holding an important meeting to discuss the negotiations between deposed Haitian president Jean-Bertrand Aristide and the man who had orchestrated the coup against him, General Raoul Cédras. It pained me to miss the meeting but missing the meeting with Kaykay at my apartment would be a major blunder. As soon as I arrived home, the phone rang.

"Where were you, naughty boy?" Nana's voice growled.

"You know I was at work. I got out late. I was going to call you. Save the food for me tomorrow."

"You should have called me. I had to go all the way to Broward to get fresh grouper for you."

"Thank you, my dear sister," I said, laughing. "Please, forgive me. I have something I wanna share with you tomorrow when I get there. *Bisou*, Nana."

"You'd better get your tail here, and on time." We both laughed before hanging up.

By now, it was five p.m. I had roughly an hour to get prepared. I called a nearby florist shop and ordered a bouquet of twenty-four premium long-stem red roses. I then hurried and cleared the table of messy stuff: keys, notes from work, etc. But I left the bowl of fresh fruits, a bottle of red wine, and two crystal glasses displayed in the neatest fashion over a red velour tablecloth, a gift from my sister that I rarely used. Fifteen minutes later, the flowers were still not delivered, and I grew impatient, knowing I had a mere forty-five minutes to get everything set. I called the florist, and a lady with a high-pitched voice picked up the phone.

"I have yet to see the deliveryman," I said, growing nervous.

"He's running late. He had a prior delivery. He should be there within the hour."

"Do you mean in fifteen, or thirty, or forty-five minutes?" I asked her, becoming neurotic.

"I don't know, sir. The traffic is just another factor."

"Forget about it. I'm going to get the bouquet myself."

"But the driver has already left."

"Lady, you make me another one fast. I'm on my way."

"Wait—but—"

I did not reply. I hung up the phone and ran to my car. In ten minutes, I was there. "I need the bouquet," I said in an intense voice almost out of breath, and a lady in a white skirt rose from her seat behind the counter, startling.

"Was it you who just hung up on me?"

"Yes, lady. I need to get the flowers, or I'm doomed."

She looked at me, puzzling. "Are you on a rescue mission or are you trying to seal a last-minute love deal?" she asked.

"Please, hurry."

"What about the first bouquet? Do I call the driver and ask him to return?"

"Do what you think is best for your business, lady. I need to go."

"That girl stole your heart, young man," she teased me.

"What else can make someone so crazy? My girlfriend is coming to see me," I said with a grin, which soon exploded into a burst of laughter.

"At your apartment?"

"Yes, are you almost done with the flowers?" I became restless, looking at the clock.

"Did you get her see-through lingerie?" She teased me again, peering into my eyes while putting the final touches on a magnificent bouquet of red roses stuffed in a hearty love box.

"No. Do I have to, lady?"

"Of course, you do. After the first round, you'll need something to quicken the pace of the second one." She smiled.

"And the lingerie will do?"

"Young man, Victoria's Secret is two doors down," she said, chortling while handing me the flowers. "It's one hundred and fifty dollars, sir."

I pulled out my wallet and retrieved two hundred. I handed the money to her. "You can keep the change." I was gone.

In the car, going back home, I thought about the lingerie, but it was fifteen minutes to six. "Too late," I muttered. I got home at five minutes to six, just in time to lay the roses on the table next to the bottle of red wine and the bowl of fruits. I hurried and lit my patchouli incense stick and turned the music down low on Chopin's "Piano Concerto No 1." I took off my clothes and rushed to the bathroom for a quick shower. I wanted to look refreshed when she showed up. By now, it was five past six. I entered the closet, scanned the clothes to see what I would wear for the moment. I finally settled on a pair of pajama pants and a white undershirt, exposing my trim waist and firm upper body like a matchless chulo at the prime of his game.

Ten minutes past six, she had yet to show up. I grew feverish. From the window of my apartment, my eyes watched like a hawk the coming and going of every car down in the parking lot. Suddenly, I saw her car, a black Toyota Corolla convertible, roll in and pull into one of the empty parking spaces. Kaykay stepped out, wearing a loose button-down dress and low-heeled shoes, weaving with grace in the evening breeze like a lovely princess. Within seconds, she was at the door. As she raised her hand to ring the bell, I was already in front of her, and her arm, instead, landed on my shoulder. I held her by the waist and eased her inside. She glanced around the room and her eyes caught the adroitness with which the table was decorated.

"Baby," she said feebly. "All this is for me?" She added in a dovish fashion, arms wrapping around my neck.

"No. It's for the two of us," I said, still holding her thin waist, a bit firmer this time. She melted on me with her eyes closed, searching for my lips. Her small firm breasts, rubbing my chest, aroused me.

"Baby, can we sit on the sofa?" I said with a softening voice.

"Uh-huh."

I soon realized that the wine and roses were merely the icing that adorned the quintessential sweetness of a cake, but nothing sweeter than the passion that lies beneath the thrill of lovemaking. I had not felt this way in years. We now lay face up, side by side on the sofa, and I began to unbutton her dress while she moaned in a tenderness that grew in intensity at each move as my fingers crept downward. We soon retreated to the bedroom, interlacing, and kissing. She let her dress, now totally unbuttoned, fall to the floor.

"Do you have condoms?" She asked out of breath. She was blunt.

"No, baby," I replied with a tinge of embarrassment.

"We can't have sex unprotected." She let go of my hand, ran to the sofa where she had dropped her purse, and retrieved a small box of condoms. Under the weight of our heated passion, we went under the bedsheet.

#

The flame of passion had subsided after a prolonged moment of intimacy. We now sat at the table following a well-deserved shower. I folded her voluptuous body inside one of my favorite robes. I was in my pajama pants and my undershirt.

"We look like newlyweds on a honeymoon," she said, laughing.

"I couldn't ask God for another gift—the gift of sharing my life with you in wedlock, Kaykay."

"God has already decided on a path for our lives, our future. I think now it's up to us to stay the course," she said, taking aim at the roses and the wine on the table.

"Kaykay, tell me what's missing?"

"The food. So, where is it, Vinco?"

"I wasn't sure of what you would want. So, I was waiting for you…"

"Can I order Italian?"

"No. But I can make lasagna."

"That will take forever. I don't want you to get home late, *mi querida.*"

"I'll make spaghetti, then. Still Italian, right?" She said with a twinkle in her eyes.

"Will you want me to help?"

"Sure." She lurched for a kiss, which I promptly delivered.

We then walked to the kitchen, together, pulling all ingredients out of the cabinets. "How do Haitians make spaghetti?" She teased, trying to find a way to tell me that I didn't know how to make spaghetti.

"The same way as Colombians, Kaykay."

She laughed. "Not really, Vinco."

"How so?"

"Because I remember you told me you like yours with smoked fish."

"You remember that?"

She paused for a moment, hand resting on the cutting board over which the vegetables lay. "When the man I love speaks, details are as important as the substance." She giggled.

Her statement warmed my heart, and I reached for a kiss. "Yeah, but it's not the best time for smoked fish. It would fill this apartment with an aroma I'm sure you wouldn't be able to tolerate." So, we settled for a veggie spaghetti: olive oil, zucchini, yellow squash, garlic cloves, spinach, fresh basil, onion, and tomato sauce.

We chopped together over the cutting board, co-preparing the meal. A few minutes later, we were back at the table, having dinner over wine as Frederic Chopin's "Piano Concerto No. 1" played in the background.

"Kaykay, I have a good friend of mine I'd like for you to meet. His name is Pedro, one of my best college buddies."

"I would be delighted to meet him. He's a Latino, I presume."

"Yes, but he's married to a Chinese girl, his college sweetheart. They both invited me for dinner next Saturday evening."

"I would love to go with you."

"He lives in North Dade. Would you want me to pick you up?"

"I'm too far down in the Gables. Why don't I meet you here at five? Then, we'll go together. Besides, our love story is still a secret."

"You're right. Sometime next month I'll take you to meet my dad and my sister."

"Where's your mom?"

"Still in Haiti, along with my three other siblings."

"I want to tell my parents about our relationship, but I also want to wait until after graduation when I will no longer work at *the Bedell*."

"That makes sense."

We were done eating and back on the sofa. She leaned on my chest. "Baby, I feel so secure in your arms."

"And I feel so blessed to have you in my life, Kaykay."

"In two months, we'll be free to tell the world about our romance. And I can't wait."

"Me, too. By then, you'll be ready to move to DC, and that's my biggest dread."

"How so, Vinco?" She was startled.

"Because of what happened to me before."

"You can fly to DC, and I can fly down to spend weekends with you."

"Your parents won't approve of it."

She rose from the sofa, eyes widened like an alert tigress ready to go on the offensive. "Vinco, I want you to take a good look at me. I could have rented my own place if I wanted to. That also means we could live together should we decide to do so."

"Kaykay, I know you and I are old enough to choose the right path."

"Vinco," she said, falling back into the sofa. "I promise never to renege on my decision to be with you until…"

"And I'm committed to being by your side—always. But I have to be honest with you. I don't think I'll be able to sustain another long-distance relationship."

"We can still find another way that could be less painful for both of us."

"Also, I'll have to step up the search for my son."

"And I agree."

"I need a rested mind. I know I'll have to face Michaela someday."

"To rekindle?"

"Rekindle what? I never left her. She did. I feel obligated to be part of my son's life. Every time you talk about Miguelito, I see my son, too. A boy I have yet to hold in my arms. But that won't happen until I find Michaela."

"Any luck so far in the search?"

"No. But Pedro told me last week he's found an address for me. If it's true, I'll be in France in November or December."

She said nothing but looked pondering. "Kaykay, I know this is a delicate subject, but I feel I have to let you know of this process so you won't feel surprised if and when I tell you I'll have to go to France on such a mission."

"Let's hope the address takes you to your son."

"I know he may never live with me, but I want to be part of his life. He'll know he has a father to whom he can turn."

"And not just in time of need. You'll make sure you and his mother share responsibility. I wish Miguelito's dad was a father like you."

I realized this conversation was out of place. But I wanted to remind her of my ordeal, despite our flourishing love. I wanted her to still be supportive of my search. She became pensive, briskly. "Baby, this is our moment. Let's enjoy it to the fullest," I said in a timid voice.

We went back to the bed and lay next to each other. "Will you take me to Haiti someday?"

"Of course. If you marry me, we'll spend our honeymoon there. We'll probably buy a vacation home on the hilltop overlooking the coastal town of Saint Louis, my hometown."

"And we'll make love all day long, Vinco."

"You got that right." In an intense moment of passion, we wrapped each other's bodies and went under for another round of lovemaking.

Chapter 23

The next day after work, I drove straight to Nana's home. When I pulled into the driveway, I met Papa sitting on the porch, listening to a local Haitian radio station. In those days, like most Haitians in Miami, my father was passionate about what was going on in his homeland, but more so about the negotiations going on in Governors Island, New York. At the heart of the talks was the return of Jean-Bertand Aristide to the presidency in Haiti. Most Haitians were skeptical, and they had good reasons for that. The brutal nature of the military regime in Haiti was the main factor. That skepticism was soon reinforced as news broke out of New York that General Cédras walked out of the meeting, refusing to agree to the restoration of democracy in Haiti. In Miami and elsewhere in the Haitian diaspora, people were outraged. My dad's anger boiled over. As soon as he saw me coming, he rose from his seat.

"I was about to call *you*," he growled, slapping the radio as if it was the one responsible for the bad news.

"What's wrong, Papa?" I asked, a bit worried.

"Didn't you hear the news?"

"Yes, I did. But Papa, you need to keep your calm. Cédras will never leave of his own volition. He will leave when he's forced to do so," I insisted, getting closer to him as we shook hands.

"This is unacceptable," he said in a much calmer tone. "Can we go to 54th Street? The community leaders have just called for a massive protest."

"Okay, Papa. Give me a few minutes. Where's Nana?"

"She's in the back."

I went in, passing through the living room and making my way outside into the backyard where I met her in her compact garden, tending to her flowers. "Hey, naughty boy," she cried, laughing, putting away her garden tool and gloves.

"I won't be able to stay long as promised. Papa is impatient, waiting for me to take him to 54th Street."

"For the protest?"

"Yes."

"Papa is losing his mind. He's glued to the community radio twenty-four/seven. Even when he's asleep, the radio must be on."

"If he's so anxious, I'm afraid, Nana, this might raise his blood pressure."

"I took it this morning. It was quite high."

"Nana, didn't you reason with him, encouraging him to calm down?"

"I did. My husband also talked to him. But he won't listen. And I can't keep the radio from him. So, at the church, we pray for the madman Cédras to leave the country. Then, I think, Dad will be okay."

From the front door, Papa's impatience grew even higher. "Vinco, hurry *up*. There's a live report from 54th Street. Don't you hear? The demonstrators were already there."

"I'll be right there, Papa." I edged closer to my sister while lowering my voice. "Nana, I wanted to tell you I'm seeing a girl. Her name is Kayla. Like Mica, she's Hispanic."

Nana seemed surprised. "Where did you meet this girl?"

"At work."

"At work?" Her eyes widened. "How do you know she's a good person?"

"I've known her for over three years."

We walked back inside and strolled to the kitchen. On the porch outside, Papa's impatience had reached the boiling point. "I'm afraid of these Hispanic girls after what Michaela did to you."

"Sister, I understand your concern. But Kayla is not Michaela in many ways. I'll bring her to meet you and Papa."

"And when do you plan on doing this?"

"I'll let you know." I moved away from the kitchen, keys in hand and ready to go. It was painful to tell her about Kaykay. She was still hoping for the day I would call her to let her know that Michaela had been found.

"Vinco, why can't you date a Haitian girl?" She followed me to the dining room where I stood.

I turned around. "Does it matter, Nana? Does it? Love has more to do with personality. It has nothing to do with ethnic or racial background. I don't think you're ready to forget what Lucien, your old boyfriend, did to you. And yet, he was Haitian. Dating or marrying someone who's not Haitian doesn't remove my Haitianism, my patriotism. It's a trait I have that Michaela as well as Kayla admires."

Though still skeptical, the wrinkles on her face now lessened. "Make sure you tell me a few days in advance before bringing her here. You know I'm busy at church."

"I will, dear sister." I hunched for a hug, and we embraced. She refused to let go of me. "Vinco, what about your son? Will you give up looking for him?"

"Not at all. In fact, I'm making preparations to go to France before the end of the year."

"You can't find your son without finding Michaela. And I'm almost positive if you guys ever meet again, that love will spring in a blink of an eye."

"I've always known finding Michaela is something I must do. It's my dream, but finding her has more to do with being in my son's life. I have to tell you, Nana. I pray for her to be safe, but I no longer believe in Santa Claus."

"What do you mean?"

"I mean whatever we had, if it was true love, has long been extinguished."

"What if she never marries or never had anyone in her life?"

"It could be, but this also would never excuse the way she treated me. And what *kind* of question is this? It's been *three years*, not three days. My phone number never changes. I wrote to her, called her, and she never replied. Nana, do you really want me to wait for something that no longer exists? Do you want me to forever remain your miserable little brother? There's nothing Michaela can say or do to justify what she did to me."

"How could I want you to feel miserable? Vinco, you know big sister loves you. At your age, I dream of the day that I can see you create your own family and live happily; and I understand why you feel so hurt. But you continue to feel hurt because that love is not dead, and it would take a single spike to trigger it again."

I said nothing. Her words of wisdom resonated with me. She was speaking the truth. She then let go of me, and I was ready to step out to the front porch. She held me back again.

"Vinco, I don't want you to think that I approve of Michaela's behavior. It surprised me. But I still don't think she had decided one day to walk away from you at a critical time when the two of you needed each other more than ever. So, before you embark upon another serious relationship, think of this reality. I wouldn't want you to hurt this new girl in your life."

"Nana, Mica may still love me, whatever that means, but I think she can no longer be the woman with whom I should share my life. Anyway, Nana, don't worry. I'm a grown man now. Papa's waiting for me. Before he goes bananas…"

"Okay. Be careful out there, naughty boy." She exploded into bursts of laughter.

"I'll bring Papa back before nightfall."

Within minutes, Papa and I reached the Haitian Refugee Center. Nothing seemed out of the ordinary. The traffic on North Miami Avenue as well as on 54th Street was lighter than usual. No cops were on site regulating traffic as was usually the case on occasions like this. There were no folk musicians singing revolutionary songs, but a small group of die-hard compatriots congregated in front of the HRC, discussing the way forward. We parked by the roadside and joined them. Papa was disappointed.

"Whatever happened to the demonstrators?" He snarled. His face hardened.

"Papa, this is Tuesday. Folks must work. They have bills to pay. Despite our problem as a people, we can't forget about our obligations." Papa said nothing, but he became pensive.

All of a sudden, a tall, hairy-faced gentleman in a trench coat walked out of the refugee center and sauntered up to us. He looked mean. "Comrade," he said, "do not get discouraged by the latest events in New York. We knew from the start, Cédras and his flunkies were never serious in the talks to allow Aristide to return to finish his presidential mandate. You want Aristide to go back to Haiti, you'll have to chop off the snake's head."

"Speak clearly, comrade. I was born here, I don't understand this Creole," said a skinny boy wearing a straw hat. He stood next to me and Papa.

"The solution is a second revolution," the tall man replied, dismissing the skinny boy.

"How can we do it from here?" The skinny boy asked again.

"We'll do it in Haiti, of course."

"Stop giving people false hope, comrade. How're you gonna get to Haiti? In your car?"

"We're gonna get there in due time because we *are* revolutionaries." The giant guy looked annoyed and began to display an arrogant posture. His brows contracted while lurching from one side to the other like a witch man processed by a voodoo god. He started looking down at the skinny fellow, scolding his every word.

The skinny man did not seem intimidated. "Who do you think you're fooling? Maybe yourself. Revolutionaries don't throw empty rhetoric. They act, and their bold actions sway undecided or scared people to follow," he said, shaking. His patriotic emotions were unambiguous.

Papa and the rest of the group agreed with the skinny man, who was feeling empowered to hold his ground. The man who was light-skinned, almost like a mixed-race fellow, turned red like a ripe tomato.

"You need to have deep conviction, brothers and sisters," he uttered in a clumsy move to gather support for his revolutionary preaching. But no one believed him.

A middle-aged woman then rose from the back of the group, poised to take on the light-skinned gentleman. "I've lived in this community years before Baby Doc fled Haiti, and every time I come here, it's always the same speech. For a while, I believed you. When Baby Doc left, everyone wanted to go to Haiti, to try to make the most out of this political space. I expected you and your so-called revolutionary bunch to go down there to take the fight to the remaining thieves. You didn't, like many other cowards before you. Now, you're preaching about going back to

Haiti to lead a revolution when the criminals are back in power? *Shame* on you." Her body shivered.

"You got that right, young woman!" Everyone applauded.

The giant guy felt cornered. "I'll spit on your face if you don't step away," he lashed out at both the skinny man and the young woman.

"Yeah, *dan pouri se sou bannan mi li gen fòs*," said a red-eyed woman in a calico dress. She was furious. *Rotten teeth always gain strength over ripe bananas.*

"Yes, you're right!" The rest of the group cried.

Feeling besieged, the man tried to ignore the insults and began to pass out leaflets with revolutionary slogans. A very short, gray-haired man grabbed one of the leaflets and gave it a quick glance.

"You see, this leaflet, you gave it to me more than eleven years ago. It's the same words, the same commas, the same sentences. More than a decade later, with all the madness going on in Haiti, you don't even have the decency to revise the wording. And now, you're talking revolution. What planet are you from?"

The truth seemed to have crept under the man's skin. His eyes turned scarlet red, like the devil in his worst moment of anger. "Get the *hell* away from me before I break your neck," he let out with shivered lips and started mumbling words like a stuttered wild goat.

"Go ahead. I'm waiting for you," the short man said.

The madman turned around, and like a savage hawk, he dove down on the short man, trying to pin him down with a severe blow. But the crowd moved in and pushed him away. My dad was in disbelief.

"This is too serious to let a crazed fellow like you, comrade, lie to us," he said. "Calm down, comrade. Go easy on the young man. Like all of us, he's frustrated."

The tall fellow then walked out of the group, crossed the street, and disappeared behind one of the apartment buildings. The group soon dispersed. Disillusioned, Papa raised his head in disappointment.

"Let's go, son. Haiti doesn't have much of a chance with these bluffers," he said.

#

It was six p.m. when Kaykay and I pulled into the driveway of a townhouse in the Miami Lakes neighborhood. It was a cozy place built inside a gated community with an elegant, landscaped garden. As soon as we stepped out of the car, Chen and Pedro walked out, standing side by side, in total elation. They had been waiting, eager to meet us. Kaykay and I walked hand in hand and stepped up to the front porch, and the couple greeted us with hugs and kisses.

"Dear friends, it's with great pleasure I'm presenting to you Kayla, the new girl in my life."

"The pleasure is ours," both Chen and Pedro replied in unison with uncontrolled glee.

"Kaykay, this is my longtime friend and my brother, Pedro, and his lovely wife, Chen," I said, pushing Kaykay forward.

"Nice to meet you," Kaykay said with a smile that heightened the glow of her golden face.

She clung to my arm as we stepped inside following Pedro and Chen, who invited us into their lovely living room decorated in red fabric curtains and Persian rugs. Kaykay was molded inside a chic two-piece dress with a cap-shoulder top, leaning on me as we sat on the sofa. Soon, little Charlito, their son, came running toward us, arms outstretched, until he crashed on Kaykay's arms, who lifted him up and carried him.

"Even Charlito can see your distinct beauty," Chen said, laughing. We all laughed too. Chen then rose from her seat and made her way to the kitchen to make final preparations for dinner. Charlito followed her but he soon went back to his room to play with his toy. I watched Chen moving up and down her spotless kitchen, busy getting things done. She no longer looked petite as she did back during our college days. She had gained a few pounds, but she still bore the elegant fashion, wearing her magnificent hoop rings. Pedro, always in his trademark blue jeans and white T-shirt, looked quite relaxed as we waited to be called.

"Kayla, you can never imagine how happy I was when Vinco called me to tell me about you," Pedro said, looking straight at my girlfriend.

With a tinge of blush on her face, Kaykay smiled but said nothing.

"Kayla," Pedro continued, "thank you for opening up your heart and allowing Vinco to venture to the most intimate part of it. I'm delighted to see my dear friend happy again."

Kaykay smiled once more. She seemed moved. Her face lit up as she leaned on my chest. "Kaykay," I said, touching her chin a little. "I have two great friends in this world: Pedro and Ronel, another college buddy."

"By the way, how's Ronel doing?" Pedro inquired.

"He's doing okay. He graduated last year. He now works as a computer programmer for a firm near the Omni International Hotel on Biscayne Boulevard."

"Vinco, what about that slim Haitian girl who used to bring fried fish and rice to school?"

"You mean Chantale?"

"Yeah," Pedro confirmed. "We used to call her Chantoutou."

"She's now married to a young physician, and they live in Sanford, near Orlando. From time to time, we talk over the phone."

While chatting, Chen called to us. All three of us got up at once. "Kayla, it would be best to take off the shoulder top of your beautiful dress," Chen suggested. "These two friends are chatty when they meet, telling each other jokes of long ago. We'll laugh a lot. Come with me."

"I see that," Kaykay said, laughing. "They never gave me a chance to even say a word."

Kaykay followed Chen while Pedro and I sat at a table sumptuously garnished with a blend of Chinese and Puerto Rican cuisines. From vegetable eggrolls to arroz con pollo to chicken fried rice over dark sauce, and a series of Chinese delicacies that until then I knew nothing about.

"What a great wife you have, Ped!" I complimented him.

"I can't complain, man. But listen, Vinco. Kayla is very pretty. I like her demeanor, respectful, assertive, and articulate. She looks a bit like Mica, too."

"Yeah, but she's nothing like Mica, personality-wise. She has a strong character I admire a lot. But I must admit, Ped. I don't think I'll ever be able to get over Michaela."

"Even I myself think of her sometimes, also thinking of your son, for whom you must find her. I don't know how you'll manage this if you find her. If you never find her, I think, in due time, you will get over this sad story, Vinco." There was a quick pause in our conversation. "You know, Vinco. Don't fully commit to Kayla, at least until you return from France. I wouldn't want you to hurt her."

"Ped, you sound like my sister. How can I hurt her?"

"We'll talk."

The ladies returned. Kayla was now relaxed with the topless shoulder cap. "Now, we all can eat informally," Kaykay said laughing, starting to feel more comfortable.

"I'm thrilled to see the two brothers at the same table. These are inseparable brothers. And like brothers do, they also argue over the phone. I always like to see them doing that, too," Chen tittered, placing a bowl of Chinese noodles on the table.

Everyone held their chopsticks so well, as if that was all they knew as a feeding tool, except me. I stumbled at every try, and Kaykay had to come to the rescue.

"Vinco, it looks like you're going to need a *lot* of practice." Chen teased me.

Then, Charlito came running again toward the table. "Mommy, I can't find my robot toy," he cried, burying his little creamy face on Chen's lap.

"I'll get it for you, son," Pedro said, grabbing him from mom's lap and lifting him up with an admirable love, the profound affection that one can find in a father's eyes.

My heart sank, thinking of my own son, Yrvin Junior. The little boy wrapped his arms around his dad's neck and soon fell asleep. Pedro quietly rose from his seat and took Charlito to his bed. A minute later, he was back at the table.

"Oh, I missed those college years," Chen said. A bittersweet chagrin popped on her face.

Kaykay looked at both of them with great admiration. "So, how did you guys first meet?" she asked, curious to know.

"Well, I was at the library searching for a book when this crazy boy came from behind and asked to help."

"And then?" I intervened, supporting Kaykay's curious question.

"Of course, I refused. But he insisted. I said to myself, this guy is very stubborn. He doesn't seem to take no for an answer. So, I let him help in the search. I soon realized he wanted something special out of me. We then walked outside, sitting by the bench for a prolonged chat. There was a chemistry between us. Since then, we never let go."

"What a fascinating story!" Kayla was excited.

"And you, Kayla? How did you meet Mister Right?" Chen's eyes widened, unblinking.

"Our story is so bizarre," Kaykay chortled.

"How so?" Pedro queried.

"This young man crept into my life while I was sleepwalking."

"You mean, he's stolen your heart?" Chen asked with an amicable tease.

"Indeed," Kaykay affirmed. "And I succumbed to his charm and surrendered my heart."

"Wow! When do you guys plan on tying the knot?"

"Soon. But no specific date yet," I said, preempting Kaykay.

We joked all evening over a delicious meal. In the end, the couple walked us outside. We got in our car and drove off. While in the car, Kaykay was pensive. "What a lovely evening, *mi amor*!" I tried to cheer her up.

"Yes," she replied. "Our situation is so strange, Vinco."

"So, it goes for every love story—odd or strange. But Kaykay, that's life itself. It was a set of circumstances that brought me to your path, and I haven't been so happy in a long time."

"Baby, thank you for letting me know. I love you more than I could ever explain, which makes me so scared."

"Why would you be scared? Losing me?"

She let out an exasperated sigh as if she wanted to say something too burdensome to express. Instead, she reached for my arm, squeezing it. About a block from my apartment, a lusty urge took hold of me. "Baby, I want to make love." I was blunt.

"Me, too. Maybe more than you do."

"I know it's getting late. But can you wait for another couple of hours?"

"I can. I'll have to call mom when we get inside."

As soon as we entered the apartment, she picked up the phone and called her mother. "Mama, I'm still at the friend's home. Is Miguelito asleep?"

"No. He's been vomiting since you left. I thought maybe he ate something bad earlier in the day." I could hear the conversation.

She dropped the phone without putting it back to its base, grabbed her purse, and fled without giving me the chance to walk her down. I was shocked. I went to my room, thinking how serious she was as a mother, but also how unpredictable she could be when under pressure. She acted as if I did not exist, making me feel the lovely evening we just spent was nothing but an insignificant pastime, a simple task to please a boyfriend. I was shocked, but I was hoping it was an overreaction. Obviously if Miguelito were in grave danger, her parents would have rushed him to the emergency room.

The next day, when we met for lunch, Amy had not yet arrived.

"Vinco, I'm sorry. I left so quickly last night," Kayla said with a tinge of embarrassment.

"I understood, Kaykay. A parent's concern is one of the greatest gifts for a child," I said.

Chapter 24

Since the false rumor about the brokered peace accord between President Aristide and General Cédras in New York, the community had been on edge. Tensions continued to flare. Across the Haitian diaspora, street protests had intensified. On July 2, Raoul Cédras, under pressure from the United Nations and the OAS representative, Dante Caputo, agreed to step aside to pave the way for Aristide to return to the presidency in Haiti.

In Miami, the mood began to shift from outright despair to a sense of cautious optimism. Educated and progressive Haitians, however, still had some reservations about the agreement. They had always regarded the overthrowing of Aristide, elected in a landslide in 1990, as a coup against Haitian aspirations for democratic rights and the rule of law. The agreement reached in New York said Aristide would return by October 30, but no specific date was given, and that had contributed to the worries. Trapped in a dubious diplomatic game, Aristide was unable to deliver the victory speech millions, both in Haiti and the diaspora, awaited.

The coup leaders did not sign the accord directly with him. They signed it with the United States, and in doing so, they trapped the exiled president into bowing to some of the worst humiliating conditions. Although the agreement called for Aristide's return, it also called for an unopposed US military intervention in Haiti as well as an amnesty for the brutal Haitian military, including the coup plotters. That was a bitter pill to swallow.

To the Haitian people, the memory of US military occupation of their homeland decades earlier constituted one of the dark chapters of Haiti's history. They wholeheartedly believed that popular democracy was incompatible with foreign military occupation. The thought of seeing American soldiers patrolling the streets of their country had sent chills to the hearts of millions of patriotic Haitians. In Miami, it was consternation. They accused Aristide of trading Haitian dignity in exchange for securing his own selfish interests, his petty-bourgeois aspirations.

Saturday, Ronel called me. "Vinco, are you coming to the rally at the Notre Dame?"

"I didn't know about it. I just returned from the gym."

"Many people are angry about the conditions imposed on Aristide. A rally is scheduled for ten a.m.."

"Okay. I'll meet you there."

"Listen, Vinco. I met Chantale yesterday. She's in town."

"Really? I haven't spoken with her in a while. I'd love to see her."

"She'll be at the rally."

"I might be a few minutes late. I have to go see my dad first."

"See you then, Vinco."

About an hour later, I arrived at Nana's house. She was in the living room, fixing her hair. Nanouche fell asleep on her lap. Her husband wasn't home. Neither was my father. "Where's Papa?"

"He went to a job interview somewhere in North Miami-Dade. My husband drove him there. He's been really worried about Mom and the rest of the family in Haiti."

"I told him not to worry. They will get their visas to travel. I plan on hiring a lawyer in Port-au-Prince to speed up the process. I dream of the day when we all can be reunited in this room, telling jokes."

Nana laughed and alarmed Nanouche in the process. She dove onto me, raising her little hands in the air, cheering.

"Vinco, you know your father more than I do. A man who will do everything in his power to preserve and protect his dignity. Although he appreciates what we do for him, he would prefer to be the one leading this process. That can happen if he gets a job."

"What is that supposed to mean, Nana? We're all one and indivisible."

"Finding a job will do us a great favor. It will give him a positive state of mind, seeing his provider's status restored. It'll also help to keep his mind busy, away from the political situation in Haiti."

In my arms, Nanouche had fallen asleep again, and I laid her back on her mother's lap. "Nana, I've been asking him to come to live with me, but he refuses."

Nana was done fixing her hair and rose from the sofa while grabbing one of the cushions and stuffing it under Nanouche's head to deepen her sleep. "He has a point, Vinco. You work long hours, and you live in a world far removed from the one he's used to. Papa can't be detached from his Haitian traditions. The closer he can get to living in Haiti, the better he feels. And Little Haiti provides that."

"Yeah, but he can still listen to his Haitian radio, and when I come home, we can go to eat, to the gym, like father and son."

"Vinco, you know your dad's world has always been a Haitian one."

"Nana, I live alone, and that doesn't seem to tell you anything?"

"Don't even go there. You know how I feel about this."

"Nana, at my age, I need some structure in my life." I felt saddened all of a sudden.

"I pray every day for a miracle to happen. I have faith. You'll find Mica."

"Finding my son is my top priority. I already told you I'm seeing a new girl."

"Vinco, we had this discussion before. How the *hell* can you find Yrvin Junior without going through Michaela? I still think your story with Mica is not over. Time will tell."

"Nana, you're joking, now." I felt there was a form of mockery in my sister's statement. "I will find Mica, for sure. I now have the means to do so. I can travel. I know my son's birthday, and he bears my name. The French registry will put me on the right path to them if they're still living in France. If and when we meet, I think, it will be a surprise, for sure, but with no trace of emotional love. I have concluded that Michaela has decided to move her life in a new direction."

Nana moved closer to me, peering into my big black eyes. "Joking? Again, time will tell," she reiterated. She walked toward the kitchen, and I followed her.

"What is love then? A shallow gift from a candy store?"

"Vinco, there's a lot of truth in your reasoning. Yes, Michaela is a weak person who doesn't have the guts to fight for her man."

"And I *am* that man. Your lovely, little brother."

She paused for a moment, pondering. "Baby bro," she said in an odd mixture of sarcasm and soberness. "The biggest mistake Mica made was to agree to go to Europe to please her folks. Not many girls in town would agree to this. And I'm questioning her parents' motives. Yes, it was their right to be angry. Yes, it was their right to take whatever steps necessary to protect their daughter; but sending her off to Europe did not make any sense to me. One shelters his prized possession in times of adversity. Their action seemed more an act of embarrassment and rejection rather than a move motivated by love. I understand your predicament, Vinco. You also must bear part of the blame. You got her pregnant." Her eyes turned moist, and I could see the pool of tears ready to splash down her cheeks.

"I know I share a part of the blame, Nana. But this incident allowed me to discover the weak side of her. Being pregnant is no mortal sin, not the biggest sin of the world. Michaela knew I offered to marry her, and she agreed. You can blame her parents all you want, Nana. In the end, it's Michaela's life."

Unexpectedly there was a squeak in the front door, and Papa walked in followed by Nana's husband. Both wore dark sunglasses and straw hats. Papa was smiling.

"Nana told me where you guys went," I said, edging in to shake their hands.

"By the grace of God. I got my first job in America!" Papa was overjoyed.

"Papa's a lucky man," Nana's husband said, chortling while making his way to the kitchen for some food.

"Yes, I'll start working as a tailor in one of the factories in North Dade."

"Really? You got the job, Papa?" Nana was amazed.

"I'm so happy for you, Papa," I said, applauding, not only because he now found a job, but also because of the positive state of mind accompanying that job as Nana stated earlier.

Then, Papa changed the conversation. "Vinco, I've received a package from the US consulate in Port-au-Prince. It's about your mother and the rest of the children."

He instructed me to follow him to his room. There, he grabbed a big brown envelope from the top of his dresser. He handed it to me. It was filled with a stack of forms that Papa needed to fill out to speed up the process of reunification. On top of the forms, there was an approval letter, confirming that the petition for family reunification in the United States had been approved. I read it loud and clear. Delighted, Nana soon joined us in the room as we celebrated.

"Why didn't you tell me about the package, Nana?" I said, still jumping for joy.

"I was going to tell you, but we were too busy talking about Mica." All three of us strolled to the dining room table. There, we sat. One by one, I filled out the forms while Papa and Nana filled me in with additional information I did not know. Papa sighed in relief when it was over.

"So, you're going to mail them on Monday, right?" Papa asked.

"No, not Monday."

"Why?" His face wrinkled.

"Because some of the forms must be notarized. Monday, during my break at work, I'll come here to get you so that we can go to the bank where there is a notary public. Tuesday morning, I'll mail them on the way to work."

"Sounds like a plan!" Papa rejoiced.

"I have to go, now." I rose from my chair, grabbing my car key. Papa walked to his room. Nana walked me to my car outside.

"What about your new girl? You said you're going to bring her to meet us?" She asked.

"I didn't forget. I will soon."

"But, Vinco, you gave me a date last time."

"I know I said this weekend. Now, I've been thinking that it is too premature."

"Is she pretty like Mica?"

"You bet. And she has something Mica doesn't have. She has a very strong personality, a girl ready to fight for what she believes in."

"So, what's keeping you from bringing her?"

"There are a few things she and I need to iron out. When I bring a girl to you and Papa, I have to be absolutely certain she *is* the girl who is going to be my wife. Let me go, now, Nana. *Na pale pita.* We'll talk later."

Fifteen minutes later, I pulled into the Notre Dame's parking lot. There was a crowd, but nothing to compare with the large crowds we used to have during the old days of the refugee struggle. As soon as I stepped out of the car, Ronel called to me. Chantale was with him, wearing a T-shirt with the Haitian flag emblazoned on it. Out of excitement, we fell into each other's arms in a tight and prolonged hug.

"I miss you, Vinco, one of the few good friends I had in my college days," she said, giggling in her usual way, like a young filly.

"What do you mean? We're not friends anymore?" I teased her.

"We still are, but it's a friendship both of us can no longer enjoy. You're busy with your big important job downtown. And I'm as busy as you are, going to work, tending to a husband, and raising two children."

"Vinco, do you see? Chantoutou doesn't change both in look and in style," Ronel said, joking.

"You *stop* it, Mr. Macho man," Chantale said, laughing while pinching him in the arm.

"So, how long you're gonna be in town?" I asked her.

"I'm leaving tomorrow. I came down to see my folks. Mom was not doing well."

"Is she okay, now?"

"She's fine. She suffers from hypertension, and she doesn't want her doctor's recommended diet. You know those old folks. They're so hardheaded."

"I know. I'm facing the same thing with my dad. So, how's married life?"

"Stressful," she laughed.

Then, one of the leaders at the rally, a tall man in an olive-green outfit, called everyone's attention, ready to give the latest news from the negotiations in New York. Ronel moved closer to the crowd to listen.

"Nothing has changed since yesterday. We have yet to have a specific date for President Aristide to go back to Haiti. The putschists in Port-au-Prince are dragging their feet. So, comrades, we must continue the popular mobilization and remain vigilant," the man said, holding a microphone in his hand.

Chantale and I remained stationary under a large oak tree near the church building, trying to catch up on lost time. We could not stay there too long, however. Folks from the neighborhood began to arrive. Some of them came from a laundromat across the street. Others came from farther away and rushed to fill the ranks of frustrated compatriots. Consequently, we retreated to my car.

"Vinco, I think of you and Michaela all the time. I know you're suffering."

"I really was. There were times I could see darkness, sweeping over me coming from all directions."

"Vinco, you're speaking in the past tense. Is the darkness behind you, now?"

"No, but I must reclaim my life. I still have faith. I'll be able to see my son someday."

"Don't stop looking for them. Right now, what we're doing is just making assumptions."

"I'm going to France next fall."

"But Vinco, France is a big country. Don't let blind passion guide you to nowhere. If you travel to France and come back empty-handed, it will be a major blow."

"I think it might have the opposite effect."

"You mean it might bring you closure?"

"Perhaps, yes."

"My friend, you need to speak with sound reasoning. There will never be closure until you find Mica and Vinco Junior."

"I know they're in Alsace, perhaps still in Strasbourg. Let's not forget, Chantoutou, I now have the means to travel to France. My son bears my name. I will first try my luck with the French registry. I know the date and the hospital he was born."

"This is a brilliant idea. You know, Vinco? Michaela surprises me in a big way. She's different from many girls I know from the Dominican Republic. She doesn't know how to stand up for herself."

"You're right Chantoutou. Nana, Pedro, Ronel, and a colleague from work I'm now dating make the same observation."

"Really?"

I pulled out my wallet and retrieved a photo of Kayla. I handed it to her. "Wow, she's gorgeous!" She tittered. "You always date beautiful girls. Régine, Judy, Mica. What's her name?"

"Kayla. I also have to tell you she has a child from a previous relationship."

"That's nothing. People make mistakes all the time in life, like you and me. The truth is that she loves you and she wants to live with you. Have you guys talked about living together?"

"Vaguely, but there's a strong and undeclared understanding that she and I will ultimately live together."

"A little advice, Vinco. Don't make any serious move with this girl until you return from France. Whether you find Michaela or not, it's going to help you make that firm commitment with her."

"Why do you say this, Chantoutou? Do you think I might find Mica and reconnect?"

"It might be true. Remember, it takes two to tango. Yes, Mica seems weak, and her actions show it. But you're strong. If you guys were to be together, your resilience, your strength would eventually make up for her deficiency." She paused for a moment while I sat near her, thinking. She was speaking the truth. "And then, Vinco. Tragedy falls on Mica because of you."

"How so?"

"What you mean how so? You got her pregnant. You could have protected her, using condoms."

"Chantoutou—"

She stopped me. "I'm not saying you should spend the rest of your life in solitude because of your stupid mistake. All I'm saying is that it's important to do the best you can to find her and your son. And as pretty as this new girl is, I think you should wait until you make a serious move in the search for Mica because you wouldn't want to break her heart. Meeting Mica has the potential to change the narrative."

While talking, the rally was over. One by one, the politically charged Haitians vacated the parking lot. Ronel came back.

"How was it?" Chantale and I asked.

"Nothing new. The same news. So, we wait. Hopefully, Aristide will go back in October."

Chantale walked out and joined Ronel. Before leaving, we made a commitment to staying in touch and to talk more often. After my friends left, I drove to Morningside Park, where Mica and I went to consider our next move after the pregnancy test result. I was thinking of what Chantale and my sister told me that day. Two people who barely knew each other came to the same conclusion. "You must find Mica or at least make your best effort before committing yourself to any other person." Truth hurts. Honestly, I did not know how I would react if and when I met Michaela. I still harbored deep in my heart the unwanted sense of betrayal—a lingering anger that I could not erase because my love for Michaela remained dormant in my heart. I felt stuck in the depth of this love.

Reaching the park, I walked out, passing some couples in their romantic promenades as I strolled toward the tiny bench across which was the bay area of Miami Beach, where I had proposed to her. There, I sat, contemplating the waves pitching against each other, wishing my story with Michaela was nothing but a nightmarish dream. It had been more than five years, but I felt as if it had happened yesterday. I could feel Mica rubbing her head against my chest, seeking the comfort I could provide. Unable to mitigate the pain, I walked back to my car and drove home.

Arriving at home, the first thing I did was to grab the Yellow Pages off my little bookcase and went to sit at the breakfast table to ponder what I was going to need to travel. Out of my briefcase, I then took out a pen and a note pad on which I jotted down the most pressing things I would need for the journey to France, including a passport, airplane tickets, train tickets to travel from Paris to Strasbourg, hotel reservations, and more.

Among them, the passport was the most crucial at this stage of the preparation. To get a Haitian passport, I knew I had to go to the Miami Haitian Consulate located downtown on 13th Street, not far from where I worked on Brickell Avenue. I would also need a tourist visa for the trip. So, I thought. The French Consulate is located two buildings down from the Bedell Tech Firm. I could walk there from my office. I had never been to any of them. Neither did I know their phone numbers. So, I retrieved their numbers from the Yellow Pages along with the numbers of several airline companies to compare prices. American, Air France, and United were the main ones.

Chapter 25

Monday during lunch, I headed straight to the Haitian Consulate, bringing with me my birth certificate to confirm my Haitian identity. Located in a two-story building across an empty parking lot where most of the people who came, like me, did so to either get their passports or for other services. I parked my car, across the street and walked in. There was a line of people seeking services, but it was rather small. I didn't recognize any of them. After a few minutes in line, I reached a glass window where a young woman sat. She was dressed in blue and red, the color of the Haitian flag. I didn't know why. It was not the flag day which is celebrated on May 18th.

"How can I help you?" She asked.

"I'm here to get a passport," I replied.

"Here, fill out this form. When you're done, bring it back along with your birth certificate and 150 dollars," she said, handing me the form.

I then moved to the corner of the room, sat in one of the reception chairs, and filled out the form. In a few minutes, I was done.

"Your passport will be ready in two weeks," the young woman said as I was handing her the required materials.

I left and went straight to the French Consulate. In the lobby, I met a receptionist, an older lady in a blue suit. She told me that no visa was required for green card holders who traveled to France or to any other country that belonged to the Schengen area. I was happy.

One Friday morning in May, I was getting ready to leave for work when the phone rang. At first, I ignored it. My mind was on the traffic jam that awaited me on Biscayne Boulevard. As I grabbed the car keys, the phone rang again. I picked it up this time. Before I answered, Nana's voice shrieked from the other end of the line.

"Vinco, Vinco, Vinco!" She was ecstatic.

"What's the news, sister?" I asked.

"Mom and the kids got their reunification visas." I could hear the jubilant voice of Papa in the background.

"When did you get this phenomenal news?" I was thrilled as well.

"They just called. Mom said it was yesterday when they went to the US consulate in Port-au-Prince for a scheduled appointment."

That was the best news I had in years. "Nana, I'm on my way out. I'll call you as soon as I get to my office. I need to beat the traffic."

We hung up, and I left for work. While in the car, a sense of pride, an awed sensation of *joie de vivre* took possession of my being. For years, I dwelled in an ocean of homesickness, of an emptiness I could not fill, a void that never ceased to ache. Now, the dream of seeing Manman and the rest of my siblings was on the verge of becoming a reality. I could not ask for more that morning.

When I walked by Kaykay's office that morning at work, she was not there. I wanted to share the news with her. I knew she would have been happy for me. When I entered my office, Amy was there, getting my schedule of the day ready. She noticed the joy on my face.

"What's going on, *Mister*?" She asked, laughing.

"I just got the greatest news. My mother and my other siblings will be in Miami soon!"

"When?"

"No date yet. But soon."

I called Nana as soon as Amy left my office. We arranged for ticket purchasing and other logistical needs required for traveling. Throughout the day, I was in sheer delight. Kayla did not make it to work that Friday, and I did not know why. I avoided calling her, for I figured if she did not call me, it was because she could not. By three o'clock in the afternoon, I was about to leave when she called my office. Amy was with me, and she picked up the phone.

"Hey, princess, whatever happened to you?" Amy asked, teasing her.

"I had to take the day off. You know I told you graduation is this afternoon." Kayla's voice came through on speaker phone.

"I'm sure you don't wanna talk to me now. Here is the *boss*," Amy said, tittering.

Amy then passed me the phone, and she left as if my phone conversation with Kaykay was something she wanted to avoid at all costs. And my urge to talk to Kayla did not help either.

"Baby, sorry for not calling you sooner. I had to go get ready for graduation," she said with an unusual politeness, as if trying to preempt a negative reply.

"I thought you told me graduation was next week, Kaykay?"

"Did I? I must have given you the wrong date." We went on to talk for a few minutes about other matters and we hung up.

As soon as we hung up, Amy came back. "You weren't eavesdropping? Were you, Amy?" I said. I was deliberate.

"Have you known me to be an eavesdropper?"

I did not reply. I laughed instead. Then I went on to review the work of the week and assignments for next week as we usually did. But before we began, Amy sighed in a deep breath.

"Vinco, you know you've been playing a dangerous game? Did you realize that?" She said in a firm tone of voice.

"What do you mean?"

"I'm no kid. I know you and Kayla had been deep in a relationship, and I'm very scared for you."

"Amy."

"Don't try to deny it. She told me."

"She did?"

"Not because she wanted to, but because she had to."

I could not do anything but throw a guilty stare at her. "Vinco," Amy continued, "you seem quite naïve. Kayla was supposed to be helping you find your lost true love, and she ended up being your *true love.* How serious were you in finding out what had happened to the mother of your son? How true was that love when you're ready to give it up without putting up a serious fight to learning the truth?" Her eyes went moist.

"Amy, I'm sorry for having to conceal this story from you."

"No need to be sorry. I would do the same if I were in your predicament. Besides, your status here would be in jeopardy. Vinco, Kayla understood what she did was wrong, but she said she could not resist under the weight of your charm. She loves you passionately, but she knows she'll never be able to fill the emptiness in your heart, the love for your son and Michaela. For that she says she must sacrifice her love for you so that you could be free to continue on your search to find Michaela."

"Amy, that last line can't be further from the truth. Kayla knows I'm not giving up the search for Michaela; she also knows I can't lose something I no longer have. Michaela is no longer mine. She was the one who had decided to sever all contact with me, preventing me from reaching my son. I've discussed all this with her, and she agreed. If she's having second thoughts, that means the passion she claims to have is shallow at best—skin-deep to be precise."

"No Vinco, she's being realistic. As long as you're in that search for Michaela and your son, her love will never get your full attention, and she's afraid of that. She's been crying. Did she tell you she's moving to Washington DC with her son?"

"No. I know she's going there for her graduate studies."

"Did she tell you her son's father is now heavily involved in her son's life?"

"No."

"Did she tell you her son's father lives in suburban Maryland near Washington? He's an important official at the Ecuadoran embassy?"

"No." I was horrified. I took a deep breath to digest the news. "Amy, I wouldn't be surprised if she calls me someday from DC to say she is staying there permanently."

"Vinco, go find out what happened to your Michaela and son. You can. You have the means to do it." She paused for a moment. "My brother, I'm sure you're different from many men I know, some of whom I've dated. Some men would simply write Michaela and the son off their minds and go on with their lives. And because you're not like them, your suffering will be everlasting unless you find out the truth about your son and his mother."

I dove into her arms like a child seeking the sheltering love of his mother. "Thank you, Amy, for sharing these hard truths with me."

"Vinco, one last thing. Don't pressure her in an attempt to rip these truths out of her mouth. Wait until she tells you, and if she doesn't, you already know. See you Monday. Be strong. Your family is coming to America. That should be enough to keep your mind away from Kayla."

As soon as Amy left, I grabbed my car keys, shut my office door, and drove to my sister's home. They were still in that same delirious state of mind. An explosion of joy shook the small house as I walked in. They all surrounded me, and we began to jump out of happiness, including Nanouche who could not understand the motive behind such sudden joy. But I struggled to keep my mind away from Amy's latest revelation. We congregated around the breakfast table, talking about finding a place for Papa to rent. I invited him once more to move in with me so that he would not have to deal with the monthly rent. Again, he refused; but he asked me to help with household expenses until my brothers could find a job.

"And whenever you feel lonely, don't hesitate to come and sleep with us," he added, laughing.

He knew when Manman came, the temptation to go and spend some nights with them was going to be irresistible. Yes, he was right. I could not wait for Manman to arrive and tell her stories that, until now, remained untold, and to make up for lost time in the merriment of her motherly love. I craved her tales, new and old, nighttime stories of childhood friends I left behind, the struggling neighbors of whom I sometimes thought, the rustic life of peasant men and women in my grandma's village, and of the innocent and naïve children, running wild and naked in open fields in rural Saint Louis.

For years, I longed for those legends of walking zombies in the *cric crac* hours when the crepuscular rays seemed distant, tales told in a tiny room, tenebrific enough to spook your mind. Those fairytales were an integral part of me, of my culture, of my childhood, of all that made me who I was. The coming of Manman, my brothers, and my baby sister would fill a void that ached day and night, would bring the other half of a whole that I terribly missed and because of which I was forced to dwell in a web of profound nostalgia.

#

Later at home, I lay in bed, thinking of what Amy had told me. I felt smashed by the vicissitudes of life, by yet another sense of betrayal. If it was true what Amy had told me, my relationship with Kayla could be on the verge of collapsing. Kayla claimed she may have given me the wrong graduation date. It was difficult to imagine she could err on that important date. Maybe she had a reason for not telling me. The pattern of action seemed to follow Amy's story. She never told me who her son's father was. Nor did she ever tell me that he worked in the DC area. At the same time, she was adamant about moving to Washington, and pursuing a graduate degree. Could it be she was seeking a rapprochement with her son's father in a quest for some form of happiness?

In fact, Kaykay's attitude brought weight to Amy's story. It had been a week since she and I had an intimate conversation, and she did not appear to show any eagerness to have one. Was it the beginning of a sad story, foretelling the demise of our burgeoning romance? Right there in my bed, I made a bold decision not to seek answers to these questions. I had learned over the years that romance at its purest form is an enigma that cannot be controlled, just like the complexity of the human heart. From the start, we had taken the wrong steps; Kayla had warned and urged me to avoid taking this train of love that could be fatalistic for both of us. Those sexual stirrings, however, that catapulted us into bed did not spring out of a pristine love, but rather out of a shared and uncontrolled desire, which could not be rekindled once it had reached the climax of its satisfaction. Reality was fast catching up with her. Michaela's unsettled story, despite the unknown, overshadowed the romantic pathway that Kaykay and I had to navigate. Determined not to let myself be dragged into another state of melancholy, I got out of bed, walked to the fridge, grabbed my bottle of Haitian rum, and poured it down my throat. Then, I went back to bed. Within minutes, I fell asleep.

The next day, which was Saturday, I spent a big part of it looking for the best deal from several airline companies. I settled on Air France. It was cheaper, and the accommodations pleased me.

Now, it was time for me to look for a hotel to stay in Strasbourg. My phone book did not offer this help. The worldwide web could help, I thought. So, I drove to my office for a better connection. Few colleagues were at the building when I walked in. I waved and they waved back as I was rushing to my office. After an extensive search, I found a hotel called Hotel D Strasbourg. I dialed the number.

"*Que désirez-vous?*" said a female voice from the other end. *How may I help you?*

"I'd like to make a reservation for one person?" I replied, a bit anxious.

"What date, sir?"

"Check in on November 15th and check out November 31st with the possibility of expanding it if necessary."

There was a brief silence, and in about a minute later, the reservation was confirmed. I was thrilled.

The weekend came and went. She did not call, which was not part of her character. I made no attempt to call her either. Despite the pain, I remained strong and ready for any eventuality. Maybe this time, life wanted to spare me from this painful sequence of disappointing romantic adventures. Monday arrived. At work, I kept the same demeanor, focusing on the task at hand.

As usual, Amy, Kakay, and I ate lunch together, telling jokes until the end of lunchtime. She called me as soon as I was back at my office. I did not pick up. She seemed to have been surprised by my unconcerned and professional attitude. She called me again on Tuesday right after lunch. Still, I did not pick up. It was truly hurting, ignoring her call. She did not call again. I knew she wanted to have a conversation that could not be held at the workplace. Friday evening, she called me at home. I was in the kitchen when the phone rang.

"Vinco, I know you're angry with me," she said with a breaking voice.

"Why would I be angry?" I interrogated.

"Because of my behavior. I'm sorry."

"Don't apologize for something you didn't do."

"I should have invited you to my graduation. I didn't because I knew it would've created unwanted attention."

"How so?" I gave a ridiculous laugh.

"Vinco, it's not a laughing matter. I knew just close relatives were going to be there." She paused for a quick second. "Well, except for my son's father, who flew from DC for the occasion."

"Really? I'm sure he must have been the guest of honor with a vested interest."

"What do you mean, Vinco?"

"Obviously, it wasn't your son's graduation…"

"Vinco. What are you trying to say?"

I did not reply to her question, for I could not say everything I wanted to say. I knew Kayla, a shrewd young woman, and for her to bring the father of her son into the conversation in such a sordid fashion was not a mistake. It was a carefully planned move designed to implicitly remind me of the impasse in which we dwelled.

"Anyway, Vinco. I'm moving to Washington with my son. Lately, he's been very close to his dad. Being in Washington with him and being closer to his father would help change his attitude toward school at a time he's been slacking off in his academic performance."

"I agree. You're doing the right thing. A son needs his father—always," I said.

"You didn't even ask me when."

"I figure it must be soon. You start school next term. Right?" I was vague.

"But anyway, it's next Friday."

"You guys are going to have so much fun, mother and son!" I foiled her provocation.

"Can we talk tomorrow after work, Vinco?"

"I can't promise that. I have an urgent meeting which begins at five-thirty. I'm afraid it might be too late to call afterward."

The line went cold for a few seconds. "Vinco," she said with lowered, guilty voice. "I don't want you to think I'm trying to run away from you."

"You're not *trying* to run away from me, Kaykay. You *are* running away; I'm simply left with one wish for you: that you have a safe trip. I'm confident you'll live a productive life as well as a successful one. Remember what we always joke about? Be *jam* (strong) in the face of adversity. Always keep your head high as you have always shown it at the firm. And as for me, don't you worry. You know I'll be okay. I've been through a lot of hardships in my young existence, but that has also shaped my character. That's what gives me the strength to speak with absolute certainty."

She burst into tears. "What are you talking about, Vinco? You're talking as if this is the end of the road for us."

"I'm convinced this is the terminus. If it isn't, show me the way; for beyond this point, it is an emptiness with no end, an aimless ride, an endless field of suffering, a mutually inclusive demise. And if we persist, we'll do one thing: delaying the inevitable."

"I never thought it could be that easy for you to write me off your heart and mind, someone you claim to have loved so much," she growled.

Then, I remember what Amy had told me, and I became stronger. "Kaykay, I don't think I need to remind you that I'm no kid, certainly not an empty-headed loser. Yes, you've warned me about what we were getting into. I went ahead and crossed that line because I thought you would never leave me stranded along the bank of the river of hope. You give your son priority over our love, and I respect that because as much of a caring individual I would be to your son, I will never be his dad."

"Vinco, you're talking nonsense. I didn't call to say our relationship is over."

"Actions speak louder than words, Kaykay. Remember I told you never will I force myself again into a long-distance relationship because I know the pain it entails. You're moving to Washington to be closer to your son's father, a man with whom you once fell in love. So, what's in it for me? I don't think you're interested in a shallow love affair, exchanging courtship missives like those who believe in fairytales."

"Vinco."

"Goodnight, Kaykay. Stay in peace."

"Goodnight, my love," she said. Her voice was breaking.

I did not reply as we hung up.

On Monday, we kept the usual demeanor at lunch. Wednesday was her last day at the firm. I ordered Amy to organize a farewell lunch in her honor. I did not take part in it. I purposely went up to Palm Beach for a business meeting to avoid facing her during her final hours on the job. I did not have the courage to stand and watch as everyone congregated around her, showering her with kisses and hugs. Instead, I entrusted Amy with a postcard to deliver to her on my behalf and to encourage her to read it in front of everybody. In that note, I congratulated her for her academic success. I also thanked her for her professionalism, her *franc-parler,* and her meticulousness as an office organizer and manager. I concluded the note this way: *Kayla, you are irreplaceable in every way. I will surely miss you.*

The next morning, when I walked by her office and glanced at the empty chair, I felt a sense of gloom that I could not describe. With a heavy heart, I walked to my office where Amy was waiting. Her eyes were moist and red.

"How did it go?" I asked.

"Just as expected. Everyone showed up. Jason made a sober introduction, telling everyone Kaykay was moving to Washington. Tony then moved to the center of the room and spoke on your behalf; on the value and the trust you've placed in her. I could not speak. I was too emotional. She was teary throughout the whole lunch in part because of your absence on an occasion like this. After everyone was dispersed, I walked her to the car, helping her carry the many gifts she had received."

"So, what happened when you guys reached the car?"

"We hugged each other and did not want to let go. She has been like a sister to me, obedient and respectful. She left in my heart an emptiness that I will never be able to fill."

"Did she feel disappointed at my absence?"

"When I handed the card and asked her to read it, she broke into tears. And I had to move closer to comfort her. But in the car, she said your action was cruel. She said she was crying the whole time because of your absence. She went on to share with me her last conversation she had with you, and you punctured her heart at every word. She said she'll never love another man the way she feels for you."

At that point, I fell into Amy's arms, and we sobbed together.

Chapter 26

It had been almost ten years since the last time Manman and I shared a laugh under the same roof. Despite the distance, however, her touch, her frown, and most of all her advice felt like a protective magnet in my heart and mind. It was her words of wisdom that gave me the strength to get off the boat and run to safety on that dreaded night at the Port of Miami. "I have faith in you, son. No matter the odds, you will succeed." Through the years, these words served as the light that guided me through trials and tribulations in my quest to reach the ridgeline of salvation. The idea of being reunited with the woman who gave me life, who fed and sheltered me and my siblings amid countless times of uncertainty, filled my heart. I was delighted to find myself counting the hours before meeting Manman and feeling so safe in her warm embrace.

The night before, I slept at Nana's home. In fact, we did not sleep at all. Papa, Nana, and I spent the whole night chatting and telling jokes about the good old times in Saint Louis. A week earlier, Papa and I had rented a modest two-bedroom apartment in northeast Miami to house the family. However, on the eve of such a historic arrival, we felt it was necessary to be together.

It was finally morning. Arrival time was eleven a.m. on board an American Airlines flight. Nanouche, who had slept all night, was totally bewildered by the sudden elation in the house. Nana had Nanouche stay with her dad, although she wanted to come along. By ten a.m., we pulled into the Miami International Airport parking lot. We knew arriving ahead of time at that airport swamped with travelers was the best way to deal with the anxiety, in particular on a day like this. Luckily, we found a parking spot several meters away from the main entrance where people arriving on the international flights came through. We walked out of the car and carefully crossed an alleyway that led to the main entrance. Nana leaned on Papa, who held her hand, and I walked a step behind. We now had entered the moment of truth. I watched Papa trying to suppress his anxiety by holding Nana's hand tighter and keeping his head high on the walkway from where the passengers from Haiti would be coming.

By eleven-fifty, passengers started coming out. They came in waves. My anxiety heightened at each wave, and Manman and the kids had yet to show up. Papa began to stroke his bald head, smacking his lips out of nervousness. At last, we saw them coming, walking like wayfarers moving in uncertain directions. Guyto, one of the older children, walked ahead of my other brother Compa. Royo, my youngest sister, walked with Manman, pulling their luggage along. We waved, and they spotted us. We ran into each other's arms, hugging, squeezing, kissing, and shedding tears. I grabbed Manman's luggage, which was very small, as we hurried back to the parking lot. Though my car was fit for five people, we were able to squeeze in since driving from the airport to Papa's new home was a short distance.

In the car going home, Manman leaned on Papa as if trying to make up, in one short moment, for the long-awaited time spent in unrelenting loneliness.

"So, did you guys bring my sugary cassava?" Nana asked.

"I have it in Manman's luggage," Royo replied with a big sigh of relief, as if to say *Finally, I'm in America.* The boys, ever curious, glanced through the car windows at the high rises and the network of highways over which lines of cars weaved at full speed.

"This is clearly America," they said with a burst of laughter.

At last, we came to our destination. I hurried and helped the boys carry the luggage inside. Manman went in, strolling hand in hand with Papa, followed by Nana and Royo chatting, trying to make up for lost time. With a mixture of anxiety and pride, Manman surveyed her new home, but focusing on the kitchen in which she was going to spend a lot of time because she loved cooking those delicious Creole dishes. We all converged in the living room, squatting on the carpet floor, digging through the luggage for the gifts—artisanal clothes, pictures of the old neighborhood where I grew up, rare delicacies unique to that part of Haiti, and even a few varieties of mangoes from my old backyard. The feeling of hope and empowerment that escaped me the night I left Haiti had returned with an indescribable joy. Everyone dear to my heart, whose love and commitment toward me were unconditional and unwavering, sat next to me.

After three hours of chatting, talking about relatives they left behind, their endless hardships, Manman started feeling tired; I let her go for a well-deserved rest not before she told me about the deteriorating health of my grandmother, who lived on a hilltop overlooking Manman's backyard. Nana was also tired. Before she left, she helped Manman organize the home the way she liked it, for Manman was a woman obsessed with neatness. Then, she went home to her waiting husband. But I stayed and spent the weekend with them, catching up with my siblings. The week that followed, I took the children to register for school, reminding them of the power of an education in a country where opportunity for those with college degrees was limitless. Officially, life in America had begun.

I spent the rest of the month helping my siblings to understand the school system in Florida, an experience that reminded me of my first days in America. I would stop by every afternoon going home from work. Manman would leave me delicious meals. I did not have to tell her; she knew she had to save me a plate. Nana had gotten jealous, saying I no longer liked her food. But she understood the feeling of being able to enjoy Manman's meals after so many years. She herself would bring her husband and daughter over on Sundays to enjoy Manman's delicious pastries.

Meanwhile, the protest movement in the community began to wear off. Reality set in. Aristide had agreed to the terms of his return. So, there was not much the patriotic Haitians could do to prevent the embarrassment. Indeed, on October 15, 1994, Aristide returned to Haiti under the protection of twenty thousand US troops who had landed in the country a month earlier. Many Haitians, who had hoped to go back to Haiti to help with the democratic process, felt they had been forced to forego such a lofty goal. Integration into American society had become their main aim. Some of them turned out to be highly successful in their American journey.

#

On a very chilly night in mid-October, my phone rang, just as I walked home after a long day at work. I refused to pick it up. I was too tired. But after two rings, the phone went silent, and the person left no voice message. The phone rang again after a couple of minutes. Still, I did not pick up. This time, the person left a message. "Vinco, it's me, Chouchou. I'm in town, and I wanted to hear from you and perhaps see you if you're not busy."

I figured a moment with Judy would be nice. There were times that I honestly thought of her, thinking my life could have been different if I wanted to give her love a chance. Now that she is a married woman with a promising career, I certainly would not want to interfere. Judy was one of the rare cases where hope died while love lived. Irresistibly, I called her.

"Chouchou, sorry I missed your call. I just walked in, and I'm dead tired. So, how are you and the family?"

"We're okay. I've been here since Monday on a business trip. I wanted to see you before leaving tomorrow."

"I will have to be the one to go and pick you up, but I'm exhausted."

"Don't worry. I have a rental. I'll be there in a few."

She hung up without giving me the chance to say no. Fifteen minutes later, she was on the porch, and as soon as I opened the door, she strolled in, forever stylish, wearing a button-up midi shirtdress with a pointed collar. We hugged each other rather casually, *bisous* on the cheeks, like two young doves in a platonic friendship. I invited her to the sofa where we sat side by side. She then took off her shoes, head back on the cushion and cross-legged.

"Chouchou, I thought you were going to bring me some souvenirs from Freeport," I said, teasing her.

"I could have done it with pleasure, but I didn't think you would want anything from me," she replied in a firm voice, bearing boundless pride. "Maybe on my next visit, Vinco."

"Chouchou, I'm just kidding."

"Vinco, you look tired."

"You sound like a concerned wife."

"A concerned friend," she corrected me with a flirtatious smile.

"You want me to fix you dinner?"

"Chouchou, you're my guest, remember?"

"Let's swap roles for a minute, Vinco." She laughed while rising from the sofa and sauntered down toward the kitchen. I followed her.

"Chouchou, you're making it seem as if we've never left each other."

"That's how I feel. I find meeting you again is the greatest gift from God."

"And what can this gift do for us?"

"I don't know about you. As for me, it brings happiness. Now I know there's a place I can go where I can feel indescribably joyful." She then pulled frozen fruits out of the fridge to make a smoothie.

"Chouchou, let me do it for you."

She turned facing me. "It's for the two of us," she said with a twinkle in her eyes.

Soon after the fruit drink was done, we went to the dining table, sitting on opposite sides facing each other. "How's married life?" I asked.

"It has been okay. Just the way I anticipated it."

"What do you mean?"

"My marriage is transactional at best. I hope it will be very different for you when you decide to embark upon such a journey." Her oval face was drawn as she pondered her next words.

"I don't think I'll ever get married if it can't be a soulful, sentimental decision."

"Really, Vinco?"

"I've come to realize that skin-deep love cannot survive moments of uncertainties in a marriage because it's too lopsided, contractual, and shallow."

"So, what truly happened to that Spanish girl?" Her eyes widened, peering into mine in a search for the truth.

"The last time we talked, I told you, it didn't work." I felt the need to tell her the truth this time. "Chouchou, I met her a year after you left. We were deeply committed to each other. She got pregnant a few weeks after my graduation. I offered to marry her, and she agreed. When her parents found out, they manipulated her, forcing her to move to France to live with her uncle."

"Then, what happened?"

"The morning of the flight, I begged her not to go, but she refused. In France, we kept a long-distance relationship. A few months later, the baby was born—a boy she named after me, Yrvin Junior. By then, my sister had gotten married, and I was left alone in the apartment. Then, I asked her to return to Miami where we would live together, raising our child. Once again, she agreed. Then, she walked away from the arrangement. We haven't talked in almost six years."

"*What?* Vinco, you never found out why she did that?"

"No, but I'm going to France in two weeks. The purpose of my trip will be to find my son."

"And also *her*," she corrected me once more.

"Of course, finding my son also means finding her."

"Have you done some preliminary searching?"

"I have a childhood friend who lives in Paris. I'm sure he'll be able to help me in the effort. Also, Pedro has gotten me some contact information."

"I remember *Pedro*, Vinco. How is he doing?"

"Great. He and Chen got married a few years ago. They have a son, always cheery. We talk about you sometimes."

"Chen, you mean the Chinese girl?"

"Yes. They had gotten deeply involved, and she turned out to be the love of his life."

"I'm happy for him. But Vinco, your Spanish girl didn't have much faith in you. She seemed a weak-minded person."

"Just like you who didn't want to give up your Mark for fear of alienating your parents."

"No, Vinco. The reason why I kept Mark was because leaving him and going public with you would have prompted my parents to send me to Europe. And I was terribly afraid of that.

But if I were to be pregnant, I would have no other choice but to tell the truth, no matter the consequences."

"Had you told me your story ahead of the party, I probably would have reacted differently. I loved you unconditionally. That was why after I saw you with Mark, I felt wrecked, and I could never recover."

"I saw it differently." She looked saddened and stopped sipping on the smoothie.

"How differently, Chouchou? If I didn't love you, I could have simply played it along, making love whenever we felt like and having a good time. I knew you wanted more than just having fun, but you blundered on your strategy."

"And I paid the heaviest price for it, too." Her eyes turned misty. "So, when are you leaving?" she asked. Her face was drawn as sadness crept in.

"Two weeks from today."

"Will you call me from France?"

"I don't have your phone number. How?"

She pulled out a card from her purse and gave it to me. "My secretary will pick it up and she will pass me the phone. You can call me any time before five p.m. on weekdays. I wanna know how your search turns out to be."

"Thank you, Chouchou."

"I hope you find your son and his mother. I want you to live a happy life."

"Happy like you."

"When I'm with you, of course." She laughed.

"Wish me luck, Chouchou. My son is my top priority for the moment."

We went back to the sofa. She leaned against my chest this time, dozing off—a resting princess after a long voyage. We both soon fell asleep. She did not wake up until four a.m..

"Chouchou, remember you have an early flight to catch."

She got up, took a shower, and made breakfast for the two of us before she left.

"Have a safe trip and let me know when you get there."

She turned around and looked at me, her eyes swelled with tears. Misty-eyed gratitude, ablaze with mounting desire, which beheld me with shivered lips. "I will, my prince." She then adjusted herself in the car and drove off.

Long after she left, I sat on the couch, thinking of her, of her predicament. "But Judy, well-settled and structured in society, cannot be the woman with whom I should flirt," I kept saying to myself. She herself reminded me of our dangerous situation. Having sex with me would certainly mean the demise of her marriage. I was terrified of that prospect; and that fear of falling into a love trap had succeeded in repressing that raging fire of lust that threatened to seize control of my heart and mind.

#

Since the day Kayla left the firm and then moved to Washington, I heard very little of her. From time to time, Amy would tell me about her and that she had found a job in DC and she was not interested in returning to Miami. Amy and I had gotten very close. She had become a sister, making sure my work assignments were done in the highest professional manner. She was such a dignified young woman and a pleasure to work with. Every day after work, she would tell me stories of failed romances, of hopes and hard-earned romantic victories. I knew most of them were fairytales drawn from her own fictional world. But I longed for those stories, for they made me feel evermore empowered to embark upon the journey to find Michaela and Yrvin Junior.

On Friday, before I left, as we usually did, Amy and I would review the tasks for the following week. As we sat at the table, I told her what she had long been wanting to hear. "I'm leaving for France on Monday. I wanted to surprise you." She was delirious.

"Do you have the flight tickets?" She asked.

"Yes. Pretty much, I think I have all that I need. Listen, last week, I had a meeting with Tony and Mike on my upcoming vacation. You'll work with them until I return, possibly in four weeks. Make sure you put off all meetings and appointments until the third week of December. Here is my sister's phone number in case you wanted to know more about the search while I'm in France."

"I'll be praying for you, Vinco."

We talked, going over a few more work-related tasks. Then, we rose from our chairs and went for a tight hug. She soon left, returning to her office.

I then called my friend Ronel to brief him about my trip. "I'm leaving for that historic mission, man," I said with a laugh.

"This trip is long overdue. Guess what?" He said in his usual joke-telling manner.

"What?"

"I was with Laurette yesterday."

"Doing it again?" I teased him.

"No. We were talking about you, your suffering. She said she has been praying for you. She hopes you find your son and his mother, although she never liked her."

"Man, I welcome all the best wishes."

We talked for a few more minutes and we hung up. I drove home shortly thereafter. On the way, I stopped by my parents' home to spend some time with them before departure. When I arrived, my dad and my brothers were not home. They had gone to see some relatives in Fort Lauderdale, my mother told me. But Nana was there, as she always did on her way home from work. Royo, my youngest sister in a floral dress, was there with Mom. She was the most beloved, always with Mom.

"Last night at the church, Vinco, all of us from our group celebrated when I told them you're going to look for your son and his mother," Nana chortled as we all squatted on the floor to talk.

"Really?" I was moved.

"Let's pray," my mother commanded. We then closed our eyes, held hands, and bowed our heads for a lengthy prayer. In the end, we all shed tears, but they were tears stemming from feelings of mixed emotions, not knowing if my trip was going to be successful. Nana soon went home to her husband and daughter Nanouche. I stayed a little.

When I was leaving, my mother and Royo followed me to the car.

"We'll be fasting the whole time you're away or at least until we hear from you, and that your son and his mother are with you," they both said with one voice. We hugged each other and I drove home.

I had never been to France, but I had a friend named Frankel, who had been living in Paris for more than a decade. He was an old friend from my primary school years in Haiti. Although we had not communicated for a number of years, he was delighted when I called him the next day to inform him about my arrival in France as well as the purpose of my trip.

"Man, I thought I'd lost you," he said from the other end.

"No, man. I've always thought of you. The problem is, I live in a community where most of my fellow Haitians are from the northern part of the island. Little Haiti is not Port-au-Prince where you're from," I said, equally rejoiced.

"But you had my number."

"I did. But calling France was very difficult for me as I was going through hardships and other logistical problems associated with living in immigration."

"You are *so* right. I myself went through a lot during my first couple of years in this country."

"The most important thing, Frankel, is that we're now reconnected. And I need your help."

"What is it, Vinco?"

"I have a child who was born in France, in Strasbourg to be precise. I have yet to meet him because I lost track of his mother shortly after he was born. I'm traveling to France in two weeks."

"The first thing we need to do, Vinco, is to check birth records in Strasbourg. Then, we'll need to look for a possible address. It's not going to be easy. I've never been to Strasbourg, which is a city in Alsace on the German border. But I will go with you on the search. What's your son's name and his date of birth?"

"Yrvin Junior Monsalve, and his mother's name is Michaela Monsalve. He was born on October 17th, 1987."

"I have a friend who used to live in Alsace. I can ask him for help if we run into problems locating them."

"Thank you, my friend."

"I need the flight date. I'll have to pick you up from the airport. Which airport, by the way?"

"Flight date is November 14th, arriving from Miami at Charles de Gaulle International Airport at seven a.m. Paris time on board an Air France flight."

"Vinco, you'll also need a train ticket to go to Strasbourg, and I will purchase it for you from La Garre de l'Est, which is the eastern train station that goes to northeast France."

"Thank you, for the offer, but I've already bought that ticket. See you next week."

Soon after Frankel and I hung up, I called Pedro. I wanted to update him on the final preparations for the trip. "Ped, I'm edging closer to the travel date."

"You've already purchased the ticket?"

"Yes, November 14th."

"Did Hector call you? I gave him the number."

"No, he didn't."

"I'm surprised. But do you still have the number and the address I gave you?"

"Of course. And I have an old childhood friend in Paris who will help me in the process."

"Perfect. So, how's Kayla?"

"That's history."

"How come?"

"You remember I told you she was going to Georgetown for her graduate degree."

"Yes. So, what happened?"

"That was a major point of contention. I refused to be trapped in a long-distance relationship again."

"But you knew about this before you got involved with Kayla. Right?"

"Yeah, but she has changed plans since then. She has decided to literally move to Washington with her son so that he can be closer to his dad, who lives in suburban Maryland."

"*What?*"

"This has hurt me tremendously. And I'm afraid people might think I *am* the one who can't manage a relationship."

"I'm so sorry, man. But you have a serious mission ahead of you, and that should be your focus."

"Pray for me, Ped, so I can find Yrvin Junior."

"I'm optimistic you'll find both Mica and your son. And when you do, don't be vindictive in your words. I know you're seriously hurt. Speak with Mica with humility and intellectual reasoning, no matter the conditions in which you find her. She could be settled with another man, embracing a French life or whatever. But always remember she is the mother of your son. You'll always need her if you want to play an active role in your son's life. Meanwhile, I'll be waiting for your call."

"Thank you, brother."

We hung up.

Chapter 27

November 14 had arrived. Departure time was seven p.m.. It was a Monday. By six-thirty, all passengers were ordered to gate number nine, bound for Paris. I was the first in line. A young woman in a Pierre Balmain uniform and a silk scarf greeted me with a smile. I handed her my boarding pass and was allowed to proceed down a cold alley that led to the plane. To lessen the stress, I carried light luggage—a gift for Junior and a few personal items. All were stuffed in a small carry-on. Once inside, I was directed to my assigned seat. I was near a window, and that pleased me. One by one, the other passengers streamed in, taking their seats. Within minutes, the plane was full. Flight attendants were ordered to shut the door and get ready for departure. Soon, the plane started to pull its way along the tarmac and headed toward the airstrip. Flight attendants then asked all passengers to tighten their seatbelts and requested everyone's attention as they went over the safety rules. Shortly after that, it became quiet as the plane was poised to take off.

I peered through the window and glanced across the vast airfield beyond which was a network of highways filled with cars weaving up and down amid twinkling lights, which grew distant and small as the plane took off and gained altitude. I had prepared my mind for a seven-hour flight, my first time on a long flight like this. To kill the time and keep my mind occupied, I had brought my favorite novel to read. By 6:30 a.m. local time, the plane began its descent over Paris. The feeling of being in European airspace could not have been more exciting. I pulled up the window shade and peered through thin, gray clouds over which the plane navigated its way toward the landing strip. My eyes eagled Paris, vast and luminous. Fifteen minutes later, we were on the ground. Slowly, the plane made its way toward the terminal.

We soon emptied the plane and followed a straight line that channeled all passengers to French Immigration and Custom Services. I reached a French Immigration agent, a tall young man of mixed races and blue eyes. I handed him my passport. He scrutinized it and then looked at me.

"Monsieur, bienvenue en France," he said, laughing. *Welcome to France.* At last, I was officially in France. I walked behind some other passengers who seemed to have known their way out to the taxi stand.

Someone called my name. "Vinco!" I turned around. There, stood Frankel in a black jacket and blue jeans. We rushed toward each other for a long hug.

"Look at you, man!" He said. We were thrilled like children in a schoolyard.

"Look at you, too!" I reciprocated.

"Let's get out of here," he said, snatching the luggage from my hand as we crossed to where he had parked his car, near the curve of a dead-end street.

We got in the car and drove toward a stretch of highway leading to downtown Paris. My destination was Alsace, but to get there, I had to catch a train at *La Gare de l'Est*, the eastern train station, one of the busiest in Paris. My reservation was scheduled for three in the afternoon. So, I had a few hours to cruise around town, discovering Paris in autumn, gray and cold. After a short drive, we rolled into the tail end of the *Avenue de l'Opéra* where le Palais Garnier is located, and Frankel told me it was one of the city's most venerated monuments—an imposing opera house.

We veered toward the *Place de la Concorde* already swamped by fast-moving pedestrians, going up and down, weaving in a cold morning breeze, to their destinations.

"Let's go have breakfast, Vinco," Frankel said like a concerned big brother. He was older, and he had always played this role ever since we were teenagers back in Haiti.

"Can we have a late breakfast, instead? I ate something on the plane just before landing," I replied. I then glanced across the street, and my eyes caught an enchanted esplanade across which was a large open waterway. "Isn't it the Seine River we're looking at?"

"Yeah, man. Let's find a parking spot, so that we can go for a quick walk. We're here in the ninth district, the most famous for its many historical landmarks."

Luckily, we found a spot close by. In haste, we walked out and sauntered down toward the esplanade, a captivating boardwalk on the bank of the Seine River. Despite the chilly morning, we saw more than a dozen *Bateaux Mouches* downriver and myriad of tourists who flocked the southern station near the Eifel Tower, waiting to get on board for a riverboat ride and discover Paris in one of the most intimate and elegant ways. Mica came to mind.

"This would be a great site for a romantic promenade," I said, laughing.

"Wait until you find your girl. It would be the perfect place to rekindle that lost love," Frankel said, teasing me.

He stepped closer to the bank as one of the tour boats filled with tourists was sailing upriver. I wanted to follow him, but the chill had become unbearable—too cold, far colder than the Miami winter.

"I need a winter jacket," I said, shivering.

"You didn't know where you were coming, man? This is Paris, not the French Riviera."

"Oh, man. I should have bought one back in Miami."

"Let's go to FNAC. It's a major department store."

We rushed back into the car and drove down the *Avenue des Champs-Èlysées*, the famous boulevard framed by fancy stores and boutiques. By then, it was eight-thirty, and the atmosphere became rowdier. Halfway through, Frankel pulled to the side of the street and parked the car.

"This is FNAC, Vinco." We went in, and it did not take me long to find a good winter jacket made of faux fur.

"It feels very comfy inside, Frankel," I said, trying it on.

"You really need one like this, especially for Strasbourg, which is much colder than Paris," he chortled.

I paid for it. We went right back into the car and continued down the *Champs-Èlysées*, on through *Arc de Triomphe* and *Avenue des Grandes Armées*. I purposely avoided talking about Michaela, for I needed to enjoy this moment of Paris, and perhaps, I thought, it could be my only dazzling moment in France.

"I think I'm ready for that breakfast, Frankel."

"There's a little place, not far from here, where they serve tasty pastries."

"Let's go there, then."

Frankel drifted off the avenue, rolled into a narrow street whose name I could not remember, and parked behind a line of cars with frosted windows. We walked out and strolled down toward *Buffet Parisien*, a small diner painted in red. We went in. It was a two-storied buffet. A few customers were inside. A young woman in a white apron greeted us with a smile.

"*Vous désirez, messieurs?*" she asked. *What would you like, gentlemen?*

"I'll have a croissant and a *crème brûlée*," I replied, eyeing the food.

The young lady walked us to a corner table and seated us there. *Crème brûlée*, a delicious dessert with a rich custard base and a hardened top caramelized with a blow torch, had always been my favorite French dessert. It was a delicacy they used to serve at a French bakery in the city of North Miami. Mica and I ordered it each time we went there. That was enough to bring me back to reality. Frankel opted for the buffet. As soon as we were seated, he ran down for a tray and rushed to fill his plate with an untold number of French pastries—from macaroons, to financiers, to *pain au chocolat*, etc.

"You're going to choke yourself with food," I teased him.

"I can't resist," he laughed. "Vinco, I have gotten some information for you."

"Really? Did you talk to your friend from Alsace?" My eyes widened.

"No. I couldn't find him. But I did my own search. I went on the World Wide Web, and I typed the info you gave me. The child's name and his date of birth. I found an address and also found his mother's name: Michaela Monsalve, just as you told me."

My heart jumped. "*Merci beaucoup*," I said with an odd feeling of joy and anxiety. "Did you find a phone number associated with the address?"

"No. But I think that address should be a great point to begin the search, and if you're lucky enough, it might be the correct one."

He handed me the address and I glanced at it. Then, I pulled out of my wallet the address Pedro had given me to compare. They were different. Pedro also gave me a different phone number. A tinge of disappointment filled me.

"It doesn't mean neither of them is right. It means you have more options or more leads in the search." Frankel paused for a moment, pondering. "Let's call that number now," he suggested.

We rose from our seats and rushed to a public phone right outside the main entrance. Frankel dialed the number and passed the phone to me. It rang several times, but no one picked up. We tried again and again and again. Still, no one picked up. Frankel urged me to leave a message. I refused, thinking if the number was right and I left a message identifying myself, it could be counterproductive. I did not know if Michaela would ever want to talk to me. I came to France to find my son, and I did not want to jeopardize the search. I figured a surprise meeting would have more of a chance of success. Sadness now descended on my mind and heart and chased away all appetite for food.

"Vinco, don't worry. Be optimistic. Remember, you've come this far, and you have yet to reach Strasbourg. That means your official search has not yet begun. I feel I should go with you, but I just started a new job. We will communicate daily if not hourly. If necessary, I'll join you in Alsace this weekend. I'll be off."

"Thank you, big brother."

After breakfast, we spent the morning hours exploring Paris's chic neighborhoods, and grand boulevards. Then it was time to head for *La Gare de l'Est*. Within minutes, we were there. The eastern train station was a major hub for travelers going east and even to countries like Germany, Luxembourg, Belgium, and Switzerland. Understandably, that afternoon, the place was thronged with busy people going in and out of shops, boutiques, and restaurants to serve those waiting for the arrival of their trains. I checked out my ticket. My train was scheduled to arrive in ten minutes on platform nineteen.

"Call me when you get to the hotel," Frankel said.

I nodded in agreement. We then hugged goodbye. He left, and I walked toward the platform.

Chapter 28

The train was there, and passengers were boarding. I handed my ticket to a blonde woman in a cap and a blue jacket. She took it without looking at it and allowed me to get on. Although I was assigned to a specific seat in the center of the train, I was able to switch seats with an older woman who did not like to sit by the window. The train left exactly on time, just as an afternoon sun struggled to pierce the gray clouds on the horizon.

Soon, Paris was behind us as the train rolled into the countryside. I had brought my camera with me, and I used the moment to capture scenic landscapes, small towns, and villages fit for a postcard. About two hours later, the train reached *La Gare Centrale*, Strasbourg's railway station. Everyone walked out and left the platform. I felt cold, lost, and alone. I made my way toward the taxi stand. It was far smaller than the one near the mega railway station I had just left in Paris. A few cars stood by. A driver, a short man in an overcoat, walked up to me. He sensed I was a stranger.

"Vous allez où, monsieur?" Where are you going, sir?

I took out the address of my hotel and handed it to him. "Hotel D. Strasbourg on *Rue du Fossé des Treize*." He carefully read it and smiled.

"*Mais c'est pas trop loin d'ici*," he boasted with an air of confidence. *But it's not far from here.*

"*C'est combien cette course pour arriver à l'hôtel?* I asked. *How much does it cost to get to the hotel?*

"*C'est dix euros, monsieur*," he replied, opening the back door to let me in as I began to shiver in the cold. *It's ten euros.*

"*C'est pour la première fois que vous êtes ici à Strasbourg?*" *Is it your first time in Strasbourg?*

"*Oui. Monsieur.*" *Yes, sir.*

"*Alors, vous venez d'où?*" *So, where're you from?*

"Florida, USA."

"You'll love Strasbourg. It's sometimes referred to as Little Paris," he said in English.

"You speak English? That's nice," I said with a smile.

"Yes, sir. Most of the taxi drivers here understand English. Some of them speak it fluently," he said. A glow of pride lit up his face.

"Are you from here?" I asked. I was curious.

"Yes, I was born here. But my parents were from Morocco."

"So, you speak Arabic as well, right?"

"Yes, I do."

"Coming from Florida, how do you get to speak French so fluently?"

"I was born in Haiti."

"I see." While talking, we had arrived at the destination. "I told you it was close by."

I gave him fifteen euros. "I give you five euros as your tip."

"*Merci, monsieur!*" he said. He was very happy. *Thank you, sir.*

Before he left, I called to him. "Can you come to pick me up tomorrow morning around nine?"

"Of course. But where will we be going? Cruising around town?"

"No. I'm here on a special mission to find my son, who was born here, and I don't know my way around."

"*Avec plaisir, monsieur. Je serai là.*" *With pleasure. I'll be here.* He drove off and I went in.

#

A young man about my age greeted me at the concierge. "You've booked for two weeks monsieur."

"Yes."

He checked me in and handed me two electronic cards for my room. The first thing I did after dropping my luggage was to run to the shower to cleanse my exhausted body. By now, it was six p.m. and I was hungry, but I felt no strength to put food in my mouth, and when reality set in, realizing the purpose of my trip, all desire to eat had disappeared. I called Frankel to let him know that I was okay. I told him about my worries, for I dreaded the prospect of failing to locate Michaela and my son. A failed trip would almost mean losing any hope of ever meeting Michaela and my Junior or ever finding out what had happened to them.

As these thoughts raced through my tormented mind, I grabbed the telephone and dialed the number I had tried already in Paris. Still, no one picked up. I tried several times thereafter. Still, there was no answer. A long night awaited me. I realized I should have asked the taxi driver for his phone number. I became restless. I put on my clothes and ran down toward the concierge.

"Can you call a taxi for me?" I asked a young woman with hollow cheeks, dark hair, and thin eyebrows.

"Do you want the same gentleman who brought you here?" She asked with a captivating smile.

"That would be fantastic," I replied.

She made the request, and within minutes, the same gentleman arrived, and he was happy to meet me again. "I thought we had a deal for tomorrow?" He said.

"Yeah. I still need you for tomorrow, but now I have an urgent need to go to these addresses," I said, handing him a piece of paper that contained the two addresses.

He gave each of them a deep look. "I can take you to both. One is about fifteen minutes from here, somewhere in the European quarter. The other is a bit farther away in a village outside of town."

"Let's go to the closer one, then," I said.

We left the hotel and headed east, driving through Strasbourg's historic district packed with tourists mixed with local people going in and out of fancy stores, all in jolly moods, enjoying a moment in paradise despite the autumnal chill. It was mid-November, and no one could escape the Christmas carols.

"This is dazzling. What a beautiful site, a wonderful atmosphere!" I cried.

"*Oui, monsieur.* It's going to be like this until Christmas Day. This city has the most fascinating decorations in the country. Tourists from all over the world visit Strasbourg every year to enjoy this special Strasbourgish moment."

"Listen. I'm Yrvin. And you?"

"Ahmed."

"Ahmed, I would probably come back here sometime in the future."

"You won't regret it."

We rolled into an avenue called *Avenue de l'Europe* which led to the European Parliament. Before Ahmed pointed it out to me, I had already seen the signs and the flags of the countries that belonged to the European Union. However, instead of going straight to the direction of the building, Ahmed turned to the right and drove into a narrow street. Halfway down, he stopped in front of a townhouse.

"We have arrived," he said.

My heart sank. "Wait for me," I said, stepping out of the car. My legs buckled as I walked to the front porch. I rang the doorbell, and an older woman came up and opened the door.

"*Que désirez-vous, monsieur?*" she asked, looking perplexed. *What do you want, sir?*

"I'm here to see a lady named Michaela Monsalve."

The woman looked at me with such an unwelcoming stare as if trying to fend off an intruder. "*Il n'y a personne ici qui porte ce nom.*" *There's no one here by this name.* She stepped back and shut the door before I had a chance to ask further questions.

I went back to the car, a humiliated man ravaged by fear and apprehension. "I had a wrong address. Let's go back to the hotel," I said to Ahmed.

"How about the other address?"

"Let's wait for tomorrow. You say it's a bit far away."

He saw the disappointment on my face. "You were not sure about this address?"

"To tell you the truth, Ahmed, I'm not sure about the other address either," I said. I felt I had to tell him the truth. I needed his help.

"How so?"

"I'm here to try to meet my son I never had the chance to meet. He was born here. His mother and I were dating when she got pregnant in Florida. Her parents sent her away as a result. At the beginning, we kept our relationship despite the distance. But soon after the baby was born, she stopped calling me. I tried and tried to find out what had happened without success. I called her several times without any reply. Then, the phone number was no longer working. It's been almost six years."

"Do you have any piece of identification that could confirm you as the father?"

"No, but I remember the place and date of birth. He was born on October 17, 1987 at the maternity hospital on Rue Philippe Thys. He and I have the same name. He's Yrvin Junior."

"The hospital is not far from here. The boy should be six years old, now. Right?"

"Yes."

"While you were talking, I was thinking. Tomorrow at nine a.m., we'll go to the other address. If it's a wrong one, too, we'll try public records. I can see you would be a good father for your son. I myself didn't grow up with my dad, and I suffered from his absence—a lot."

Later in the room and alone, I lay in bed, feeling saddened by my failed attempt to find Michaela. I wanted to call Pedro, but the six-hour time difference made it impossible. My optimism had lowered; I started thinking maybe this was not going to be easy. However, I remained hopeful—I had to—hoping Wednesday might bring some luck in the search. After all, I had just arrived in the city. The prospect of not being able to father my son had deepened my pain.

The idea that Junior would never meet his father, would never know his uncles and aunts, countless cousins, and everything that made him a replica of his dad frightened me. My search on European soil must *not* be in vain, or else those wants that constitute the core component of human existence would be shrouded in Junior's mind like a mystery. I was thinking perhaps Michaela would at least tell him I did all I could to be involved in his life, but the tide that would send me to him never flowed my way. Feeling restless, I paced to the window. Outside, darkness had already engulfed Strasbourg. So, I paced back to bed, dwelling in a bittersweet dream, dreaming about my son, a prince attired in fine clothing, in the shelter and care of his dad.

I knew too well the infinite angst that seized upon the mind of a young man being raised in the absence of his father. I had lived it when Papa went to work in a foreign land. It was painful, but it was different. Papa had to make a necessary sacrifice to make sure his children would always be well-fed and sheltered. So, I had a reason to be hopeful of his return, and Manman always told me that Papa would someday come home, and he did. As for me, what would I say to Junior? Most importantly, what would he think of me?

"I have to find my son. No matter how long it takes," I muttered to myself.

I remembered what Mica told me shortly after Junior was born, and that he was a photocopy of his father, looking too much like him. His smile, his frown, even his bald forehead. I wished she did not say those words, which never stopped pounding my heart. Memory is *so* mysterious, boundless, powerful, and everlasting like a headstone in a loved one's graveyard. "I have to find my son," I kept on saying, to spare him from walking down that lone road, in search of his missing half, in search of his sense of whole. But here in this hotel room, in this Alsatian, autumnal night, alone and downhearted, I felt resolute in my quest to end Junior's lone road, to be the wellspring of the story of his life. As for Mica, I was ready to face the truth—whatever that truth was. The night was long and sleepless.

The next morning, Ahmed showed up on time, eager and ready to take me to that second address. Not knowing how long my day was going to be, I had to eat a small breakfast to keep me going.

"Bonjour Yrvin," Ahmed said with a confident smile.

"Bonjour, Ahmed."

"Are you ready?"

"I think I am, Ahmed, for anything the day has in store for me."

We hurried and got into the taxi, which was parked right across the street from the main entrance of the hotel. Then, we drove toward the historic district. It was colder and grayer than the day before, but the chill seemed to have done nothing to force people into hibernation. Strasbourg was fully awake. Folks were wrapped inside their winter coats, walking in gigantic strides, crisscrossing each other on sidewalks and the city's intersections, which were filled with cars waiting for the green light. On every street corner, *jongleurs* dressed in Santa outfits waited for their next chance to make some much-needed cash.

"Où est le vieux clochard du coin?" I asked with a repressed laugh. *Where's the old beggar from the street corner?*

"You're not going to find him today. Not until next year," Ahmed said with an explosion of laughter.

"Why? They've been rounded up and shipped somewhere else?"

"No. They've all become Papa Noel. Didn't you see them at every corner?"

"I did. And the Santa outfit will keep them warm. Strasbourg is such a cold place, Ahmed."

"This is the fall season. It's going to get colder next month. But we have snow tomorrow in the forecast. The first real one of the year."

"Wow! I never saw snow before. I'd better get my camera ready to take some souvenir pictures. I hope today will be our lucky one."

"Let's keep our fingers crossed. But I'm absolutely positive you'll meet your son if he and his mother still live in the city."

"That's reassuring, Ahmed."

"Yrvin, I don't think you would come this far if you weren't sure you could find your son. This is basically Day One. I'm with you until you find him."

While talking, we rolled into an area unique from what I had seen so far in Strasbourg. The street was made of cobblestones with canals and old half-timbered homes. I glanced through the car window, and my eyes caught a large terrace atop Barrage Vauban, which offered a panoramic view of that section of town. There were eateries everywhere, along with shops selling all Alsatian souvenirs such as teas, wine, and crockery.

"Where are we, now, Ahmed?"

"We're driving on Grande Rue, and this area is called La Petite France, a major hub for tourists as you can see. From your hotel, you can walk to this area. You'll enjoy it."

We now left town, taking Rue de Strasbourg, which then turned into a stretch of highway called Route Nationale. About fifteen minutes later, we rolled into a small community called Kilstett, just west of the Rhine River. Ahmed pulled the address out of his shirt pocket and took a frantic look at it. I remained tightlipped. My heart began to race. He pulled by the side of a street near several apartment complexes.

"Let's get out," he said.

I followed him toward one of the apartment buildings behind an iron gate.

"The first unit on the right is the place," he said, pointing it out.

He stepped back to let me go and knock. I rang the bell, but no one came to the door. I knocked again, and again. There was no response. Disappointed once more, we reclaimed the road back into town. From that point on, I felt I had hit a dead end.

"Ahmed, you said we can use public records to try to locate them?"

"I think you can," he replied. I could see the disappointment on his face. He sincerely wanted to help in the search.

"Before we do so, let me return to the hotel and make some phone calls. Meanwhile, you can go back to work. I'll call you later this afternoon."

"Sounds like a plan," he said.

Back at the hotel, I went up to my room, grabbed the phone, and called the same number I had been calling. It rang, but still no one picked it up. By now, it was close to midday in Strasbourg and six p.m. in Florida. I knew Pedro might be home. I called him, and Chen picked up.

"Hello, Chen," I said with a firm voice. I didn't want her to know of my worries in Strasbourg.

"Oh, Vinco! Glad to hear from *you*. We've been thinking about you, hoping you're successful in the search. Have you found your son?"

"Not yet. I've already used all the contact information I had. None of them worked. Where's Ped?"

"He's right here. Vinco, don't lose faith. I'm optimistic you'll find them." She passed the phone to Pedro.

"Vinco, I heard what you just told Chen. Don't feel bad. You got this far. Your sacrifice will bear the desirable results. Listen, call me in fifteen minutes. Let me make some phone calls."

Meanwhile, I came down to the hotel lobby where there was a snack bar. I figured I needed to eat something to hold me a bit. Behind the desk stood a black girl, and like all hotel employees, she looked quite fashionable in her hotel uniform, eager to throw that sincere smile to everyone who walked into the lobby. The minute I stepped out of the elevator, which was adjacent to the front desk, our eyes met, and her brilliant smile greeted me. I thought it would have been nice to ask her some questions about the city.

"Your name, mademoiselle?" I asked rather politely.

"Isabelle," she said. Her smile was welcoming. "Is it your first time in Strasbourg, monsieur?"

"My very first, Isabelle," I replied, edging closer to talk. The lobby was empty. "Do you have a map of the city? I need to learn how to navigate around the historic district."

"Sure." She stepped back and grabbed a booklet that had everything a visitor would need, including restaurants, bookstores, shopping centers, etc. She handed it to me. "What is your name, sir?" She asked with a curious stare.

"Yrvin."

"You're here for one week?"

"No, I plan on spending two weeks. I wish I could spend more time here. Strasbourg is worth exploring."

"Yes, it is. But two weeks is more than enough to move around town, to travel across the border into Germany, and to even visit other historical cities in Alsace."

"I'm not here as a tourist. I'm here on a mission to find my six-year-old son. I have never met him."

"What do you mean by being 'on a mission?' You don't know where he lives?"

"I'm afraid not. I came here with some contact information, but none of them proved to be right. So, my search has hit a wall. I figure getting to know Strasbourg more might help."

"I see. Knowing this city can certainly help." An old couple walked in. "I'll talk to you later."

"Do you know my room number?"

"I know. I'll call you."

I went back to my room and called Pedro. Fifteen minutes had already passed. "Man, the address I gave you should be it. A place called Kilstett, outside of Strasbourg."

"I was there earlier in the day with a taxi driver who knows the area very well, obviously. We knocked several times. No one came to the door."

"Vinco, go try again. I just got off the phone with one of Mica's cousins. He was one of the few people who had the address I gave you. Michaela wrote to him from that address. But that was three years ago. I'm thinking she may no longer live there, but that address should lead you to somewhere much closer to where Mica is if she still lives in Strasbourg."

"The taxi driver told me the same thing. That I must go back because the place did not look abandoned. Maybe people were at work."

"I'm praying for you, Vinco. I wanna see you happy again."

We chatted for another ten minutes and hung up. Pedro's voice was uplifting. A renewed optimism had taken control of my being. I noticed his voice sounded so distant, which made me realize I was indeed far from home, and perhaps the distance might have played a role in Michaela's change of heart. Strasbourg was certainly not Miami, subtropical and sunny with beautiful beaches. Here in this European city, gray and cold, I found myself in a strange urban environment in which people moved at a fast pace.

Chapter 29

By now, it was two p.m., and for the first time, hunger seized my stomach. I took the booklet Isabelle had given me and began flipping through the pages, looking for a restaurant not too far from the hotel. I zeroed in on La Marseillaise, a fifteen-minute walk away. I put on my jacket and scarf, closed the door behind me, and went down the elevator. On the way out, I waved to Isabelle. She waved back with a smile, still busy with folks checking in.

That afternoon, though still windy and cold, the sun had finally risen, and it was the perfect moment to walk down the *Centreville* of Strasbourg, which was light-laden with Christmas trees. I crossed the street, ambling past tree-lined promenades bejeweled by autumn gold as the wind blew fragrances of burning leaves. I then ventured along Canal du Faux-Rempart and on to Rue de la Nuée-Bleue, passing a myriad buildings of lush contrasting architecture, including French baroque, German Renaissance, and modern high rises—an aesthetic play in the theater of nature I could not ignore despite my painful longing. This autumnal scenery and its cold air reminded me of Paris along the banks of the Seine and its surrounding parks and gardens.

I soon reached a cobblestone street in which older folks walked their thick-furred hounds in the afternoon quietude amid the inclines of its architecture and its vibrant hues of fallen leaves. La Marseillaise stood where the street met Place Broglie, a historical venue fully alive as shoppers went to and from Marché de Noël, bags in hands. They quickened their steps against the backdrop of a stunning architectural décor, a blend of Alsatian half-timbered and baroque, which was not far from where Claude Joseph Rouget de Lisle sang France's national anthem, *Chant de Guerre pour l'Armée du Rhin* (now known as *La Marseillaise)*, for the first time in 1792. Not surprisingly, being located close to this historic site, the restaurant carried the perfect name.

I went in, and a slim young man in white and blue attire greeted me. He spoke perfect English. "Party of one?" He asked.

"Yes."

"Follow me." I trailed him down toward a table near the window. There, he seated me. "Your server comes shortly," he added and left.

Through the window, I watched people going up and down the street, some hands folded inside their jacket pockets to keep warm from the cold. I looked for Michaela in the face of every young woman who walked by. Soon, I saw a young couple with a mixed-race boy, sauntering down and quickening their speed. My heart leaped. I rose from my seat and rushed outside to the blazing eyes of the server coming my way and the young man behind the welcoming stand.

"I'll be *right* back!" I yelled before she had a chance to ask any questions. By the time I reached the pavement, they were already a half block away. "*Mica!*" I screamed.

The couple and the boy turned around and saw me coming. When I realized I had the wrong person, I walked past by them, still crying Mica. They looked at me as if I was crazy.

"*Il est cinglé, quoi?*" Said the man as his wife and son stared at me. *Is he crazy or what?*

I returned to the restaurant a man with a tormented mind. I reclaimed my seat, looking at the menu. La Marseillaise was a French bistro, which suited me well.

"We have a very selective menu. What would you like?" The server asked, ready to write the order. She was an Asian woman, blue-eyed and frizzy-haired, who spoke with a strange feminine voice, deep from the base of her throat.

"I'll go for a *sandwich de thon* with onion, lettuce, and tomatoes."

"And what would like to drink, sir?"

"*Du pamplemousse pressé* (fresh-squeezed grapefruit) with a couple of drops of vanilla extract."

"We don't have extract. We do have essence of vanilla. Will that work for you?"

"That will be fine."

A few minutes later, the food came. I struggled to take a few bites, knowing I needed to eat to keep going. Halfway through the food, however, I stopped and I began to ponder my next move. "I must find my son no matter how long it takes," I said to myself. The more I thought about my predicament, the angrier I became. Humans are selfish beings, as David Goldstein, the old Jewish rabbi near my home, used to say.

I started to wonder how I would react when I came face to face with Michaela. Depriving someone of his son, his most prized possession, is the cruelest blow one can inflict upon the heart of a loved one. But beyond the search for my son stood my love for Mica. My anger boiled over precisely because I continued to love her. So, the search for Junior was also the search for a lost love, and going back home without finding them would undoubtedly leave beneath the fibers of my heart an everlasting anger, an unremovable stain of anguish that I wanted to avoid at any cost. I stood up from my table, paid for the food, and left.

When I returned to the hotel, Isabelle was still there. She was alone behind the reception desk. I walked straight to her.

She noticed how I struggled to put forth a smile. "The cold has taken away the joy, huh?"

"You're right, Isabelle. But it's not just the cold."

"The search, too. I know. By the way, I just got off the phone with my brother. I asked him if he knew of any Dominican or Hispanic community in Strasbourg. He said no."

"Really?"

"Yes. I know there's a large North African, mainly Arab, community here."

"You were born here?"

"Yes, but my parents were from Cape Verde."

"So, you're familiar with zouk and kizomba?"

"I love konpa, too. They're my favorite music."

"Listen, I'm going to my room. I have to think about my next move."

"Monsieur Yrvin, do you still have the addresses with you?"

"Yes, I do."

"I can go with you if you don't mind. I get off work in fifteen minutes."

"Thank you so much, Isabelle. One of the addresses is too far. It's in Kilstett."

"Kilstett? I never heard of that place."

"It's a small village outside of town. But the other one is not far from here. It's in the European quarter."

"Very good. I'll call you to come down when I'm ready to leave."

I went up thinking Isabelle might be a Good Samaritan sent from God to help me find Junior and his mother. A few minutes later, she called me.

"I'm ready. Meet me at the corner by the courthouse."

"Okay."

I rushed down and met her standing at the edge of the streets, shivering. "My brother is coming to pick us up," she said, laughing.

"This is a bone-cracking chill," I said with a chortle. "But, Isabelle, you're a *Strasbourgeoise*. For me, it feels like living in the North Pole."

She laughed. "My brother should be here any minute. I gave him the address. He said he knows exactly where it is. It's not far from the European Parliament building."

She was a pretty girl who reminded me of Régine because of her smile and her fine diction in expressing her carefully worded sentences.

"There he comes," she said, waving at her brother so that he could see us as he maneuvered his car to get to us.

We ran to him as he pulled by the side of the road and pushed the door open, and Isabelle and I waltzed in. I knew I was taking a risk by getting in the car of people I barely knew. However, I knew I came to Strasbourg for a noble cause, and life itself is about taking risks.

"Jean-Michel, this is Monsieur Yrvin Lacroix I told you about."

"Nice to meet you, Monsieur Jean-Michel. I hope I'm not interrupting your schedule on such a busy Wednesday night."

"No. Not at all. It's a pleasure to help."

As we drove through the busy streets, I could remember the areas Ahmed and I drove through the day before. I remained tightlipped, ravaged by anxiety.

"Wish me good luck," I said when we reached the townhouse's front door.

But Isabelle walked out with me. "Let me knock," she said.

"Sure," I said, giving way for her to walk to the front steps and knock. She rang the bell, and a young woman this time walked to the door.

"I'm here to see Michaela and her son Junior," Isabelle said with a smile.

"No. Mademoiselle, there's no one here by those names. Sorry." She shut the door.

"It was the same thing as last night," I said, feeling devasted.

"I would suggest, Yrvin, that you go back to the other address again tomorrow. I can take you."

"Don't worry, Jean-Michel. I've hired a taxi driver. I'll ask him to take me back there again tomorrow."

"Very good. If that attempt also fails, we'll try public records."

"It was the same thing my driver told me this morning."

They drove me back to the hotel, a disappointed man. "*Du courage*, Yrvin," Isabelle said. "I work tomorrow. If you need anything, let me know." *Be strong.*

"I will." They drove off, and I went up to my room, bracing for another sleepless night.

Indeed, the night was long and painful. In the morning, I called Ahmed and asked him to take me back to that village again. However, we did not get there until it was almost midday. Just as the day before, Ahmed stepped back and let me knock. After the third ring, I saw a young lady peering through the front window. When our eyes met, she stepped away from the window and pulled the curtain down. I was devastated. I turned around and looked at Ahmed, whose disappointment on his face could not be hidden. As we veered to head toward the car, the voice of a woman called to us.

"Que voulez-vous, messieurs?" asked an elderly woman in a white silk dress. *What do you need, gentlemen?*

We went back to speak to the woman. "My name is Yrvin Lacroix, and I'm looking for a young woman named Michaela and her son Junior."

"You're looking for *who?*"

"Michaela Monsalve and her son, Junior. I was given this address and was told they live here."

The woman became pensive. She called to the girl we had just seen standing by the window. She rushed to the front and came to stand behind the old woman. They said something in a language I could not understand. It sounded like German. Soon, the old woman became hesitant and aloof.

"I don't know such person," she said and shut the door.

I wanted to cry as I hit my head against the door. I sensed they knew something. "Yrvin, they know her. I heard them say that in Alsatian, a local Germanic language."

"But you don't speak that language. Do you?"

"No, I don't. But I understand some words, and I could hear the young lady say your son's mother has a cousin who works downtown."

"Wait, Ahmed. Let me go back." I pushed open the car door and headed back to the apartment front door. I knocked, and the young woman walked out.

"Monsieur, la personne que vous recherchez n'habite plus ici," she said, looking sideways. *The person you're looking for no longer lives here.*

"Do you know where she now lives? Please, mademoiselle. *Aidez-moi. Je viens de loin*," I said, begging her. *Help me. I came from far away.*

"She lived here for two years. She rented a room. She and her handsome boy named Junior, who so much looked like you. A year ago, she found a place closer to her job, and she moved out."

"Where does she work? Do you know?"

"No, I don't. But it's somewhere inside the European Union building."

I called to Ahmed, who rushed to join me. "This young lady just told me Michaela works inside the European Union building," I said in a frenzied movement.

"She has a cousin who is my friend. We both work for the same company."

"You mean Josefina?"

"*Oui*! Do you know her?"

"Yes. I met her in Miami six years ago."

"What's the name of the company you two work for?" Ahmed asked, hungry for an answer.

"Les Galeries Lafayette. It's on Rue du Vingt-deux Novembre, in the heart of downtown, Strasbourg, Grand-Est. You can't miss it."

"Don't worry. I know every inch of Strasbourg."

"And your name is Vinco?" The young lady asked.

"Yes."

"Josefina used to tell me stories about you and Michaela."

"Your name, mademoiselle?"

"Martine. Let me call my job to see if she's there."

Martine got on the phone and made the call as I held my breath. She spoke to someone and asked the person to go get Josefina on the phone. In that moment of silence, I asked the young lady to let me speak to Josefina when she came.

"Of course," she replied, seeming relieved now and honestly wanting to help. A minute later, Josefina came to the phone.

"Dear friend, with me is an important person who urgently wants to speak to you," Martine said with shaking hands, knowing the intensity of the moment.

"Martine. Don't tell me you call me to let me know that loser Pierre-Henri wants to talk to me. I'm extremely busy. You know that." Her voice through the phone was loud enough to be heard from where I stood.

Martine then passed me the phone. "Tell her," she said.

"No. It's not loser Henri. It's Yrvin, Vinco I mean."

"Junior's dad?"

"Yes. I'm in town in search of Michaela and Junior."

"Am I in a dream?"

"No. I'm real, still living despite the odds. Josefina, I'm coming to see you now."

"Yes, yes, yes!"

I passed the phone back to Martine, hugged her goodbye, and Ahmed and I returned to the car and sped away under the blazing eyes of the young lady watching us from her front porch, feeling proud for having made an act of kindness and generosity.

"Yrvin, I told you today was going to be different in the search."

Without replying, I kept touching the car to make sure I wasn't in a wild dream. We ran into expected traffic when we reached downtown, and I became restless.

"How far are we from Les Galeries Lafayette?"

Ahmed looked at me and laughed. "Relax, we're just blocks away."

Chapter 30

Soon, traffic eased up and Ahmed drove on. After two intersections, we ran into a very busy parking lot. It was wide and filled with cars coming and going. Ahmed found a spot just off the street, across which was a sign for Les Galeries Lafayette. Ahmed walked with me to the main entrance. In the middle of a slew of shoppers, we strolled in with restless glances, searching for Josefina. All of a sudden, a voice wailed from behind.

"Vinco!"

We turned around. There was Josefina in a winter coat and boots, arms spread like a golden eagle, advancing toward me. She was jubilant. I ran toward her, and when we met, we fell into each other's arms. We went for a long hug while shedding tears, but tears of joy.

"You've changed in physical appearance, Vinco. You look well-built, but still quite handsome," she said, grabbing my hand.

"You now look like a mature young woman, pretty and stylish. I would have missed you if you didn't call." I presented Ahmed to her. "He's my driver who has been doing all he could to make this moment possible."

"Thank you, sir. You don't know what you've just done for us. My cousin's ordeal is finally coming to an end."

"I'm glad to help," Ahmed replied. "By the way, do you have a car, mademoiselle?"

"No, I don't, but you can leave us. I'm not going back to work."

"Yrvin, you don't need to pay me. It's been a pleasure to meet you. I'm happy for you."

"No, man. I can't do that." I pulled out my wallet and retrieved two hundred euros and handed the money to him. "You're such a Good Samaritan!" I said, laughing. With reluctance, he took the money.

"Call me, if you need me, Yrvin."

"I will."

Ahmed left us on the step of the store and disappeared amid myriad shoppers perambulating up and down the busy street.

"Where's Mica, now?" I said, shaking.

"She's at work."

"And Junior?"

"At school."

"Josefina, I wanna see them, now!"

"Not yet, Vinco. We have to plan this. Vinco, how did you get to find Martine's address?"

"A good friend back home helped me."

"Wow! Let's cross the street. There's a pastry shop on the corner. Let's go there." She kept looking at me with a disbelieving stare.

In a few long strides, we reached the pastry shop. Like the rest of the businesses, the place was packed and rowdy. We went in and claimed a remote spot, away from the commotion.

"What do you mean we have to plan this? Michaela is now married?"

"No, no. She's been a different person, fighting anxiety and depression. She's completely withdrawn from any kind of social life. She only lives for Junior."

"She still lives with your parents?"

"No. She moved out a year after Junior was born."

"To go where?"

"She'd found a job, working as an interpreter at the European Union building. So, she'd decided that it was time to live on her own with Junior."

"Did you ever hear her talking about going back home?"

"Yes. But she said she knew you would never forgive her for what she did. And every time I raised the issue with her, she would cry. And when Junior asks for his father, she simply says, 'He will come for us. I don't know when. But he will.'"

"And what did your parents say when she moved out?"

"She was an adult. There wasn't much they could do to stop her. Besides, my parents felt so guilty for going along with her parents to send her here. In some ways, they bear responsibility for Mica's sadness and depression. She goes to work and comes home, taking care of Junior. The rest of the time, she spends thinking of you and crying."

"Oh, gosh!" I was in tears. "Does she keep in close contact with her parents back home?"

"No. She refuses to talk to them, saying they're the root cause of her suffering."

"Let's go find her, *now.*"

"I know where she works, but I don't know her precise office. We'll have to wait until three p.m. when she gets off to go get Junior from school."

"I know you're hungry. Why don't you order something?"

"I don't think I can put food in my mouth, right now. The joy has chased away my appetite."

"How about some hot tea? It's cold outside."

"That's fine. Let's order two cups."

She called to one of the servers, a young woman about Josefina's age. "What would you like?" She asked, pen and paper in hand.

"Two cups of tea."

"Which one?"

"Would green tea be fine, Josefina?"

"Yes."

The waitress left with the order. "Tell me, Vinco. What have you been doing?"

"I graduated with a degree in software engineering, and I now work as a director at a software engineering firm in Miami."

"Wow! I knew you were smart."

"But despite all that I have accomplished in my life, nothing can bring back the happiness I lost the day Mica left me to come here. I've never been happy since then. But few people knew of my ordeal after all these years. I worked hard to move on with my life, but I couldn't."

"You've never tried to find someone?"

"When it became clear to me that Michaela would not come home as promised, I tried to make some sense of my life. But I failed because my heart only beats for two people: Mica and Junior. Remember what she told me in the van?"

"I remember. That she was going to return the next year. After Junior, she tried hard to go back, but my parents opposed the idea and alerted her parents, especially her mother. So, they called her and warned her of the consequences. So, Mica got scared."

"Did they ever say what the consequences would be?"

"They probably did, but Mica never told me."

I figured Michaela did not share everything we had planned for the return. So, I refrained from telling her. The waitress came back with the tea. After a couple sips, I stopped.

"Josefina, take me to Junior's school, and we can wait for Michaela there."

"Vinco, I don't know what his reaction will be."

"I know. He will be in shock, and no matter where it happens, Junior will be in *shock*. Perhaps, when he sees you with me, the shock might be lower."

"You're right. Let's go."

We left the crowded pastry shop and headed toward a tram station. With a firm grip, I held her hand. At last, I was on a path that was leading me to Junior.

"Am I in a dream?" I muttered to myself. Then, "So, Josefina. You're still at school, right?"

"I'm a law student at the University of Strasbourg."

"Very good. I'm proud of you."

"Thank you."

"No boyfriend yet?"

"Not now. I had a couple of failed experiences."

"And that Pierre-Henri you were talking about with Martine?"

"He's a loser who likes me. Remember. I'm Michaela's cousin. I don't fall for losers." She laughed.

While talking, we reached the stop where we had to get off the tram. From the tram's stop, we walked two blocks to an elementary school buried behind some giant trees on a dead-end street. By now, it was early afternoon, and I felt I was living a historic moment of my life. After years of living in agonizing solitude, at last, I was going to get the chance to hug my son. It was a feeling I could not describe.

To appease my fear and regain self-control, I held Josefina's hand firmer amid the autumnal chill of Strasbourg. We walked in silence over dry leaves, passing through a line of birch trees with naked branches to reach a walkway leading to the main entrance. Despite the cold, droplets of sweat poured off my face. I did not know how my son was going to view me. He was six years old and maybe had grown prematurely, perhaps spending time, questioning the facts of life.

"I used to come in with Michaela, picking up Junior," Josefina said, trying to lower my anxiety. We went in and strolled up to the front desk.

"*Puis-je vous aider?*" Asked a green-eyed lady in a dark suit. *May I help you?*

"*Je suis venu voir mon fils,*" I replied, struggling to keep a firm demeanor. *I'm here to see my son.*

"*Vous êtes venus chercher votre fils, vous voulez dire?*" the woman asked, taking a frantic look at me as if scrutinizing me. *You mean you come to pick up your son?*

Josefina intervened. "He's from America, and he's eager to see his son he hasn't seen since he was born."

"What is the name of your son?"

"Yrvin Junior."

She looked in the computer. "You mean Yrvin Lacroix Junior?"

"Yes."

From the intercom, she called for Junior to come to the front office. I held onto Josefina. The next few seconds were crucial. Suddenly, a boy wearing blue trousers and a fur jacket over a white shirt trod up to us, holding his little backpack in one hand. Instantly I said to myself that Michaela was right. He truly shared my features. He was fairer in complexion, dark-haired but wavier, and like me, he had a dark spot on the left side of his little nose. He knew Josefina, and he seemed to like his cousin. In a few small steps, he strolled up to her, weaving in a world of innocence.

"*Maman ne vient pas aujourd'hui?*" he asked Josefina while paying little attention to my presence. *My mom won't pick me up today?*

"Yes, but Papa is here first," Josefina said with a reassuring smile.

He raised his head and looked at me. I was hesitant to move and hug him for fear of rejection. "*Vous êtes mon père?*" *Are you my father?*

"*Oui, c'est moi, Junior. C'est Papa.*" *Yes, it's me, Junior. It's Dad.*

"*C'est pas vrai. Vous n'êtes pas mon père. Mon papa vit en Amérique.*" *That's not true. You're not my father. My dad lives in America.*

"*Parle-lui en anglais. Maman luit parle toujours en anglais,*" Josefina said. *Speak to him in English. His mother always speaks to him in English.*

"It's me, Junior. Your dad. I couldn't come to see you all these years. Now, I can." We switched to English.

"I don't believe you. I don't believe you. Mom didn't tell me. I wait every day for Papa, every day, every night. Mom cries all the time." He began to cry.

"I'm here, now, son. I promise I'll never leave you." I opened my arms, trying to hug him, but he refused.

"I don't know you," he said. He was emphatic.

"Junior, it's true. It's your dad. He came yesterday, looking for you and Mom," Josefina intervened again as the woman behind the front desk watched with blazing eyes.

With some hesitance, he then let me hold his hand. "It's okay, son. I will always be by your side from now on." I held him firmer now, stroking his wavy hair.

"Josefina, can you ask the lady at the front desk to call Mica?"

"I already did. And she's on her way," the lady said.

"Did you tell her who is here?" Josefina asked.

"Yes, I did."

Junior had now gone quiet. He knew Mom was on her way. He kept looking at me as if trying to discover himself through the features of a man, a father about whom his mom talked all the time. Now that we were speaking in English, he seemed to begin to see some frankness in my fatherly words of affection.

"How are you doing in school?"

"Fine."

"Do you like your teachers?"

"Yes."

He was not ready to exchange words with me, and his mono-syllabic replies suited me well. I knew he was in shock. Josefina drifted away and sauntered up to the main entrance, eyeing the porch to catch a glimpse of Mica. Junior and I paced to the corner and sat side by side in the reception area. Through a window, I watched Josefina, whose eyes were fixed on the porch. Soon, she saw Michaela. She pushed the door and ran outside. Junior and I rose from our seats, stepped out of the reception room, and stood in the middle of the vast empty office hall. The green-eyed woman behind the desk was on the phone but made an abrupt stop and hung up. From her seat, she watched with glaring eyes.

Michaela walked in unsteady steps, moving toward the door. I held Junior's hand and walked closer to the door. Through the glass window, I saw her standing midway talking with Josefina, who held her hand, exchanging words I could not discern. A red shawl was wrapped around her neck. A pair of golden hoop earrings adorned her still flawless, oval face. She wore a winter coat and a pair of blue jeans tucked inside shiny boots. Then, Josefina let go of her hand and stood there watching Mica, golden hair floating in the crisp air, as she made her final steps toward me.

She pulled the door and ran toward us, eyes welled with tears. Junior ran toward her and buried his face in Mommy's coat. I stood there almost motionless, frozen in place, showing no emotion.

"*Vinco!*" She cried in a high-pitched voice. She dropped her purse under the weight of her emotion and spread her arms to hug me when she reached me. I avoided her embrace.

"I'm sorry, Vinco, for all the pain I've caused."

"What *for*? You could have done otherwise. I'm here to show you that I'm not as selfish as you. I'm here to tell you there wasn't much you could do to keep me out of my son's life. *Nothing*."

"Oh, Vinco, oh, Vinco."

"*Don't* Vinco me. For almost six years I waited in vain for a glimpse of my son, for a word from you, waiting to relive the love we once shared, to be there for us, to shelter my son from this dangerous and cruel world. In vain, I waited, like a hopeless beggar who lives in a dark alley with no end. When your phone went silent, I tried and tried and tried without success to reach you. Denying a father the right to raise his son is the greatest pain one can inflict upon his heart. It is also the greatest misfortune to befall a child. Look at Junior. *Look* at him. *Look!* He doesn't even see me as his dad. I'm a stranger to him. How does it make you feel? I can see the pain in his eyes when I hold his hand. I can see how he struggles to rest his hand in mine, the man who claims to be his father. Isn't he right? *Isn't* he? Until now, he knew he was fatherless." My eyes stung as I glared at her.

"Oh, Vinco, I always talk to him about you, about us."

"What could that do for Junior, who needs his dad at a very critical stage in his young life? Michela, there isn't anything you can say to justify your action, your reckless action."

"Vinco, I think of you day and night."

"But I was a phone call away."

"I was too ashamed to call you."

"Too ashamed to pick up the phone to call the man you once said you were born to love. Is that *right*? Meanwhile, I was left alone to wallow in a hellish world of solitude, in a web of sleepless nights, of hazy days, and of romantic backstabbing."

"What do you mean by 'romantic backstabbing'? I never betrayed you." She had gone subdued and seemed unable to utter another word. Her misty eyes turned to an avalanche of tears.

Junior stepped in and stood between us, holding both of our hands. "Papa, don't be upset," he said in a soft and innocent voice.

"I think we must go before nosy people start pouring in," Josefina said.

Michaela went over to the front desk and signed Junior out. Although she did not speak English, the woman behind the desk understood the story.

"Go in peace my children," she said. "Hot heads can't raise a child. Cool heads can. Remember this," she said in French as we were leaving.

Chapter 31

It was colder outside than when we entered the school. "How far is the home?" I asked.

"Not far. It's at the turn of the street," Michaela said, still shaking.

I held Junior's hand as if trying to make up for six years of absence in one short instant. He seemed to understand. He leaned on me as we walked in silence. When we reached the place, it was the same place Ahmed and Isabelle took me before. I said nothing. Michaela lived in a studio apartment tied to the main house. It was well furnished, including a small eating table and a small kitchen. It felt warm inside. I took off my overcoat and handed it to her. She hung it in a winter closet, along with hers and Junior's. Josefina did not want to take hers off. She was leaving.

"Vinco, you're not hungry?" Michaela asked, hoping I'd say yes.

"No, I'm not. And you?"

"No, but Junior is."

"No, I'm not, Mommy."

"Vinco, what hotel are you staying at?"

"Hotel D, near the historic district."

"I know. It's on Rue du Fossé des Treize near the courthouse," Josefina said. "Look at you three, *une petite famille si mignonne*," she said, smiling. *A beautiful little family.*

"Me, too. I know where Hotel D is. It's a bit far from here," Michaela said. She seemed to want to stall me without begging me to stay.

"I'll sleep here then."

"Vinco, where did you think you were going?"

"What about Josefina?"

"Don't worry. I'm a *Strasbourgeoise*. This is my city. I have to get going."

"Not yet, walleyed girl."

She laughed. I walked her to the front door. I pulled out my wallet and gave her two hundred-euro bills. "Go get some food," I said, poking her cheek.

Before she opened the door, Mica called to her. "Please, don't tell anyone Vinco is here. I wanna be the one to tell them. I'll ask Vinco if he wants to visit them this weekend," she told Josefina.

"I know the story, remember? How could I do that?" She laughed again, hugged me goodbye and left.

"I feel sorry for her, walking in that cold," I said.

Now, just the three of us were in the room. Junior could not keep his little shining black eyes off me. He was still trying to make sense of this dramatic turn of events in his life. "Mommy, is it true you could call Papa and you did not?"

"I could call him, but it was not easy for me to do it."

"Why wasn't it easy, Mica?" I said. "You owe your son an honest explanation. Tell him why you deprived him of six years in his father's life. Tell him."

"I'm sorry. I thought you were going to be very angry once I told you I could not come."

"But in essence you did. You found all kinds of excuses, using false pretexts about learning French, finding a part-time job... And when the lies became fruitless, you stopped all contact with me. I went to bed every night alone and worried, not knowing how you and Junior were surviving. For six years, I lived with an unbearable torment, working hard to keep my sanity, to go on."

She came and sat next to me at the edge of the bed. Her eyes turned red, filled with remorse. "Vinco, you're right. There's nothing I can say to justify my action. Remember at the maternity hospital when I told you my uncle never came to visit me?"

"Yes."

"Well, when I came home, he transferred me with the baby to a small room, and life was precarious at best. So, I told him I was going to Miami to live with you. He and his wife were furious. I told him I'd always believed it takes two parents to raise a child, and raising a child is a lot of responsibility that I did not wish to delegate to anyone. He listened and then called my parents shortly thereafter, telling them of my intentions. Within minutes, my mother called me. She threatened to make me pay if I went back to Florida with a child. So, I felt trapped, like a caged bird. I thought of sharing the ordeal with you, but I knew you weren't going to believe me. I could have asked you to send me plane tickets, but I didn't know how and where to go get them and then travel to Paris to board a plane. I felt hopeless. As days went by, I figured you'd moved on with your life and found someone else. So, I'd resigned to raise Junior on my own. For years I suffered from depression and anxiety. I used to cry in front of Junior, but I had to stop doing so because the last time he watched me crying, he asked too many questions." Tears streamed down her cheeks.

"Mica, I already knew your parents' intentions, loaded with prejudice. It bothered me at first, not because of what they did, but because of your inability to stand up for me, for Junior, and for our future in wedlock. I could not believe you accepted to be bundled out of your parents' home and shipped across the Atlantic because you got pregnant by the boy you were dating."

"They kept saying they had to do it out of love, and I felt guilty for betraying their choice in me."

"They had to do it because they loved you? It's hard to believe your folks honestly loved you. If they did, then we need to redefine the meaning of love. You don't throw away what you love. You cherish and preserve it. In your case, you had become an embarrassment to the family, worse than your sister Gabriela, who used to have a new boyfriend every six months, as you yourself told me."

"Vinco, it took me a while to understand my parents' selfishness. When I finally did, I was able to move out of my uncle's home with Junior. I haven't spoken to them in three years. I live because of Junior and because of the hope I'll be able to take him to you someday, even if you had moved on with your life. As you can see, Vinco, I never mistreated your son, our son. I watched him grow before my eyes, looking more like you every day, a constant reminder he is the fruit of our love."

"Remember what you told me at the library?"

"We said so many things in the library. Which one are you referring to?"

"That you came to this earth to love one man, and that man was me."

"And I'm still committed to this vow. I never loved anyone. I could not love anyone. I walked through life unable to see any other man. No other man has ever touched me."

"Do you mean no man has ever approached you?"

"Yes, men did, but I always use my stare as a repellant. And they flee like spooked rats in the middle of the night." She paused for a moment, and then looked at me straight in the eyes. "And you, you've never met anyone?"

"I have, and I even worked hard to move on with my life. But I could not. I simply could not marry any other woman once I knew you and Junior were out there somewhere. People thought I was crazy. I dated a girl in an effort to bring some sense to my life. But she walked away, saying she will never earn my heart, which belongs to someone else. People thought I was naïve to still nurture a hope that somehow the mother of my son, who turned her back on me long ago, would still be waiting on the other end of the road. I knew otherwise, however. I knew too well what they did not know, that you were a person with such a weak personality."

"Even Nana and Pedro thought so?"

"No, my sister still believed in you and was afraid something terrible had happened to you and Junior. Pedro was skeptical, but still hopeful. However, he said he would not have waited all these years before going on this mission to find out what had happened. In fact, he was overjoyed when I told him I bought plane tickets to go on a search for you. Ronel, Chantale, and even Laurette, the girl who never liked you, all are now praying for me to find you, including a young lady at work with whom I share my ordeals every day."

"Do you still work at that data-entry job?"

"No. I worked there two years while I was in graduate school. But after graduation, I found a job at a software engineering firm in Miami where I've been working ever since. Now, I'm the project manager for the firm."

"I'm happy for you, Vinco."

"For *us*, now. And you? I know you work in the European Parliament building. What do you do there?"

"I work for the Irish mission as an interpreter and secretary."

"Every day I go to work, thinking of you, Mica. Sometimes, I think of buying a home. Then I choose not to, for I wouldn't want to live in a big home alone. What I did was set up a fund for Junior and hope that someday he would inherit my savings if something were to happen to me. There are days it is harder to sustain the pain, like when I see my coworkers bringing their children, especially on Fridays, walking past me, all in jolly moods. I think of you, of Junior. My personal secretary, who prays every day for you and me to be reunited, has to come to comfort me, telling jokes to make me laugh. And every time I think of you, thinking how weak you were, unable to stand up for us, Junior and I, a rage seized up my mind."

"*Mi amor*, I'm sorry. Now that you've found me, don't leave me. Don't leave us. Your strong character will make up for my weakness. I'm sure you didn't come this far just to see how your son and I were doing. *Mi amor*, I need to reclaim my life the way we've always wanted. You don't have to believe all my excuses. If your heart still has a place for me, hold me. When I needed you, I had to close my eyes and plunge into dreams I wished would never end. That was how I have been satisfying my sexual needs." She lowered her voice so Junior, who was falling asleep in my lap, would not hear.

"And you never went back to school as you told me?"

She turned her face sideways. "I could not. I had to find work wherever I could to support myself and Junior."

I did not force her on that. She was still young. Junior had fallen asleep like a boy ravaged by fatigue after a long voyage. At last, he had found the other half of him that was missing.

"I have to wake him up. In the winter, it's always a fight to get him to shower after school."

"Let him take a nap. It's still early."

Now that the cloud of uncertainty was behind us, it was time to make up for lost time. I was hungry for food all of a sudden. "You know, *amorecita?*" That word appeared to warm her heart.

"*Di me, amorecito.*" *Tell me, my love.*

"Now, I'm hungry."

"I have food in the fridge. Rice and beans I cooked yesterday."

"That's too heavy. I need something light."

"I can make rice pudding for the three of us."

"That's fine. Do you speak Spanish with Junior?"

"Not really. But he knows some Spanish. When I was at my uncle's, they used to speak with him in Spanish. And sometimes, we exchange words in Spanish enough to make sure he can survive in it. But I focus more on English. So, we speak Frenglish in the house."

She smiled and leaned her head on me, like she was seeking a comfort she knew only *I* could provide. She took off her boots and now lay in bed, resting her head on my chest, letting her long golden tresses fall on me. A few minutes later, she got up and went straight to her small kitchen to make rice pudding. I joined her, leaving Junior in bed, in his deep slumber. Watching her, alive and eager to make supper for us, thawed my heart. She moved back and forth with grace; with the same elegance and agility I had known her for.

I've found my wife, I said to myself.

"Vinco, how's Pedro doing?"

"Very well. He married his college sweetheart, a Chinese girl named Chen. They have a boy named Charlito. Every time I go to see them, I always leave with mixed feelings, thinking of you and Junior. And I could see Junior playing with Charlito."

"Where does he work?"

"He works for the city of Miami as a civil engineer."

"Good for him. And I'm surprised he's a married man, now. I thought he was a player. I used to see both him and that Chinese girl kissing behind the library."

"Just like you and I." She laughed.

"And Ronel?"

"He's still the eternal player. He has yet to settle down with a girl. I don't think he ever will. But he asks for you all the time."

"Really? He was such a player." She burst out laughing.

"Mica," I said, my voice went coy.

At the coyness in my voice, she turned around to face me. "Shhh. Junior is…"

"I can see, Mica. But…." I said with almost muted lips.

"You didn't change. You never will." She smiled. Her voice lowered.

In bed, Junior moved and stretched as if he was about to wake up; and that brought us back to reality. I changed both demeanor and conversation.

"I need to take a shower, Mica, but I have nothing to put on afterward."

"Go take your shower. I have a robe you can put on." She then went to her closet and grabbed a brown robe and handed it to me before I stepped into the bathroom and got undressed.

Later, after we all took a shower, we sat at the table, eating rice pudding.

"Mica, can you call in sick tomorrow morning?" I said, hoping she would say "yes."

"I was thinking about it, Vinco. Of course, I can."

"Thank you, Mica," I said with a smile. "After we drop Junior at school, we'll have to go to the hotel. I'm looking forward to tomorrow, our first full day in more than six years, Mica."

"Six years, seven months, and eighteen days, Vinco," she said, letting out a heavy sigh.

"Plus twelve hours, thirty-five minutes, and fifty seconds. I was also counting, Mica."

Nana soon came to my mind. She was right when she kept on insisting my love for Mica would never die, and that the moment we met it would ignite again. There at that little table, I kept looking at both my son and Mica with adorable eyes. I knew I could not return to America without them, the priceless prizes of my life. But I was hesitant to tell her to quit her job on the first day we met.

Meanwhile, Junior could not take his little eyes off me. He was trying to digest this sudden, dramatic moment of his life.

"Papi," he said. "Is it true I am Haitian, too?"

"Yes, you are because Papi is Haitian."

"My teacher said Haiti is a bad place. Is that true?"

"No, it's not, son. But everywhere you find good people and bad people."

"Papi, are you taking Mommy and me to America?"

"Yes."

"When?"

"When I leave in two weeks."

"And we'll all live together forever?"

"Yes. Until you grow, mature, and marry your sweetheart and create your own family."

"No. I don't want to leave you and Mommy. I want to stay with you forever, too." His creamy young cinnamon face glittered under the fluorescent light.

Michaela knew I was talking to her. Enough to convince her to put in her resignation at work the following day. I couldn't be happier. All three of us shared the same bed, the way I had anticipated it, the way I had always dreamed of. Junior slept all the way until daylight. But Mica and I spent the night in each other's arms, catching up.

Chapter 32

The next morning, we ate breakfast together before walking Junior to school amid the snowflakes that blanketed our path as we walked in the cold.

Then, we made our way to the tram station to catch a tram to the hotel. Before we got up to my room, I stopped by the front desk and requested a suite for three. I did not see Isabelle. I knew she would be happy for me. The receptionist asked us to wait while she got the suite ready.

"Do you remember Fontainebleau Hotel?" I asked Mica, pecking her cheek.

"How could I forget where we first made love and Junior was conceived?" She laughed. "And you lied to the receptionist that day, telling her that we were husband and wife."

"If I say this now, it won't be a lie because you are my wife."

"But, Vinco, we'll have to make it official."

Isabelle walked in, shivering. "Bonjour," she said with a smile that seemed to tell Mica and me that she understood the girl standing next to me was indeed the mother of my son. "I'm happy for you," she added. Mica and I laughed as I presented her to Isabelle. We chatted for a minute, and Isabelle walked away to begin her workday.

A few minutes later, a chambermaid came down and said the suite was ready. "What about my belongings, which were in the other room?"

"No. They're all in your new room, now, sir."

We went upstairs and dove into a two-room suite bathed in the sensual fragrance of amber. Instantly, it reminded us of Fontainebleau.

"Baby, it feels like yesterday we were in a venue like this. Doesn't it?" I said with a voracious stare, communicating the lusty feeling that had been boiling inside of me since the night before.

"Yes, it does, Vinco," she said, dropping her purse onto a plush sofa across the room.

We now stood by the side of the bed, holding hands, peering into each other's eyes, rediscovering the rarity of our love—pure, pristine, and profound. It was the roots of that love, so deep, that despite the distance and the passage of time, we were able to win over the uncertainties of time to give our lives, our future the sense of purpose and belonging enshrined in human dignity. I lifted her hands and wrapped her arms around my neck. Then, I held her by the waist.

"Vinco," she said, breathless and full of joy. "It's hard for me to describe how happy I am right at this moment, folding in your arms. Two days ago, I was dwelling in the deepest hole of solitude. I only had the happy memories of long ago to keep on going, dreaming of our first kisses, our first lovemaking. Now, I will dream no more. It's real, Vinco. It's real, *mi amor*. I'm in your arms, forever yours." Her voice quivered in those soulful words.

"I'm forever yours, too, my love." I held her tighter, leaning forward for a sugary, lip-locked kiss. The tips of her firm breasts began to rub my chest. Our kiss now became voracious. We soon fell into bed, undressing each other.

"Baby, what if I'm pregnant again like the last time?" She said, almost out of breath as I softly stroked her luscious, feline, and voluptuous outline.

"That will be a blessing, *amorecita*. Junior would have a little brother or sister to play with," I teased her. She smiled, tickling me.

I pressed on, caressing her naked body. In my arms, she groaned and moaned. "Vinco, make love to me. Make love to me like there's no tomorrow. I had longed for your sweet caress, your magic touch. Take me, Vinco. Take me to the final frontier of intimacy."

Under the weight of our voracious love, we went under the bedsheet. The intimate moment lasted more than two hours. Long after it was over, we remained interlaced, breathing in the smell of our sweat.

"It feels so refreshing," she said pressing her naked body against mine. We did not want to let go, and when we finally let go, it was past midday. But we still lay in bed.

"Baby, would you marry me?" I said, my eyes unblinking.

"Vinco, you asked me that already, and I remembered saying yes."

"That was years ago."

"Yes, I want to marry you and live with you until death."

Hearing those words from Mica's emotional voice, which was unthinkable a week earlier, healed the deep longing and emptiness inside of me, stirring me to tears.

"Baby, we'll have to do it, now. Today, I mean. Can't we do it at the courthouse next door?"

"We can always call and find out." I picked up the phone and called the front desk.

"*Vous désirez, monsieur?*" Asked the receptionist. *What would you like, sir?*

"*Savez-vous si on peut se marier au Palais de Justice de l'autre côté?*" *Do you know if one can get married at the courthouse next door?*"

"*Non, monsieur. Vous devez aller à la mairie.*" *No, you must go to the mayor's office.*

"Let's go then," she said. "I think we'll need two eyewitnesses."

"Call Josefina and let her know we'll come to get her in an hour. I'll call Ahmed, the taxi driver who has been helping me since Monday."

"We'll have to go get Junior, too, Vinco."

"Call his school while I call Ahmed in the meantime."

"Yes, *mi amor*. Josefina might be at work, but I'm positive she'll be ready once I tell her the reason why we need her."

While we waited for the taxi driver, we got dressed and walked to the courthouse across the street. We wanted to make sure we could be married at the mayor's office or perhaps at the courthouse just like in America. It was a nineteenth-century neo-Greek building with a snow-covered rooftop, wide-open doors, and an inner courtyard. We went in, walking hand in hand when a stocky man attired in a puffy jacket stopped us. His face looked dull, mustachioed, and droopy-bearded, like an old wizard in a security uniform.

"How may I help you?" He said, stroking his beard.

"We're here to get married," I said. Mica and I stood firm, still holding hands.

"No. You have to go to the mayor's office."

"Thank you, sir." We turned around, ready to leave.

"Don't wait too long. The office closes at three p.m.."

We went back to the hotel but stayed in the lobby, eyeing the street, waiting for Ahmed. Five minutes later, we saw his taxi parked by the side of the street. We walked outside to meet him. I greeted him with a handshake.

"*Mi amor*, this is Ahmed, a new friend. Thanks to him, I was able to find you so quickly." I presented her to Ahmed. They also shook hands.

"*Très heureux de vous faire la connaissance*," he said with a big smile. "*Elle est jolie*," he added, turning to me to congratulate me. *Happy to meet you. She is pretty.*

"Thank you, Ahmed."

"I understand why you went stir crazy yesterday," he said, opening the door to let us in. Mica looked immensely pleased.

"Ahmed, we have to go back to Les Galeries Lafayette."

"To get the young lady of yesterday?"

"Yes. From there, we'll go pick up our son from an elementary school not far from where you took me Tuesday night. Then, we'll go to the mayor's office. We're getting married."

"Wow! I'm happy for you." With glee, he drove off.

From our seats in the back, Mica kept looking at me with dreamy eyes and unspoken admiration. She tilted her head toward my chest like she wanted to be sure what we were about to do was truly real. I, too, wanted to make sure my Mica was now and forever mine. In my mind, a slew of thoughts swept through. But one of them stood out. "If faith can shake someone's soul and lift mountains, love can certainly make what looks impossible possible." I could never get rid of the lingering love that dwelled in my heart for so long. Though I tried to ignore it, I could not, for this dormant passion was powerful enough to take me across the Atlantic in search of Mica and Junior. I wrapped my arm around her neck.

"Mica," I said in a soft, filtered voice.

"*Oui, mon coeur,*" she replied in French, lifting her head and twinkling her eyes. It was the first time she spoke in French to me in such a sentimental manner. *Yes, sweetheart.*

"*Je ne pourrai jamais vivre sans toi, ma chérie.*" *I will never be able to live without you, my love.*

"Vinco, we've finally found that happiness that has eluded us for so many years," she whispered in my ear.

Our arms folded about each other's shoulders as Ahmed drove us through the milky streets of Strasbourg. Outside, it started to snow again, but it did nothing to chase the Christmas shoppers away. Jolly faces garnished with snow, they wandered up and down the enchanted streets, moving in and out of stores festooned by multicolor ornaments, all in the merriment of the Christmas season.

I thought of the ski resorts of the Vosges mountains now covered in snow a few miles outside of town, over the ridgelines. Josefina had once promised to take us there once we were in Alsace. I wanted to talk to her about that, but she had become pensive, and her occasional sighs revealed that my presence had ultimately brought to bear a peaceful and resting moment of her life, which she had yearned for after a long and excruciating climb while carrying the weight of an agonizing guilt. She seemed to have been freed from the yoke of depression and anxiety.

About twenty minutes later, we reached *Rue du Vingt-deux Novembre*, and Galeries Lafayette was in sight. Through the windshield, Mica spotted Josefina stepping down from the department store's entrance and treading up to us in quick, long strides. Ahmed pulled over by a newsstand near *Club de la Presse Strasbourg-Europe*. I pushed the door open, and Josefina poured herself in, still shivering from the cold.

"I can't believe it! This is going so fast. You guys are getting married?"

"It couldn't come fast enough. Six years is a long time to wait," I said, laughing.

Sitting on the other side of me, Mica's eyes brimmed with pride. "It was truly meant to be," she said, holding me tighter.

A few minutes later, we made it to Junior's school. We met the same woman from the day before. Without even asking, she called for Junior to come to the main office. When he walked out, he ran to us with spread arms like an eaglet at the height of its bliss. He buried his little creamy face on me this time. The receptionist watched in awe as my boy tightened his grip on his dad.

"What a difference a day makes! I have never seen him so happy," she boasted.

Now that we had the witnesses, Mica and I became evermore confident this was *the moment*. The one we had been waiting for. The one we had never ceased to think about since the day we exchanged our first kisses. In the car, Junior looked bewildered as we drove by his house without stopping.

"Mommy, we already left home."

"We know, son. Don't worry," I said, pulling him against me. "Mommy and I are with you. It's all that matters."

A moment later, we arrived at the mayor's office, also called Hotel de Ville. It was in the center of town and a busy place. Finding a parking spot had become impossible. So, Ahmed decided to pull to a small taxi stand across the street.

"I'll wait here for you," Ahmed said.

"No, Ahmed," I said. "You must go with us."

He obliged, laughing.

At the entrance, we met an officer in uniform just like the man in the puff jacket Mica and I met earlier at the courthouse. When we told him why we were there, he smiled. "Go to the third floor," he said. "*Mes félicitations!*" he added, laughing, as we walked past him on our way to the third floor. *Congratulations!*

"*Puis-je vous aider?*" Asked a young woman behind a glass window. She was about Mica's age. *May I help you?*

"*Nous voulons nous marier.*" Josefina and Ahmed stood right behind us. I held Junior's hand. *We're here to get married.*

"*D'accord. Attendez un instant.*" She pulled out some forms and asked Mica and me to fill them out. *Okay, wait a minute.*

"Papi, you're marrying Mommy?" Junior asked. He began to get a sense of what was taking place.

"No, son," I teased him. "I asked Mommy to marry me, and she agreed." Mica pecked his little face. We then walked to the corner of the room and sat on some chairs, filling out the forms, and turning them back to the young woman.

"*Ça vous coûte vingt-cinq euros,*" she said, taking a frantic aim at us as Mica unzipped her purse and handed the twenty-five euros to her. *This will cost you twenty-five euros.*

"*Assayez-vous. La greffière arrive dans quelques minutes.*" *Take your seat, and the clerk will be here in a few minutes.*

A thin woman in a dark dress and boots, maybe in her fifties, walked out and instructed us to follow her to a small room on the other side of the hallway. We went in.

"*Alors Monsieur Yrvin, Mademoiselle Michaela, vous voulez vous unir aujourd'hui par le lien du mariage? So, Mr. Yrvin and Ms. Michaela, you would like to get married today?*

"*Oui,*" we both answered. *Yes.*

She then went over some rules as we listened with the highest of attention. Then, she asked Mica and me to stand facing each other to say our wedding vows.

"Monsieur Yrvin, enlevez votre bras droit et répétez après moi." Raise your right hand and repeat after me.

As I raised my right hand and began to repeat after the woman, I watched Mica's eyes swell with tears and they swelled even more when I said that I was committed to upholding my solemn vow no matter the odds until death. When it was her turn, a sudden charge of romantic emotion seized my heart as she echoed my words, vowing to remain faithful to our union to the very last breath of her life. Her lips quivered as each word filtered through, pounding my heart.

"Maintenant, je vous prononce mari et femme." Now, I pronounce you husband and wife.

She then instructed us to kiss each other. Mica and I jumped in each other's arms and went for a prolonged French kiss. We did not want to let go until the woman said, *"Ça dure trop!"* That's too long!

"Yes, this takes too long," Junior said, looking at both of us with a strange, funny stare.

The woman stepped out of the room and left without a trace. Her role was purely ceremonial. Our role was holy and pure. "Ahmed," I said. "Find the best restaurant in town, fit for the moment."

"Yes, *sir.*"

"I have one in mind," Josefina said. She was cheerful. Her cousin had won over what seemed to be an infinite, unmitigated loneliness.

"Which one?" Ahmed asked.

"*La Casserole* near the Cathedrale de Strasbourg. It's fine dining."

"I know that one. It's on 24 *Rue des Juifs*. You have great taste, Mademoiselle," Ahmed said.

"I had *un p'tit ami* (a boyfriend) from the university who took me there twice. He wanted to impress me."

"Wasn't he Pierre-Henri?" I asked, teasing her.

"No, Vinco. I already told you he's a loser." She laughed.

Mica laughed, too. Junior looked at his mother. "*Mommy, mais tu n'as pas ta belle robe blanche comme font les autres,*" he said, looking at me as if looking for an answer. *Mommy, you don't have your beautiful white gown as other people do.*

"*Mon fils,*" Mica said. "*L'important c'est notre amour. C'est pas la robe.*" *My son, what's important is the love, not the gown.*

It did not take long before we arrived at the restaurant parking lot on a quiet street glittered with Christmas lights. Shops and boutiques were on both sides. We walked in silence.

"I'm glad to be part of your successful mission, Yrvin," Ahmed said with an awesome pride.

I held Mica and Junior's hands tighter. Josefina pulled the door, and we walked in, coming face to face with a young receptionist who stood erect behind the greeting stand.

"Party of five?" She asked in a show of extreme politeness.

"Yes," I replied.

Chapter 33

The place was nearly empty, albeit two restaurant goers who sat in the middle of the room in a tête-à-tête conversation. She instructed us to follow her down a hallway with a marble floor that led to a reserved room fit for the moment. Crystal chandeliers sparkled overhead against the backdrop of low-volume classical music. I did not know how she understood the importance of the moment. There, she seated us. "The waitress will arrive shortly," she uttered softly with a smile, leaving menu cards on the table for us.

Mica and Junior sat next to me while Josefina and Ahmed sat on opposite sides of each other and dug through the menus for the perfect entrée.

"*Ma chérie*, choose for both of us. You know I'm not Alsatian," I said, lifting her face, shifting it toward me, and delivering an amorous, lip-locked smooch.

"Me neither, my love. But I'll try."

"I'll go for the homemade duck foie gras," Ahmed said.

"What is that?" I asked him.

"It's marinated in pinot noir, poached fruit and walnut crumbles," he said.

"Well, whatever that is, enjoy it, my friend."

"Me, I'll go for the duck breast from the southwest," Josefina tittered.

"It must be enough to fill you." I made fun of her.

"Yeah," Mica said, smiling. "Do you remember the Chinese buffet in North Miami Beach?"

"That was a long time ago. Now, I watch every single thing I put in my mouth," she confirmed with a laugh.

"And you, Junior?" I asked him, pecking his narrow brownish face.

"Papi, I'll do like you. I'll let Mommy choose." He hunched toward Mommy, hungry for a kiss, which Mommy lovingly delivered. Then his little black eyes began to scrutinize the menu. "Mommy, can you add this, too, for me?"

"Which one, son?"

"*La bettrave et le cassis*," he said, grimacing.

"What's that, Mica?"

"It's vanilla baravoise and beetroot sorbet."

"Great choice, son. I love you."

"I love you, too, Papi."

"What about us, *chérie*?" I said.

"I already made our choice. We'll go for the Langoustine. Basically, it's a roast, variation of butternut, chestnut bisque, and WAH whiskey."

"Mica, I'm afraid of that whiskey. You forgot. I've always been a chicken head."

Everybody laughed, except Junior, who did not understand the expression "Chicken head." "What's that, Papi?"

"It's another way to say I can easily be drunk after drinking alcoholic beverages. So, the whiskey will make Papi's head spin, and I'm sure you don't want that. Right?"

"Right, Papi. Don't order it."

"I'll go for the filet de sandre, then. It's pike-perched fillet, roasted green cabbage leaf, cranberries, and smoked sauerkraut sauce."

"That sounds great," I said just as the server, a young man in black-and-white attire, showed up, and we all placed our order. A moment later, our table was garnished to the fullest.

Before everyone grabbed their silverware, I rose to speak. "Mica, today is the happiest day of my life for two reasons," I began as everyone looked on. "I came to Strasbourg to find my son. Not only did I find him, but I also found your love, which I thought I had lost long ago. Now, look at us, a family at last. I can say with absolute certainty that I've found the missing part of my life that had escaped me. I now found *you*, Mica, my darling, my inspiration, next to whom I will wake up every day with the sense of purpose that I had been yearning for. We don't know what tomorrow will bring, but one thing is certain: If the passage of time was unable to efface our entrenched feelings, as long as we have each other to lean on, to care for Junior, there won't be any storm, no matter how powerful it might be, that we won't be able to withstand. I love you until death and beyond."

I then dropped back into my seat. Mica's eyes brimmed with tears. I wrapped my arm around the nape of her neck. Junior was moved. His creamy face brightened in a smile that soon burst into a titter. So too were Josefina and Ahmed, who did not seem to believe that true love could still be found in a world where most of us are guided by selfish interests.

"May God bless your union," Ahmed said.

Mica then rose to speak, using her multilinguistic ability to address me in both French and English.

Chéri, il y a un p'tit secret que je ne t'ai jamais révélé jusqu'à ce soir. Depuis le jour où ton regard amusé et heureux croisa le mien dans ce petit magasin de chaussures, j'étais déjà conquise. D'un seul coup, une vague chaude et heureuse m'emportait. Quand je suis rentrée chez moi ce jour là à la tombée de la nuit, je me suis renfermée dans ma petite chambre où j'ai passé toute la nuit à rêver. Je voyais déjà toi et moi dans une aventure infinie. Un beau film. Un long métrage dans lequel nous serions heureux pour toujours. Malgré toutes les pènes que j'ai moi-même infligées à nos deux cœurs à travers les années, regarde, regarde mon amour où nous en sommes ce soir. À l'instant même,	Honey, there's a little secret that I never revealed to you until tonight. Since the day your happy and charming gaze met mine in that little shoe store, I knew I had been conquered. Suddenly, a warm, joyful wave swept me away. When I got home that day at nightfall, I locked myself in my little room where I spent the whole night dreaming. Already, I saw you and me on an endless adventure. A beautiful film. A feature film in which we would be happy forever. Through the years, despite all the hardships that I have inflicted upon both of our hearts, look, *look* my love, where we are tonight. I feel

je sens que toutes les fibres les plus profondes de mon coeur sont en train de vibrer..., une sensation impossible à d'écrire. C'est plus que magnifique.	that all the deepest fibers of my heart are vibrating, a sensation impossible to describe. It is more than magnificent.

She then fell back into her seat as tears continued to spring out of her eyes. But they were tears of joy stemming from the purest of emotions.

"Mommy, why are you crying when this is supposed to be your happiest moment?" Junior said. He was afraid for his mother.

"These are happy tears, little boy," Josefina chortled.

Over jokes and laughter, we wolfed down our food. We had the best of times. Later, in our hotel room, as Junior watched his favorite television show, we sat on the sofa, thinking of where we had been, and how we were now a family.

"Baby, I have to make some phone calls," I said, pulling away to go grab the phone.

First, I called Frankel in Paris to give him the happy news and introduce Mica to him. He was overjoyed and he said he was waiting for us in Paris to give us a romantic taste of the city. Then, I called home to deliver the news. On the first call, Nana picked up the phone.

"Nana, it's me. I have Mica with me," I said, laughing.

"Hallelujah! Glory to God! And Junior?"

"He's right here, watching TV."

"Can I speak to Mica?"

"Baby, here is Nana."

"Hello, sister, how are you?" Mica laughed.

"I'm okay, now. I had been praying every day for you and Vinco. I had faith…"

The ladies talked for a few minutes, and I told Nana we would be home in two weeks. I also called Pedro. He was jumping for joy as I talked to him, and I could hear Chen in the background celebrating. I had come to realize how my loneliness was such a pain for so many of my loved ones.

While Mica and Nana chatted on the phone, I ceased the moment to call Judy in the Bahamas. I knew it was still early like in Florida. I was lucky I did not have to go through her secretary as she had instructed me. She picked it up on the first ring. "Judy," I said, my voice was cheery. "I found Michaela and my son."

"Wow! I was praying for it to happen. Now, you'll have the peace of mind that you deserve. When are you guys coming home? I presume they're coming with you. Right?"

"In two weeks. Thank you for your support, Judy."

"You know I always want you to be happy."

"Bye. Hug your little princess for me."

"You do the same, Vinco."

We hung up. It was something I felt I had to do, for despite everything, I knew Judy would want nothing more than seeing me happy.

Mica was done talking to Nana. We went to check on Junior in the next room. He had fallen asleep without taking off his clothes. Mica woke him up.

"Go take your shower," Mommy ordered him.

"We're not home yet," he said.

"We won't be going home tonight. In fact, for now we'll stay here. And in two weeks, we'll go home to Florida," I said, holding him.

"I won't go back to my school anymore, Papi?"

"No, son. You'll have a new school when you get to Florida," I said, taking him with me to the main room while retrieving the little gift I bought for him back in Florida. It was a box that contained a bronze soccer ball. I handed it to him. "This is what I bought for you, Junior."

"For *me*, Papi?" He was delighted. "So that we can play together in Florida?"

"Yes. We'll play after school while Mommy makes spaghetti," I said, pulling Mica next to me. Until now, she was watching with adorable eyes Junior and dad, the two most important people in her life, united at last.

"I can't wait to be home, Vinco," she tittered, pulling me down in the bed as Junior followed us.

"But I'm going to lose my friends, Papi."

"You'll have new friends, son. I make you a promise."

"Yes, Papi."

"We'll be back here next summer so that you can see your old friends."

He wrapped his arms around me. "Papi, do I have a grandma in Florida?"

"Yes, you have two of them."

"How about grandpa? I have two of them, too?"

"Yes. And you'll be able to spend time with them, and uncles and aunts."

"And Aunt Nana, too?"

"Yes. And you'll play with her daughter who's about your age, your cousin Nanouche."

"Yeah, I'll talk to Nanouche every day. Does she know French, Papi?"

"No, but you too can speak Creoglish."

"What's that?"

"A mixture of Creole and English."

"You'll teach me Creole, too?"

"Of course, or you won't be able to speak Creoglish with Nanouche."

"Will Aunt Royo teach me, too?"

"Sure. Aunt Royo will call you every day to practice with you. Aunt Royo is funny. She'll make you laugh all the time."

"Not funnier than Dad," Mica injected. "Is Royo your baby sister you used to tell me about?"

"Yes."

"I can't wait to meet all of them."

Later, after we all took our showers and were ready to go to bed, Junior came to sleep with us. He did not want to sleep alone, for he had never done so before. He always slept in Mommy's arms. So, we went to sleep with him. When he fell asleep, we went back to our room. But we were unable to sleep.

"In one day, baby, look how much you've already accomplished," I said.

"Yes, Vinco." She rested her head on my chest. "Baby, tomorrow is another busy day."

"I know, but these will be formalities as you're going home to Florida."

"I know. Many of my things in the apartment I will donate to a neighbor. I'll submit my resignation to my job."

"As soon as we get home, you must register for school, taking the remaining courses to get your business degree."

"I'll take them online."

"Of course. As soon as you're done with the program, I'll look for a job for you at an investment firm near my office, in the same building. That way, we'll be able to go to work in the same car."

"Yes, *mi amor*. May God bless our family."

"Baby, how about your parents?" You won't call them?"

"I will, but it's not the time. In Florida, I will. I won't even call my uncle. I'll let Josefina do this for me. This is our moment. We don't wanna spoil it. I haven't spoken to them in three years…"

"*Amorecita.*"

"Not tonight. They nearly destroyed my life, our lives…"

I did not force her. I understood how she felt.

Saturday morning, we went to La Bresse, the best ski resort in the Vosges. Neither of us could ski, but we wanted to do this to fulfill a promise we made back in Florida. Josefina wanted to come, for she was skilled when it came to skiing. But she had to work, so we went without her. We reached La Bresse around ten a.m.. Already, the platform was full of skiers.

"Vinco, I'm scared to be on the slope."

"Me, too. But they said the base depth is perfect here."

"I can imagine. Look at this snow. It's powdery, the best in Alsace."

"We can try snowshoeing," Junior suggested.

"Let's do that," Mica and I said at once.

It was sunny. So, we went up to the station and ordered our snowshoes and gear. After a short training session, we went for a hike down a trail amid snow-covered trees and hilltops. Several families hiked with us in a long row like a church procession. The trail soon meandered up to a mountain flank where there were resting stations for hikers who wanted to rejuvenate their bodies before continuing their journey. We went into one of them. To the east, our eyes caught snow-blanketed rooftops of tiny German villages below the Black Forest. The scenic landscape warmed our hearts. We were alone, but we felt strong. Holding our son tight, the product of our romance, Mica and I were in utter delight.

Chapter 34

The morning before we left Strasbourg, Josefina came to see us for the last time. She met us in the hotel lobby where we waited for Ahmed to take us to the train station. Her face was drawn as if ravaged by fatigue. Even her fashionable hoop earrings and her forced smile were not enough to conceal her sadness. Her dear cousin and best friend may forever be out of her reach.

"Mica," she said, "when will I see you again?"

"Perhaps in a year or two," I replied, preempting Mica who, under the weight of her emotions, was unable to find the perfect words to console her cousin.

For more than six years, they lived like beloved cousins do, sharing their pain and their worries. Now, Mica must move on. Another life was waiting for her back in America; the one she had longed for.

"We'll talk over the phone. I will make sure of that, Josie," Mica whispered.

Junior understood. He moved closer to Josefina and grabbed her hand. "Josie, Papa promised me we'll visit every summer." He looked to his dad for confirmation.

"Yes, my son. Also, we can always send plane tickets to Josie so she can travel to Florida and spend some time with us."

That last word appeared to have reassured Josefina. A smile beamed across her face—a natural one, this time. She pulled Junior toward her, burying him under her fox fur coat in a tight hug.

"Josie, you're going miss your boy, huh?" Mica teased her.

"I'm missing him already," Josefina replied.

"By the way, Josie, did you tell Uncle that I'm going back to Florida?" Mica asked.

"No, I didn't."

"*Really?*" Both Mica and I were shocked. Our voices rose and shuddered.

"I was going to tell him like you asked me. Then I thought about it and came to this conclusion. If I tell him now, he will hurry and call your dad. That would create a crisis even before you get to Florida. I think it would be best to wait for when you get home with your husband and your son. Then you yourself can call Uncle Emilio and Aunty Lucrecia. I think the impact would be more powerful if they learn this important milestone in your life from your own voice. As for my father, he won't know anything until I hear from you."

"You're right, Josie," I said, wrapping my arm around my cousin in-law's neck, complimenting her for her words of wisdom. "Thank you for having the foresight to ensure our journey back to Miami."

"Let's go. Ahmed is outside," Junior chuckled. He was cheerful with a boyish innocence. Josefina's explanation meant nothing to him as we lifted our belongings to get going.

Pushing our luggage out through the main entrance, we met the taxi driver who was racing to join us. "Bonjour Ahmed!" We greeted him with one voice just as Isabelle was rushing in. She was late for work.

"You're leaving?" She said in a hurry.

"Yes, we are. Thank you for all the help," I said.

"Have a safe trip, Mr. and Mrs. Lacroix." In a few hasty steps, she was gone. Those words "Mr. and Mrs. Lacroix" set my heart aglow. They made me, as well as Mica, believe we are indeed one forever.

Ten minutes later, we arrived at the central train station. Before we left Ahmed, we thanked him for everything. He and I exchanged phone numbers in the hope of meeting again someday. Josefina walked us all the way to the platform where the train bound for Paris was already stationed. Passengers were boarding. Josefina dove into Mica's arms for one last hug. They both shed tears. Junior and I joined them in the hug. We hugged and squeezed, and then we let go.

From the train, we watched Josefina shivering in the cold, waiting for the train to depart. Then, the train pulled away, and Josie faded from our sight.

"She's such a sweetheart," I said, putting my arm around Mica's shoulder as she rested her head on my chest.

Mica sighed. "I don't think I'll ever find a cousin like her. If it wasn't for her, I don't know where Junior and I would be today."

Two hours later, we arrived at the Paris Eastern Train Station. Frankel was there on the platform waiting for us. I presented Mica and Junior to him.

"What a beautiful little family!" Frankel uttered with a burst of laughter.

"Mica, Frankel is just like Pedro and Ronel. He's like a brother to me, my childhood best friend."

"I was ready to travel to Strasbourg to join in the search, Vinco," Frankel affirmed, holding Junior's hand. "Without a doubt, your son is the pure product of a charming wife and a very handsome husband."

"Papi, where are all these people going? They're all walking fast," Junior said. His little black eyes tracked the motion of hundreds of travelers crisscrossing each other.

"This is Paris, son. Everything here is done fast. These people must hurry because they don't want to miss their train just like we did back in Strasbourg."

"I'm surprised also to see all these folks in one train station," Mica muttered, looking dazed.

"How did you get to Strasbourg?" I asked her.

"I remember we took the train from the airport."

"There's a train station outside of Charles de Gaulle International Airport," Frankel confirmed. "But Vinco, what time is the flight?"

"Twelve-thirty pm."

"I was going to take you guys to a cozy place for breakfast," Frankel said.

"Don't worry. We ate at the hotel before we left." Mica assured him as the car weaved through the busy streets of Paris. The wintry weather had turned the city gray and cold.

"Let's drive straight to the airport then," Frankel suggested. "You're talking about a busy place; Charles de Gaulle is one of the busiest airports in the world. It can be a nightmare for travelers who are late."

"Yes, Frankel," Mica giggled like a young, curious girl. "I'm dreaming of the sunshine state already. I can't wait, *amorecito*."

"You'll be in Florida soon, where it's sunny and warm," I said, teasing Mica as if she did not know. Junior was at the paroxysm of his elation.

As a quick treat, Frankel drove us through the city center on the way to the airport, rolling through the enchanted boulevards of Paris as the Eifel Tower loomed in the distance. "Next time you guys are in Paris, I'll give you a tour fit for a royal family," he said, feeling proud of himself.

"That would be nice," Junior chuckled.

"You won't be in the tour, son. It will be for Mommy and me," I said, making fun of him.

"*Pourquoi, Papi?* He frowned, grimacing what was a little happy face a few seconds earlier. *Why, Dad?*

About an hour later, we pulled into the airport's main entrance. Frankel helped us retrieve our luggage from the trunk.

It was hectic as the drivers behind us put pressure to move quickly. They were blowing their horns while pulling in as well. In a rush, we thanked Frankel for his generosity.

"I can't wait to see you guys back in Paris again!" He reiterated his earlier promise, as he pulled away from the chaotic scene—a venue swamped with weary faces of travelers hustling and bustling as teary-eyed relatives said their last goodbyes. In gigantic steps, we pushed our way toward the custom service area. After a stressful moment of going through all the inspections, we made it to the plane.

"Baby. I can't wait to see Miami again. It feels like a lifetime has passed." Mica confessed.

"You'll see. Nothing has fundamentally changed. It's the same city you left almost seven years ago," I said with a grin. Junior listened; his eyes gleeful as he smiled.

The flight was long but smooth. It was past midnight, local time, when we arrived at Miami International Airport. I thought of Nana and Pedro. Either of them would have been happy to pick us up, but it would have been unfair to ask them this late. So, we had to get a taxi home. Junior fell asleep in the car as soon as we left the airport. He missed seeing the city landscape as the car rolled through the empty streets. Mica leaned on me, dozing off. Forty-five minutes later, we pulled in front of "The Grenoble." At last, we reached our destination. I led Mica and Junior up to my apartment.

"This is our new home," I said, holding both Mica and my son in a tight hug. We shed happy tears.

"This is exactly how I've always anticipated it to be. The home I've dreamed of for all those years," Mica stated as the tears continued to drop. "Vinco, it's not just the coziness of our place. It's the love, the commitment, and the will to wake up every day with a sense of purpose, knowing we're no longer suffering. Our nightmarish moments are behind us."

Listening to those words from my wife, I could not help thinking of Nana who had never ceased to believe in Mica's love for me. I felt ashamed for not sharing my sister's unwavering faith.

"*Amorecita*," I said, raising her face toward me. "We have a future to build, and it formally begins today."

"Yes, Vinco. But I'm confident we're up to the task."

Later, after we took a shower, all three of us crammed into bed. For the first time, I realized how small my apartment was. Like I told Mica back in Strasbourg, the need to purchase a house that would be suitable for us was unavoidable.

Early the next morning, we woke up to the blaring ring of the phone. Mica picked it up and handed it to me.

"Why don't you answer it? It's time for people to know there is a woman in the house." We both laughed.

"Hello," Mica answered.

"Mica! Hallelujah! God is great!" Nana was jubilant. Mica did not have to say who it was. The phone was on speaker. Junior jumped out of bed and joined us.

"I missed you, Nana. I can't wait to see you," Mica said with a surge of excitement.

"Nana, where's Nanouche?" I asked. "Junior wants to talk to her."

"She's in the room with her dad. The main reason I called you guys this early is that we're having a welcome back gathering at Manman's house. It begins at seven."

"Already, Nana? We're all tired after such a long trip." I tried to postpone the event.

"What do you mean, Vinco? Yes, it is this evening. Manman, Papa, Royo, and the boys, and some other friends from church have worked all week for this moment. Let me hear Junior."

Junior grabbed the phone before Mica could hand it to him. "Bonjour *ma tante* Nana," Junior said. He was thrilled. "Where's my cousin, Nanouche?" He asked in English.

"Wow, Junior knows English. How about Creole?"

"Not yet, Aunt Nana. But my dad told me Nanouche will teach me."

"Dad was right. Yes, she will."

"How was your first night in America, Junior?" Nana asked, laughing.

"Fine. I'm happy to be with Mom and Dad."

We chatted for a few more minutes before we hung up. I was shocked. I had the suspicion something was cooking for us, but I never anticipated it to happen so soon. We all got up and went to sit on the couch in the living room. I watched Mica surveying the room with extreme pleasure. She then got up and walked toward the window to get a glimpse of the neighborhood. Saturday morning, fancy cars of all brands filled the lot. Farther away, lovely homes with lush green yards lay dormant in the morning sunrise.

"This is North Miami Beach, Mica," I said. "Aventura Mall is roughly two miles away."

"And Jade Garden, our Chinese buffet is few blocks down, Vinco," Mica chortled as she made her way toward the kitchen. Junior and I followed her.

"There's everything we need for breakfast, Mica. But we'll have to go out later today for grocery shopping."

"Why don't we wait for tomorrow, Vinco? I can see we have enough to last a week. Remember this evening? We can't look tired when we get there."

#

All day, I had been trying to reach Pedro and Ronel without success. It annoyed me. I wanted to brief them about the trip. I knew they were eager to know the details. Even though the event at my parents' home had preoccupied my mind, I wanted to hear from my buddies.

"Mica, you know it's strange. I've been trying to reach them both."

"Ronel and Pedro? I can see the disappointment on your face." She preempted me. "You managed to find me, I'm sure, you'll find them." We laughed.

Six p.m., we were ready—well, somewhat. Mica wore a knee length, Houndstooth, red burgundy dress like a mature woman who dwelled in the fashion world of haute couture clothing. It suited her well with her golden hair held together by a vintage French rhinestone hair clip. Junior was dressed in a two-piece navy-blue suit like a young prince. Mica wanted our son's

424

appearance to match the pride of his lineage, as he was on his way to meet his father's family for the first time.

I was going to put on some casual clothes. Upon seeing Mica in such a formal outfit, I realized how important the moment was for her. Except for Nana, she had never met any of my relatives. She wanted to impress them, and perhaps her appearance and demeanor might help assure my parents that her love for me was pure and that her behavior over the past seven years was the result of a simple misjudgment. I went to the closet and pulled out a two-button blazer, an off-white shirt, and Italian wool dress pants.

Before we set out of the apartment, Mica held my hand. "Baby, I'm nervous," her voice shook as she spoke.

"You should not be, Mica. We're going to meet people who love us, who will have nothing but good wishes for our marriage."

"Papi, why are we so well dressed up?" Junior asked.

"We're going to see members of your family. Aunty Nana is having a little party for us."

"Are we going to have a lot of food, Papi?"

"A *lot*, son." He was delighted.

I held Mica's hand tighter to reassure her. "*Amorecita*, they'll be excited to meet you. You'll see."

Under a starry sky, we strolled toward the car in the parking lot, passing bushy impatiens and red hibiscuses in full bloom in the garden. Mica smiled as we walked in the evening breeze. A silvery moon beamed on her cinnamon face. "Without a doubt, Vinco, the wintry world of Strasbourg is behind us."

"Yes, *amorecita*. This is the lovely Florida that missed you so much. Now that you are back in its fold, I couldn't be happier," I said, whispering the words as we drove down Biscayne Boulevard.

Junior sat in the back, discovering Miami, a place his mother had always talked about. Fifteen minutes later, we arrived at my parents' apartment building. Cars lined up on both sides of the street, and we figured this could be other residents who parked their cars there. We were lucky to find a spot right next to the entrance. As soon as we stepped out of the car, we saw Nana in a floral dress, arms outstretched running to meet us halfway. My younger sister, Royo, and my mother followed her. When they met, Nana and Mica jumped into each other's arms. Manman and Royo were astonished. Junior and I stood behind.

"Junior," Manman called to him. "Look at my handsome boy!" Manman was ecstatic. Royo joined her, delighted.

Junior then crashed into Manman's dress. *"Grandma! Grandma! Grandma!"* He kept saying out of exhilaration. It looked as if he had known her all his life. I was convinced that my little boy had longed for that moment. He had yearned for it in silence all his life.

After a long tight hug, Nana and Mica let go. She then walked toward Manman who grabbed her hand. *"Pitit mwen, pitit mwen, pitit mwen,"* Manman said in Creole. *My girl, my girl, my girl.*

Mica did not speak Creole, but she understood the joy. My mother's welcome had lessened her nerves. When she and Royo met, she seemed more relaxed. I did not know why, but she later told me her biggest fear was not to meet my parents, but to see how they were going to receive her. Papa and the boys now walked out to join the celebration. Junior moved to talk to his uncles while Mica and Papa talked below the front porch.

"It is an honor to welcome you, my lovely lady, to our home," Papa said.

Mica was moved upon hearing those words. Then, in his usual, authoritative manner, Papa ordered us inside. I was astonished. A huge crowd was there, greeting us in jubilation.

"Hooray!" They all screamed. Pedro and his wife Chen, Ronel and Laurette, Onès and his wife Clautide, Chantale and her husband from Sandford, and the entire crisis group were there to welcome us. I knew then why I could not get a hold of my best friends. Even Amy, my secretary from work, was there to be part of this historic moment. She had been communicating with Nana since I left as I instructed her to do. She could not keep her eyes off Mica and Junior.

"We planned all this, Vinco!" Nana and Ronel shouted together.

"Nana called me a week ago to talk about the idea. I agreed. Then, I called Ped. We were with Nana when she called you this morning," Ronel affirmed.

Mica and I were stunned. Chen and Amy pulled me to the side. "You have such fine taste, Vinco. We're glad you've found your sweetheart and your son," they chortled.

Mica exchanged words with Laurette and Chantale. She knew them back in the day at Barry University. She did not seem to remember Laurette's shady maneuverings in her desperate attempts to disrupt our relationship. Maybe she did and had already forgiven her. Royo, ever playful, took Junior and Nanouche with her, holding their hands, moving to the center of the room, and asking the guests to be quiet for a grand announcement. At her command, the apartment went silent. All eyes were on them.

"None of you here can describe the joy in my heart. My lovely niece Nanouche and my handsome nephew Junior are with me tonight. Aren't they adorable?" She tittered.

The guests went wild. "*Yes!*"

Although the place was small, we all felt warm and cozy. Manman, Nana, Chen, Amy, Laurette, and Chantale moved back and forth from the kitchen to a long table in the corner on which they displayed all the delicious Haitian food and drinks. Some of the crisis members helped as well.

"Mica," I whispered in her ear. "It's time to make our own announcement."

"Yes, *mon amour.*" She murmured.

Until now, we had kept our marriage a secret, waiting for a moment like this, a venue in which all my beloved relatives and friends were present.

"Ladies and gentlemen, Mica and I would like to say a few words," I said. The room went still. The women fixing the food on the table also stopped. "We are pleased to announce that Mica and I are, and forever will be, husband and wife. While in France, we've made a vow to never let go of each other. I asked Mica to marry me, and she agreed, and to formalize our commitment, we went to the Mayor's office as it is customary in France. We both felt it was the best decision, not just for us, but for Junior, and for our future as we moved on in life. The minute we met in Strasbourg, I knew it was true what Nana, Pedro, Chantale, Amy, and Ronel were saying. My love for Mica was suppressed by sets of circumstances beyond my control; but it was neither dead nor dying," I said with shivering lips. Mica's eyes now brimmed with tears, but they were tears stemming from the deepest of emotions.

The noiseless room had now become uproarious. Rounds of applause vibrated the windows. My Mom and Dad, who stood across from us, could not find the words to express their happiness. They looked at Mica and me with admiring eyes.

"It is a pleasant surprise," Manman admitted.

They then moved closer to us. "Do you guys plan on having a wedding reception?" Both of my parents asked.

I looked at Mica. "This may come sometime in the future. As of right now, it's not on the agenda," I said.

Mica smiled but said nothing. The chatting had resumed. Although the food was ready, most people wanted to talk to us first before they went for their plates. All of a sudden, Pedro and Nana pulled us over to the next room. "You guys did the best thing. You did what every responsible parent would do," Pedro said as he hugged me.

"I'm happy for you two! Mica, you're officially my sister in-law," Nana cheered.

"We did not do this for Junior alone. We did it because of our love. A love strong enough for our marriage to survive. Right, Mica?"

"There's nothing more to add, Vinco." She was blushing.

Pedro then turned to Mica. "Do your parents know you're here?"

"Not yet. But I plan on calling them this week. As you know we arrived late last night. Besides, I have to be prepared for that call."

"When was the last time you talked to them?" Nana asked. Her eyes widened, curious to know.

"It's been three years."

"Three years?" Nana seemed surprised. "That's a long time. You and Vinco must plan this."

"Listen," Pedro intervened. "I met your sister last week when I was walking out of my office downtown. She was with an older lady who needed a building permit. She said she still lives with your folks. You haven't talked to her in three years as well?"

"More than three years. In fact, I only talked to her twice during my stay in France," Mica admitted with unadulterated pain.

"I was afraid of making any reference to you while Gabriela and I were talking," Pedro assured Mica.

"You did the right thing, Ped," I said with a grin.

"As she was leaving, we exchanged phone numbers." Pedro said, pulling a business card out of his wallet on which Gabriela's name was written. "Here it is. I think you might need it, Mica, in order to reach your family."

"Thank you, Pedro."

"Don't wait, Mica. Listen to Pedro. Do this as soon as you can," Nana urged her.

"And Vinco, you'll need to help her in the process. And if you guys need my help, I'll be there," Pedro told us.

Meanwhile, the party in the other room was in full swing. Compa, my youngest brother, morphed into a master DJ, kept the guests on their toes with the latest Haitian music. Out of the blue, Junior burst into the room, searching for us. He looked nervous.

"What's wrong, son?" I asked.

"I wanna dance with Nanouche. But she doesn't know how."

"Where's Nanouche?" Nana asked.

"She's waiting for me on the dance floor."

"Let me go teach you both," Nana said, laughing while grabbing Junior's hand to go join Nanouche.

"This boy is a photocopy of his father. Even the way he walks," Pedro observed, smiling. "Mica, even if you wanted to forget about Vinco, Junior's presence would not have allowed it."

We all laughed and returned to the other room. The party went on until close to midnight when we told my parents and the guests that we had to go because we needed to rest. But we were the last ones to leave out of respect. Amy was ecstatic as she was leaving. When she reached where Mica and I stood, she edged closer.

"What a charming wife!" She giggled. "We have so much to talk about, Vinco. I'll wait for when you return to work next week." She then weaved on.

Chapter 35

Back at home, we were exhausted. Junior fell asleep the minute he took off his clothes. Mica and I could not. We knew the moment had arrived to face Mica's parents. Despite everything, she still loved and respected them. Afterall, they gave her life and raised her with the care and love every child would deserve. As she once told me before this regrettable decision to send her off to foreign land, she had never suffered from the young woman's angst, the urge to break free to prove who she was. She was the princess, and they trusted her. She never believed a mistake, however grave it might have been, could render her ineligible for family love. Her animosity came when the spring of her life was shattered, and she was forced into womanhood like a fragile spring leaf snapped at its stem even before it develops and blossoms.

As she lay on my chest, pondering, I knew she would find the courage to speak to her parents. When times were dark with a baby to raise—alone—she did what she thought was necessary: relying on her own propulsion and inner strength. The man, for whom they sent her away, was now her husband; and the baby, for which they thought shame had befallen them, was now a lovely boy that any parent would cherish.

"Mica," I said, "You're going to do what Nana and Pedro told us. The time has come to meet your parents."

"Vinco, I need some more time. Please, my love."

"No, you don't. You're scared, I get that. But avoiding them will never heal the rift. In the morning, you'll call Gabriela."

"Baby, please."

"Mica, remember we have a busy week ahead. We must find a good school for Junior, start looking for a bigger home, and you will register for the remaining courses as we've discussed back in Strasbourg."

"But we can do this while I'm gathering the strength to meet my parents."

"Yes, we can. But I'm afraid if we keep postponing this meeting as a means of avoidance, we will never be free from that ghost of fear. I know you're scared of rejection. I am, too. But this is a part of life. You know, Mica?"

"Yes, darling."

"Your parents' decision may be harsh, but I can't deny I'm part of the blame. I should have used protection."

"Vinco," she rose from the bed and pointed at Junior who slept like a prince. "This thought is no longer valid. Look at our son, our lovely son. What we did may have been a mistake, but it was in no way a crime. I take full responsibility for what I did. I could have stopped you if I wanted to. But I loved you then and I always will. In allowing myself to be pregnant, I may have misused or abused their trust in me. But getting pregnant by you, the man I love, I believe, did not amount to the punishment, this pain they had inflicted in me. I'm not afraid of meeting them. I'm afraid of saying things that I might later regret."

"Mica, you will not go alone. Junior and I will be with you. Now, let's try to get some sleep."

On this thought, we wrapped ourselves in each other's arms. Early the next morning, I woke up and found her sitting next to me. "Mica, I thought you were sleeping."

"Vinco, I've been up since five."

"What time is it?"

"It's seven, Vinco."

I sat up, grabbed the phone from the lamp table, and handed it to her. "Call Gabriela, *amorecita*."

Without any hesitation, she dialed the number. She put the phone on speaker so that I could hear. No one picked it up. She dialed again. Still, there was no answer. But the greeting confirmed the phone was her sister's.

"Hello Gabby, this is Mica. I'm in town. Call me when you get this message," she said in Spanish.

"Baby, give it an hour. Then, you'll call again," I said, comforting her.

Junior was still asleep. Mica then went to take her shower. While in the shower, the phone rang, and I picked it up. "Hello," I answered.

"My name is Gabriela. Can I speak to Michaela? She is my sister, and she just called...."

"She's in the shower. You wanna call her back?"

"Isn't it Vinco?" She asked. There was a shaking in her voice.

"Yes, Gabby. It's me. Mica and I and our son came home from France Friday night."

"*Really?* I'm in shock. Where are you guys now?"

By then, Mica was done in the shower. "Here is Mica."

"Mica, Mica, Mica, my lovely sister. I thought I was never going to hear from you again."

"Yeah? By the grace of God, I have survived," Mica replied with a vague tone of voice.

"I know the anger. I can't talk here. Give me the address, and I will be right there."

As the phone was on speaker, I could hear. I gave her the address and instructions about how to get to "The Grenoble."

Thirty minutes later, Gabriela showed up, wearing her old trademark blue jeans and button-down blouse. She looked as sharp as the last time I saw her. The second she entered the apartment, she dove into her sister's arms, and they began to cry. Junior woke up to the cry of tears from his mother. He went and held my hand out of fear.

"Who is this woman hugging my mom?" he asked with apprehension.

"She's her sister, your aunt. They're only shedding happy tears," I said. This was too complicated for Junior.

After a long hug, they let go. Michaela invited her to sit on the sofa. She obliged. Junior and I joined them, but only for a short moment, just to exchange a few words and let Junior meet her. Then, we left the two sisters and strolled to the kitchen where I made breakfast for all of us. While in the kitchen, I listened to their conversation.

"Mica, since you left, the house was no longer the same and, maybe it never will be. Mama has been depressed. Papa is angry all the time, blaming Mama for everything. He even blames himself sometimes for having to let his brother play with his emotions and convince him to send you to Europe."

"Gabby, if this is true, why did they never ask me to come home? When I tried to do so, they vehemently opposed, relying on Uncle's accounts, not wanting to know how I was coping with a pregnancy in a country whose language I did not know, living with an uncle who could barely provide for his family."

"That wasn't what Uncle told them. Remember?"

"You also were there in the room. I was hoping you would stand up for me. You didn't. When Mama kept saying I had become an embarrassment, when Papa called me a bitch, you did not defend me. I wrote to you, you never replied…."

Gabriela turned her face sideways. The truth was too raw. A river of tears streamed down her cheeks. "Mica, you have every right to be angry. I was selfish, too selfish to stand up for you. I'm sorry. They had always treated you better than me, and I thought this was my moment to take revenge. But soon after you left, I found out I was swimming in an empty ocean with no rescue on the horizon. I missed you so much to the point I moved out and went to live with Hector. But every time I visited them, I found them to be like two angry birds living in the same cage. I thought of reaching out to you, but I was embarrassed to do so, knowing you will never forgive me."

"Too embarrassed to call your only sister in this world?"

"Yes, Mica. I'm still ashamed. Look at you now, living with Vinco and your son. Tell me. How did you survive?"

"I've survived and so have my husband and my son—despite the cruel world I was thrown into. But I'd rather not talk about my ordeals in Europe right now. I don't want to relive the painful moments of the last seven years. If I keep dwelling on them, I will never speak to Mama and Papa again."

"When did you guys get married?"

"Few weeks ago, in France." Mica then changed the conversation. "So, how are you doing now?" She was not interested in sharing her stories with her sister, at least not yet.

"Three years ago, Mica, things got worse when Uncle called them and told them you had moved out and that he did not know where you lived. Mama went days without eating. Papa became angrier. Since then, he has spent his days in the little backyard garden or sitting on his rocking chair on the patio, contemplating old pictures from when you were young. One day, I went to see them, and I saw a "for sale" sign in the front yard. When I asked why they were selling the house, they said the memories were too painful. A few weeks later, they sold the house and bought one in Hialeah Garden. Hector and I got separated. Things didn't work out. So, I moved back home."

"Gabby, I just made vegetable omelet with Haitian buttered rolls for all of us. You and Mica, come join us," I said, trying to water down the emotions.

"No, I'm not hungry," Gabriela replied. "I ate something early this morning."

"But you can still join us," I insisted. She laughed. The two ladies rose from the sofa and strolled to the table.

"Hmm! It smells good," Gabriela cried. "Let me try a bit."

"You got it, Gabby." I put a small portion on her plate.

"Mommy, you're not happy. Why?" Junior then asked, ever curious and sometimes confused, questioning why unhappiness was never far from him.

This was a reality Mica knew too well. The boy questioned that often. She then threw a repressed smile to conceal the sadness on her face. "Mommy is fine, Junior. Let me share with you," she said, taking a spoonful of omelet from her son's plate and spooning it in her mouth.

"Gabriela, no babies yet?" I inquired in a playful manner.

"No. Maybe never." Her eyes fixated on Junior, her only nephew through whom the reflection of both of his parents was unmistakable.

"He looks so handsome, so cute. I'm proud of you, guys. I'm looking at you three, a proud little family. Your love has endured. Mica, I remember you once told me it's either Vinco or no one," Gabriela said, looking at her sister with profound admiration.

But Michaela was in no mood to accept her sister's praise. She struggled but failed to put forth a normal demeanor.

"So, Vinco, what have you been doing all these years?" Gabriela asked.

"If you remember, I graduated from Barry a few weeks before Mica left. Then I went to graduate school. Now, I'm a System Information Engineer and Project Manager at the Bedell Tech Firm downtown," I replied.

"Wow! I'm impressed!" She chuckled. "And you, Mica?"

"I could never continue with school. I tried, but raising Junior was a lot. I plan on registering this coming week. I should complete the business major in May if all goes well," Mica replied with a fictitious smile.

"And you, Gabby?" I asked, being quite inquisitive.

"Nothing much. I have an Associate Degree in Information Technology from MDCC- Miami Dade Community College, as you remember, Mica. After you left, I found an entry level position at Saint Mary High School. I still work there," she said but soon switched the subject. "Mica, when do you plan on visiting home?" She was uncomfortable talking about her slacker behavior, which did not surprise Michaela, knowing her sister was not an ambitious person.

"Vinco and I would like to go this afternoon."

"Please, do. That would be the best gift to Mom and Dad."

I took out two business cards from my wallet and handed them to my sister in-law. "Gabby, write the address down on the back of one. Then keep the other," I said with pride. In that instant, I thought of Pedro's words 'They would not have sent Mica two thousand miles away if they knew then what you are now.'

"Thank you, Vinco."

"Mommy, I'm going to see my other grandma?" Junior asked.

"And Grandpa, too," Mica replied, poking his chin with a love that can only be found in a mother's eyes.

"To lessen the shock, I'll tell them you're coming. Around what time, Mica?" Gabriela asked.

"Six p.m., right, Vinco?"

"Yes," I replied.

Mica then walked her sister down to the parking lot where they talked some more before Gabriela departed.

#

Michaela leaned on me as we drove down One-Hundred-and-Third Street leading to Hialeah Garden where her parents now lived.

"Baby," she sighed. "I don't think this is something I can do. Too much is going in my mind. Among them was the night of the meeting after you and Nana left. The way they treated me while Gabriela, my spoiled sister, sat there laughing. They had always known me to be an obedient child, and they took advantage of that. They would have never done it to my sister. But does obedient mean submissive, Vinco?"

"Mica, I'm sure you know one reinforces the other. Not only did your parents know you would obey whatever the order was, but also, they knew you would submit to their will, regardless of whether you agreed or not. In Gabriela's case, it was different. They knew she would challenge their authority if the order did not please her."

"Vinco, I'm still bitter. Please, help me."

"Junior and I will be there. That will be enough. But you know, *amorecita?*" We reached an intersection, and I turned her face towards me, raising her chin a little. "You'll have to reconcile with your parents. Junior's presence will be your victory. How can you still be afraid after winning this struggle? You have survived the rough times in Europe. We're not sure how they will react when we get there, but whatever their reaction, be conciliatory. Be positive."

Junior sat in the backseat and appeared to be enjoying the ride, discovering Miami on a beautiful Sunday afternoon. Cars on both sides of the streets weaved on while Spanish music blasted away. Consumed in his sightseeing adventure, he was unable to listen to Mom and Dad. His attention returned to the car when I said, "We have arrived."

The car soon pulled in front of the iron gate of a small home with a hacienda covered porch design built in the middle of a large courtyard. It was a sparsely inhabited street, which was the reality of that part of Miami at that time for being so close to the everglades. A beige Toyota Corolla was parked on a concrete driveway.

"It's Gabriela's car," Mica said. "At least that was what she drove this morning."

We all stepped out, opened the gate, and walked to the main porch. Mica rang the bell. On the first ring, Gabriela walked out, wearing an open collar dress.

"*Come in!*" She tittered, as Mica, Junior, and I strolled in.

Lucrecia, who stood behind the door, took Junior's hand and edged closer to talk to me. "Vinco, how are you?" She wailed in a lacerating pitch.

"I'm doing fine," I replied with a smile.

Michaela showed no emotion. Junior followed his mother's attitude. Although he knew he had arrived at his grandparents' home, he was reluctant to show the same enthusiasm he had displayed the night before at my parents' home. The fact that he watched his mother standing and shaking with her eyes swelled with tears in front of people who were supposed to be her close relatives made him even more reticent.

From the back, Emilio rushed in. "Vinco, look at you! Strong and built! Look at my little prince!" He kept on saying as tears sprung out of his eyes. I sensed this was one of his most torturous moments in life. His macho culture crumbled that afternoon. A father's lost daughter had come home. Nothing could be sweeter, even if it was under one of the most uncomfortable circumstances.

Lucrecia now let go of Junior's hand and dove into Mica's arms, crying. Her hair had gone gray. Wrinkles had invaded her light-skinned face. She now wore glasses perched on the tip of her nose. Her robust figure had shrunk, ravaged by years of living in sheer pain.

Emilio's body looked firmer in a pair of blue jeans and Polo shirt. His face wrinkled a bit when one looked up-close. He joined Lucrecia in the embrace as if trying to protect their daughter from danger. Gabriela joined them, too. I was tempted to join them as well in this solemn moment. I was afraid, however, of alarming Junior.

After five minutes of shedding tears, Lucrecia and Emilio invited us into their living room neatly decorated with family pictures and historical artwork from the Dominican Republic. We sat on a brown leather sofa, facing them.

"I know you may not be hungry, but Mama has made rice pudding and banana cake, your favorite, Mica," she said, running to the dining table and came right back. "Why don't we sit at the table, and have rice pudding while we talk?"

We all rose at once, sauntered up to the table, and took our seats, except Michaela. She stood next to me, looking at the cake which was designed like a birthday cake with her name written on it. That may have irritated her.

"I don't wanna eat. *No tengo ambre.* I'm not hungry," she reaffirmed again in English. "I didn't come here to celebrate. I came to see you because you are my parents, and I will forever love you despite everything. I will be forever grateful. Afterall, you gave me life and supported me with the parental love and care that you thought I needed—until I became an embarrassment. I also came here to show you that I *have* survived with my dignity intact." She then sat down near me as an avalanche of tears flooded her cheeks.

I knew there was a lot more she wanted to say. Before she got carried away with her blistering remarks, however, I tapped her under the table as a reminder of what we talked about earlier in the morning. She understood.

Lucrecia and Emilio turned their faces away. They did not have the courage to look their daughter in the eye. An eerie silence took hold. The cake and the rice pudding no longer meant anything. Everyone seemed to be looking at each other as if trying to find the perfect words that would ease the grief. Emilio then broke the stillness.

"Mica, Mama and I are not trying to justify what we did. It was painful and ill-judged. It was a rush to judgement which caused us seven years of living in agony. As you know, after you left, we tried to support you however we could. We believed in my brother's promise to provide for your needs. But unfortunately—. His voice quivered, and he began to swallow his words.

"I wish I could take back those years," Lucrecia said. "Vinco, I'm sorry. Mica, I'm sorry."

Junior, who seemed to have understood what was going on, made no attempt to ask any questions, which would have worsened the moment. Afterall, it was because of his conception that his parents and his grandparents had to go through such a long and excruciating period of living in darkness. However, he did not have to say a word. His presence, his charm, his attire, all loudly spoke the unspoken words too agonizing to express.

I, too, was in pain. There at that table, many things went through my mind. Life is a journey full of uncertainty, like a minefield that requires courage, the will to learn those survival skills that are quintessential to navigating to safety unharmed. Every human being needs the wherewithal that will make it possible to be productive for the good of oneself and others. In this journey, we all make mistakes along the way, for none of us is perfect; but imperfections do not always drive human interactions to the sinkhole of oblivion. Once recognized, our flaws could be a catalyst for change—change of heart, change of behavior, change of will, and all other undescribed but well understood changes that are required to render our journey through life an enjoyable one. Mica's parents' acknowledgment of their misguided decision was good enough for me and for Mica as well. Her head tilted to my side, she smiled at last. Maybe we were thinking the same thing.

"Mama," she said as the smile widened her face now turned rosy and moist from teardrops. "How is Grandpa doing?"

"He passed away two years ago in Las Matas," Lucrecia replied with a sigh of relief. At least, there was something we all could talk about with the same interest.

"How did that happen?" I asked.

"Well, he went to see some relatives in Haiti. When he returned, he became very ill. Every time I talked to him, he complained about chronic pain all over his body. His thoughts had become more and more incoherent. He mixed Creole with Spanish, and he got irritated when I asked him to rephrase in Spanish."

"Really?" Mica asked in horror.

"That reminds me of my Haitian heritage," Lucrecia smiled again, a captivating smile directed at Junior and I who are also Haitians, confirming the family's multiethnic reality.

"You should've seen it, Mica. We all went. It was a sad moment, but I'm sure you would have enjoyed the family reunion. Many of his living relatives came from Haiti, including his two younger sisters and their children and grandchildren, many cousins, and friends from the Haitian town of Ouanaminthe where he was born and became a well-respected businessman. We all were one, crying with the same level and intensity of our emotions."

"It was amazing," Emilio said.

"Vinco, you wanna do like Mica? You're not even going to take a piece of that cake on which your wife's name is emblazoned?" Gabriela said in a teasing manner, changing the conversation. "Mama made it with such a love that I had never seen her display since the night at your birthday party when you and your sister were there."

"Yes, I am, Gabby," I replied with a grin.

I knew her parents were sincere in admitting that their actions were unacceptable. *If I was the man who caused the rift, let me be the bridge of reconciliation.* I said to myself. I then grabbed the huge bowl of that rice pudding and the large silver spoon that was designed to serve everyone. "I'm the waiter," I said, chortling while filling everyone's plate.

Mica's plate was the first to be filled. She took the first bite too. We ate, joked, and laughed. Junior talked about his Haitian relatives, Grandma, Grandpa, cousin Nanouche he had met at the party the night before. When it was time to leave, they all walked us out to the car. In warm embraces and tight hugs, we said goodbye with a promise to meet again very soon.

Back at home, we felt relieved the reunion went as we had hoped. The haze that clouded our minds was now behind us. A life free of any constraint awaited us—a happy married couple backed by an army of well-wishers from both sides of their families. Junior went to sleep after taking a much-needed shower. Mica and I sat on the sofa, our bodies entwined. With one gentle motion, I kissed her lips. In soft moans, she reciprocated as my fingers skimmed across her breasts.

"Amorecito," she whispered. *"Te necesito. Te quiero. Acaricia me."* *My love, I need you. I want you. Caress my body.*

"Me Tambien, amorecita." I replied with an uncontrolled urge to increase the tempo. *Me, too, my love.*

But Junior slept in the room. So, I refrained from roaming the rest of her body. Into each other's arms, we fell asleep. We spent the following week getting things done. Junior was enrolled at a Catholic elementary school located a few blocks away. Mica was registered for the remaining courses at Barry University. We hired a realtor with instructions to look for a home on the eastern side of Biscayne in the Aventura neighborhood. Mica and her mom and dad chatted on the phone almost every night, making up for lost time. Nana called every day, still playing her big sister's role, which pleased Mica a lot.

The following Sunday, we drove to Morning Side Park on Biscayne Bay. When we arrived, a few cars were parked deep near the edge of the shorelines, the way it was the morning after the pregnancy test. We pulled up to a parking spot close to a little pathway that ran straight towards the benches facing the high rises of Miami Beach on the other side of the bay.

"Papi, let's go sit over there," Junior suggested, pointing at a bench over which a pair sea birds had just flown away. We obliged. We were alone as we sat, but we felt strong.

"Mica," I grinned. "I think we can now safely say love can indeed bring happiness."

"Yes, *mon amour*," she replied.

Taking aim at the wave-beaten shorelines and listening to the cacophonous squawking of the early morning gulls flying overhead, we both held our son tighter.

"L' amour pur l'a remporté," Mica mumbled in French.

"What was that?" I could not hear her.

"Pure love has won," she reiterated this time in English.

448

9 798986 508634